STRANGE NATURE

Books by Mary Watson

STRANGE NATURE

MARY WATSON

BLOOMSBURY
LONDON   OXFORD   NEW YORK   NEW DELHI   SYDNEY

BLOOMSBURY YA
Bloomsbury Publishing Plc
50 Bedford Square, London WC1B 3DP, UK
Bloomsbury Publishing Ireland Limited
29 Earlsfort Terrace, Dublin 2, D02 AY28, Ireland

BLOOMSBURY, BLOOMSBURY YA and the Diana logo are trademarks of
Bloomsbury Publishing Plc

First published in Great Britain in 2025 by Bloomsbury Publishing Plc

A catalogue record for this book is available from the British Library

ISBN: PB: 978-1-5266-1937-2; eBook: 978-1-5266-1935-8;
ePDF: 978-1-5266-8940-5

2   4   6   8   10   9   7   5   3   1

Typeset by RefineCatch Limited, Bungay, Suffolk

Printed and bound in Great Britain by CPI Group (UK) Ltd, Croydon CR0 4YY

To find out more about our authors and books visit www.bloomsbury.com
and sign up for our newsletters
For product safety related questions contact productsafety@bloomsbury.com

For my cousin, Ayesha Price, whose smile
could light up a room

'The world was to me a secret which I desired to divine.'

Mary Shelley, *Frankenstein*

ONE

It was a summer's day, wet and warm, when Jasmin learned that monsters wore ordinary faces.

She was eight years old. Grandma Georgie had been making pasta sauce, humming along to old love songs. Jasmin was in the adjoining room, loading her Sylvanians into their blue van. The baby Milk Rabbit toppled as Jasmin drove the van from home – a cushion beneath the table – to school.

She didn't hear her grandfather's heavy tread going from bedroom to kitchen. She didn't see his face when he loomed over Georgie, because she was unloading the Sylvanian rabbit children at their school. The smell of anchovy-infused tomatoes filled the air. On the radio, the Beatles sang about love.

This memory was a seed. It had grown into a twisting, hungry thing. It had changed her, that moody day when disaster happened only metres away.

Because on that day, playing with her toy rabbit family, Jasmin didn't look up.

She didn't look up when she heard her grandfather's deep voice in the kitchen, rumbling three words, 'You did this.'

Jasmin drove the mama Milk Rabbit to the shoebox that was her office, whispering, 'Oh lord, I have a ton of work to get through,' as her own mother would often say.

It was the smell of burning that finally drew Jasmin's attention. When she turned to the kitchen, she saw tomato pasta sauce seeping across the floor. Red dripped down the oak cabinets from a saucepan upended on the stove. Steam rose, hot and urgent, from a large bubbling pot. *All you need is love*, the loud, happy music insisted.

Jasmin saw Georgie's arm waving. No, not waving, flailing. She saw Georgie's body jerk as it was pulled into an awkward embrace. She saw Georgie's eyes bugging, her face contorted. She saw her grandfather's hands squeezing her grandmother's neck. She finally registered the sound she'd blocked out. Those three guttural words repeating: *You did this*.

Jasmin stood up, the mama rabbit falling from her hand.

'Georgie?' she'd said uncertainly.

This was the part she hated most: the way she'd just stood there. Georgie had clawed at her grandfather's hands around her throat, *You did this, you did this, you did this*, and Jasmin couldn't breathe. Couldn't move. Georgie gurgled, and slumped to the ground, her pretty yellow dress patched with red sauce.

Jasmin finally ran. She tore out of the house with a wild, animal howl. She ran outside, screaming until her throat burned.

Next door, the gardener was trimming ivy from the boundary wall. He took one look at the frightened girl, dropped the shears and leaped right over the wall.

Jasmin didn't go back inside. She couldn't.

She felt soft hands on her shoulders, a murmuring voice telling her that she was safe now. But she still screamed. She heard hushed voices: *Georgie's been hurt.* Someone called an ambulance.

Georgie might die. And Jasmin could have stopped it. If she'd just looked up.

You did this.

Jasmin shook herself out of the gentle hands. She walked towards the house. Someone called her name but she didn't stop.

She should have looked up. Then she could have stopped it. If she had paid attention. If she'd been aware. If she'd noticed the clues.

If she'd been watching.

Inside, her grandfather had sunk into a kitchen chair, a neighbour hovering behind him. He was quiet now, his eyes losing that feral light. He glanced up at her.

'Jasmin, love.' His voice was rough with emotion. 'My girl.'

They'd been so close. Jasmin had adored her grandfather. He was a giant teddy bear of a man with a thick grey beard who played endless games of snakes and ladders with her. He'd walk with her to the newsagent's for jellies, saying, *Don't you tell your mother now.* He'd sit with her, guiding her as she sketched, and beamed when she held up her finished work. He let her

3

name the mice in his study. Sometimes he'd take them out of their cages, and they would run up her arm to her shoulder. But looking at him in the kitchen chair, she flinched and turned her head sharply.

Jasmin saw Georgie's legs on the kitchen floor, her crooked toes in her soft sandals, the red sauce on the skirt of her dress.

She made herself move closer. Jasmin made herself watch.

And now, watching was habit.

Jasmin thought of that day as she walked along the river to the university.

Logically, she knew that she had only been eight years old. That by alerting the gardener, she had saved her grandmother's life.

Still, guilt had taken root that day.

In the near distance, the ivy-covered arts buildings signalled that Jasmin was near her destination. The day was bright, hot for October. As usual, she entered the campus through the south gate, a wide arch that broke through the line of trees. She preferred this to the far side with its modern architecture. She liked the old buildings, the twisting ivy and the courtyards sheltered by mature trees.

She wasn't supposed to be there. She was an imposter, a schoolgirl, barely eighteen, walking among adults. Maybe that was part of the reason she loved it.

She'd discovered this spot at the start of the term, after she quit soccer. She'd ended things with Callum, her boyfriend of two years, at the beginning of summer. It was a few weeks before she'd left to visit her dad in Italy. At first, it had been OK between them. They had agreed to stay friends. But then when term began again in September, things had felt weird. Callum had been cold. Mean, even.

One Friday afternoon, she'd headed with the girls to soccer practice. Across the pitch, where the boys trained, Callum's eyes held hers with bland indifference.

'You made a big mistake,' Amy had said. 'But it's too late now.'

Jasmin had followed Amy's gaze across the field to where a girl now stood beside Callum. She didn't need to hear their conversation to know that this was Callum's new girlfriend. The way he smiled at her, the way she popped her hip. Then Amy and the others were jogging over and Jasmin was left behind.

Watching her friends in their closed circle, she had felt raw. She'd unbalanced their little gang by breaking up with Callum. She had only fitted in while she'd been with him. Now, they saw her for the girl she truly was. The girl who didn't belong anywhere.

Jasmin had walked off the soccer field. She knew she would never go back. She'd walked along the canal until she found herself at the university's south gate. She was on the narrow path behind the quadrangle with its stern but familiar architecture of grey stone walls and Gothic embellishment. Taking in the pointed arches, the detail carved into the stone, for the first time since coming back from Italy, Jasmin found peace.

She felt like she belonged. She knew this place – a place

she'd come to as a child, with her small hand held in a large, comforting one.

She came back the next day, and the next. Before long, she spent most afternoons roaming the campus. She began to find her way around, to recognise the students who sat at picnic tables beneath the autumn trees.

Now, Jasmin continued down the tree-lined avenue, eyeing the narrow lane to the left. Her body knew the way. It always veered in that direction, a sunflower turning to the sun.

Yielding to the urge, Jasmin left the avenue. She walked towards the Old Science building, where the much-lauded Professor Eamon Larkin had once had an office.

As usual, she stopped outside a three-storeyed, ivy-covered building. It was off the main path, tucked away behind the botany department and beside the greenhouses. It was called the Old Science, because most of the science faculty had moved into a newer, better-equipped facility.

Jasmin trained her eyes to a window on the far right. Her grandfather's old office. She stared at the window with a guilty longing. She had been his. *My girl*, he'd said before they'd taken him away. After that terrible day, her mother, Sonia, had changed Jasmin and Dash's surname to hers in an attempt to shield them from the fallout. When Georgie came out of hospital, they tried to stitch their lives back together, but it wasn't easy. The town wouldn't stop talking about it, wouldn't stop their vicious scrutiny laced with faux sympathy. There'd been more than a little *Schadenfreude* at one of the town's old, rich families reduced to tabloid headlines.

Her grandfather had been sentenced to ten years. More than nine had passed, but Jasmin didn't know if he was still in prison or if he'd got out on early release. There were some questions she knew she couldn't ask. Wasn't sure if she wanted to ask.

Jasmin gave herself one minute to look. That was all she allowed herself. A small peek at the past. Then, as she always did, she turned her back to the building and walked to the path and away.

Ahead was the Edith Donnelly Theatre, and beside it the Three Divas, the theatre cafe. This was where Jasmin always ended up on the days she wandered the campus.

The Three Divas was intimate, with deep green walls and wooden chairs. Posters from plays dating back to the 1970s hung on the walls. Sepia photos of actors celebrating opening nights smiled down at Jasmin as she surveyed the room. In the corner, a young man read Sartre, and at another table two women talked animatedly.

They weren't here yet.

It was a quiet time of day, too late for the lunch crowd, too early for the evening. After ordering her decaf oat latte, Jasmin took her usual seat at a small table beside a window, partially hidden by a pillar. Close to the alcove, she could both observe and listen. Taking out her homework, she opened her book to where she'd left off, but her mind wandered.

In her family, her artistic, clever, beautiful family, everyone had a role. Her brother, Dash, was the thoughtful, dreamy poet. Her mother, Sonia, was the organised one, who ran both home and office with indomitable efficiency. Her grandmother, Georgie, was the bubbly socialite, and her partner, Benedict, the storyteller. Jasmin's dad, long absent, was the wanderer who, much as he tried, could never keep still. She had learned to forgive his compulsion to explore, and looked forward to each new postcard from some faraway place. And as for her grandfather, no one spoke about him.

Jasmin, they all insisted, was the curious one. Jasmin liked to know. She liked to watch. 'Like a little cat,' her mother would say.

The curious one. Jasmin wasn't sure if this was good or bad.

The bell above the door to the Three Divas jingled and Jasmin's heart skipped a beat.

TWO

It was them. She could tell from the way the room suddenly felt full. The light scent of coconut and vanilla and mint. Laughter.

Jasmin kept her eyes on the page of her homework – *King Lear*, which was frustrating her no end. She couldn't understand why a man who was meant to be powerful was so fragile.

'Man, I could eat a horse.'

That was Rían. He was always hungry. For food, but also, Jasmin sensed, for life.

She'd first seen them, three weeks ago, from her little nook in the window. Four of them gliding down the tree-lined lane, detached from everyone else. They carried themselves like rock stars, like they danced at midnight in the dark part of the woods, or in the underground chambers of forgotten castles. These four knew how to find the secret parties where they'd stain their lips with red wine, then dance and argue ideas late into the night. They would lounge on velvet or moss and be beautiful, and kiss and touch and discover.

Jasmin glanced up to see Rían sauntering to the counter. The cafe served only wraps and sandwiches from the display fridge at this time of the day, but the women behind the counter made an exception for Rían, saving him hot pie and chips, and saying things like, 'Sure, he's a growing boy.'

Jasmin was certain that Rían, tall and lanky, was not a growing boy. He had black, curly hair and laughing brown eyes. He was charming, but appeared genuinely interested in others. He asked after grandchildren and husbands, about bad knees or shoulders, and so the women at the cafe made an exception for him. She guessed that a lot of people made exceptions for Rían.

Hot drinks in hand, the friends made for the alcove, to their usual cosy table set into a recess in the wall. They dropped coats, nudging into the booth. Arms touching arms, they talked over each other, a gentle, familiar ribbing. Allie playfully smacked Damien's hand as he poked her side. Imogen checked her lipstick in a small compact, prompting Rían to remark, 'Ah sure, you're gorgeous.' She pulled a face and snagged chips from his huge plate. They were close, easy, and it made Jasmin ache.

In her three weeks of watching, she had gathered that they were journalism students. That Imogen was the daughter of the well-known current affairs TV presenter Síle Barrett, and carried a switchblade in the front pocket of her bag. Allie was struggling to keep on top of her coursework, while Damien raked in good results. And Rían, with his dark eyes and long lashes and silk waistcoats, had lived in his mother's native Senegal until he was six. He drank espresso. Imogen drank cappuccino. Allie didn't like coffee and always ordered hot chocolate. Damien only ever ordered the bottomless filter coffee.

Jasmin watched as they talked about essay deadlines and rigid professors, a new bar in town.

'Come on, Rían, let's check it out tonight,' Imogen said, flicking back jet-black, chin-length hair that fell against pale, pale skin. She favoured vintage dresses and jackets, and always looked immaculate. Her features were sharp and her eyes an ice blue, making her appear shrewd.

'I can't this evening, we have to cover that alumni event for the *Answerer*,' Rían groaned. He had the kind of face that demanded attention: a regal nose, sensual lips and mischievous eyes. 'Unless Allie doesn't mind doing it by herself? Allie?'

'What?' Allie had been lost in thought. She often was, like an edgy Alice in Wonderland with her short blonde hair and eyeliner and faux leather leggings. She fiddled with a coin in her hand. 'No way. I'm not going alone.'

Imogen sat back, dissatisfaction settled on her mouth. 'I survived Mathieson's test this morning. I need something fun. Damien?'

'Come with us to the alumni event,' Allie said.

'I said something *fun*.'

'We make our own fun, you know that, Imogen.' Rían wagged a scolding finger at her.

'At least come to the cocktail reception,' Allie urged. 'The drinks are free.'

Rían rubbed his hands. 'Yes, come. Bring your camera, Damien. Your pictures will be so much better than ours.' He slung an arm around Allie's shoulders. 'No offence, Allie-cat.'

'None taken.'

'I don't know.' Damien seemed reluctant.

Of all of them, it was Damien, the most ordinary of the four, who'd captured Jasmin's attention. Conventionally handsome, straight out of a sports drink ad: lips full and kissable; hair thick and mussed in just the right way. He favoured muscle tops and joggers, and his only concession to the encroaching cold weather was a battered army jacket. The very first time she'd seen him, walking in a shaft of sunlight down the tree-lined lane, Jasmin hadn't been able to take her eyes off him. It wasn't just his looks. It was something else that drew her. A sadness in his eyes. The way he moved. She watched him the way you looked at an exquisite painting, at a distance, across a barrier. Never wanting to touch.

'We'll ask the coins,' Allie declared. The others groaned, but Jasmin smiled. Allie and her coins. Any uncertainty and she would whip out the divining coins she carried in her backpack.

Allie gave a slight roll of the eyes at the theatrical objections, but she was grinning. She didn't seem to mind that the others had little patience for her coins. She shook a small velvet pouch, then dipped her hand inside. She reached her closed fist to the centre of the table while the others shifted impatiently.

'Come on, Allie,' Rían said, drumming his fingers.

'Don't rush the coins.' She drew her hand back to herself, placing it on the table in front of her.

'Well?' Imogen said teasingly. 'Do the coins approve gate-crashing the drinks reception?'

Allie raised one small dulled gold coin between her forefinger and thumb. Jasmin couldn't see the image on it.

'The Burning Heart?' Rían raised an eyebrow. 'Romance, passion, am I right?'

Imogen held up her hands as if in surrender. 'Not me then. I'm still licking my wounds after Thuli.'

'Must be Damien or Allie,' Rían said, before adding slyly, 'or Damien *and* Allie, if that's still on the cards?'

Jasmin was sure that Allie flushed. She looked away, pretending she hadn't heard. 'Coins, Rían,' Damien said. 'These are coins. You're mixing up your divination tools.'

Jasmin noted that Damien also sidestepped the question of him and Allie.

Allie held up a second coin. 'The Noose.'

'This is why I hate these coins,' Imogen complained. 'Really, Allie, I ask for fun and you give me death?'

'It doesn't have to mean death. The Noose could mean feeling stuck. A need for release.' Allie gathered both coins and held them in her open palm. 'And we have to consider the coins together.'

'Passion and death? Then we're definitely going,' Rían said, thumping his hand on the table.

'C'mon, you know cards or coins can't tell the future,' Damien said, getting to his feet. 'I mean, they're entertaining but that's all.'

'You're leaving?' Allie glanced up at him.

13

'Yeah, I have to study. Test tomorrow.'

'Will you come tonight?' she said.

'Please? Maybe take a few pics for the *Answerer*?' Rían added.

Damien hesitated. 'Sure. I'll meet you there.' He smiled at Imogen. 'We'll have fun.'

'Promises, promises,' Imogen muttered.

As Damien pushed through the cafe door into the autumn afternoon, Jasmin's phone buzzed with a message. It was Dash, asking if she was home.

On my way, she fired back and returned her homework to her bag. With a final glance at the friends, she made for the door. Leaving the cafe, she saw a woman in a blue striped T-shirt walking briskly, her head down. Jasmin stepped to the left, trying to avoid her, but the woman mirrored her movement. They both stepped right and Jasmin let out an apologetic laugh.

Then the woman looked up and Jasmin's laughter ended abruptly. Her eyes were red-rimmed, mascara smudged.

'Are you OK?' Jasmin said, but it was obvious the woman wasn't OK.

'I—' the woman started, then pressed a shaking hand to her mouth as a sob escaped.

'Did something happen?' Jasmin pressed gently. 'What's your name?'

'Niamh.' The woman appeared distracted, looking around the avenue as if she were searching for something. Or someone.

'Come,' Jasmin said, finding herself using Georgie's voice,

soothing and confident. 'Let's sit on the steps there and gather ourselves.' *Gather ourselves.* Georgie's words too.

Niamh suddenly froze and Jasmin wondered if she'd gone too far with the grandma talk. But she was focused on something behind Jasmin. Her eyes were wide and frightened.

Jasmin whirled round to see what the woman was looking at, but class had ended and the tree-lined lane was swirling with people emerging from the buildings on either side. She searched the crowd, looking for something that could have caused such a reaction. Something scary. Something that could make the woman's face twist with worry and distress. A monster, a demon. But there were only chatting students moving easily to their next class. A couple stopping for a kiss. A lecturer talking to a small group of graduate students. No monsters.

'Did you …?'

Niamh was hurrying away. Jasmin watched her blue striped T-shirt retreating, the blonde ponytail bobbing.

Instinct told Jasmin to follow. She made her way through the now thinning stream of students. Niamh took a sharp left beside a building, into a narrow alley and down a flight of stairs. From her roaming, Jasmin knew these stairs led only to a maintenance door. It was a private, hidden spot with no throughway.

Niamh disappeared at the landing. After a moment came the sound of rustling, then her bag falling. Jasmin crept closer.

'C'mon, c'mon, c'mon, pick up.' The woman's whisper travelled up to where Jasmin waited at the top of the stairs.

Then she said, 'It's me.' Her voice was thin and shaking. 'Can I see you? This evening? Please.' Jasmin heard the trepidation in that last word.

What was Jasmin doing? She needed to stop eavesdropping and leave.

Then Niamh's voice dropped. 'I have to get away. My dad's picking me up early tomorrow, so it has to be today.' She let out a loud, pained exhale. 'I'm not safe here.'

Jasmin was rooted to the paving. In her mind's eye, she saw red sauce dripping down oak kitchen cabinets.

Niamh spoke again. 'OK. Will I find you there?'

Jasmin wished she could hear what the other person was saying.

'Thank you,' Niamh breathed, then added, 'I'm so scared. He's a monster.'

THREE

It was just gone five thirty when Jasmin let herself into the front hall at home.

'Jasmin, that you?' her mother called.

For the last few weeks, Sonia had been working late, as she did when she was in crisis management mode. Jasmin was no stranger to returning to an empty house, especially as Dash had been away studying physics in Dublin these last few years. But her brother had returned in the early summer, deciding to do his postgrad here. These days, Jasmin would come home to find him digging in the fridge for leftovers as if he were eighteen again.

The bouquet on the hall console was large and fresh. The house smelt of rosemary and lamb and something jazzy played in the background. Laughter and familiar teasing voices reached Jasmin as she hung up her jacket. She walked through the kitchen and into the dining room, where the table was set with candles. The chandelier glowed and the red embossed walls made the room seem both elegant and intimate. A couple in their seventies stood near the window, the woman opening her arms when she saw Jasmin.

'Georgie,' Jasmin exclaimed, as she flew into her grandmother's arms. 'You're home.'

She pulled back to drink in her features – the short grey hair, the thin lined skin that folded around her watery blue eyes. They'd been away for four months, and she'd missed Georgie something fierce. She and her grandmother had always been close, and their bond had only grown stronger after her grandfather was imprisoned.

'School off to a good start?' Georgie studied her, and as always, saw too much.

'It's school.' Jasmin shrugged, shifting away from her grandmother's keen eye. Georgie knew her inside out. That's what happened when you lived next door to family.

Jasmin turned to the distinguished man who stood beside her and gave him a hug. She breathed in the familiar woody scent of his Aramis aftershave. Benedict was nothing if not steadfast. 'Hello, Benedict. Looking good.'

'Flattery will get you everywhere, my dear.' Benedict's eyes twinkled as he handed her a small blue box. 'We saw this in a jewellery shop in Perugia and thought of you at once.'

'They're beautiful,' Jasmin said as she saw the garnet earrings inside, then chided, 'You two spoil me. You'll make me insufferable.'

'Impossible.' Benedict pulled out a chair for her beside Dash.

18

'Yeah. You're already insufferable,' her brother said, smiling and shaking his head. In front of him was a new fountain pen, no doubt picked up by Georgie and Benedict on their travels.

'Really, Dash? Is that the best you've got?'

'Now she's gone and poked the hornet's nest,' he goaded her playfully.

'Oh, stop it. You two will give me more grey hairs,' Sonia said as she returned to the room holding a heavy casserole dish, the smell of garlic and spicy slow-cooked meat filling the air. Her dark hair, lightly lined with silver, was pulled back in a loose bun. When Jasmin had returned at the end of August after visiting her dad, she'd been struck by how Sonia was ageing – the new folds around her mischievous brown eyes, the determined jaw getting a little softer. The incremental changes that Jasmin couldn't observe up close.

Georgie clasped Sonia's hands, saying, 'Oh, my dear, this looks delicious. We have missed your excellent cooking.'

Sonia once let it slip that Georgie had initially had reservations about her, that she would have preferred that Richard, her only son, marry a nice Irish girl, by which she meant a white woman. Then, years ago, Richard left, needing to find himself. By that time, Georgie and Sonia had grown close, bound in no small part by shared exasperation, an inside knowledge of what it meant to love someone who wouldn't be held, who couldn't keep still. Richard was flighty, a free spirit, and sometimes Jasmin wondered if that's why her mother worked so hard to keep her and Dash grounded.

19

'Do you need a hand, Mam?' she watched her mother turn to the kitchen.

'*Now* you ask,' said Sonia, though Jasmin knew that her mother would have everything under control. *Just get it done, and don't make a fuss*, she'd heard her say so many times.

Sonia had tried to teach this to her children too, drilled into them how to fix a dinner, stay on top of laundry, keep the house in shape. Work before play. Jasmin's dad might have come from old money, but Sonia didn't, and she had ingrained in them the value of getting things done, quickly and without hassle.

'Tell us about dad,' Dash said to Georgie as Jasmin pushed back her chair. 'Was that scorpion still occupying his bathroom? You should have heard Jasmin scream.'

'I think you're confusing me with yourself.' Jasmin glared at him as she left the room.

In the kitchen, Sonia lifted a tray of roasted vegetables from the oven. 'Bring in the water, would you?'

Picking up the jug, Jasmin's eye fell on a pile of envelopes, most of them still sealed but a few opened, addressed to both Georgie and Benedict. Sonia had been collecting their post while they were away. They were close to a spill of water and a few of the already opened letters were wet at the edges. She moved the letters, pulling out the damp pages to let them dry.

'Now where is that bottle of red?' Georgie said, coming into the kitchen. 'I think you'll like this one. There was this gorgeous vineyard in the South of France …'

Jasmin's attention was caught by an invitation card from the university. Georgie still received correspondence from them, particularly if it involved fundraising. Usually Jasmin wasn't interested, but this time her heart picked up. *The Annual Alumni Lecture. Speaker: Professor Theo Merrick.*

The four in the cafe had been talking about going. Damien was going to take pictures …

Her heart beat even faster. She would see them.

She held the card up. 'Are you going to this?'

'Not tonight,' Georgie said regretfully. 'We're only just back, so it's an early night for me.'

'I think I might like to go.' Jasmin drew the card to her chest. 'If you don't mind me using your invitation.'

'I don't mind.' Her grandmother was looking too intently again. 'You've never wanted to before though.'

Jasmin glanced down at the invitation. She couldn't tell Georgie that she wanted to see the four away from the cafe. That she wanted to watch Damien take photos, see if Allie's coins were right.

'It's that Theo Merrick, I suppose?' Georgie said. 'The handsome professor? It seems he's all over the newspapers these days.'

Of course, Jasmin knew of Theo Merrick. Everybody did. He was a professor at the university, but one that was often on the radio or the TV, the go-to media personality for anything science-related. Tall with dark blonde hair, and good-looking. He spoke in easy soundbites and had a sense of humour. He had a podcast too, *Hot Science*, a conversational show.

'Yes,' Jasmin said, relieved that Georgie had given her an out. 'He's so interesting.'

Georgie raised an eyebrow. 'Is he now? You know your grandfather taught him. Theo was one of several starry-eyed students who'd come round to the house.'

'No,' said Jasmin quietly. 'I didn't know that.'

They were silent for a moment. Georgie never mentioned her grandfather and Jasmin didn't know what to say.

At last, Georgie smiled. 'Well, it's fine by me if it's all right with your mother. You'd better come in and have your meal. That lecture starts at seven.'

FOUR

Jasmin had only ever been to one lecture at the McKellan Galleries before. She'd been eight years old, and she'd sat in the car while her grandparents argued at the gate.

'She will be bored, Eamon,' Georgie had said, exasperated. 'It's no place for a child.'

No place for a child. It had sounded like Eamon was going to take Jasmin some place dark and dangerous. But when they arrived at the McKellan Galleries, a brightly lit neo-Georgian building at the edge of the university's main campus, Jasmin had been awed. The size of it. The grandness of the oval entrance hall with its wide marble staircase that curved so elegantly. Her grandfather always took her to beautiful places. But her grandmother had been right. Jasmin was bored. She'd sat on the hard chair, trying her best to keep her eyes, so thick and heavy, from closing. She hadn't understood a word, but she was a good girl and pretended to listen. At the end, Eamon had

23

smiled at her and she'd glowed. He was proud of her, and that was what mattered most.

Now, this evening, Jasmin stood outside the McKellan Galleries once more. The ivy had been cleared, exposing sharp grey stone that gleamed in the evening light.

'Are we going in or daydreaming outside?' Dash said, checking the time. 'We're late.'

'I didn't know you were a secret fan of *Hot Science*.' Jasmin eyed him, stepping ahead.

'You underestimate my dedication to getting out of the washing-up,' Dash replied.

They were indeed late and the lecture had started over ten minutes ago. The room was as Jasmin remembered. Large, with tall windows and white wood-panelled walls. The lighting was soft, the room elegant. Rows of burgundy padded chairs faced an image of an old manuscript projected on to a screen at the front. A man, Theo Merrick himself, stood at the lit podium beside it, addressing the audience as Jasmin and Dash tried to slip in quietly. He was handsome, she supposed. More so in person than he was on the TV. Like one of the heroes in Georgie's romance novels with their rich white men, all blue-eyed and square-jawed. His audience was oddly hushed, a little solemn even, hanging on his every word. It felt as if they'd walked in late to a funeral rather than a lecture.

Jasmin searched the back rows but couldn't see any free seats. She noted Rían next to the aisle, leaning back in his chair with his ankle crossed to his knee. Allie was beside him, scribbling in a notebook, and Imogen further down the row.

Her eyes flicked over the middle rows, then the front, where she finally saw two seats in the second row. She hesitated. People started looking at them. Heads craning to see the pair who were hovering in the aisle. Jasmin suddenly felt very visible.

'Please, do come in,' Merrick said, noticing them. 'Glad you could join us.' He gestured with a welcoming hand, like a gracious host.

Now everyone really *was* looking at them.

'There.' Dash pointed triumphantly to the seats in the second row. And that's when Jasmin saw Damien, standing in the front corner. He was pointing a camera at Merrick, thankfully oblivious to her grand entrance. And while she stared at Damien adjusting his camera, Dash started towards the second row seats.

'No. Not up there,' Jasmin whispered, but he led the way with his usual swagger. She'd always envied Dash his easiness in the world.

Merrick paused, giving them a moment to get to the front. The audience watched her and Dash as they walked down the centre aisle. After what felt like an eternity, they reached the row. Dash smiled pleasantly as a man shifted his legs with a long-suffering sigh. A young man with a neat side parting tutted loudly.

When they finally sat down, Jasmin's cheeks felt hot. The woman next to her muttered something under her breath. She wore a heavy perfume that tickled Jasmin's throat. She looked down at her hands, certain that if she glanced back, she'd see

Rían smirking at the mild disturbance they'd caused. She was sure that the people in this room were looking at her and Dash like they didn't belong.

'I don't think I ever made a lecture on time,' Merrick said. His voice was warm, his eyes kind, sympathetic, as though he could feel Jasmin's embarrassment.

The thing about being an observer, the person who watched, was that Jasmin hated it when eyes were on her. And now there were so many eyes. She had that unpleasant tingle, the one that always came before the unbearable lightness that signalled the beginning of a panic attack. She pulled in a slow breath, feeling the air expand her lungs.

'Yeah, Jas, don't mind them,' Dash whispered, placing a reassuring hand on her shoulder. It felt solid and grounding despite Jasmin's discomfort. Someone shushed him, casting a disparaging eye over his worn T-shirt, his favourite even with the small hole on the sleeve.

'So, I was just telling everyone – I have a digression. A confession.' The speaker's words finally drew her attention. They sounded low and strangely intimate despite the packed room. *I have a confession.* She looked up.

'Sometimes, in a certain light, I believe in immortality.' There was a rumble of laughter. He smiled wryly, holding up his hands. 'Right, I can see I'm losing you. Why am I speaking of magic in a lecture that's meant to be about science?' His voice became more serious. 'But sometimes we forget that the line between science and magic wasn't always so clearly drawn. Think of the alchemists of Prague, who believed themselves men of science, who grounded their search for the philosopher's stone – which was meant to grant immortality – in scientific principles and observation. That's what we want, isn't it, when we pursue scientific inquiry? To investigate mystery. And maybe magic is not as far-fetched as we might think. What if, by finding the right answers, we could be more? Maybe even live forever. While I don't believe that some unknown, inexplicable alchemy can extend the human lifespan, I do know that with good science, we can live longer, healthier lives. The average human life has already been extended over the last six hundred years. What if we could extend it by another twenty, another fifty years? Why not … a hundred?'

The audience turned quiet again. Jasmin considered his words. Of course, she'd have Georgie around forever if she could.

'A personal interlude, if I may.' Merrick stepped away from the podium, moved closer to the audience. 'It feels serendipitous talking about my latest research into wellness and longevity at the McKellan Galleries this evening. You see, it all started right here in this building, when I was a young PhD student more than ten years ago. Like many others, I made my dutiful pilgrimage, standing beside tourists to glimpse a thirteenth-century manuscript in its glass cage. The jewel in McKellan's crown. *The Book of Monsters.*'

The manuscript on the screen. Jasmin should have known. Eamon had brought her here to see it on her eighth birthday. He'd arranged for a visit outside of official viewing hours. It had been just the two of them in the temperature-controlled room with the Book behind thick display glass. Jasmin hadn't been sure what the fuss was about. An old text, full of strange drawings and words she didn't understand. But her grandfather's eyes had been shining.

Merrick's voice lowered, like he was admitting something personal. 'What I hadn't anticipated was that *The Book of Monsters* would change me.'

His eyes tracked the audience. It felt to Jasmin like he held her gaze a moment longer. But then maybe everyone in the audience thought that. Merrick clearly knew what he was doing.

The screen changed, now showing a faded pink and green illustration of a serpent eating its tail. A famous image, Jasmin knew.

'*The Book of Monsters* contains four short, terrible myths. Stories about the everyday monsters that walk among us. And of these four myths, the one that is most disturbing, and least understood, is the *Immortalis*.'

The *Immortalis*. Jasmin could almost hear her grandfather's voice from all those years ago. *Everything man is or wants is in this book*. The *Immortalis* had been his favourite. He had told her the stories at bedtime, despite Sonia's protests.

'The *Immortalis* is believed to be based on true historical events from the eleventh or twelfth century,' Merrick continued. 'It's a short, almost abrupt story of an old, battle-worn king in the last months of a war. The king and his army had been besieged for many months. The last animal had been killed, the last grain eaten. The army had been ravaged, with many soldiers lost. The king and his nobles were desperate. They were elderly men, and weak. They could not withstand much more.'

Jasmin could hear the echo of Eamon's words as Merrick spoke. She felt as though she were curled against her grandfather, listening to the strange tale in the comfort of his sitting room. The tick of the clock, the licking of flames in the grate.

There she went again. Thinking about her grandfather. Maybe coming here tonight had been a mistake.

'The old king summoned the remaining army for a special blessing. The next day, every last soldier was found dead, scattered around the sacred altar. All the young, strong foot soldiers who'd fought for the king suddenly drained of life. Terrible mourning swept the city. But the king and his elite were glowing with vitality. Somehow, overnight, they'd gained an almost supernatural strength, seeming to have shed years in just one night. Younger, stronger – invincible. They fought their way out of the besieged castle, defeating the enemy.

'Rumours grew that the king had made a dark sacrifice that night. But perhaps the strangest thing,' Merrick paused, giving his words weight, 'is that there was no sign of a struggle. It appeared that the soldiers gave up their lives willingly. For strong as the human impulse is to survive, it is also in the nature of humans to sacrifice themselves for the right cause.'

Jasmin had a sudden image of the soldiers on a slow march to the sacred ground, eyes bright with conviction.

'As the myth goes, the soldiers offered up their youthful blood, and the king and his elite drank it while chanting an incantation. The king had become a young man again, with the strength of ten men. Vitality coursed through his altered body. But this change could only be sustained through sacrifice. And so the king lived, young and strong, but always hunting. Always hungry.

'The last line states, "The immortalis roam the earth to this day, searching to preserve their strength."'

The audience hung on Merrick's every word. They were enthralled, gazing at him like the willing victims might have gazed upon the ancient king. A strange tension gripped the room, an anticipation that she could see in widened eyes, shoulders squared towards Merrick. Jasmin had a sudden thought: the king outside, in the beautifully landscaped McKellan Galleries gardens. Hungry.

'I understood something that day, standing in front of *The Book of Monsters*,' Merrick's voice turned thoughtful, looking inward. 'A simple truth. A truth as old as time: *human beings, essentially, want to live.* We are hardwired to survive. I was young myself then, no old king – but even then I knew it. Which brings me, somewhat indulgently, to the Wellness Formula.' He laughed, and the atmosphere in the room relaxed. 'My revolutionary project for optimal well-being that is firmly grounded in scientific research. The Wellness Formula is an interdisciplinary, biopsychosocial study spearheaded by myself and Dr Candice Greene. It has been developed in conjunction with top researchers looking at the big picture of the conditions for good health and well-being. It's a longitudinal study, both observational and interventional …'

Merrick continued talking, but for the first time in years, Jasmin found herself thinking about the immortal king. The hungry king had always frightened her. She would have dreams of him outside her house on the lawn, looking up at her window, waiting to drink her blood. And the worst thing was she would go to him willingly. Jasmin would wake up in a cold sweat, clamping a hand over her mouth to stop from screaming out loud.

'That was surprisingly entertaining.' Dash grinned at her, jolting her out of her thoughts. The lecture had ended, the lights were up and Jasmin, lost in the past, had missed most of it.

People around them stood to leave. 'Do you want to go home or in there?' He inclined his head to where the folding doors had been opened. Most of the guests were migrating to the drinks reception, where they'd be served wine, finger food and asked to make donations.

Jasmin watched the gathering crowd. 'In there.'

FIVE

While Dash went to the bar, Jasmin roamed the room, watching.

Merrick was at the centre, of course, surrounded by a circle of admirers. Jasmin could see why the university had made him their star. He was a walking advertisement. Their perfect result. Tall, smart and charming. *This is what we make here.*

Her grandfather had been like that.

Around that inner circle, people clustered in groups as waiters circled the room with trays of wine glasses. Scanning the room, Jasmin recognised some of Georgie's friends, women with pearls and a weekly blow-dry, laughing. Usually, Georgie would be right there in the middle of them. Jasmin admired her for it, that even after the scandal, Georgie had refused to give any ground. She had resumed her usual place in the world, and carried on as before. Almost as before.

Jasmin searched the room, but she couldn't see the four friends. With a dart of anxiety, she wondered if they'd gone to that new bar after all. Disappointment fizzed in her stomach.

'Took you long enough,' she grumbled as Dash finally appeared, handing her a sparkling water. She glimpsed his watch, two minutes before eight – he'd been gone nearly ten minutes.

A passing waiter stopped and offered a tray of canapés, prawns with guacamole and cucumber, that smelt fresh and lemony. Jasmin took one.

'Got chatting with the guys at the bar, sorry. Come over, we can hang there.'

She bit into the canapé, enjoying the explosion of flavours on her tongue.

'You can finally meet Javier,' Dash said. 'He's fun.'

Jasmin peered over to the bar, checking out the group of men bunched around it, bantering. They did look fun. In the early summer, before they'd left for Italy, Dash had met Javier at the gym, and was always heading out with him, biking, or a barbecue, or hanging out at Javier's digs.

But then, peeling away from the bar, Jasmin saw Imogen, in a 1950s-style red flared dress, balancing a tray of cocktails.

Jasmin tracked Imogen as she wound her way through the room, meeting up with the other three, who'd just come in through the double doors.

No one could miss them. It was in the air around them, in the way they stood, taking up space, a hip jutted out here, a straight back there. They shared a self-possession that came from their togetherness, from having discovered something in each other, and it made them shine.

Jasmin took in Allie in double faux leather and eyeliner so thick Jasmin could barely see her eyes as Imogen handed her a cocktail. Rían, in a long crimson duster coat, sipped from a hip flask.

Then Jasmin's eyes tracked, as they always did, to Damien.

He didn't need unconventional clothes to set him apart. Nor was it the pleasing symmetry of his face, his thick tousled hair or the pensive brow. What drew her to Damien was a recognition of sorts, that there was something in his soul that was familiar to her. Something she longed for.

'I'll find you and Javier later,' Jasmin said. 'I see some friends over there.'

It wasn't a lie, they were friends. Just not hers.

As she made her way through the crowd, Jasmin wondered exactly when did observing become stalking? Watching a group of friends in a cafe was one thing. Following them to an event was more calculated. A teeny bit unhinged, maybe.

Because you need to catch trouble fast, Jasmin thought. *Before someone snaps and tries to murder his wife. Before your dad ups and leaves to another country. Before your boyfriend replaces you. Before your friends forget you were there at all. That's why you have to stay watchful.*

'You're blocking the way,' came a voice from behind her, cold and annoyed. Jasmin spun round to find it was the girl from earlier – the girl who had been crying.

'Hey, Niamh,' Jasmin said. 'Feeling any better?'

'Oh, you again. Yeah, I'm fine.' Niamh's tone was clipped. She looked like she was going to a job interview, almost as if she was trying to compensate for her previous lack of composure. Her make-up was perfect and she wore a knee-length black dress, her blonde hair in a low ponytail. Her suede pumps had a chunky heel and she carried a neat black bag with a long gold chain. Around her neck was a heavy gold pendant, oval-shaped with gentle scalloping. Scales. It was a dragon's egg. It looked cheap, the kind of thing you'd pick up at a flea market, a contrast to the rest of what she was wearing. Her gaze was loose, searching without focus.

'I was worried about you earlier,' Jasmin said, still worried.

'Were you now?' Niamh narrowed her eyes.

'No,' Jasmin said, feeling like she'd been accused of something but she didn't know what. 'I mean, yes. I just thought – you looked like you might need help.'

'Why would I need *your* help?' Niamh looked decidedly unfriendly. 'Wait, how did you know my name?'

Jasmin was taken aback at the suspicion clouding her features.

'You told me. Earlier.'

Uncertainty settled in Niamh's eyes. Then she shook her head and let out a short, nasty laugh. 'You can help me by leaving me the hell alone,' she spat. Her fingers tightened on her glass of wine and she lowered her voice. 'He sent you, didn't he? Is this his way of "managing me"? You tell him, I'm done being managed.' Irritation clouding her features, Niamh marched off.

What just happened? Jasmin thought. She glanced behind her and saw a woman also watching Niamh's departure. The woman was in her thirties, wearing a silky bronze dress with a white blazer. She was striking, the bronze complementing her brown skin. At that moment, Merrick appeared at the woman's side, sliding a familiar hand around her hip and murmuring in her ear.

The party had spilt out on to the wide veranda despite the chill in the October evening air. People clustered together like penguins, drinks in hand as they talked and networked. Jasmin saw Niamh there, hovering at the edge of a group, looking at her wine, shoulders rigid. Someone nudged Jasmin from behind, a firm knock on the small of her back.

'I'm sorry,' came a familiar voice.

Jasmin turned. It was him. Damien. Her cheeks grew warm.

'Didn't see you there,' he said pleasantly.

You never do, Jasmin thought.

He smiled at her curiously, as if to say *Cat got your tongue?* Which was what Georgie always said when Jasmin went quiet.

'Are we going to take this picture then?' a loud, jovial voice intruded. A group of older men in suits gestured to the camera, Merrick among them. He was shaking hands and uttering his customary charming phrases.

He side-eyed Damien. 'Well, what are you waiting for?'

Merrick hadn't been rude, far from it. But there was something dismissive about the way he spoke. The way he looked past Damien like he didn't matter. Damien faltered, and Jasmin sensed he noticed it too. She watched him as he fumbled with the camera, with his worn jacket and scuffed shoes, while the older men in their expensive suits joked about how their time was money and if he was lucky maybe he would know that too one day.

'Of course. I'm sorry.' Damien stepped forward to take the picture, and Jasmin felt a prick of irritation on his behalf. He didn't need to apologise to these men.

Merrick directed Damien to take another photo, and Jasmin began to suspect that his appearance of being in touch, a man of the people, was a mask he slipped on only when it suited him.

Jasmin studied Merrick, and wondered what he was like when he was alone.

SIX

A jewelled hand touched her shoulder, followed by the strong notes of white floral perfume.

'Jasmin, hello, it's so nice to see you here.' One of Georgie's friends stood beside her. 'How is Georgie? She due back from her travels soon?'

Jasmin beamed at the older woman. 'They got back today.'

'I'll call her up, I want to hear all about the cruise. Your grandmother is a lucky woman. All this glamorous travel – and with such a handsome man … Tell me, did they seem awfully happy?'

Georgie's friends fluttered around Jasmin, closing in on her. They asked about Georgie's travels, about Richard, who they hadn't seen in years but were still interested in. Genuine affection and concern for her grandmother showed in their expressions and smiles.

Over their shoulders, Dash grinned at her, raising his beer.

He knew that she was trapped in that embrace of silk blouses and tailored trousers and musk. She was fond of them, but Georgie's friends could *talk*.

After fifteen minutes, Jasmin's gaze darted around, plotting an escape from this elegant, perfumed snare. Peering through the open veranda doors, she saw Niamh come up the garden path, stumbling on the uneven paving. Jasmin frowned, wondering why she'd been down there in the dimly lit garden.

Again, unbidden, the image popped into her head: the hungry king, his eyes huge and demanding, his skin sinewy and taut, luring people down to the garden. His teeth bloodied. She saw his hands ending in unnaturally long shadowy fingers, reaching out, as if to caress. As if to take. She saw the shadowy fingers stretching to cross the garden paths, creeping over the shrubs, the autumn trees …

As Niamh climbed the steps to the veranda, Jasmin could see pure rage on her face.

'Tell me, my dear, what are your plans for next year?' The women drew her attention back to them, cooing in delight when Jasmin confirmed yes, she would apply to the university, but had not yet decided on a programme.

She began initiating her extraction, *So lovely to chat*, when a deep voice interjected.

'Excuse me. I'm taking photos for the *Answerer*, the university newspaper. Would you mind?'

Looking over her shoulder, Jasmin saw Damien with his camera. He was smiling at the women in their pearls and silk.

Her heart beat faster, and her skin prickled at his proximity. She scarcely dared look up at him.

'Of course you can take our picture,' one of the women declared, delighted. 'Jasmin, come here. Stand right in the middle. Georgie's going to love this.'

The women arranged themselves, bombarding Damien with questions. 'What's your name?' 'That's a magnificent camera.' 'Are you studying journalism here at the university?' 'My father was president, you know. Sixty years ago.'

'Law, actually,' he replied, adjusting the lens of his camera. 'My name's Damien.'

'Law? Good career options there. My Emmet is a barrister.'

'What a fine-looking young man you are, Damien. What is your last name?'

'McHugh?' another woman said when he answered. 'Anything to the Roscommon McHughs? No?'

They threw question after question, like birds pecking at bread.

'Jasmin, did I hear that you broke up with your boyfriend over the summer?'

Jasmin scowled. They were being playful. Deliberate. *A perk of old age*, Georgie called it, that coy breaking of social rules. Damien smiled at her, then his face was hidden by the camera.

'That's a great shot,' he said, glancing at the camera screen. 'I'll just get your names?'

Behind Damien, Jasmin caught a glimpse of Niamh talking to a waiter. Niamh swiped a glass from his tray in a clumsy move that had wine slopping over the sides, and the waiter stepped back.

Jasmin frowned. Something was clearly off with Niamh.

Not your business, she reminded herself.

The women introduced themselves and Damien jotted down their names in a small notepad. He turned to Jasmin, slipping the pad in his back pocket.

'So, you're Jasmin.'

'I am.' She'd recovered her cool, thankfully.

'Jasmin Malik,' one of Georgie's crew added helpfully, then melted away, not so subtly winking at her.

Jasmin shook her head. 'How come you're the photographer for the *Answerer* if you're not studying journalism?'

'I'm not with the *Answerer*. My friends are.' He lifted the camera again. 'I'm doing them a favour. I like taking pictures.'

The camera clicked. The picture taken, Damien kept the camera aloft, his eyes holding hers. Jasmin felt something bright and hot inside, a spark, a flare.

'What do you like about it?' she asked.

'I'm interested in people. You capture all sorts of things in a picture. Look.'

Glancing down at the screen, he moved to stand beside Jasmin, arm to arm, and showed her. It was an intimate shot, something in the way she was looking at him made it seem like she was the only one in the room. Her skin glowed in the soft lighting, and there was a knowing in her eyes that she hadn't seen before. A boldness and confidence that she liked. Her

41

small smile made her look like she had secrets. She looked strong.

He was right. It was a good picture.

'Give me your number and I'll send it to you.'

'You want my number?' she blurted.

He grinned. 'So did you,' he said, 'break up with your boyfriend over the summer?' He raised his hand, reaching for a strand of hair that had fallen over her face. He tucked it back, his fingers lingering near her cheek, his eyes steady on hers.

Two things happened at once.

'Damien, there you are,' Rían said, throwing an arm around his friend.

A loud crash sounded from the far side of the room.

Heads turned to find the source of the noise. Across the room, near the bar, a large blue and white vase lay in pieces on the floor. Niamh stood next to it, mouth open, eyes wide. The broken shards and wet, tall-stemmed flowers were scattered like pick-up sticks, the water seeping across the stone floor.

A sudden hush overtook the room, the silence ringing in Jasmin's ears. Only a few seconds passed but it felt like minutes.

'Always a sign of a good party when the china gets smashed,' Rían commented, breaking the quiet. 'A bit too much of the free wine, I'd say.'

But Jasmin could see that Niamh looked … desperate. Her mouth moved with inaudible words, an apology or a plea to the room. A waiter ran over, crouching down with a dustpan and brush to sweep up the smaller shards. Slowly, people began to resume their conversations, filling the room with noise once

42

more. A few looked at Niamh with disdain as she took a stumbling step forward.

Impulsively, Jasmin went to her just as Niamh stumbled again, putting a hand out to the wall to steady herself.

'I'll have whatever she's having,' Rían said, bringing his flask to his lips.

'Niamh,' Jasmin called as she pushed her way through the crowd. 'Niamh, wait!'

'Do you know that woman?' Georgie's friends drew around Jasmin, their disapproval clear. 'That vase was not cheap. Honestly, these students …'

When she finally extracted herself, Niamh was no longer in sight. Jasmin searched the room, trawling the sea of unfamiliar faces, but couldn't find her.

She steeled herself and went down into the garden, moving away from the light and noise. Niamh was not there either.

Jasmin shivered, the cold setting in. What was she doing, chasing after a drunk girl who'd told her to back off? But the desperation in Niamh's eyes niggled at her.

He's a monster.

Something glinted from the paving. Jasmin reached down and picked up a small gold object. She immediately recognised it – Niamh's necklace. It must have fallen, maybe when she tripped over the uneven steps. Jasmin peered out at the dark garden but couldn't see anything. Only the branches, reaching out like thin fingers. Shivering, she closed the necklace in her palm and turned back.

Inside, people still flocked around Merrick and Candice.

Georgie's friends still gossiped. Allie and Imogen were still knocking back cocktails and laughing. The broken vase had been cleared up.

'You ready to leave?' Dash said as Jasmin returned to the bar, his friends now working the floor. 'This is getting boring.'

'Yeah, sure.' Jasmin felt out of sorts. She waved at Georgie's friends, realising that she'd lost her chance to give Damien her phone number. She groaned.

'What?' Dash sounded amused.

'Nothing, nothing. Let's go.'

He raised an eyebrow, handed her the car keys and said no more.

SEVEN

The McKellan Galleries were every bit as grand and imposing in the afternoon light. Jasmin walked up the steps, running the tip of her finger over the rough texture of Niamh's pendant. She'd be looking for it. There must be a lost property box here, and maybe she'd find a way to speak to Niamh again, to know that she was really OK.

Inside, Jasmin inquired at reception, who sent her to find someone called Curtis, who managed the lost property.

'He's out in the back.'

Jasmin went through the event room, observing a new vase had replaced the one Niamh had broken. She walked down the veranda stairs, thinking about how Niamh had seemed when they'd spoken. *I'm done being managed.* She hadn't seemed drunk then, Jasmin thought. And yet, she'd clearly been inebriated just a short while later when she broke the vase.

That was odd.

A bad break-up, Jasmin thought. It had to be. Niamh must be a dramatic sort. Jasmin had to laugh at herself. This was what happened when you watched too much. Other people's stories became more real than your own.

Ahead, Jasmin saw a young man with friendly eyes carrying stacked crates of empty wine glasses.

'Excuse me, have you seen Curtis?' Jasmin stopped him to ask.

'He's fixing a post at the bottom of the garden,' the man said. He seemed familiar. He'd been there the previous evening, Jasmin was sure. One of the bar staff.

'You're friends with Dash, aren't you?' she said tentatively.

'You know Dash?' His face brightened into a wide smile.

'He's my brother. I'm Jasmin.'

'Of course. You were here last night, he pointed you out. Said you're his clever little sister. I'm Javier.'

'Oh, you're Javier,' Jasmin laughed. 'We've heard all about you. Nice to finally meet you.' She gestured to the crates of wine glasses. 'You with the caterers?'

'Just helping out. My sister runs Wild Thyme, the catering company, and needed a last-minute fill-in.'

'The canapés were really good.'

His smile broadened. 'I'll tell her you said so.' He shifted the load in his arms and added, 'Curtis is that way. Through the garden and turn left.'

'Thanks.'

But before Jasmin could move, a shrill scream filled the air. Rooks flew from the trees where they'd perched. Javier stiffened. Jasmin felt a coil of alarm in her stomach. They looked at each other.

Putting down the crates, Javier sprinted along the path. Jasmin set off after him, and even though she was fast, she couldn't keep up. At the end of the path Javier paused, looking around. There was that scream again, closer now and even more distraught. He turned right and Jasmin followed.

She emerged from a cluster of trees to see a large stone shed. From the broken wheelbarrow and tyres outside, she guessed it was where garden equipment was stored. Jasmin stopped, feeling a paralysing trepidation. She called out, 'Javier?'

'Jasmin, don't come in here.' Javier's voice was wild. She could hear another voice, from inside the shed – a voice whimpering, 'Oh God, she's dead,' over and over.

Jasmin felt eight again, bracing herself to walk back into Georgie's house. Her reluctant feet on the stone path. That hot pulsing in her ears. The scent of garden cuttings, leaves prised from stems and cut branches. Knowing that her worst nightmare was through that door. Time passed and she could not move. She was unaware of the running footsteps behind her. Just her own thudding heart.

She thought about her odd conviction last night that the old king from the stories had been out in the garden. Her childhood embodiment of terror. And she'd been right, there had been something terrifying out here in the garden. Maybe not a dead king from ancient stories with fingers like the tips of trees in winter, but a beating heart stopping. The last breath of an unknown woman. A body coming to a final halt.

47

Two gallery staff rushed inside the shed. Jasmin stayed rooted to the spot.

Oh God, she's dead.

Javier emerged from the shed, his tanned skin now pale. The sparkle in his eyes had been extinguished.

'I'm going to call the Gardaí,' he said.

Suddenly, Jasmin was released from whatever had bound her to the gravel. She stepped forward. She had to know what was inside the shed. Javier tried to catch her arm.

'Jasmin, no.'

The pulsing in her ears was a constant drumbeat. The fumes of lawnmower petrol made Jasmin's nose tingle. She had to go in. She pushed the door open –

Javier's broad hand pulled it shut. 'Don't.'

'What did you see?' She squeezed out the words.

Because Jasmin had seen something too. A single black suede pump lying on its side. A small black bag with a long gold chain.

She had seen them before. Only last night.

They belonged to Niamh.

When Sonia came home, Jasmin was in the living room.

'Have you eaten?' Sonia called, dropping her bag in the study.

'I'm sorted,' Jasmin said, her stomach rebelling at the thought of food.

When Sonia came in minutes later cradling a mug of hot tea, Jasmin was still staring at the blank TV screen.

'What are you doing?' Sonia looked at her curiously.

'Deciding on my art project,' Jasmin lied.

She'd heard the whispers, as she and Javier were told to go back to the McKellan. *Found hanging. Taken her own life.* He'd walked with her through the garden, clutching her arm as if he needed it to stay afloat. His eyes were red, his distress obvious, and Jasmin had felt a pang when she left him, his head bowed as he waited to talk to the guards.

And now, her mind was tangled with thoughts. Of Niamh, her eyes wide and frightened. The desperation in her voice when she'd made that call. *I'm so scared. He's a monster.* The pendant that was still in Jasmin's pocket.

She couldn't tell Sonia what had happened. She didn't have the words. Sonia settled on the armchair and turned on the repeat of the six o'clock news. There were reports about fuel prices rising and a knife attack, but Jasmin didn't take any of it in. Until she saw a reporter outside the McKellan Galleries.

Jasmin shifted to the edge of her seat. She felt ill. She wanted to look away, but morbid fascination drew her attention.

'… on the university campus after a young woman's life came to a tragic end'.

'That poor, poor girl,' Sonia said, her eyes soft. 'And her family.'

'… while deeply distressing for the university community, Gardaí do not suspect foul play,' the reporter continued sombrely.

Jasmin leaned forward, trying to glean every bit of information she could. Then a university official was on-screen, extending his condolences. As Jasmin watched him talk about rallying behind students, extended counselling services, she realised that she didn't believe it.

'They're under so much pressure, students nowadays,' Sonia said sadly, turning off the TV. 'Remember, Jasmin, nothing is more important than your health.'

Jasmin's mind was elsewhere. She thought about how unsteady and uncoordinated Niamh had seemed when she knocked into the vase, apparently in the far stages of inebriation. *I'll have whatever she's having*, Rían had said. Would she have had the presence of mind to navigate the dark garden all the way down to the shed, find a rope and end her life? Jasmin's instinct said no. Because she'd heard Niamh explicitly say that she was afraid, that she needed to get away. Her dad was coming to collect her this morning. She was running out on her coursework and life here, because she was afraid. Afraid of someone she'd called a monster.

Now Niamh was dead.

In her intoxicated state, she could have easily been over-powered by the person she feared. The hanging could have been staged …

It wasn't suicide, Jasmin thought. It was murder.

But what could she do now? She could go to the guards, but an eavesdropped conversation wasn't exactly convincing evidence. Jasmin didn't know Niamh, and they might say that she'd misunderstood, or that she was making drama. Jasmin needed more evidence.

Sonia sighed and picked up her empty mug. Before leaving the room, she paused. 'Is everything OK, Jas?'

'Just thinking about that student.' She hesitated before adding, 'I saw her last night at the alumni lecture. She was pretty wasted.'

'Oh, Jas, I'm so sorry.' Sonia's face was etched with concern.

Jasmin glanced up. 'Do you think it definitely *was* suicide?'

Sonia frowned. 'Sounds like they think so. There'll be a post-mortem though, and an inquest. The guards will be interviewing her friends and family. They'll find anything suspicious.'

Unless Niamh's monster had covered his tracks.

Sonia left the room and Jasmin stared again at the blank TV screen. If she could find out who Niamh had been talking to on the phone, that would be a start. Whoever Niamh had been confiding in might know who this monster was. They would know why she had been so upset.

And this person had been at the lecture last night. Jasmin tried to think who she'd seen Niamh talking to. She'd been on the outskirts of a group of students Jasmin didn't know, spoken to a waiter who she'd blanked because she'd been so hyperfocused on Niamh ... Jasmin groaned, sinking into the suede sofa. If only she'd taken pictures –

Immediately, she sat up again.

She hadn't taken pictures, but she knew who had.

EIGHT

In the weeks after her grandfather was taken away, Jasmin had nightmares.

She dreamed of the hungry king, strong but somehow desiccated, waiting in the garden. She dreamed he had long fingers made of shadows. Thin, long, *wanting* fingers that stretched and stretched, through the garden, into the kitchen. They reached over red-stained cabinets and bubbling pots, until they wrapped themselves around her grandmother's neck and squeezed. When Georgie fell, they turned, searching for her.

Today, stepping through the south gate and into the tree-lined lane, Jasmin felt the shadow touch of those long fingers. Like the monster from her nightmares was awake again. Like she had never really been safe since that summer's day in the kitchen.

As she walked towards the theatre, Jasmin saw Gardaí on

campus. She caught snippets of conversation from the students she passed.

Isn't it awful?

Can't believe what happened.

So sad.

Niamh Cunningham. Her name was Niamh Cunningham.

She heard the name again and again. *Niamh Cunningham.*
So sad.

Stepping inside the Three Divas, Jasmin saw the friends at the alcove table. She hesitated in the doorway, then walked up to them. They were deep in conversation, but as she approached Damien glanced up, his face brightening with recognition.

'Hey! You ran off the other night.' He grinned, his full lips curving up and making his green eyes shine. It came easy to him, Jasmin saw. The flirtatious grin, that inviting way he looked at her. Not a player exactly, but no choirboy either, she guessed. He had both hands wrapped around his coffee cup, as he often did, and Jasmin wondered if he was cold in that thin army jacket. 'You were going to give me your number.'

Jasmin was sure the others were rolling their eyes. 'Sorry about that. It's just – she was at the party, wasn't she? The girl who—'

'Yeah, I know.' Damien was more subdued now.

'You were there at the alumni lecture?' Allie said.

'I was. Do you mind if I sit for a minute?'

Rían shifted along the bench seat and patted the place beside him as he introduced himself, adding, 'This is Allie and Imogen, and this charmer here is Damien.' *I know*, thought

Jasmin impatiently. *I know who all of you are.* 'Can I pour you a glass?'

She noticed the carafe of red wine on the table. She didn't often drink, alcohol didn't pair well with her panic attacks. But slowly sipping a glass of wine would give her a reason to stay longer.

'Just a splash.'

With the wine in front of her, Jasmin searched for what to say. 'I met Niamh the day she died. It was … odd.'

'What do you mean?' Damien said, leaning forward slightly.

Jasmin studied the friends. Rían was watching her with a lazy interest. Imogen was inscrutable. Allie picked at an empty sugar sachet, shredding it into strips and twisting them.

'Did any of you know her?'

'No,' Imogen said. 'She was in her second year on the maths teaching programme. Our paths didn't cross.'

'But we noticed her,' Allie added. 'At the drinks party.'

'She knocked over that huge vase. I think everyone noticed her.' Imogen was being cagey, Jasmin realised. She kept her cards close to her chest, as usual.

'I saw her in the ladies before that,' Allie said. 'She was searching through her bag, unpacking everything. She looked stressed. I asked her if she'd lost something.'

'And had she?' Jasmin said.

'Painkillers. She said she got bad tension headaches and always carried them with her. She was sure she'd put them in her bag, then she asked me if I had any. I didn't, no surprise.'

'Did she seem drunk?' asked Jasmin curiously. 'Only she didn't seem drunk to me earlier in the evening.'

Allie thought about it. 'Not even a little. She was trashed when she knocked over that vase, which was, what, thirty or forty minutes later?'

'Why would a drunk woman go all the way down a dark garden and into a maintenance shed?' Rían said.

'They didn't say they found her in the shed on the news,' Jasmin said quickly.

Rían raised an eyebrow. 'All right, detective, calm down.'

'We don't listen to the news. We get our information through the campus whispering network.' Imogen lifted her glass to her red-stained lips and drank. She sounded bored but her eyes were sharp.

'But we don't know when she died. She could have passed out somewhere after the drinks party and gone to the shed when she woke up,' Damien pointed out. 'It could have happened hours later.'

'True.' Imogen emptied her glass and reached for the carafe.

'I don't think she killed herself.' Allie twisted a strip of paper, seemingly fixated on the wine glugging into Imogen's glass. 'I think someone did it to her and wanted it to look like she killed herself.'

'Allie Vaughn,' Imogen snapped, spilling a drop of wine in her irritation. 'This isn't fiction. You've no basis for saying something like that.'

Allie closed her fist around the twisted-up paper. She met Imogen's eyes defiantly. 'I checked the coins.'

'Oh, well then,' said Rían. 'If the *coins* say so.' Jasmin was reminded of the coins that Allie had drawn before the alumni lecture. The Burning Heart and the Noose.

'They found a note,' Imogen said.

'They did?' Jasmin was surprised. 'Do you know what it said?' And how did Imogen know?

'It was short. Handwritten with a Sharpie, and found in the shed on top of her coat. It said, *I'm sorry. N.*'

They fell silent for a moment. Jasmin pictured the note in the shed. She shook her head, not convinced.

'The afternoon before she died, I ran into Niamh,' Jasmin said tentatively. 'She seemed distressed. And – and I followed her.' She was nervous to admit this, as it didn't exactly paint her in a good light, eavesdropping on a private conversation. 'I wanted to make sure she was OK. She was talking on the phone, she told the other person that she wanted to see them that night. She sounded afraid and was making plans to leave town the next day.'

'Seriously?' Imogen said, sitting up. 'You followed her?' She muttered something that Jasmin didn't quite catch, but sounded an awful lot like '*Stalker much?*'

'She was afraid?' Allie said.

'You should take this to the guards,' Damien said, his eyes troubled.

'Take what? An eavesdropped conversation? All it does is prove that she was not in a good place. It makes her sound paranoid, and perhaps she was.' Jasmin's throat tightened. 'Maybe Niamh wasn't well.'

'Do you know who she was talking to?' Imogen sounded more eager now. 'Did she mention a name?'

Jasmin shook her head. 'It sounded like they arranged to meet that evening, presumably at the lecture. If we could just find out who they are and talk to them ...'

'Well, this changes things.' Imogen sat back in her chair, her cherry-red nails tapping the table. Her eyes darted as her speech picked up. 'It also makes a damn good investigative piece.' Noticing the others' questioning looks, Imogen added, 'How better to honour Niamh's memory than to write the truth of what happened to her?'

Damien snorted. 'Honour her memory? You didn't even know the girl. None of us did.' He drank the last of his wine, shaking his head when Allie pushed the nearly finished carafe over.

'So?' Imogen challenged. 'We can still honour her, can't we?'

Allie slumped a little further in her seat. 'Imogen, Niamh's death isn't a way for you to ...' She clammed up, not finishing her thought.

'I saw her talking to you at the party, Jasmin,' Rían said. 'Did she say anything then?'

Jasmin shrugged. 'Told me to get lost.'

'I saw her coming up from the garden,' Allie said. 'I thought, there's the girl with the headache and figured she'd gone down to escape the noise for a few minutes. I wondered why she didn't just leave if she was so miserable.'

'She couldn't leave,' Imogen said, snapping her fingers, 'because she'd arranged to meet her mystery friend.'

'We could check the pictures,' Jasmin said. 'Damien's pictures. She might be in the background, if we're lucky.'

'Excellent thinking,' Imogen said. 'You took loads, didn't you, Damien? And not just the posed group shots.'

'Yeah. I haven't had time to go through them yet,' Damien said.

'Let's do it now.' Imogen was already gathering her phone, putting it in her bag. 'We can see if Niamh is in any of them, and who she's talking to.'

'I have a paper due,' Damien said.

'Which means you'll have had it finished days ago. You're always on top of your work.'

'And I'd like it to stay that way.'

A look passed between them.

'I know.' Imogen softened. 'But this is really important. We'll be fast. And then you'll have the rest of the evening to work.'

'Fine,' Damien relented. 'But they're mostly posed shots of alumni donors. Don't get your hopes up.'

'It's a lead, isn't it?' Imogen stood, her jacket on and bag slung over her shoulder. Her eyes were bright now. Jasmin smiled: Imogen was like her, curious.

'Are you a journalist?' Jasmin stood up, eyes level with Imogen's. She knew the answer, of course.

'Studying to be. Because I am a bloodhound. Like you, I think.' Imogen gave a wolfish smile. A hungry smile.

She was nearly right. They both craved knowing things. But Jasmin needed to know so that she could control her world. So that nothing would take her by surprise. She wondered what drove Imogen's curiosity.

'You're in your second year?' Jasmin asked as they walked. 'How old are you all?'

'I'm nineteen,' Damien said easily, falling into step beside her. 'Imogen's nineteen for a few more weeks, Rían twenty-one, and Allie's twentieth was Sunday. And you?'

'Eighteen,' Jasmin said, leaving out the *still at school* part. 'And you three are studying journalism?'

'Allie's in print,' Imogen said, 'and Rían and I are majoring in broadcast.'

'With these good looks, how could I not?' Rían flashed a smile fit for a toothpaste advert. He was good-looking, Jasmin thought. But it was Damien she was aware of. Damien, with his strong shoulders and arresting features. Damien, who was charming, but so very guarded.

They drew attention as they filed out of the Three Divas. Admiring glances. Raised eyebrows.

And this time, Jasmin walked out with them.

NINE

The late afternoon light had turned everything golden. The October skies were tinted purple, casting a dreamy hue over the campus. Fallen copper leaves scuttled in the wind. They all piled into Allie's tiny car, with Jasmin squeezed between Imogen and Rían in the back seat. Black faux fur covered the steering wheel and an air freshener shaped like a cherry was clipped to the vent. The sickly sweet, artificial smell hit the back of Jasmin's nose.

Damien and Rían rented rooms in a house on Burgess Street, about seven minutes away in a slightly rundown part of town. Allie parked, hitting the brakes a little too late, too hard, and they unfolded themselves outside a two-storey, terraced house.

In the sitting room, a bunch of guys were entranced by an action sequence on the large TV screen. The air smelt of popcorn and beer and boy.

'Damien and I are upstairs.' Rían gestured to Jasmin to go up the narrow staircase. 'I'm the room at the end.' He smirked. 'Mine's bigger. But Damien gets the garden view.'

'Go ahead,' said Damien as they reached the upstairs landing. 'I'll get the camera.'

'I think I left my jumper here,' said Allie, following him.

Jasmin watched Allie's slim figure disappear behind Damien's door, then trailed after Rían and Imogen. They went into the end room, the one overlooking the street. She paused at the threshold of Rían's room. It was decorated with soft blues, greens and reds. Silk tapestries and paintings hung on the walls, a Persian rug on the floor. A low divan was tucked into the corner and the room smelt like clove and cinnamon. Rían went around lighting candles. Imogen sank down on the cushions arranged around an intricately carved coffee table. She stretched out, almost purring. Outside, rain had begun to fall softly.

'No need to hover like the devil in a church.' Rían glanced at Jasmin. 'Come in. Make yourself comfortable.'

Jasmin stepped into the room, feeling like she'd gone through the looking glass. She took in more details as she entered. The room was filled with treasures from faraway places, bead art, stone sculptures, a large green bronze leopard.

'That's from Benin.' Rían saw her stop to touch the leopard. 'My mam picked it up at a market, while away on her travels.'

'It's beautiful,' she breathed. 'All of it.'

'Beauty and magic, that's what matters most,' Rían said, his eyes burning with an indefinable knowing.

'You believe in magic?'

'Not in the way most people understand it,' he replied, lighting the last tapered candle, which was wedged in an empty wine bottle covered in old, dripped wax. A flickering light glowed softly in the room. 'I don't believe in wands or cauldrons or abracadabra, or anything obvious.' He stepped towards Jasmin, reached for her hand. He held it. His hand was cool, hard in hers. He looked into her eyes, searching. 'Do you feel that?'

'Feel what?'

'Close your eyes.'

Jasmin shut her eyes. Rían's hand left hers and she missed the cool comfort of it.

'Keep them closed.'

She did as she was told, feeling suddenly dizzy. The scented candle wax was sharp in her nose. The rain hit the windows in a gentle repeating tap. She felt the room closing in on her, something in the air pushing against her, a barely-there caress of something insubstantial yet indisputably there.

'Keep them closed,' Rían said again. 'Who is standing near you?'

'You are. And Imogen.' Then she added, with certainty, 'And Damien.'

'Open your eyes.'

Jasmin opened her eyes to see Rían stood where he'd been before, now joined by Imogen and Damien. From the doorway, Allie watched, a coin turning in her fingers.

'How did you know we three were here with you and not Allie?'

'I don't know. Just felt it,' Jasmin said, a little uncomfortable. She didn't like this conversation.

'Magic is art, where beauty may be created. Magic is connection, where you're in tune with others.' Rían's words sounded like an incantation. 'Where you're in tune with the people who are yours. Magic is science, where the most marvellous things are possible.'

Jasmin glimpsed her fingernails, the charcoal embedded in the hard skin there from this morning's art class. She remembered years ago, when Eamon had taught her to draw.

'The true artist,' Eamon had said, holding her hand in his as they reworked the details of the face she'd sketched, 'always leaves something of themself in their work. They infuse their creation with something that is uniquely them. But it goes two ways. The work marks the artist, alters them.' He lifted their hands, showing the charcoal stains down the sides. 'True art recreates the artist, as the artist creates the work.'

Right now, standing in Rían's room, Jasmin felt she was being remade. As if just by being together, they were making something beautiful. She knew that it would forever change her.

Maybe that's what Rían meant by magic.

'You'd better take a seat.' Imogen tugged Jasmin's hand and drew her to the low bench. 'Once Rían starts on ordinary magic, he can go on all night.'

'Let's take a look, shall we?' Damien took a seat beside Jasmin, opening his laptop. 'You asked for posed and candid shots, so there's a lot.' He clicked on a thumbnail, and started flicking through them.

'Wait, slower,' Allie said, crouching behind him, carefully studying the screen. 'Niamh was wearing a black knee-length dress with her hair tied back. What else?'

'Black suede pumps and a bag with a gold chain,' Jasmin said. The image of one of those shoes on the floor of the shed flashed in her mind's eye. She swallowed hard.

They searched through the photos of smiling groups. These were disappointing because Damien's shots were clean, with little clutter in the background. As they moved through picture after picture, Jasmin began to feel a crushing disappointment.

'Hey, there's Jasmin,' Rían said, at the photo of her standing with Georgie's friends. 'And all the university old guard's wives. They look like a fun crowd.'

'My grandmother's friends.' Jasmin smiled. 'They are.'

'I bet they have some stories to tell.' Rían clicked to the next picture, the closer shot of Jasmin staring right into the camera. The picture that Damien had taken of her on the veranda. 'Now *this* is interesting.'

Jasmin felt her cheeks burn.

But Rían wasn't talking about Jasmin. He was pointing to the background. At the edge of the screen was the knee-length black dress. The blonde ponytail. Niamh.

'Who is she talking to?' Allie said.

The other person wasn't in shot. Only part of a white blazer was in frame.

'I know who that is,' Jasmin said. 'Go back a few pictures.'

Damien went back until Jasmin said, 'Stop.' In the picture was an older couple, and beside them stood Theo Merrick and the woman wearing a bronze dress and white blazer. 'See the piping on the edge of the blazer?'

Damien flipped between the two pictures. 'You're right. That's Candice Greene.'

Rían whistled. 'The person out of shot that Niamh is talking to is Theo Merrick's partner, both in life and work.'

'Are we thinking that Doctor Candice Greene is Niamh's secret friend?' Imogen sounded sceptical.

'Maybe,' Jasmin said slowly, frowning at the picture of Candice with Merrick and the older couple. 'Or they could have been making small talk. Wait, is that a scratch on her face?'

Damien leaned in. 'I can't tell.'

Imogen shifted nearer to see the red line along Candice's cheek, which was partially obscured by her hair. 'It could be. Is it in any other pictures?'

They flicked through the pictures again, but couldn't get a clear enough view. Imogen leaned back. 'Hard to be a hundred per cent certain with her hair down, but it looks like a fresh scratch. I think someone scratched Candice's face at some point during the drinks reception.'

'That's wild,' Allie shook her head. 'How?'

'Candice does not look like the type to enjoy a good bar brawl.' Rían was getting fidgety, his interest moving on to something else.

Jasmin went back again, finding the shot Damien had taken of her, with Niamh in the background and Candice out of frame. 'This was taken right before Niamh knocked into the vase.'

'She was definitely drunk then,' Allie said. 'She was unsteady and slurring. But what if it was more than that? What if they'd argued earlier, maybe when Niamh was down in the garden, with her scratching Candice's face? What if Niamh was picking up where she'd left off, and in her agitation, she smashed the vase?'

'They spoke and then the vase broke,' Rían sounded bored, done with the ins and outs of Niamh and the vase and the scratch on Candice's face. 'Doesn't mean the two were connected.'

'It's not too much of a stretch to say that Niamh might have scratched Candice,' Allie protested.

'Maybe.' That was all Imogen would allow.

'That's the posed pictures done.' Damien returned to the thumbnails and clicked on a separate folder. 'Here are the shots from the lecture.'

In the first picture, Merrick stood in front of the audience, his expression open and engaging. He gestured towards the image behind him on the screen. The women in the front row had their faces tilted up to look at him with rapt expressions. With his black shirt and trousers he looked like a high priest at some sacred ritual.

'That's really good,' Jasmin said. Damien smiled, and it ran through her like a small shiver.

They scrolled through, until Rían leaned forward. 'Wait, is that Niamh?'

Damien had photographed the audience head-on. Niamh was sitting near the front. The people around her were beaming at Merrick, entranced. But Niamh – Niamh was scowling. The anger on her face was all the more marked for the soft, smiling expressions around her.

'Wow,' Allie breathed. 'What do you think that means?'

'I think we shouldn't leap to any conclusions just yet. She could have been thinking about something else. Let's earmark that picture, make a note and keep going.' Imogen was scribbling in her expensive-looking notepad.

A few photos later, Damien stopped again. 'Hey, that's Niamh talking to Rory.'

It was a picture of the veranda. Niamh was stood to the side, her back to the camera, talking to a young man. His hair was curly on top, buzzed at the sides, and his shirt was open at the neck. He looked like he worked out a lot.

'Who's Rory?' Jasmin said.

'Surely you've heard of Rory,' said Rían. 'Have you been living under a rock? His parties are infamous.'

They thought she was a student, Jasmin realised. But before she could say anything, Imogen spoke up.

'Rory's a real dog,' she said, making notes in her book. 'Always trying to get in some girl's pants.' She gave a mischievous grin. 'Doesn't have the same charm as our Damien here though.' Her eyes rested lightly on Jasmin's before winking at Damien, then she broke into an easy giggle as he reached to ruffle her perfect hair. Jasmin wondered if Imogen was trying to tell her something.

'He's often at the gym where I work,' Damien added. 'Might as well move in there.'

By the time they'd gone through all the photographs, they'd only found two more that showed Niamh in the background.

In the first, she was talking to a serious-looking young man that Allie said she recognised as Merrick's research assistant, but none of them knew his name.

The figure in the second photograph was more familiar. While Jasmin hadn't seen his face at the time, it was obvious from where they stood that this was the same waiter she'd seen talking to Niamh.

'That's Javier,' Jasmin said, pointing to the picture. 'His sister did the catering. He …' She remembered the moment when they had heard the scream. How they'd both run. How Javier saw Niamh in that shed.

'She was probably only getting a drink from him,' Rían said. 'But we need to find him, and everyone else, and talk to them.'

'Rory's having a party on Friday night,' Imogen checked her phone. 'We'll go. We should be able to track down Javier through the caterers, and Merrick's RA through his department.' She snapped her notebook shut.

'What about Candice?' asked Jasmin.

'We'll come back to that,' said Imogen, shifting uncomfortably. They all seemed reluctant to approach Dr Candice Greene. 'I suspect she eats nosy students for breakfast, that one.'

Damien pulled the photos of Niamh into a separate folder and was about to close his laptop when Jasmin had an idea.

'Could I see those pictures again?' she asked, pulling the computer on to her lap. She examined the photos side by side, noticing the time they were taken. 'See, her glass in the earlier picture with Rory is half full. In this picture, there's a quarter left, and then here she must have a new glass. She only had two glasses of wine, and I saw her taking a third but it's unlikely she had time to drink that.'

'Unusual to be falling over her own feet and smashing vases after two glasses,' Imogen mused.

'Maybe she hadn't eaten, or didn't metabolise alcohol well,' Allie said. 'She could have downed that third glass like a shot.'

'Or maybe someone spiked her drink,' Imogen replied.

'You said she was looking for painkillers,' Jasmin said to Allie. 'What if she asked someone else? What if someone gave her something … ?'

'Something that made her seem drunk,' whispered Allie.

'Why?' Imogen was staring into the middle distance. 'Why would anyone want to drug Niamh? Kill her even? She seems like an ordinary student, just like all of us. What makes Niamh different?'

'OK,' Rían clapped his hands. 'I'm calling it. That's enough talk of death. We need to do something else.'

'What do you have in mind?' Allie said, brightening.

'Messy Jack's?' Damien named the student bar. Jasmin had only been inside it briefly, and found the crowded room with its red lighting too much.

'No,' Rían said. 'We're not going to a bar after talking about spiked drinks and murder. That's just asking for trouble and bad vibes. Let's take a walk.'

'But it's raining.' Jasmin gave a disbelieving laugh.

'Oh no, she said it.' Rían shook his head.

'That's right, she did.' Imogen had a wicked glint in her eye.

'I'm afraid you said it.' Damien gave her a pitying smile.

'Said what?' Jasmin looked around, unsure what was going on.

Rían leaned into her and smiled. His eyes were large, and his thick brows made him appear demonic. He whispered, 'The forbidden words.'

'We've forbidden "but it's raining",' Allie explained. 'There's nothing that can't be done in the rain.'

Jasmin tried to get her head around the double negatives but Rían was up like a bullet, Damien behind him. Suddenly, they were both just boys, unbounded vigour coursing through them.

'You know what that means,' Rían said, edging to the door.

'Punishment.' Damien raised his eyebrows.

'Jasmin, you're sentenced to a rain dance,' Imogen declared, standing up.

'We'll come with you. This time,' Damien said. 'Let's go.'

They were all rushing out of the door, not stopping to take jackets. They raced down the stairs, elbowing each other out of the way. They ran out of the kitchen door into the small back garden, hustling Jasmin with them. She heard herself giggling, exhilarated, maybe even a little scared.

The rain came down hard. Rían was leaping around the shrubs, all legs and arms. Allie twirled around, lifting her face to the rain. Imogen gave it full welly, wiggling her hips and snaking her arms to the sky. Damien danced, laughing in the twilight as the rain drenched his T-shirt.

Jasmin lifted her arms and danced. The rain plastered her hair to her head, her top to her skin. She couldn't stop laughing, and raindrops fell into her open mouth. She jumped and twisted to an inaudible song, the music in her heart. Around her, everyone danced. Rían spun Allie around. Imogen shook her shoulders and Damien let out a whoop.

Jasmin hadn't felt this content, this joyful, in a long time.

Maybe Rían was right. Maybe this was magic. Ordinary magic.

Suddenly, an acute sorrow squeezed her heart. Whatever had happened to Niamh, her life was over. Jasmin remembered Merrick's words from the lecture: *human beings want to live.* Jasmin had heard that in the tone of Niamh's voice when she'd confessed her fear to the secret friend. She had wanted to live.

Dancing in the rain, Jasmin was more certain than ever that someone had snatched Niamh's life from her. And she was determined that they wouldn't get away with it.

TEN

Jasmin was late. She could see Imogen and Allie, waiting beneath the oak tree outside Latimer House. Behind them, blackberry vines trailed up the stone wall, the leaves reaching up to the purple-blue sky. Fat berries hung in clumps, like jewels. The sky was a dance of light, shifting and glinting between slow-drifting clouds.

'You made it.' Imogen sounded pleased. She was wearing a full-skirted green velvet trench coat today, which stood out against the silver light of the autumn afternoon. Everyone who passed craned to look at her, but Imogen didn't seem to notice.

It hadn't been easy. When Imogen had texted to say she had an idea to find out more about Niamh, Jasmin had decided to mitch her afternoon classes. During her lunch break, she had gone to the office and given a rundown of her crippling period pains to the young receptionist. He'd signed her out hastily, reminding Jasmin to get her mother to authorise her absence on the app.

'This is where Niamh lived?' Jasmin said, looking up at the four-storey grey building that looked like it had stood there for a hundred years.

'Yeah,' Allie said. She had an elfin face, and it seemed to Jasmin that her tentative nature was etched into her delicate features. 'It's one of the better ones. We're in Elizabeth House, down that lane.'

Jasmin looked at the building doubtfully. She wasn't sure about going inside and asking questions about Niamh, but Imogen seemed adamant. 'Are Rían and Damien coming?'

'It's just us. Rían has a media lab this afternoon,' Allie explained, 'and Damien hasn't replied yet. He doesn't always check his phone if he's at work.'

Jasmin caught something in her tone – an amused irritation, like she knew Damien better than the others. There was definitely something between Allie and Damien.

'What's the plan?' Jasmin said as they walked towards the door. 'Ask people what Niamh was doing the night she died?'

'That would be a terrible idea.' Imogen grimaced as she pulled open the outer door to Latimer House. 'We'd look like ghouls.'

Aren't we? Jasmin thought.

'We're working an important story, Jasmin.' Imogen seemed to hear her unspoken question. In the small glass porch, she pressed the bell. 'A young woman died under mysterious circumstances and it's been covered up. If we don't do this,

Niamh will never have justice.' Imogen held up an imperious hand to halt Jasmin's response and spoke into the intercom. 'We're meeting a friend. Aoife. Second floor.'

'What if no one called Aoife lives there?' said Jasmin.

'There's always an Aoife.' Imogen smiled at her when the door buzzed open. 'Jasmin, you start on the first floor with me, and, Allie, you start at the top. We'll meet in the middle.'

They stepped inside on to speckled grey vinyl flooring. Allie headed to the lift while Imogen walked towards a wide wooden staircase with a decorative iron banister. From beyond the stairs came the hollow, steady thwacks of a ping-pong rally, a burst of raucous laughter when the rhythm broke. And further away, the clattering of dishes from the shared kitchen. The lingering smell of lemon-scented chemicals reminded Jasmin of school.

Imogen marched up the stairs to the first floor, turning left into the corridor. She gave a bold, loud knock on the first door. They listened a moment, but no one answered. They moved to the next door, and this time a young woman with tortoiseshell glasses opened the door.

'Imogen?'

'Thuli?' Imogen looked unexpectedly flustered. 'You're in Latimer this year?'

'Obviously.' Thuli sounded uncomfortable. 'Why are you here?'

'Sorry,' Imogen said quickly. 'We're doing a mental health survey. For the *Answerer*. I'll move on. Didn't mean to bother you.'

Thuli studied Imogen for a moment, her eyes softening. 'You're not bothering me.'

Imogen retreated before Thuli could say anything else. The door clicked shut behind them and Imogen exhaled. 'We'll start with the next room, so.'

'Is Thuli an ex?' Jasmin pried cautiously. Imogen kept looking straight ahead, her eyes determinedly bright.

'Brief summer romance. I'm over it,' Imogen replied with a rigid smile. She rapped at the next door and a tall woman wearing a rumpled tracksuit answered.

'Hello,' Imogen said brightly. 'I'm Imogen Barrett from the *Answerer* and we're interviewing for an article about students' mental health. Would you mind if we spoke with you for a few minutes?'

'About what exactly?' The woman kept the door at forty-five degrees.

'We want to understand if students are aware of the support structures in place and if they're enough. Should the university be doing more to ensure the well-being of its students? We won't ask any intrusive questions and it will be anonymous and confidential, I promise.'

'OK, five minutes. I have a paper to write.' She opened the door wider and Imogen and Jasmin stepped into a small room. Books and papers were spread on the desk beside an open laptop, and the room smelt of sugared jellies. 'I'm Agnieszka.'

'Five minutes is all we need.'

'So the answer to your question is pretty simple,' Agnieszka said cheerfully. 'I don't know much about the support structures here. I'm lucky in that I've never needed them. Personally, if I was in trouble, I wouldn't look to the university for help.'

'And why's that?' Imogen said curiously.

Agnieszka shrugged. 'I don't need to. I have family, my GP, to look after me.'

Jasmin thought of Niamh, hiding by the maintenance door to make that call. Scared her unknown friend wouldn't pick up. Niamh might have lived in this building bustling with other young women, but she seemed to have been very alone.

'Is there something else?' Imogen said gently, picking up on something unspoken.

'Look, it's obvious you're writing this article because of Niamh. I don't want to speak ill of the dead, but it's easy to see why she was … on her own. She wasn't the friendliest. She kept to herself. She was cold, to be honest. She never chatted to anyone in the laundry room or kitchen, and she rarely went to the common room. One of those humourless, sporty types. Kept telling people to keep the music down. Obsessed with clean eating and all that. Though,' Agnieszka paused, 'she did take a lot of headache pills. Popped them like candy. Everyone knew if you needed little white tablets after a big night out, Niamh would have them.'

'She didn't have any friends?' Imogen nudged the conversation back on topic.

Imogen was compelling, Jasmin realised. Her hard edges were dropped and that haughty exterior gone. Instead, Imogen had shifted into the girl you thought was your best friend.

She was like honey, luring Agnieszka into sharing more than she might intend. Imogen was going to make a damn good journalist.

'She didn't go out much,' Agnieszka said. 'I never really saw her hanging out with anyone. Not even with the other gym girls.'

'She went to the gym often then?'

'Niamh was rigid about it. She exercised every day from what I could see. Like I said, she ate carefully too. No sugar, no white carbs.' Agnieszka shook her head sadly. 'All that saying no to chocolate and now she's dead. What did it matter?'

ELEVEN

'No one seems to know her,' Jasmin said as they trudged up to the third floor, Niamh's floor. 'Not really.'

With every conversation, they gained a picture of an aloof, controlled young woman. One with a high degree of discipline. One who batch-prepared her calorie-counted meals in the shared kitchen and studied while waiting for her laundry. She did OK in her academic work, and appeared to spend more time at the gym than the library. She never attended residence activities or joined in the chats. It was like her real life happened somewhere else.

They knocked on the door beside Niamh's room, casting a furtive glance at the firmly shut one next to it. There was a longing in Imogen's eyes, and Jasmin would not have been surprised if she was calculating how she might break in.

The door they'd knocked at suddenly flew open, and a cheerful-looking, red-haired girl peered out.

'Sure, I'll answer your questions,' she said after Jasmin made the introductions. 'I'm Becky, what do you want to know?'

This one was a talker, clearly. She spoke fast, like she had too many things to say and not enough time. 'Let's start with the existing well-being support services,' Imogen said. 'Are you aware of them at all?'

'Well, the university does try,' Becky began. 'There are services and programmes, but they could definitely work better, if you know what I mean? I have a few ideas …'

Becky, it turned out, had many ideas, and it took a lot longer for the conversation to segue to Niamh.

'Tragic,' she said, shaking her head sadly. 'I just feel if I'd had somewhere to channel my concern, like a peer-to-peer encouragement programme, maybe I could have reached out more to Niamh. I like to be involved, you know? Helpful. My mam says I was like that even when I was a toddler.'

From what Jasmin had heard, Niamh would have run a mile from a peer-to-peer encouragement programme.

'Reached out *more*?' Imogen pounced on the word. 'You tried to help Niamh then?'

'Of course. She was my next-door neighbour. And she seemed troubled.' Becky hesitated, then continued, 'One night, say, two weeks ago, I was coming home late and her door was ajar. I could hear her arguing with some guy.'

'Do you know why they were arguing?' Imogen said, her voice even and contained.

'It wasn't a loud fight,' Becky replied, 'but you could tell she was furious. He was saying, "I'm doing the best I can," and she was like, "Do better" and said that she was tired of him only being there when it was convenient for him. I figured she was seeing him, but he wasn't that into her.'

'Do you know his name, what he looked like?' Jasmin said a little too eagerly. Imogen frowned at her.

'No.' The regret in Becky's voice was obvious – she had clearly tried to snoop. 'He was out of sight. I saw some of his back and arm and can only tell you that he was tallish, wearing a long-sleeved T-shirt. Good shoulders. Anyway, the next day, I reached out to Niamh in the kitchen, to make sure that she was OK, that she knew she had friends, you know? But when I brought up the boyfriend, she blanked me. Said she didn't *have* a boyfriend. Well. They sure argued like they were together.'

Becky looked like she was going to say something else, but then pressed her lips together. Uncertainty flashed in her eyes, and perhaps worry that she'd said too much already. 'You're not going to print this in the paper, are you?'

'We told you we wouldn't.' Imogen checked her watch. 'Thanks for your time.'

Jasmin wanted to object, push Becky a little harder. She knew more, Jasmin was sure of it. But Becky was looking down, a nervous hand tucking her hair behind her ear.

Imogen made for the corridor, somehow striding with her usual poise despite the tiny room. She tilted her head for Jasmin to follow.

They were at the door when Becky stopped them.

'It wasn't the only time I heard them.'

Jasmin caught the small triumphant smile on Imogen's face before she turned round. As if she knew that Becky had been holding back, wrestling with herself and her tendency to over-share. As if Imogen knew that pushing would only make her retreat.

Becky dropped her voice. 'I think he threatened Niamh.'

'Threatened her?' Imogen said, alert.

'Yeah. About a week ago I heard someone leave her room around one in the morning. I was asleep but I heard voices, arguing again, louder this time. It woke me up. As he left, he growled at her, then slammed the door.'

'Growled at her? What did he say?'

'He said … "You're going to regret this." Exactly those words.' Becky's eyes were wide. 'And now she's dead.'

Dash was in the kitchen when Jasmin got back home. In front of him was a heap of batch bread with chicken, crisps and lettuce that he'd made into three-layer sandwiches – his favourite from when he was a young teen.

'I thought you'd outgrown that particular abomination.' Jasmin dropped her bag on one of the bar stools.

'And I thought you were home sick. That's what Mam thinks anyway.' He took a huge bite, chewed, then said with his mouth full, 'So where were you?'

'Out walking.' She went to the sink and focused on soaping her hands. 'It helps sometimes.'

She felt him looking at her. Dash suspected that she'd bunked off. He knew her too well.

'You've been home a lot lately.' She leaned back against the sink, drying her hands with a towel, and narrowed her eyes at him. 'Women trouble?'

He chuckled and gestured to a chair. 'Come, have a sandwich. I won't bore you with my romantic woes.'

'So there *are* romantic woes?'

'Eat.' He pushed the plate towards her but Jasmin shook her head.

'I'm not hungry.'

'Too bad.' Dash gestured to a brown paper bag on the sink. 'I'll have that then.'

She picked up the bag and peered inside – chocolate and Sour Patch Kids.

'For your womanly troubles,' he said.

'Someone has trained you well.' Jasmin laughed and took the bag. 'Whoever she is, tell your latest conquest that I am grateful.' Dash didn't often bring his girlfriends home, and seemed to change them with each season. That part of his life was a mystery to Jasmin, and one she didn't particularly care to uncover. *He'll find the right person when he's ready*, Georgie always said.

'I'm not seeing anyone,' Dash said, sombre now. 'Not any more.' He took another bite of his sandwich, clearly unwilling to talk about it.

'OK,' Jasmin said, ruffling his hair as she passed him. He hated it when Sonia did it, but Jasmin understood the urge. To reach out and touch. To say, *I'm here*, without making a huge fuss of it.

'I have a ton of homework.' She tucked the bag under her arm. 'If you wanted any of the chocolate, too bad.'

In the sunroom, her homework abandoned, Jasmin opened a new spiralbound blank notebook. She usually used them for quick sketches, but she had other ideas for this one. Turning to the first page, she wrote *WHO WAS NIAMH?* She thought for a moment, and began to make a list.

- *Aloof, isolated, not friendly*
- *Strict about diet and exercise*
- *Distressed about something*
- *Was frustrated in her friendship/relationship with a man*

That was it. They'd spoken to maybe thirty or forty women that afternoon, and that was what they had.

Maybe that in itself was saying something. That Niamh wasn't easy to know. Jasmin stared at the list again. One thing was sure – Niamh didn't seem happy.

But the afternoon had delivered a potential suspect. The maybe-boyfriend who growled at her only a week ago, saying *You're going to regret this.* A night-time visitor to Niamh's room, one that busybody Becky had only glimpsed in passing. Her description, 'tallish with a long-sleeved T-shirt', summed up too many male students.

Jasmin rested against the fainting couch behind her and stared up at the glass ceiling. The room was filled with exotic plants,

Sonia's biggest frivolity. There were potted lemon and olive trees, bougainvillea trained along the glass walls. Summer plants from faraway countries that responded to sun and heat. They couldn't really be happy in this room that was so cold in the winter. Sometimes Jasmin wondered if the exotic plants in the glass room were a metaphor for Sonia herself.

Jasmin shut her eyes and, in her mind, she saw Niamh outside the cafe, walking away. Her blue and white striped top, her bobbing ponytail disappearing in the distance.

She'd chased after Niamh then, as she was chasing her now. But Niamh seemed to slip away, ever elusive, the white rabbit to Jasmin's Alice.

TWELVE

When Jasmin first saw *The Book of Monsters*, she was eight years old. Nearly to the hour, because it was nine in the morning, a little after her time of birth.

The McKellan Galleries were empty. Eamon had arranged a private viewing with the director, a friend of his, before it opened to the public at ten. It made Jasmin feel special, venturing into the carefully guarded room where the invaluable manuscript rested in its glass cage.

Jasmin walked up to the large book. She examined the rough edges, the faded ink. It was open to a page with writing she couldn't understand.

'What does it say, Grandpa?' She glanced at him. 'What's it about?'

'That is *The Book of Monsters*. It's a famous text – one of the most famous in the world. It dates back to the thirteenth century, and it's a little different. In those days books were transcribed, carefully and exquisitely, by monks, and they tended to be interested in religious matters. But this one tells four stories about monsters who pretend to be people.'

'Are they scary monsters? Do they bite?'

Eamon let out a loud laugh. 'Yes, I suppose all monsters do. Monsters have to use their teeth, if they are to survive.'

'I don't like it if they hurt.'

'It is the monster's nature to do what it must to survive. We can't change the nature of the beast. We shouldn't try.'

'Why not?' Jasmin said. 'Georgie says we must all try to be good and kind.'

Eamon bent down to her. 'Maybe it is good and kind to let monsters be monsters. When you trap something, cage and force it to be what goes against its true nature, it will only grow frustrated. It will grow angry and become reckless.'

Jasmin looked at the manuscript again. The writing that made no sense to her. The margins decorated with birds and beasts. They had scales and talons, wings and long, thin tails that ended in thick skin stretched between bone, like bat wings. Some monsters smiled, and were all the more terrifying in their softly coloured flatness.

'What is your true nature, Grandpa?'

He put a hand on her cheek and beamed at her question. 'My nature? To think unfettered. To discover and explore, without constraint.'

'Have you read the stories?'

'I've read versions of them. Shall I tell you them?'

'Yes please.'

And Eamon had told her each of the four stories in *The Book of Monsters*.

On the way to the Three Divas, Jasmin turned left towards the Old Science. She looked up at her grandfather's window. But today, instead of turning away, she went to the building's doors. She took one step and then another, and she was inside.

The wood-panelled passage was empty. The air was patched with must and sweat. The thick walls had borne witness for more than a hundred years. She passed seminar rooms, seeing students sitting at tables, listlessly watching their instructors, and a comforting familiarity stole over Jasmin.

This was her grandfather's place. Their place. Her eyes fluttered shut for one brief moment, and she could hear him. The way he filled a room with the rumbling of his voice alone.

You did this.

Jasmin opened her eyes. The wide stairs faced her. Somewhere above, a woman laughed. As if in a dream, she headed up to the second-floor landing, the next flight of stairs suddenly becoming Escheresque and gravity uncertain. Holding the rail, Jasmin continued walking.

On the third floor, she turned to the west corridor with its soft, thick carpet and varnished wooden panels. This short corridor boasted the most coveted offices in the faculty, earned only by raising millions in grants and senior author papers in the best journals.

She wandered to the last door on the right. It was a corner

office and looked out over a thick copse of trees and the botany greenhouses. Jasmin knew the view well; she had spent many hours in that office as a child.

There was no name plaque, nothing to say who occupied the room now. Jasmin remembered her small fingers tracing hearts in the whorls in the oak. She felt sure that if she pushed, she would find her grandfather on the other side of the door. The happy, laughing man who'd adored her. The man he'd been before.

She lifted a finger, tracing a heart on to the wood, and the door opened slightly. She just *had* to go in. See if it was the same old wooden desk beneath the window, the green velvet armchair with the worn patches on the arms. She wanted to see her grandfather behind his desk. She could picture it, Eamon, tall and decisive, standing there with a warm smile. Holding out his arms to her.

She pushed the door another few inches. There couldn't be anyone inside. It was far too quiet. No sound of fingers hitting a keyboard, or a throat clearing, or a chair swivelling.

Her heart thumping in her chest, she peered inside.

There was someone, at the window, looking at that familiar view. Her shoulders hunched as she wrapped one arm tightly around herself. Dr Candice Greene. She pressed a fist to her mouth, lost in thought.

Jasmin couldn't look away. Her feet were frozen, refusing to do as she commanded.

Sensing the presence at the door, Candice shifted her gaze, locking eyes with Jasmin. There was a faint line on her cheek, the scratch almost healed. Candice quickly wiped a tear, but it was too late. Jasmin had already seen it.

'Professor Merrick will be back in a minute.' Candice strode across the room. The sharp smell of expensive sandalwood lingered after she'd left.

What just happened? Jasmin thought to herself.

She took three steps into the room. That was all she allowed herself in the one minute she had.

The room had changed, but enough of the past remained. The old heavy wooden desk was in the same place it had always been. She could almost see her grandfather hunched over it, writing feverishly as he worked through an idea. Jasmin felt like the eight-year-old girl entering her grandfather's office with a Club Orange in hand.

'Can I help you?'

Jasmin started. Merrick had appeared at the door and was frowning, studying her carefully. She felt his probing gaze search her face. She felt he had seen her, down to her expensive trainers. But more than that, it felt like he saw through her. It felt like he saw inside. She didn't know what to say.

'Can I help you?' he asked again, more gently.

'Sorry, I'm in the wrong place,' she managed to say. The wrong time. She felt heat in her cheeks, an ache in her chest.

'Where's the right place then?' His lips turned up in a smile. 'I can point you in the general direction.' His blue eyes crinkled. *Charming*, Jasmin thought. A charming man.

But she would swear on her grandmother's life that those eyes were calculating.

'Not here.' Jasmin turned.

Walking away, she felt Merrick's eyes on her, still searching. She hurried down the stairs, feeling the wooden walls press against her. She felt them as she burst through the doors, out into the mild October sunshine. She couldn't shake the discomfort that his intense observation had summoned, the unpleasant penetration of being watched so closely.

If Jasmin was a watcher, Merrick was one too.

THIRTEEN

Imogen was waiting impatiently with Allie at the Three Divas.

'Finally,' Imogen said when Jasmin reached the table in the alcove. 'What took you so long?'

Oh, nothing much.

The ghost of her grandfather, standing behind his desk.

Dr Candice Greene crying at the window.

Theo Merrick, and the way he'd seemed to stare into her soul.

'We're heading to Rían's.' Imogen didn't wait for an answer. She stood up, slinging her oversized pink suede tote bag over her arm. 'You've got to hear what Allie recorded at Latimer yesterday – *illegally*.' She looked at Allie with admiration. 'Maybe there's a bloodhound in you after all.'

Imogen didn't see the two pink spots brightening Allie's cheeks, but Jasmin did.

'C'mon, let's go.' Imogen linked her arm through Jasmin's. 'The others are meeting us there.'

They drove to Burgess Street in Allie's car. Outside the row of houses, leaves lay in a thick brown-gold carpet. Ghosts hung from half-bare trees, and cheap-looking skeletons peered out of grimy windows. Jasmin reached for the brass door knocker, hearing it sound through the house. Beside her, Allie blew on her hands to warm them.

It was like falling in love, Jasmin thought as she glanced at her new friends framed by the twilight street. A blossoming of sorts, as they grew familiar with each other. She was beginning to recognise the small details, like the way Allie moved, angular and tentative, as she stamped her feet to ward off the cold. The exact slant of Imogen's eyebrows as she looked up at the window, peeved that they dared make her wait. Her white marshmallow hat was pulled low and she yelled, 'Come on, guys, hurry up.' She hit the flat of her hand against the door while giving Jasmin a wink and a dazzling smile. Jasmin couldn't help laughing at how Imogen could be such an unashamed diva.

The door swung open and there was Rían, wearing a burgundy smoking jacket and cream silk cravat with that whiskey voice saying, 'In you get.'

In the sitting room, one solitary housemate played a shooting game on the large screen. From upstairs came slow tabla and sitar music.

Jasmin followed Allie and Imogen up the stairs. Jasmin sat on the low padded bench at the intricately carved coffee table, which held a hookah pipe, a bronze teapot and a bowl of colourful sweets, while Allie made for the cushions against the wall.

Rían lit the candles and the smell of sandalwood mixed with cherry tobacco filled the air.

Damien entered next. Allie patted the cushion next to her. 'Sit here, Damien. Bring down the music, Rían.'

She had lit up when Damien came in, Jasmin thought.

Damien dutifully sat on the cushion beside Allie. Jasmin remembered him pushing the hair back from her face. His fingers brushing her cheek. *Stop*, she told herself. He wasn't interested in her. Why would he be? She glanced at him again, seeing that he'd leaned his head against the wall, his knees jutting out. He looked tired.

'We went to Latimer yesterday to get some background information on Niamh,' Allie began. She held a marker pen in her hand, pointing it like a conductor's baton. Her voice was self-important, Jasmin thought, guessing it wasn't often Allie took centre stage instead of Imogen. 'Then I had to rush off to my belly dancing class.'

'Ah yes, the Christmas showcase,' murmured Damien, a smile teasing his lips. 'Don't think we've heard enough about that.'

Allie nudged him with her elbow but she was smiling too. 'Mostly, I found the same as the others. People knew of Niamh, but not well. No one was friends with her. She appears to have kept to herself without making any real connection, good or bad, with anyone.' Allie pulled her phone from her shirt pocket and placed it on the table. 'There is one exception though. I talked to a student named Mai Jones, who let it slip that there was no love lost between her and Niamh. In fact,

93

once she got going, she called Niamh "calculating and conniving and a liar".'

'Conniving?' Jasmin said as Rían sat beside her.

'I know, right?' Allie said. 'She was only too happy to tell me the whole story. Niamh started working as a project assistant in the summer. For Theo Merrick.'

Interesting, Jasmin thought. Theo Merrick again.

'Mai's boyfriend Freddie was also a project assistant. You remember Merrick talking about that big longitudinal study on wellness? Freddie and Niamh were doing some of the boring admin.'

'What happened?' Jasmin said.

'There was a disagreement and Freddie lost his job. Listen.'

Allie reached out her phone, open to a dictaphone app, and pressed play.

AV: *Slow down. You say Niamh stabbed you in the back? How?*

MJ: *You know Merrick's spearheading that huge study? Freddie and Niamh were both project assistants for him over the summer. Boring work, but Merrick's PhD programme is very competitive and our plan was for Freddie to get the summer job, then totally impress Merrick, you know? I have no idea why Niamh got that job, since she's not actually even a scientist. Honestly, what a waste. Anyway, they were arranging logistics for a symposium. Some big name academics from Europe and the States were invited. Niamh was meant* to make a block booking for the VIPs at the hotel where the symposium was. The VIPs arrived to find that only half the rooms had been booked. And this was in July, during that big music festival when prices are through the roof.

AV: Woah. What happened?

MJ: Major disaster. The hotel was full and they had to scramble to find rooms in other hotels. The VIPs were tired and pissed off, and Merrick was livid.

AV: So what happened?

MJ: Niamh had been responsible for making the block booking. But she lied and claimed that it was Freddie who messed up. He denied it of course, but she'd been sucking up to Merrick the whole time, getting him coffee, offering to run out for lunch and so on. When it came to choosing who to believe, Merrick chose Niamh. Because she's so capable. *Yeah right.*

AV: Is it possible that Freddie might have made the mistake?

MJ: Not a chance. Freddie is very smart and very meticulous. He was desperate to get into Merrick's PhD programme. It was his dream, our dream really, because we've like planned out the next five years. When Niamh lied, she cost us everything. Freddie got upset, Merrick was furious, called him an idiot, fired him on the spot.

AV: I'm sure if Freddie tried to explain …

MJ: Merrick fired him and threatened to call security, and with some very choice words. Not really appropriate for a professor, in my humble opinion. So I very much doubt that. Wait, are you recording this? What the hell, Allie? You can't just—

Silence filled the room as they processed what they had just heard.

'So Niamh messed up and blamed it on someone else, who then lost his job,' Damien said. 'Not only his job, but any chance to study with Merrick.'

'That's if Freddie wasn't lying,' Allie countered.

'Bit of an overreaction on Merrick's part,' said Jasmin. 'Threatening to call security.'

'Mai says Freddie was upset,' Allie reminded them. 'Maybe that's code for *became violent*?'

'Violent? You're stretching so far you're bending backwards,' Imogen interjected.

'Children, please,' Rían said with exaggerated weariness as he pressed his long fingers to his temple. 'You make my head pound.'

Imogen paused. 'So you think if Freddie believes that Niamh cost him his future, it could be reason enough to kill her?'

'Exactly,' Allie said triumphantly.

'Do we know Freddie's last name?' Rían said, pounding head forgotten, typing quickly on his laptop. He called up different websites – the Science Society, Merrick's company site, the science faculty home page, which had news stories about its students. Jasmin leaned over his shoulder as he read the captions below the pictures.

'Here's Mai's Instagram.' Imogen held up her phone. She scrolled down the feed until she came to a picture of Mai and a young man, their heads together as they smiled at the camera. With his side parting and shirt tightly closed at the collar and her pearl-buttoned cardigan and satin headband, Jasmin could well believe they had a five-year plan, in spreadsheet and graph form.

Imogen clicked on the tag, which took her to his profile. She held out her phone for everyone to see.

'Freddie Campbell. We should speak to him.'

'Mai let slip that he studies in the Deacy Library most afternoons,' Allie said.

'I recognise him,' Jasmin breathed. 'He was there, at the alumni lecture. He was sitting near the front and when we came in late …'

'That was a fabulous entrance,' Rían teased. 'So bold. Daring.'

'Shut up.' Jasmin jabbed him playfully. 'Freddie was sitting a few seats away. He tutted at me.'

'Tutted?' Damien grinned.

'Tutted,' Jasmin confirmed. 'I'm pretty sure he was at the drinks reception too.'

'Maybe it's time to draw up a list of suspects,' Allie said, her eyes bright.

'Definitely Freddie, who Niamh screwed over.' Imogen began counting them on her fingers. 'What about the unidentified research assistant?' She reminded them of the other young man who'd been pictured with Niamh at the drinks reception. 'We don't have a name for him yet, do we? Someone should take notes. Damien?'

'Research assistant?' Jasmin said, as Damien pulled Rían's laptop towards him and began typing. 'Did he work with Freddie and Niamh?'

'Doubt it. RAs are usually PhD students helping academics with the meat and bones of their research, as I'm sure you know,' Imogen said, and Jasmin squirmed, because she didn't know, not when she was still in secondary school. It wasn't something her grandfather had talked about either. She'd helped him note changes in the mice he was studying, checking their responses, but not the boring parts of his work.

Imogen continued, 'Merrick's project assistants seem to be a different beast. I'm guessing that Merrick has a spin-out company, and that these project assistants work for him in that capacity.'

Jasmin didn't know what a spin-out company was either, and this time she wasn't going to ask.

'What's a spin-out company?' Allie reached for the sweets in the middle of the table. 'Ooh, cherry, my favourite.'

'It's when academics form a separate business, using their research to develop services or products.' Imogen frowned. 'I don't know the ins and outs of how they work, but it's not unusual.'

'I'll put the unidentified research assistant under "maybe",' Damien said.

Jasmin shuffled around the table until she was beside Damien. She settled in the cushions next to him, watching as he made three columns: *YES, MAYBE, NO.*

'Mai?' Allie said thoughtfully, still sucking on her sweet. 'I think she might hate Niamh even more than Freddie does.'

'Interesting idea,' Imogen mused. 'What Mai lacks in brute physical power, she more than makes up for in strength of will. They could even have worked together. Put her name down, Damien.'

'The maybe-boyfriend, definitely.' Damien shifted position, and his leg fell against Jasmin's. She expected him to move it again, but he didn't, letting it rest lightly against hers.

'The maybe-boyfriend has to be one of the guys Niamh spoke to at the drinks reception, surely?' Allie said.

'We can't know that,' Imogen argued.

'We can deduce it, based on how tiny her social circle was,' Allie hit back.

'What about Rory … Merrick … Becky even … ?' As names were thrown out, Damien's face turned tight with concentration as he typed, but Jasmin was distracted by the heat from his leg. Was it deliberate? Suddenly she felt warm, her legs, her cheeks, her heart.

'Merrick couldn't have done it.' Damien paused in his typing. 'While I was taking pictures at the drinks reception, I heard him say that he and Candice were going for a late dinner with former classmates.'

'He might have gone afterwards. We don't know what time Niamh died,' Allie objected.

'And so our malcontent remains a dark figure, obscured by shadow.' Rían shook his head. 'Let's hear it, Damien. Read out the names of the likely contenders.'

'Freddie and Mai, who both have a confirmed reason for hating Niamh. The maybe-boyfriend that Becky heard threatening Niamh. The ever eager Becky herself. Rory, Merrick's unnamed RA, Javier who was on the catering staff … Candice too. Merrick even, though we're not quite sure why.'

'So what do we do next?' Jasmin said, and Damien shifted to face her, giving her that smile, the one that lit up his eyes and warmed her from the inside.

'We put it all away.' He seemed to lean closer. 'And we do something else. Something exciting. We have a little fun.'

'Excellent idea.' Rían got to his feet.

But Jasmin felt sure that Damien had looked at her with intent. That he'd spoken those words with a meaning that had been exclusively for her.

FOURTEEN

It was the night of Rory's party. The river glinted in the moonlight and Jasmin and Rían stood at the railing at the edge of the canal. Behind them was a row of elegant houses, and ahead, in the distance, the glittering lights of the town centre. Rían leaned over the railing, his hands steepled together as he looked into the deep, dark water.

'How do you think you will die?'

Rían, Jasmin knew, didn't do small talk. 'Morbid question.' The cold night nudged her through her jacket. 'I don't think about it.'

But in a way, she did. Since Niamh died, the night terrors had come back. Not all the time, but enough to have her on edge. She had begun waking in the middle of the night, breathing hard and sweating in her cool room, with the terrifying certainty that long, cold fingers were reaching for her, roping around her neck. In her dreams, she saw the king, his body strong and taut, but only death in his eyes.

'I've always had this weird conviction that I would drown. Death by water.' Rían seemed mesmerised by the river, unmoving in his blue suede jacket. 'Dragged down into its icy depths. The most peaceful kind, I've heard said. Go on, how do you die?'

'Slowly,' Jasmin said, surprising herself with her answer. Not hands around her neck. Not out of the blue on a summer's afternoon. 'And I'll know it's coming.'

She pushed away from the railing, away from the dark water. She felt the cold more when she stood still.

'Here they are.' Rían pointed to the two figures walking over the wide pedestrian bridge towards them. He'd switched gears, Jasmin noticed, moving out of the pensive stillness that sometimes overcame him towards the exuberant exaggeration with which she was more accustomed.

Again, she had a strange subterranean sense that they were brought together by forces she couldn't quite comprehend. That's what her death would be like: a slow movement towards something inevitable, without her fully understanding how she'd set off down that path.

'Have you been waiting long?' Allie said. She was wearing her customary leather mini with a faux fur and too much eyeliner. Imogen was in a full-skirted vintage dress and a sheepskin jacket.

'Ages,' grumbled Rían.

'Not long,' Jasmin replied. 'Where's Damien?'

'Working,' Allie said. She checked her phone and sighed. 'He'll join us later, if he can get off early.'

Jasmin tried to quash her disappointment as they walked together down the lane. The further they went, the more imposing the houses became, all of them elegant and detached, with gardens larger than was customary in town. It wasn't a neighbourhood where students usually lived, and not on their own.

They stopped outside a gate, where a neat sign named the house *Riverview*. Pushing the gate open, Jasmin felt the bass beat from inside. Muffled conversations spilt into the front garden. The front door was ajar and they went in, finding themselves in an entry hall thick with people and fruit scented vape mist. Students crowded into the heaving lamplit rooms. In the living room to their left, people clustered in groups around the armchairs and couches, draping themselves over the furniture while others sat languid on the floor, leaning in to each other as they spoke. To the right, in another adjoining room, more energetic partiers shook their hips with arms pumping to loud music. A spinning disco ball rained light on to the walls.

'Do we have to?' Allie said. She looked nervous, like this was the last place she wanted to be.

'Come on.' Imogen stalked ahead, aiming straight for the drinks table. She muttered under her breath, clearly unimpressed by the selection. Finding an unopened bottle of red wine, she grabbed paper cups.

She handed one each to Allie and Jasmin, but Jasmin shook her head and held up the non-alcoholic cider she'd brought.

'This is Rory's house?' Jasmin raised her voice over the music. 'It doesn't look like a houseshare.'

'That's because it's not,' Rían yelled back. 'Rory lost his mam ages ago, and then his stepdad when he was at secondary. He only gets his inheritance, which includes this house, when he graduates or turns thirty, though he's allowed to live here in the meantime. Unfortunately, Rory is not particularly academically minded, though he does enjoy the more *social* aspects of the university experience.' He gestured to the room, the loud students, the relentless beat of the music. Through the window, on the outside deck, a group of guys tested their endurance by timing each other on the pull-up bar. They were sloppy and drunk, and Rían's disdain was etched into his face. 'We *cannot* stay here too long.' He shuddered, and reached for his hip flask.

'Rory's failed more courses than he's passed. He's changed majors a few times,' Allie said, as Imogen tugged her back into the hall. Rían and Jasmin followed, narrowly avoiding a couple slow-dancing to fast music in the doorway.

Imogen made for the bottom of the staircase, where it was quieter, and continued the rundown on Rory. 'In his second year in journalism, like us, though we rarely see him in class. But if he graduates in some form, he gets his inheritance.'

'How did Niamh know Rory?' Jasmin said. A boy barrelled into them, then staggered off, waving. 'They seem … very different.'

'That's the million-dollar question,' Imogen said. 'Here's what we have to do tonight. Approach Rory, get him talking about Niamh. If he's the maybe-boyfriend, we need to know.

Talk to his friends and see if they know anything, if they ever saw Niamh and Rory together. While we're here, we should also nose around the house, see if there's anything that links Rory to Niamh.'

Allie glanced around the room, chewing on her bottom lip.

'We should probably split up,' Imogen continued. 'Allie, you circle the ground floor, get chatting and find out about Niamh. Find out if she attended any of Rory's parties, how close they were.'

Allie looked nervous. 'I really don't want to do that.'

'*Honestly*,' Imogen sounded irritated. 'I'll never understand how you plan to be a journalist when you can't get out there and use your words.'

Allie lowered her eyes. 'This is someone's life. Her death. It's not just another story.'

'When will you get it?' Imogen said. Her face was bleached by the light of the mirror ball. '*Everything* is a story. Until you learn to see the world as a journalist does, you're going to keep raking in those shitty marks.'

Allie swallowed. 'Ah now,' Rían said. 'That's a little brutal.'

Imogen held up her hands, either beseeching or fed up, Jasmin couldn't tell. 'We're on the job. Now is not the time to be second-guessing ourselves.'

'I don't mind mingling?' Jasmin offered. 'I could come with you, Allie.'

'Forget it.' Imogen let out a long-suffering sigh. 'I'll do it. Jasmin, why don't you go upstairs and look through Rory's bedroom. Take Allie with you.'

Allie looked crushed. The tips of her ears turned red.

'I'll get talking to Rory,' Rían said, to cover the awkwardness. 'Man to man. See what he has to say for himself.'

'Fine.' Imogen turned on her heel before anyone could say anything else.

'Come, it will be quieter upstairs,' Jasmin said, gently taking Allie's elbow, thinking of how Georgie could settle her with just a few sympathetic words when she was feeling dejected.

Both girls stole up the unlit stairs. There were no guests up here. It was definitely off limits.

Rory's bedroom was clearly the one at the end of the passage. It smelt of aftershave and running shoes, a lingering scent of stale sweat. Inside, Jasmin switched on a lamp. The bed was half-heartedly made, like he'd started doing it but got bored in the middle and abandoned the job.

'I'm not sure what Imogen thinks we're going to find here,' Allie said, opening Rory's wardrobe. 'It's not like we're going to find a diary confessing to Niamh's murder.' She pulled a face at the tower of clothes on the chair. 'Gross.'

Jasmin opened the drawer of the bedside table. There wasn't much in it – earbuds in their case, a jumble of pens and receipts and an old handheld games console.

'He's so bland,' Allie said with distaste as she picked through a heap of sachets on the desk, all protein powder samples. 'No books, no comics, no photos. There's literally nothing interesting about him.' She made for a door beside the wardrobe and pushed it open. 'It's a bathroom.'

Jasmin went up behind Allie and looked inside. Half full

tubes of hair gel and curl cream were scattered around the sink, along with aftershave and a spray can of Lynx.

'Boys are so gross.' Allie pulled a face at the bath. 'I'm going to gag if I stay a second longer.'

Allie left and Jasmin looked around the small bathroom. It was a little messy, a ring of bubble bath scum around the tub, but otherwise not too bad. The cabinet door was ajar, and Jasmin couldn't resist peeking inside, seeing toothpaste, ibuprofen and pimple cream. Closing the mirrored door, she pulled out her gloss and touched up her lips, wondering if Damien would make it after all.

Allie was perched at the edge of the bed, looking a little shell-shocked, like she'd had enough. She tightened the belt of her fur jacket and fiddled nervously with the fabric. Her make-up had seeped, causing dark shadows around her eyes. She looked like a furious, very pretty pixie. She dropped her head in her hands, groaning. 'Imogen can be so bossy.'

'But that's not why you're angry, is it?' Jasmin sat beside her.

'No.' Allie breathed out, looking up. 'I'm angry because she's *right*. I don't know what I'm going to do. I hate journalism. I hate asking questions. I hate writing. I hate *using my words*. I've dreamed of this since I was a little girl, and now I hate it so much that I'm sabotaging myself and I'm failing. My marks are terrible. When I think of doing this for the rest of my life, I would rather die.'

'You wouldn't really.' Jasmin placed her hand on Allie's thin shoulder. 'Besides, if you hate it that much, there must be a way out.'

'I'm the first in our family to attend university. My parents will be so disappointed if I drop out. They wanted me to do something sensible, like law, but I insisted. And unlike Rory, I can't keep changing course and staying here indefinitely.'

Abruptly, Allie stood up. 'Let's go. There's nothing here.'

'OK.' Jasmin took a last look around the room, at the row of running shoes beside the wardrobe. The clothes piled on the chair. No photographs. Beside the bed, only a phone charger. On his desk, a pile of pristine textbooks that looked like they'd never been opened. A large, frameless mirror. It was almost like he didn't really live here. Not in a meaningful way. Which was odd, considering it was his family home.

What mattered to Rory? What did he look at before he went to sleep at night? An idea occurred to her. Jasmin lifted Rory's pillow, finding a silk sleep mask.

'What are you doing?' Allie said as Jasmin ran her hands down behind the bed.

'Just checking,' Jasmin said, as she saw the edge of something sticking out from the under the mattress. It looked like a page curling up. Before Jasmin could reach for it, Allie grabbed her arm. 'Someone's coming.'

Jasmin saw the wide-eyed panic on Allie's face. Imogen would smile and spin it if she were caught in Rory's bedroom. But for Allie, getting caught intruding would be shameful. She wouldn't live it down. She was frozen, watching the door as the sound of footsteps came down the passage.

Jasmin took Allie's hand and pulled her behind the door, pressing themselves flat against the wall. The footsteps stopped.

Jasmin touched a finger to her lips as they heard another door open then close. When no further sound came, still holding hands, they slunk out of Rory's room and crept down the hall.

Jasmin felt the faintest squeeze on her hand as Allie smiled at her. They'd shared something up there in Rory's room. Jasmin may not have learned anything about Rory, but her heart sang, because there'd been other gains.

For the first time, Jasmin felt like Allie might be able to trust her.

FIFTEEN

Glancing behind them, Allie nudged Jasmin towards a door. 'Let's hide in there.'

The girls tumbled inside the room, cast in a yellow glow from the street lights. Allie shut the door behind them, and they let out relieved giggles that they hadn't been spotted.

Clicking on the floor lamp, Jasmin saw they were in a large study with floor-to-ceiling bookshelves lining the walls. A large mahogany desk appeared to have been haphazardly pushed to the wall. In the centre was a rowing machine and a fitness bench. Jasmin guessed that Rory's stepdad had used the room as a study, that the books on the shelves were his. And that Rory had brought in the gym equipment without bothering to clear out his stepdad's things.

Allie took a deep breath. 'Can I tell you a secret?'

Jasmin turned to her, curious.

'I don't like parties.'

'I'd never have guessed,' said Jasmin, trying not to smile.

'I used to be mad shy when I was a kid.' Allie looked around at the bookshelves lining the walls. 'Still am, but I manage it better now. I can't do small talk. I never know what to say and I feel like this awkward lump, just standing there, with a mouth full of teeth. I don't like the vibe of Rory's parties. The heavy drinking. They're all so loud.'

Jasmin watched her with a funny ache in her heart as Allie examined the panelling on the door with unnecessary concentration. She was not what Jasmin had expected when she'd studied the friends from afar. She'd read her wrong. What Jasmin had thought was a cool aloofness was simply shyness. An inability to be looked at for too long.

'Some people just don't do small talk,' Jasmin said, and Allie nodded. 'Let's not go downstairs then. They can meet us here, it's quieter anyway.'

It was an odd, mismatched room. The neatly lined shelves contained spy thrillers that had likely been Rory's stepdad's. The pictures in their dusty gold baroque frames and the angel figurines looked like they could have been his mam's. Jasmin suspected that Rory only ever came in here to exercise. Or perhaps, exorcise.

Jasmin stretched out on the fitness bench and shot off a text to Imogen and Rían. Allie poked around the bookshelves, looking at the titles.

They were quiet for several minutes, then Allie broke the silence.

'The picture Damien took of you was stunning.'

Jasmin glanced up. Allie was studying the back of a book with apparent interest. 'He's a good photographer.'

'You like him.' Allie rushed the words. 'We had a thing back in September. Didn't last. We're better as friends. We're good now. So, if you wanted to … well, don't worry about me.'

Before Jasmin could think what to say, there was a light tap at the door.

'We're here!' Imogen sang as she came in, the brief tension between her and Allie all forgotten.

'Is anyone out there?' Allie gestured to the upstairs corridor.

'Just us.' Imogen retrieved the wine and paper cups from her bag. She looked around for a place to put them, saying, 'This is a weird room. Forty per cent mammy. I mean, look at those angel figurines, would Rory not ever chuck those in the bin? Forty per cent stepdad, and twenty per cent gym nut. Needs a few protein shakes and kettlebells to even things out.'

Rían came in, taking in the barbell, the rowing machine and a gold-framed sacred heart picture on the wall. 'Love what you've done with the place.'

And then, behind him was Damien. Jasmin felt suddenly embarrassed, even though she knew he couldn't have heard her conversation with Allie. Was her schoolgirl crush that obvious? *Ugh*, she thought. It was literally that. A schoolgirl crush.

Jasmin sat up and Rían took a place beside her. Imogen took the only chair in the room, a small desk chair on wheels, looking like a queen. She was one, in a way. She was the centre of the group, the figure the others arranged themselves around.

She poured four cups of wine and passed them round. Then she dug into her bag and pulled out a sparkling water for Jasmin.

Rían took his wine and touched his cup to her water. 'Did you have a successful mission?'

'Not particularly,' Jasmin said. 'What about you?'

'I got nowhere,' Rían said. 'Rory's friendly enough, but his range of conversation is ... narrow. We talked about his gym, our courses, but when I brought the topic around to Niamh, his only contribution was "Yeah that's tragic, man." Then he wandered off.' Rían raised an eyebrow. 'I don't think I'm quite his cup of tea.'

'Do you think he was hiding something?' Allie said, picking up a wobbly dog toy. She pushed the button beneath its base and its head and legs flopped.

'I'm not sure he has the brainpower.' Rían took a long drink from his cup. 'I lost twenty minutes of my life that I'll never get back. Please never make me do that again.'

'You're such a snob,' Jasmin scolded him, shaking her head.

He smiled at her. 'Absolutely. And what's wrong with that? Why bother with boring people, Jasmin?'

Allie was pacing the room. She picked things off the desk, turning them in her hand before putting them down. If Imogen had a kind of regal stillness about her, then Allie was the opposite. She was always darting, moving, shifting.

'The thief,' Jasmin blurted.

Allie's spine straightened. 'Excuse me?'

'I was just thinking that Imogen looks regal and composed. The queen. You're small and stealthy, the perfect thief.'

113

'Or assassin. Allie can be pretty deadly.' Imogen's lips curled up as she took to the game. 'Rían is the joker, flamboyant on the outside but sad and sombre on the inside, and not a romantic bone in his body.' Rían gave a jocular wave from where he sat beside Jasmin. 'And what's Damien?'

Damien looked back at them all. His face was half in shadow, carving his features as if from stone, accentuating the angle of his cheekbone, the shape of his mouth. Jasmin felt her heart skip as she looked at him.

'The warrior,' Allie said.

'The lover,' Rían corrected.

'The magician,' Imogen said.

It was strange, Jasmin thought, that they all saw him differently, and all of them missed the truth.

'The hermit,' Jasmin offered, knowing she was right. Damien was an island to himself.

'What about you, Jasmin?' All eyes were on her now as Rían spoke. 'What are you?'

'Jasmin is the priestess.' Damien was angled towards her. 'Those black eyes, the enigmatic smile. The aura of mystery. Jasmin is our priestess.'

They liked games, Jasmin realised. Was that why they were here? More than justice for Niamh, were they enjoying the game? Suddenly, Jasmin felt a little grubby.

'I got talking to some of Rory's friends downstairs,' Imogen said, changing the subject. 'Apparently he *did* know Niamh. They met back in the summer, at a barbecue. You'll never guess where.'

'Just tell us already,' Allie sighed.

'At Theo Merrick's house.' Imogen's eyes were shining. 'Every summer Merrick hosts a big barbecue for his assistants. Weird how his name keeps cropping up, isn't it?'

'Was Rory working for Merrick too then?' Allie said.

'No.' Imogen's voice dripped with glee. 'He doesn't need to work – look at this place. Get this, Rory is Merrick's stepbrother.'

'What?' Rían said. 'His stepbrother? He never mentioned anything. Now *that* would have been interesting.'

'Why would he?' Allie said. 'It's not like any of us actually talk to him. He's just around having stupid parties.'

'So Niamh met Rory at Theo Merrick's summer barbecue,' Jasmin said thoughtfully. 'Did they become friends? Was there any indication that Rory might be the maybe-boyfriend?'

'It doesn't look like it. I got talking to three of Rory's best buds, and they were clear.' Imogen spoke slowly and with relish: 'Rory hated Niamh.'

'What?' Rían said again, injecting the word with drama.

'They said that Rory was angry with Niamh. Because she had dirt on him.'

'What dirt?' Allie leaned forward.

'That's what we have to find out. According to his friends, Niamh used this mysterious dirt to taunt Rory and get him to do whatever she wanted. We need to move Rory to the top of the suspect list.'

Jasmin shivered. *Conniving*, that was what Mai had said about Niamh.

'They told you all this?' Allie said with disbelief. 'How did you get them to trust you?'

Imogen gave a small shake of the head and said fondly, 'Oh, Allie. That's what I do.' She sat tall, as if pulled up by her confidence. 'But that's not all.'

'Go on,' Damien interrupted before Allie could respond. 'Don't keep us in suspense.'

'They let it slip that Rory was always bitching about Niamh. One time, he said there was a reason she was Merrick's favourite.' Imogen's words became more urgent now. 'And it's because Merrick and Niamh were in a *secret relationship*.' Imogen sat back with her arms folded, checking the reaction to her bombshell. 'All of Merrick's students, project assistants and research assistants believe there was something going on between them during the summer.'

'Niamh? With Merrick?' Allie exclaimed. 'Surely not.'

'What about Candice?' Damien said.

'Maybe she didn't know. But it sounded pretty convincing to me,' Imogen continued. 'Remember what Becky said about the *maybe-boyfriend*, that it seemed like Niamh was involved with some guy who wasn't that into her. Theo Merrick is practically married to Candice. They're as close to A-list as this place gets. It would explain so much, like why Niamh denied having a boyfriend when Becky was so sure she'd witnessed some kind of lovers' spat. That's why Niamh kept to herself, because she had a huge secret that no one could know.'

'Becky heard the man threaten her late one night, saying,

"You're going to regret this," Jasmin said thoughtfully. 'Do you think Niamh was getting tired of being the secret girlfriend?'

'But *why* do people think Niamh was involved with Merrick?' Allie interjected. 'Is it just gossip? Or did anyone actually see something?'

'It sounds like a bit of both,' Imogen answered. 'Over the summer, Merrick would often call Niamh into his private office. She'd even work in there with him sometimes. And she would stay late. Then, last week, they were seen in a heated discussion behind the Old Science. They went to those trees beside the greenhouses, which everyone knows is for snogging or smoking.'

'Arguing, again,' Jasmin said.

'It always comes back to sex,' Rían said, sounding bored. 'Tedious. Humans are so dull.'

'You sound a hundred years old,' Imogen teased.

'I *am* a hundred years old, in my soul.' Rían sighed. Jasmin looked at him, seeing truth in his dark eyes. She suspected that, for once, he wasn't entirely joking.

'Let's say the rumours are right, and this is a romance gone bad,' Jasmin said. 'Maybe the argument by the trees was Merrick breaking up with her. Was she hurt and angry? Did she threaten to tell Candice? Did he kill her to stop her doing that?'

'Who says he dumped her?' Allie spoke up. 'What if it was the other way round? What if she dumped him, and it made him so mad and jealous that he killed her?'

'That doesn't make sense.' Damien pushed away from the

desk, moving to the fitness bench. 'If he was that possessive, he'd have broken up with Candice to be with Niamh. He wouldn't have killed her.'

'Oh, do men only kill their main girlfriends?' Allie said, and there was bitterness in her words as she glanced up at him. Jasmin did not miss the look that passed between them.

'No,' Damien said impatiently. 'I mean, Merrick doesn't seem possessive. Not of Niamh, not of Candice. I think Merrick is only in love with himself.'

'So what do you think happened?' Jasmin said.

'What if,' Damien said slowly, 'what if there was someone else entirely? What if their relationship made *another* person angry?'

'You mean Candice?' Imogen pulled herself taller in her chair. 'Interesting. She finds out about the affair … she lures Niamh to the shed, kills her and makes it look like a suicide. She's smart, Niamh was intoxicated. She could pull that off.'

'Or Freddie. Or maybe there was someone who was in love with Niamh?' Damien ran his hand through his hair.

'Candice makes the most sense.' Allie looked energised. 'She was talking to Niamh at the drinks reception. She could have slipped something in her drink. Candice is a pharmacologist, she would know how to incapacitate her without it showing up in the post-mortem.'

'I don't know. Candice seems too composed,' Damien said, frowning.

'Maybe that composure made her more likely to explode and act in passion?' Rían suggested.

'I saw her crying,' Jasmin admitted.

Imogen swivelled her head to look at her. 'Candice Greene, crying?'

'She was in Merrick's office just the other day.' Jasmin faltered, not wanting to explain why she was in his office. Luckily the others seemed too distracted by Candice crying. 'When she saw me, she left. But she was a mess.'

'See?' Allie said triumphantly. 'Candice knew about the affair. She was devastated. She's ruthless and would make an excellent murderer. Remember the photos Damien took? She was talking to Niamh just before the vase smashed. They argued. Niamh asked her for a painkiller. Candice sees her chance. She has something on her – a sleeping pill, maybe. She gives it to Niamh, telling her it's paracetamol. Niamh bumped into the vase and tried to get away. Feeling odd, she went out to the end of the garden, trying to find her mysterious friend for help – but Candice got there first. Niamh was weak and dazed now, thanks to the pill, and Candice dragged her to the shed. They fought.' Allie grabbed at the air. 'They struggled and Candice saw red, shouting, "How dare you take my man."' Allie gave a small animated noise. 'Candice overpowered Niamh and, bam, you know the rest.'

Allie swept her arm to the side, hitting the shelf. A framed picture fell on to the hard wooden floor.

They all stared in horror.

'Is it broken?' Damien said.

Allie picked it up and examined the picture. 'It's cracked.' She straightened up, her cheeks bright red. 'Rory won't notice.' She put the picture face down on the shelf,.

'We should probably get out of here,' Rían said. 'Before someone comes up.'

'Are we any closer to finding out who the mysterious friend is?' Damien said as they made for the door. 'The one she confided in and arranged to meet the day she died?'

Imogen shook her head. 'According to Rory's friends, Niamh was a friendless loser.' She opened the door, glancing at Jasmin and Allie. 'How did you get on? Find anything in Rory's room?'

'Nothing,' Allie said stiffly, as she switched off the floor lamp. The room plunged into darkness and they filed out into the upstairs passage.

As they were nearing the door, Jasmin thought about the curled-up edge of the page beneath Rory's mattress. It was probably nothing, a label, or something that had fallen behind the bed. But this was her only chance to confirm that it really was nothing.

'I have to use the bathroom,' she said to the others. 'I'll find you downstairs.'

Imogen looked at her curiously, but simply nodded.

Jasmin watched them head down the stairs, and then she retraced her steps to Rory's room.

SIXTEEN

Barely a minute later, she felt his familiar presence behind her. She knew it was him without looking. It was like Rían's ordinary magic experiment when he made her shut her eyes: she just knew.

'Thought I'd keep you company,' Damien said, catching up with her.

'In the bathroom?'

He laughed softly. 'No, not in the bathroom.'

They walked side by side, his hand less than an inch from hers. As they went down the passage, he brushed against her, and even that lightest touch felt charged. Jasmin cleared her throat, hoping it wasn't utterly and entirely obvious to Damien how smitten she was.

In an effort to hide her feelings, she focused on his usual thin khaki jacket with its military pockets, a fitted, long-sleeved T-shirt beneath. She could just about make out the red letters on the white fabric.

'*CRUSH IT?*' she read the loud capital letters.

Damien smiled sheepishly. 'It's one of the slogans at the gym where I work.'

'One of?'

'They like their two-word slogans there. *Crush it. Burn it. Work it.* That kind of thing. Hard music, men pumping iron. I see Rory there often. It's a lot of testosterone, but the pay is decent and I get to use the equipment. I'm lucky to have the work.'

Jasmin saw the fatigue in his eyes like a light dimmed. She remembered him saying he had to get good marks. 'You work hard.'

'I have to.' He shrugged and watched her push open the door to Rory's bedroom. 'This isn't the bathroom.'

'There was something I wanted to check.' Jasmin flicked on the bedside lamp again. Then she held on to the top corner of the mattress and lifted it. On the bedframe was a stack of printouts. She picked them up, and it took a moment for her to realise what they were.

'Test papers.' Two different courses, both upcoming, and then two dated to the last few weeks. 'He's cheating on his tests.'

'Dumb move, Rory,' Damien said, sounding almost angry.

Jasmin remembered what the others said about Damien studying hard, and she guessed it must be infuriating to see other people coast and then get through by cheating. She took a picture of the stolen tests, then shoved them back beneath the mattress.

Damien glanced over the room, his jaw still tight.

'Are you going to say anything?' She watched the emotion work over his face. 'About the cheating?'

'I don't know,' he said eventually. 'I don't know if I want Allie to know.'

Jasmin thought at first that Damien meant the unfairness would bother Allie, especially since she was failing the course that Rory was cheating to pass. Then she realised that Damien meant something else: that Allie might be tempted to get her hands on those stolen tests too.

'So this is your first party at Rory's?' Damien changed the topic awkwardly. 'What's the verdict? How do you rate his party house?' He shifted closer to her now, and Jasmin's breath hitched.

'I wouldn't know. I spent most of it up here.'

'You didn't miss anything downstairs.' He inched nearer, filling up her senses – the smell of him, freshly showered and minty shampoo. The slightly musty tang on his jacket.

'That's what Rían said.'

His eyes were locked on hers. 'I'm in no rush to go back down.'

Jasmin felt a delicious squirming in her chest. Damien seemed even closer.

The door opened and they jumped apart.

'Yeah, man, I don't think that's how—' The overhead light flicked on and a beefy young man, Rory, stood in the doorway, another figure behind him. 'You're in my room? C'mon, Damien, you know you're not supposed to be up here.' He didn't sound angry. He seemed amused, giving Damien a knowing look that made Jasmin want to wallop him.

'We're just on our way out,' Damien said smoothly.

Rory smirked, shaking his head. He walked towards Jasmin, smiling. 'I'm Rory. Nice to meet you.'

'Thanks for a great party,' Jasmin said politely. 'I'm—'

'Jasmin?' came the voice behind Rory.

'Dash,' Jasmin said, unable to hide her surprise. 'What are you doing here?'

'I was about to ask you the same thing.' Her brother folded his arms, looking between her and Damien.

'How do you know Rory?' Jasmin pushed.

'From my gym, you know, Power Up.' He nodded at Damien. 'I've seen you there, haven't I?'

'Yeah, I work there. I'm Damien.'

'Meet Dash, my brother.' She waved a reluctant hand.

Dash shifted his focus back to Jasmin. 'What are you doing here, Jas?'

The full horror of the situation was dawning on her. She couldn't stick around to answer any more questions, like why she was there at this party with university students when she was still at secondary school. Her brother could let that slip at any moment.

'I was just leaving,' she muttered.

Dash watched her, his face inscrutable, and Jasmin held his eye meaningfully. *Don't you dare give me away*, she communicated.

'Good,' Dash said drily at last. 'I'll see you home.'

Dash was a late talker. Sonia liked to say that he didn't speak at all until he was three and a half, and then suddenly came out with full sentences. Like he'd been listening, learning and quietly sorting it in his head. But since then, Dash always had something to say. Except tonight.

The drive home was silent until they were well away from the river, had passed the medical centre, the fire station and were on the straight road home. Jasmin was growing increasingly unnerved.

'Now, tell me why you were at one of Rory Walsh's notorious parties this evening.' As an afterthought, he added, 'And why I found you in the bedroom with a guy.'

She took a deep breath. 'I was there with friends. Four new friends who I like very much. You're being way too protective here, Dash.'

'And these friends, are they from school?' Dash said.

'No. They're at university.' She sounded petulant even to her own ears.

'Why are you hanging out with university students?'

'Because my friends dumped me.' Jasmin couldn't hide the pain in her voice. 'I met them at a coffee shop. They're only a year older than me.'

'What's the deal with … Damien, is that his name?'

She side-eyed him. Dash liked the idea of himself as a free spirit. Someone who followed the beat of his own drum. Surely he would understand. 'We're friends. Look, they're interesting and funny, and I like them. Rory's in some of their classes, so we decided to go. I just want to try new things, Dash.'

She spoke mildly, willing him to believe it was no big deal. He expelled a breath and she waited. She was sure he'd say

125

he'd have to tell Sonia that she was hanging out at college parties with older friends. Parties with alcohol and who knows what.

But when he spoke, all he said was, 'I get it.'

'You do?' Jasmin said.

'Yeah.' He took the corner, then added, 'But be careful. You're at different life stages, whether you like it or not. You're still at school while they've started their adult lives. They have to sort their own food and laundry, manage their own money—'

'Like you?' Now it was Jasmin's turn to raise an eyebrow.

Dash laughed and so did she.

'You got me,' he said.

'So, you know Rory well?' she pried. 'What's he like?'

'He's all right. Friends with everyone and their dog.' Dash shrugged. 'He's always at the gym. I knew him only a minute before he was inviting me out kayaking.'

'When did you meet him?'

'Early summer, before we left to see Dad. Along with Javier and a few others.' Dash hesitated, then continued, 'The thing about Rory is that you're his best friend in five minutes. Then you realise three months later that you barely know him at all.'

Jasmin's heart squeezed. That was what she feared about her new friends too. That they gave her an illusion of intimacy and that was all. 'Some people are like that.'

Dash pulled into the driveway of their house.

'Thanks,' Jasmin said and opened the door.

Dash said, 'Jas?'

She looked back at him. His lovely familiar face. She was so glad to have him back in town.

'Just be careful, OK?' His eyes were serious.

'There's nothing to worry about,' she said. 'Everything is going to be fine.'

SEVENTEEN

Sonia always cooked a big family lunch on Sundays and this week was no different. The easy banter, the smell of roast beef and the house filled with laughter were all part of a comforting routine that Jasmin had been lacking while Georgie and Benedict were away.

She needed this light, this warmth, more than ever now. Each night, the terrors grew worse. Shadowy fingers reaching for her through her sleep. It was as if the story of the *Immortalis* played in a loop in her brain, and she couldn't stop it. And, just as an old, familiar song or scent could bring memory to life, this story had brought her grandfather back to Jasmin in vivid detail.

Fragments of their time together came back to her every day now. If she stepped outside into the autumn garden, she would have a sudden, fierce memory of skipping through dead leaves with her grandfather beside her. She remembered him telling her again and again, *The journey to knowing is never easy. It comes from incisive observation, even when it is uncomfortable. Especially when it is uncomfortable.*

But today, with classical music playing, Georgie and Sonia bickering about washing the pots as Jasmin loaded the dishwasher, the shadowy fingers were chased away. At least for a little while.

After the kitchen was cleaned, Jasmin went to find Dash playing a video game in his bedroom.

'Hey. I've been thinking about giving your gym a try.'

'You hate the gym.' Dash didn't glance up from his game.

That was true, Jasmin did hate the gym. But Dash had met both Rory and Javier at Power Up and she realised with a sigh that she needed to see it for herself. Eamon was right again: *incisive observation, even when it is uncomfortable.*

'I do. But without soccer training I have to try something else.' Especially with all the nervous energy swirling inside her since Niamh's death. 'Are you going in later?'

Dash raised his head from his game and frowned at her. 'I'm going at five. That's when the others will be there.'

'I'll be ready.'

While she waited, Jasmin went to the sunroom. It was nearly too cold to be in there, and soon Sonia would shut it up for the winter. But Jasmin loved the exotic flowers and shrubs, the potted lemon and olive trees that filled the room, the delicate scent of the plants, even if it meant she now sat with a throw draped around her shoulders as she flipped through the notebook dedicated to Niamh's murder. She scribbled down what

129

they'd learned at Rory's party, wondering: could Niamh really have been involved with Merrick?

Sighing, she picked up her laptop and searched for Theo Merrick.

He was prolific. Loads of papers published in top journals, and involved in many high-level initiatives. His PhD programme was the most sought after in the country. Merrick and his partner, Candice, co-owned a spin-out company called Verge, where the Wellness Formula was being developed. A spin-out, as Imogen had guessed, was a company formed by academics with the purpose of commercialising their research and taking it out into the world. And, making money.

Jasmin clicked through to the Verge website. *At the cutting edge*, the tagline read. It was a biotech company, and Jasmin parsed through the jargon – 'harnessing the power of gene expression' and 'cellular reprogramming' – to glean that they used biological methods to discover and develop products, including medicines.

But the details didn't really matter. Because what Jasmin saw was gloss and money. The website looked expensively designed, as if it were showcasing some high-end product so exclusive that all the talk around it was soft and hushed. That if you needed to ask, you couldn't afford it. Merrick must have some serious investors, which meant that people believed in his research. And in him.

The company logo was striking. Unusual. It was an ouroboros, a serpent eating its tail.

Jasmin knew that image. She'd even seen it recently. Where? At school? She searched her mind, but the thought retreated.

Dash appeared at the door of the sunroom. 'Hell, Jas. It's cold in here. Are you not frozen?'

'Wuss.' The truth was that she liked the chill, how the cool air felt on her cheeks. 'It's not yet five.'

'Got bored, going in.' He nodded at her laptop. 'You studying?'

'No.' She pushed the machine away. 'I'm thinking.'

'What about?'

She considered her options, then decided. 'About that student who died last week on campus. Niamh Cunningham.' Jasmin had been thinking about her brother's friendship with Rory. If he'd been to Friday's party, then maybe he'd been to others. 'Did you ever meet her at Rory's parties?'

Dash blew out his cheeks. 'It's so sad what happened. Yeah, I met Niamh at Rory's house.' He sat down beside her, letting out a sigh.

'I talked to her briefly the day she died. What did you make of her?'

'She was all right. Quiet.'

He shifted beside her, his eyes resting on a potted olive, then flitting to a lemon tree, and she realised that Niamh's death had upset him too.

'The university is taking it seriously,' he said. 'More counselling available. Meetings to discuss how to mitigate student burnout. The Gardaí were around asking questions, but they've moved on. Still some journalists roaming campus though, looking like human Halloween decorations.'

'Glad they're doing something.' Jasmin felt suddenly guilty

about her and Imogen's imaginary survey at Latimer House. But, she reminded herself, Niamh didn't die because she was struggling with her mental health. There was something sinister going on, and Jasmin owed it to Niamh to find out what it was.

'Did you ever hear any strange rumours about Niamh?' She didn't dare be any more specific. Dash knew her too well and she had to tread carefully unless she wanted him looking over her shoulder all the time.

His eyes narrowed. 'Jasmin Malik, what are you up to?'

'I'm just curious. You know me.'

'I do know you. And I know you've taken stupid risks in the name of curiosity. It killed the cat, remember?'

'Just as well I'm not a cat.'

'Do you remember after Grandpa was arrested?' he said, and Jasmin froze. They never spoke about that. Ever. And now Dash was casually tossing it out there, like she hadn't shoved the whole experience in an imaginary box, taped up and labelled *DANGER, DO NOT OPEN*.

'I do,' Jasmin said cautiously.

'Do you remember how Georgie would sit in her living room, with a straight spine, nice dress and neatly made-up, receiving visitors who were really there for the gossip, only days after Grandpa tried to kill her? She still had the bruises around her throat. I'm sure she would rather have stayed in bed in sweaty jammies, her hair matted, and simply cried. But everyone expects Georgie to be gracious and welcoming, and so she was.'

Jasmin said, 'Georgie would never have sweaty jammies and matted hair.'

'What I'm saying,' said Dash, 'is we live up to what people think of us. Georgie lives up to the image of social queen. For a decade, you've been hearing variations of "our Jasmin is so curious" or "she's an observer, that one," but you don't have to be.'

Jasmin heard the sincerity behind his words, soft and kind. 'Thank you.' She bumped her shoulder against her brother's. 'Oof, you have been working out a lot lately.' She rubbed her shoulder with her hand while her brother smirked at her. He looked so much like their dad, the same green eyes, the same messy hair. But Dash was solid, grounded. While Richard felt elusive and hard to hold on to, Jasmin knew she could count on Dash. That he would be there.

'Speaking of,' he tilted his head to the door, 'shall we go?'

'I'll meet you at the car.'

Dash left and Jasmin reached for her laptop. It hit her then – the reason Verge's logo seemed familiar. She *had* seen it recently: during Merrick's lecture. She quickly searched for *The Book of Monsters* and clicked on an image of it. She scrolled down the page until she found it. The ouroboros, in faded vermillion and green. Beneath the caption she read: *Codex Asteran, about 1300, McKellan Galleries, Ireland. MSL3006, f. 204.*

Looking at the two images together, it was clear that Verge's logo had been directly inspired by an image from *The Book of Monsters*. Merrick had spoken about it that night at the McKellan, and she tried to remember what he'd said.

What I hadn't anticipated was that The Book of Monsters *would change me.* The words came as clear as a bell.

She shut the laptop and grabbed her gym bag before Dash grew impatient. Jasmin went outside with thoughts tumbling through her mind. *Merrick.* The Book of Monsters. *Verge. Candice. Niamh.*

They were all connected. She just couldn't see how.

Jasmin had been at the gym for more than twenty minutes and neither Javier nor Rory were there. She'd started on a cross trainer that gave her a clear view of the adjacent weight room. But someone had nudged her off it, pointing to the twenty-minute limit at busy times, and she wandered into the weight room.

Dash intercepted her, guiding her away from the free weights towards the machines.

'They look like medieval torture devices,' Jasmin complained while Dash chuckled.

She pulled and pushed at a few of them, regretting her life choices, when Rory came in. Across the room, he greeted Dash enthusiastically at the water fountain. Dash must have mentioned Jasmin because they both turned to her.

Rory's expression changed instantly. His goofy, easy smile vanished and a hardness came into his eyes. His mouth curved in a sneer.

Startled, Jasmin released the handle on the chest press machine, causing a loud clank.

'What's a nice girl like you doing in a place like this?' Jasmin turned from Rory to see Damien beside her. He was wearing a *BURN IT!* T-shirt that flattered his arms and shoulders and she allowed herself a moment of appreciation.

'If you serve in Satan's torture room,' she grumbled, forcing her eyes up to his, 'does that make you one of his minions?'

'Better to be the torturer than the tortured,' he replied with a wink. She felt it again, that pull towards him. An itch to touch, to know.

Jasmin stood up from the machine, glancing again at Rory, who was still talking to Dash. 'What's up with Rory?'

'He knows we were snooping in his room. Says one of the test papers is missing, and since he caught us in his room, he thinks we took it. I tried to tell him that we hadn't touched it, but he didn't buy it. He's furious.'

'One of the test papers is missing?'

'Yeah.' Damien frowned. 'Are you sure Allie didn't see them?'

'Not while I was in there.' But then she remembered that Allie had been alone while Jasmin checked the bathroom. Allie had seemed a little odd when she came out. Stiff and stilted, wrapping her jacket tightly around her. Jasmin had thought her upset, but maybe Allie had found the test papers and saw a lifeline. Jasmin pressed her palms to her cheeks. 'Oh crap, she was alone while I searched the bathroom. She might have found them first.'

They both glanced at Rory, who was now dead-lifting a heavily loaded barbell, his muscles bulging.

'I'll talk to her,' Damien said, but he couldn't disguise the worry in his eyes. 'But, in the meantime, keep away from Rory. He's not happy.'

'Do you think this is the dirt that Niamh had on him?' Jasmin said. 'That she knew he was cheating and threatened to tell?'

'If Rory gets kicked out of the university, he'll have to wait until he's thirty before he gets his inheritance.'

'And does Rory strike you as the patient sort?'

Damien shook his head, his expression grim.

'Impatient enough that he would get rid of his problem by any means necessary?'

'Who knows?' Damien said. 'We can't say. What would make one person murder wouldn't be the same for the next. People are motivated by different things.'

Jasmin felt a sudden chill. Damien was right. She would rather go without than kill someone to get her hands on her family's money. But people were not the same. And Rory clearly had a greater capacity for wrongdoing, since she'd never have cheated on her tests in the first place.

She slung her towel over her shoulder. 'I'll see you later this week?'

He nodded and she left. Walking down the bright corridor to the smoothie bar to wait for Dash, Jasmin saw Javier going towards the training area.

'Javier,' she said, stopping him. 'It's Jasmin, I was with you when—'

'Of course.' He smiled grimly. 'Hey, I felt bad letting you go that day. I had to stick around and speak to the guards. How are you?'

'Still a bit shaken,' she admitted. She hesitated, then continued. 'Can I ask you something?'

'What is it?'

'We're working on a piece about Niamh for the *Answerer* and I saw a picture of you talking to her that night. Do you mind if I ask what you were talking about?'

'For the *Answerer*?' Javier tilted his head, examining her. 'Aren't you doing your Leaving Cert?'

Damn – she'd forgotten he knew that. 'Just helping out. Getting experience.'

'Sorry.' Javier shook his head, starting to move away. 'I don't see why the *Answerer* would care about my conversation with Niamh.'

'Wait,' Jasmin said. She held out her hands, hoping he would see how much this mattered. 'It's not for the paper. It's because I want to know. I need to know.'

Javier exhaled heavily. 'It wasn't anything important. She wanted a glass of wine from my tray. I thought she looked a little unsteady, so I asked if she'd have a coffee instead. I had to go to the kitchen for the coffee, and when I got back she was gone. The vase had fallen by then.'

She nodded. A brief, innocent conversation, telling her nothing. 'Thanks, Javier.'

'Why are you asking about this, Jasmin?' He looked miserable. 'Niamh was an unhappy girl and she died. That's the end of it. It's better to leave these things alone.'

'I'm just trying to understand,' she said, her voice catching. Javier looked at her sadly. 'Me too.'

EIGHTEEN

On Tuesday afternoon, Imogen and Rían were waiting for her on a bench outside the Old Science, just as Imogen's message had said. They were deep in conversation, not noticing Jasmin until she stood in front of them. Their faces were serious, Imogen's brow furrowed as she talked quietly to Rían. For a second, with the way the bare tree branches hung over them, she saw the dead king's fingers reaching in to touch. To tap on Rían's shoulder, to caress Imogen's face. Jasmin couldn't shake the feeling that somehow this ancient monster had been summoned. That he was here, that the myth was true. And he was hungry.

'Everything OK?' Jasmin said.

'It's probably nothing,' Imogen said, getting to her feet. 'You haven't heard from Allie these last few days, have you?'

'Not since Rory's party on Friday night. Why?' Jasmin wondered if Damien had told them about Rory's stolen test, missing after Allie had been alone in the room for a minute or two.

'She's been a bit quiet.' Rían stood up. 'Probably spent the weekend in the library, trying to catch up on her coursework.' He put his arms around both Imogen and Jasmin as they walked. 'She does this sometimes. I'll find her this evening. I know how to lure Allie-cats.'

'Speaking of luring,' Imogen said, 'shall we go find the research assistant? That was good thinking, Jasmin –' Imogen cast an approving eye over her – 'to track him down in the Old Science.'

At Jasmin's suggestion, Rían had stopped by the department earlier and chatted to the secretaries. He'd discovered that the research assistant's name was Lorcan and he was usually to be found in Merrick's lab on the ground floor from after eleven in the morning until evening. Rían, apparently, had a way with secretaries.

They moved towards the door, with Rían saying, 'Damien's working again, so he won't make it.'

But Jasmin was staring up at the Old Science. The tall, imposing structure of the building she knew so well. Stern on the outside, warm and familiar on the inside. Just like her grandfather. She took a deep breath to banish the ghosts of the past. 'Let's go.'

Inside the building, they weren't surprised to find the lab entrance was card-controlled, but before ten minutes had passed the door opened and a woman stepped out.

'We're looking for Lorcan. Is he in there?' Imogen asked.

'No.' She walked past them without a glance. 'Try the PhD rec room, or perhaps Merrick's office.'

Lorcan wasn't in the rec room, so they climbed the stairs to the third floor. Today, with Imogen and Rían beside her, it was easier not to think about Eamon. It was easier to close a door to all those other times she'd come up these stairs, bouncing excitedly as she talked to her grandfather.

'Isn't this nice?' Imogen said with a touch of disdain as they stepped on the soft carpet in Merrick's corridor. 'Such blatant favouritism.'

Merrick's door was open a crack and Imogen rapped loudly. After a moment, she pushed the door wide.

There was no one inside this time. Imogen sauntered in, making her way to the desk. Rían followed but Jasmin stood at the threshold. Here in her grandfather's favourite place, memories crowded closer. She was struck anew by the strangeness of it all. He had loved this room, his job. Then, one day, with no warning, he had resigned. A week later, he had tried to kill his wife. Why?

Jasmin had wondered so many times over the years. Thinking about this was like reaching the dead end of a long tunnel. There was no answer. Nothing to explain what Professor Larkin was thinking in that fateful week. In the days after it happened, the neighbours would say that *his mind snapped*. That he'd filled it with too much knowledge until it gave in like an overstuffed shopping bag. Even then Jasmin knew this was nonsense, an attempt to explain the inexplicable.

In the far corner, despite how much the room had changed, was the green velvet chair that been her long-ago favourite. She could almost feel the soft fabric on her legs. The door she'd slammed on those memories was struggling to hold.

Imogen leaned over the large monitor, pressing buttons on the keyboard. 'Password-protected. Of course it is.'

At the small conference table, Rían picked up a textbook and read out loud, '*Advanced Stem Cell Biology.*' He shuddered.

Jasmin made for the green velvet chair, feeling like she was moving through molasses.

Imogen pulled open the desk drawer. She picked up a document and started reading. 'Hmm, he's starting a phase two clinical trial for a drug candidate in January –' She flipped the page – 'A Wellness Formula pharmaceutical. There'll be a hundred people in the trial.'

Rían studied a photograph of Candice and Merrick leaning in to each other. 'Not quite the happy couple after all.'

Jasmin lowered herself into the chair like it might bite. She could almost hear her grandfather's gravelly voice saying, *You all right there?*

And suddenly she thought, *I don't know, Grandpa. I don't think I am.*

'You all right?' Imogen glanced at her, the words an uncomfortable echo of what she'd just imagined. 'You have the weirdest expression on your face.'

'Fine,' Jasmin breathed, willing herself to believe that she was. Imogen frowned at her, and the strange spell broke. 'Absolutely fine.'

It wasn't her grandfather's office any more, it was Merrick's. The door to the past held firm.

'Imogen, look,' Rían sounded excited. He held up a thick cream card with gold lettering from a stack on the desk.

'Is that a wedding invitation?' Imogen said, her fingers stroking the luxurious card.

'Better. *Please join Theo Merrick and Candice Greene*,' Rían read out loud, '*for our annual Gala Dinner*.' He waved the card. 'That's in a few weeks.'

Jasmin shifted in her seat. Something was poking her thigh.

Imogen swooped down beside Rían. There were only a few invites left, but still she counted out five.

'What are you doing?' Rían sounded amused.

'Making sure we're invited.'

Jasmin glanced down to see what was poking her. She caught a flash of pink down the side of the armchair. She dug her fingers in to pull it out. It was a small planner. On the cover was a name, in careful, neat handwriting: *Niamh Cunningham*.

Jasmin gripped the book tighter. It was an academic year planner, starting in September. She flicked through the weeks, Niamh's looping writing conscientiously noting down readings and assignment due dates. Everything ticked as she completed them. She'd doodled flowers and vines on almost every page. Occasional song lyrics interrupted her diligent timekeeping. Jasmin turned to where the red ribbon marked Niamh's place.

Monday, the day she died.

There were four entries for that day:

EDU2309 Essay extension deadline!!
Theo 4.15 – his office

His office. Niamh had been here, in this office, on this chair, the afternoon before she died. Jasmin thought back to her encounter with the distraught Niamh outside the Three Divas. That had been between four thirty and five. Moments before they'd bumped into each other, Niamh had been with Merrick. Whatever happened in this office must have driven her to tears, to the point that she'd forgotten her planner here. She must have sat in this chair, the planner slipping down the side.

Did they have a lovers' quarrel? Had they broken up?

'What are you doing in here?'

At the door stood a young man wearing a navy button-down shirt and jeans. His hair was short and neat, and he looked annoyed.

'Taking a look at *Cellular Senescence*,' Rían said smoothly, pointing to the pile of textbooks. 'Sounds fascinating.'

The young man's snort was almost inaudible.

'You're Lorcan, aren't you?' Imogen said. 'I recognise you from your picture.'

'What picture?' Lorcan did not exude warmth and welcome. His eyes narrowed on the planner in Jasmin's hand. At the name on the cover. 'That's not yours.'

'It's not yours either.' Jasmin held on to the planner.

'Please put it down.' Lorcan raised his voice and stepped forward. 'Or I will call campus security.' His shoulders were tight with barely constrained aggression. Reluctantly, Jasmin

143

put Niamh's planner down. 'What picture are you referring to?'

'We're from the *Answerer*.' Imogen launched into her introduction, explaining they were working on an obituary, that they wanted to talk to people who knew Niamh and had seen from their pictures of the night that Lorcan had talked to her at the drinks reception.

'And we thought, as she knew Merrick so well,' Imogen said, 'she might also know you.'

'I barely knew her.' Lorcan walked to Merrick's desk. 'And I don't recall talking to her that night. If I did, it was in brief greeting. Nothing more.'

'You worked together in the summer, didn't you?'

'She was a project assistant.' Lorcan dropped his bag to the floor with a thump. 'I am Theo's research assistant. Our jobs are very different.' He didn't try to hide the self-importance lacing his words.

'But you saw her around?'

'Sure. But it doesn't mean I have anything to say about her. We sometimes inhabited the same space. Doesn't make us anything more than acquaintances.'

'Can you tell us about the rumours then?' Rían said, lowering his voice in a gossipy way. 'That she was seeing Merrick?'

Lorcan took a deep breath as if to control his impatience with such an idiotic question. His eyes fluttered shut briefly, then he spoke with certainty. 'Theo is the most brilliant man I know. He's on track to make some of this decade's most important scientific discoveries. He wouldn't do something that stupid.'

144

Imogen nodded.

Jasmin was itching to jump in and challenge Lorcan, but she was beginning to understand the technique – let the silence do the work.

Lorcan fell into the trap. 'There's always a Niamh. There's always an assistant who thinks they're someone special. I've been here two and a half years and there have been many Niamhs.' He gave a bitter laugh. 'Merrick likes the attention, sure. He'll humour them. It's a kindness. But he wouldn't act on it.'

'How can you be so sure?' Imogen said.

'Because they're nothing,' Lorcan said, his voice calm but filled with venom. 'They're absolutely nothing. He'll single them out, make them feel a little special. But a man like Theo is always going to have people who seek him out. What's he supposed to do?'

'Did Theo make Niamh feel special?' Imogen asked.

'She'd come to visit him here. They'd chat, go for coffee. She wasn't the only one. She was a pet.' He shook his head, as if trying to convince himself. 'Nothing more.'

'Does he favour you?' Jasmin said. 'Does he ever make you feel special?'

Lorcan blinked at her. When he spoke, his voice was even colder. 'Those rumours were just that, rumours. Niamh came on strong, but Theo isn't like that. He was fond of her, but only in an official work capacity. It's happened before with other assistants. It's nothing.' He sat down in Merrick's chair. 'I'm afraid that's all I have time for. Theo's waiting for me.'

They left the office, holding their silence. Jasmin felt her shoulders raised up to her ears. Imogen's mouth was set, but in silent agreement they didn't say anything. They burst through the main doors of the building, feeling the cold air hit their faces. Imogen's usually pale cheeks were pink with indignation.

'Ugh, he is a self-important, pompous, toxic ...' Imogen's words failed her. 'I think I need to scream.'

'He's much too young to be that old.' Rían shook his head and Imogen gave him a side-eye. They looked at each other, lips twitching. Then, unexpectedly, Imogen giggled. Rían slung an arm around her, and again something warm and melty rushed through Jasmin's heart at the connection they shared. At how so many of their conversations were wordless. It made her ache, because she wanted that too.

'Well, that was a very emphatic rejection of the idea that Niamh and Merrick were in a relationship,' Imogen said when she regained her composure.

'Too emphatic,' Rían said, shaking his head. 'Don't know if I'd consider Lorcan a reliable source. The gentleman doth protest too much.'

'Lorcan was jealous of Niamh,' Jasmin said slowly, agreeing with Rían. 'That Merrick had singled her out. He tried to diminish her, make out that she was nothing. But it clearly got to him.'

'Jealous enough to kill her?'

'That would be wild,' Imogen said. 'But I could totally see him doing it. Removing the unnecessary irritations. Make sure his perfect Merrick had nothing to distract him from his great, important work.'

'He sure does have Merrick on a pedestal,' Rían agreed.

'Which means he's doomed to disappointment,' Jasmin said, feeling her words too hard.

She'd known another man once, whom people had put on a pedestal. She wasn't the only one who'd thought that Eamon was everything. His students adored him. She remembered them coming over in the weeks after it happened. A parade of devastated young men and women. They'd cry, needing consolation from Georgie, distraught that the man they'd worshipped had fallen so far. They needed to talk about him, about how brilliant Eamon was, how much he'd meant to them. They'd been so single-minded in their adoration, their loss and disappointment, that they forgot Georgie had far more to grieve over than they did.

'Good. He deserves it.' Imogen edged away from the building. 'What was that book you found?'

'Niamh's planner,' Jasmin said, wishing she'd had another minute to take a picture of that last day. 'She'd marked four things the day she died. An essay deadline, a meeting with Merrick for four fifteen, the alumni lecture and …' Jasmin dragged out the moment.

'What?' Imogen said. 'Please tell me she wrote the name of the mystery friend? Or better, the name of her killer?'

'She had planned to meet someone at ten at Latimer.'

'Jasmin, you're killing me here,' Rían said in his usual sardonic drawl. He paused, realising his word choice. 'Sorry. Too soon. Who?'

'Freddie. The scorned project assistant. The one she got fired back in the summer. She was meeting him at Latimer at ten that night.'

'But she never made it back to Latimer,' Imogen said.

'Maybe Freddie found her at the McKellan.'

'We need to talk to Freddie,' Imogen said.

'Allie said he's in the Deacy Library most afternoons.' Rían checked his watch. 'Wanna try our luck?'

NINETEEN

'Do we have a plan?' Jasmin said, looking at the library. 'Other than ambushing Freddie?'

'We stick to the story that we're working on Niamh's obituary for the *Answerer*,' Imogen said.

'Are we?' Rían said.

'The *Answerer* is, but we are not. Freddie won't know that. We'll say that we want to get a vivid, three-dimensional picture of Niamh, warts and all. Bring her to life on the page, that sort of thing.'

Rían winced. 'Don't say "bring her to life". Makes you sound like a necromancer.'

Imogen and Rían bickered as they walked through the front entrance. They paused at the turnstile and pulled out their student IDs. Jasmin halted, thinking wildly for an excuse.

Imogen and Rían were on the other side, still ragging each other, when they noticed Jasmin frozen at the turnstile.

'What's up?' Light dawned in Imogen's eyes. 'Oh, you forgot your card?' She glanced at the front desk attendant, who was giving directions to a visitor. 'Quickly.' Imogen expertly slipped her card to Jasmin.

Swiping the card, Jasmin said, 'If the journalism thing doesn't work out, you could have a career as a party magician.'

'You'd have to be able to smile at strangers and kids for that,' Rían disagreed. 'Imogen's far too stony-faced.'

'I prefer regal,' Imogen grumbled.

They trawled the library until they found him on the second floor. As luck would have it, the chairs on either side of him were free. Imogen slipped in on one side, Jasmin on the other and Rían pulled up a chair on the opposite side of the table.

'Hello, Freddie,' Imogen said. 'We're from the *Answerer* and we'd like to ask you a few questions about Niamh Cunningham. You worked together over the summer?'

The flash of fury on Freddie's face was lightning quick.

'Briefly. We weren't friends.' He kept his eyes on his laptop screen.

'I know that,' Imogen said. 'We're not a tabloid, obviously, so we won't print her dark and ugly secrets. But when I'm writing about someone, I prefer to have a complete picture of them. When someone dies, everyone only tells the stories that put them in a good light. But if I'm to truly understand Niamh, I need to hear the bad stories too. I'd love to hear yours. Off the record.'

Freddie lasered his gaze on the on-screen journal article like he was memorising the content.

'Please, Freddie. Everyone's making out that she was such an angel. Is that true?'

Freddie pushed his chair back, his face red. 'Niamh was a manipulative liar. She sabotaged me, saying that I botched a hotel reservation when she knew it was her mistake. When I tried to explain to Merrick, she kept goading me and I lost my temper. He was about to call security. It was *embarrassing*. There's no way he'll agree to supervise me now. I came to this university because of Merrick. I planned everything around getting on his programme, and when Niamh told that lie, it cost me my future.'

From the way his hands clutched the edge of the desk Jasmin suspected that Freddie's temper was a bigger problem than he cared to admit.

'Niamh definitely botched the reservation?'

'She was supposed to block-book twenty-one rooms. She booked twelve. She switched the numbers around.' His voice raised slightly. 'She would have sucked as a STEM teacher.'

Jasmin pictured their imaginary obituary with that as the headline.

'Niamh was a snake. Like, she never got the pastry rounds, but was the first to choose the best doughnut. And then she would take one bite and throw it away. I've never met anyone more selfish.' The words erupted from him, like he'd kept them pent up for so long and the hold was breaking.

'Why did she lie?' Rían leaned forward.

'She was obsessed with Theo. Obsessed. It was important to her that he liked her. She couldn't handle him knowing that she'd made a mistake.'

'Did you hear the rumours about Merrick and Niamh?' Jasmin said.

'I did.' Then he added reluctantly, 'But I don't believe them.'

'Why not?'

He shook his head. 'Niamh was clearly fixated on Theo. Always finding excuses to go to his office or stay late. If he was interested in her romantically, he never let it show. But I left before the end of summer. Who knows what happened then?' He gave an exaggerated shrug, clearly still pissed off that he'd been forced to leave. 'They could have been shagging all over the office then. Why would I care?'

But he did care, it was so obvious he did.

'Did she ever say sorry?' Jasmin said. 'For shafting you in the summer?'

Freddie finally looked Jasmin in the eye. 'Funny you should ask. She got in touch the weekend before she died and said that she needed to talk to me. I assumed that she was finally going to admit to how she screwed me over, but that wasn't it.'

'Why did she want to talk?' Rían said.

'She had something to tell me, and it had to be in person.' Freddie exhaled loudly. 'She said it was important. That she could get Merrick to offer me a place on his course. We arranged to meet in the Latimer common room at ten on Monday night. But she never came.'

'Why not just talk at the McKellan?' Imogen said. 'You were there for the lecture, weren't you?' She glanced slyly at Jasmin. 'My friend here noticed you.'

'Sure. I was there. Stayed at the reception for less than ten minutes. I saw Niamh there, arguing with some waiter. Obviously, I'm not the only one she pissed off. Then I left to grab a bite and see Mai. We went down to the common room at ten, as agreed, and played Hearts with Mai's friends. Niamh didn't show and I left at twelve.'

'Mai never mentioned that,' Imogen said. 'She never told us you were meant to meet with Niamh.'

He hesitated. 'Mai was worried. She thought it didn't look good that Niamh and I had this big fight and then she killed herself around the time we were supposed to meet.'

'Do you have any idea what she wanted to tell you?' Jasmin said. 'What would make Theo offer you a place?'

Freddie raised his shoulders in a shrug. His patience, thin as it was, was wearing out.

'No idea. I didn't really believe her. I mean, what would make Theo change his mind? Unless she was prepared to confess the truth – but she was never going to do that.'

'If things ended so awkwardly between you and Merrick, why did you go to the alumni lecture?' Jasmin said.

'Despite everything, I couldn't resist hearing the great Theo Merrick speak in person.' His shoulders were slouched, his mouth disgruntled.

So Niamh was supposed to meet with Freddie at ten. But she never made it.

The time of death had not been released by the guards, but the three of them now knew that Niamh's murderer must have intercepted her before ten.

Imogen stood. 'Thanks, Freddie, this is really interesting.'

153

'You're not going to print any of that, are you?' he said, suddenly wary.

'No,' Imogen said. 'I told you, it's background information. Don't worry.'

Leaving the library, Jasmin ran over the conversation in her mind. Why did Niamh want to meet Freddie? What could she have to say that would convince Merrick to offer Freddie a place on his PhD programme?

Walking outside into the brisk evening air, Imogen said with relish, 'Niamh had to be blackmailing him. Merrick. About their affair. They must have fought in his office that afternoon because she told him she would tell Candice if he didn't … what? What did Niamh want Merrick to do? Take her back? Surely not?'

'Niamh was planning to leave,' Jasmin said, remembering the phone call she'd eavesdropped on. 'The next morning.'

Imogen saw immediately where she was going. 'You think she wanted money? I suppose, if she was dropping out of her career path, she might feel entitled to compensation. And maybe it gave her a chance to fix what she'd cost Freddie?'

'Possibly,' Jasmin said, but she wasn't sure. Niamh, she was learning, was complicated.

They walked down the tree-lined avenue, three abreast. Students bustled past them, huddling into their coats as the wind picked up. Jasmin tightened her chunky knit scarf around her neck as Imogen checked her phone.

Imogen nudged her. 'Damien texted. He and Allie are back at the house. Fancy a debrief?'

TWENTY

When they arrived at Burgess Street, Imogen burst inside, causing the gamer boys in the living room to look at her with mild alarm.

She hurried up the stairs, straight to Rían's room, where Damien and Allie were both on the low bench at the coffee table. Allie hastily scooped her divination coins from the table and placed them in their pouch.

'You'll never believe what we learned.' Imogen untangled herself from her coat and scarf.

Jasmin slid in beside Allie. She registered the odd mood immediately, a heavy cloud over them, despite Imogen talking nineteen to the dozen. But Jasmin couldn't tell if it was Allie that was off or Damien. Or the both of them together.

'... And then Jasmin asked Lorcan—'

'That's Merrick's research assistant. Very strait-laced, very far up Merrick's arse,' Rían clarified helpfully.

'... If Merrick ever made him feel special,' Imogen continued as if Rían hadn't interjected. She was still high from their afternoon adventures. 'This guy gave serious axe-murderer vibes. If I were a betting woman, that's where my money would go.'

'I don't know,' Rían sighed. 'Freddie, Mai's boyfriend and consummate tutter, really hated Niamh too. Sounded like he had more reason to kill her.'

'As did Rory,' Damien said. 'Niamh threatened to tell that he'd been cheating on his tests. He would have been kicked out of college at the very least, and then he wouldn't get his nice fat inheritance for nearly ten years.'

'Could any of them be the man Becky heard in Niamh's room?' Allie added.

Jasmin glanced at her. Allie sounded half-hearted, like she was trying to play their game but didn't have the energy for it. Definitely Allie, then, who was out of sorts.

'Hey, are you OK?' Imogen looked at her friend, her earlier concern etched on her face. She'd picked up on it too. 'I was looking for you all weekend. Where were you?'

'Sorry,' Allie said. 'I was behind on work.'

'Did you get your Media Theory essay back?' Rían said with infinite gentleness.

Allie gave a brief nod. 'Failed it. Mathieson won't allow a rewrite.'

'Oh, Allie,' Rían said, and for the first time Jasmin heard a note of desperation in his voice.

'You can study with me, if you want,' Damien said. 'We're

not covering the same content, but I can help with your essay-writing.'

Allie smiled, her eyes dropping. 'I'll think about it. By the way, Jasmin,' she said, and there was something in her tone that Jasmin didn't like. 'Weird that I've never seen you around before this week. You're first year, right?'

There was something hard and disquieting in Allie's eyes. Suspicion, Jasmin realised.

'I have classes,' Jasmin said. 'I've been busy.'

'And I never see you in the mornings. You just seem to pop up out of nowhere in the afternoons. And isn't it strange –' Allie tilted her head – 'that you only showed up the day Niamh died?'

'I was around before.' Jasmin's throat tightened. Rían and Damien were both watching her too. 'You just didn't see me.'

'I saw you,' Damien said quietly.

'What are you even studying?' Allie continued.

'Oh come on,' said Rían. '*That's* obvious, isn't it?'

Silence. They knew, Jasmin thought. They all knew and had brought her here to corner her. She opened her mouth to confess everything – then stopped. Rían was pointing at her hands.

'Look at her fingers.' Everyone stared at the charcoal around Jasmin's nails. 'She's obviously at the nunnery.'

The nunnery. It took a moment for Jasmin to understand. Then she remembered. The old convent on the other side of town, close to her school, housed the fine art department. Rían had looked at her stained fingers and surmised she was a fine art student, and that she had most of her classes there.

They all stared at Jasmin, waiting for her to confirm. She had to decide – the truth or a lie?

If she told the truth, she would lose *this*. Sitting here with her new gold-dusted friends, this silk and velvet room, the stalactite candle wax dripping down the empty wine bottle on the coffee table. She would lose the one thing she'd been searching for: a place to belong. They'd think her too young, not worldly enough. They wouldn't want her any more.

And Jasmin had fallen for them, even aloof Allie, with her eyeliner and short skirts and shyness. She treasured that moment of vulnerability Allie had shown, upstairs in Rory's house. She loved Rían's goofy sense of humour, the deep kindness she sensed inside him underneath his world-weary demeanour. His relentless style, both in dress and in manner. She felt the sun on her when she had Imogen's approval. And then there was Damien, with his deep green gaze. A gaze that seemed to linger on her sometimes, making her feel hopeful. She was almost queasy at how much she wanted him to look at her.

She thought about them, all of them, almost all the time. She even chose her clothes wondering what Imogen and Allie would think. And in her Leaving Cert year, Jasmin knew where her head should be. But school, home, everything was biding time until she was with them again.

'Yes,' Jasmin said, 'I was at the nunnery earlier.' It wasn't technically a lie, she had cut through the wooded campus on her way here.

Allie's shoulders loosened but her eyes were still watchful.

'Most of my classes are on the other side of town,' Jasmin said, and it was almost the truth.

Allie gave a slow exhale. 'I'm sorry. God, Jasmin, I'm really sorry, you must think ... I'm just ...'

'Stressed,' Imogen supplied. 'I know, Allie. I know you're worried about your courses. That you've missed deadlines.'

But she'd been so mean to Allie before, Jasmin thought. Imogen's frustration with Allie's journalistic instincts was clearly a source of tension between them, but now guilt flashed in Imogen's eyes.

'It's not ...' Allie began.

Imogen burst right in. 'I haven't been supportive. I'm just worried, and when I'm worried I get mean. I'm sorry, Allie. I've been too hard on you. You're a good journalist, you just need confidence. I can help you study too.'

Allie's eyes welled up.

Imogen reached across the table and squeezed Allie's hand. 'Don't go all silent on us, OK?' She shifted, reaching for her phone, which buzzed impatiently. 'Hang on, that's my mam calling.'

She went to the other side of the room to answer it in private. They were all quiet, giving Imogen a chance to talk to her mother. After a couple of minutes, Allie looked at Jasmin sheepishly. 'Sorry, Jasmin. I was rude.'

'Over it already.' Jasmin waved an airy hand that didn't match the heavy knot inside her. They had so nearly caught her out.

'I thought you were a weirdo who was latching on to Niamh's murder for some kind of cheap thrill,' said Allie with a faint smile.

'Are *we* not weirdos latching on to Niamh's murder for a cheap thrill?' Rían said lazily. He was wearing guyliner today and had fluffed out his curls, and he looked like Drama.

'We are journalists trying to find the truth,' Imogen said as she returned to the table. 'Sorry, my mam has been swamped lately. Sometimes she forgets she has four children. If I don't answer when she calls, it might be a few days before I get to speak to her.'

'Do journalists still do that? Find the truth?' Rían was deliberately provoking her, his expression sly. 'I thought your mam preferred to ask searching questions like, "What new hair product is taking the celebrity world by storm right this minute?"'

'You're horrible.' Imogen kissed him on the cheek.

'And you need to have some fun. We need a party soon. A real party, not that nonsense at Rory's. One with wine, beauty, wildness. Debauchery.'

'You're right.' Damien brightened. 'It is that time of year after all. Time to open up to the dark side.' He raised an eyebrow at Jasmin. 'You in?'

Jasmin hesitated. It was so much easier to party with wildness and debauchery when you didn't have school in the morning.

Damien seemed to read her mind. 'Rían is exaggerating, by the way. It doesn't have to be a night of debauchery.' Then his lips curled up in a smile, just for her. 'Unless you want it to be.' Jasmin felt his words deep in her gut.

'Maybe,' she said, feeling young and awkward. 'I guess it is Halloween.'

Rían gave her a pained look. 'We don't do Halloween, little flower. Halloween is for … the ordinary people. The people who order pumpkin spice lattes and plastic wreaths while wearing sexy kitten costumes.' He was hamming it up, but Jasmin suspected that there was an element of truth. That whatever most people were doing, the four eschewed.

'Ignore Rían,' Imogen said. 'We do celebrate the end of harvest time and the beginning of the darkest part of the year, even if we don't call it Halloween.' She waved her phone. 'I've checked with my mam, we can use our cottage in Lough Drinagh again.'

'Perfect,' Allie clapped her hands, a smile lighting her eyes for the first time that day. 'A little cabin in the woods. Where better to let the darkness in?'

'And,' Imogen said, drawing out the word, 'I have some news. You know my mother has … certain connections. I told her about the article we're working on and asked her to let me know if she hears anything.'

'And?' Damien leaned forward. 'What did she hear?'

'The post-mortem results aren't finalised but word is that there was diazepam in Niamh's system. Her blood alcohol content was high. Much higher than two glasses of wine.'

Allie let out a gasp. 'Diazepam? Is that Valium?' she said, and Imogen nodded. 'Does the Valium prove that she was drugged?'

'Depends how you look at it,' Imogen said. 'It could also prove the reverse, that she really was trying to kill herself. Mam says they found a half empty bottle of tequila in the shed and an unlabelled bottle of diazepam in her handbag. Everything is consistent with someone who was in a highly depressive, destructive state. And with the note, they're near certain that Niamh died by her own hand.' Imogen's eyes grew determined as she regarded each one of them in turn. 'They're never going to pursue this. There will never be justice for Niamh, unless we find out the truth.'

The words sat heavy on Jasmin's shoulders. Part of her had felt that once they started looking into it, the authorities would have to realise the truth.

But even kings made mistakes. And it looked like it was up to them to set the course right.

TWENTY-ONE

'So they really believe it was suicide?' Allie said. She sounded almost relieved, and Jasmin looked at her curiously.

'The report isn't final,' Imogen reminded her. 'And the inquest hasn't happened yet, it won't for another six weeks. Probably longer.'

'The problem now,' Rían sighed, 'is that we have several suspects and they all seem dodgy as hell.'

'Angry Freddie, who lost his dream because Niamh shafted him,' Imogen said, counting them off. 'Or his girlfriend, Mai. Doctor Candice Greene, the high achiever who never fails, not in her work or her relationships. Even if Merrick denied the affair, she might think there's no smoke without fire.'

'Then there's Rory with his stolen test papers,' Damien added. Jasmin wondered if he'd told the others about Allie stealing one of them herself.

'Don't forget Lorcan, who has serious psychopath vibes. All buttoned-up and secretly jealous because Merrick gave Niamh more attention,' Imogen said. 'Jasmin, you said you tracked down the waiter in the picture?'

'Yeah, Javier. I saw him at the gym,' Jasmin said. 'He says Niamh wanted more wine but he offered her coffee because she looked unsteady. When he returned with it, she'd already smashed the vase and left.'

'That's very kind, going out of his way to get her a coffee.' Imogen sounded suspicious. 'Damien, do you know Javier from the gym? What's he like?'

Damien shrugged. 'I've seen him around. He's quiet. He and Dash seem tight.' He looked at Jasmin for confirmation. But his gaze lingered, his eyes on hers, and she felt that familiar galloping in her heart.

'And Niamh? Did she ever come in during your shifts?' Allie said.

'I'm sure she did,' Damien frowned. 'I know that I saw her there, but can't tell you more than that. I didn't pay attention to her. My feeling is she just worked out and left.'

'OK, maybe we need to backtrack a little,' Imogen said, paging back through her notepad. 'Let's return to Monday and retrace Niamh's steps through the night.'

'We need a murder wall.' Rían stood up. 'If we're going to do this right we have to have a murder wall. Damien, can you print out the photos of our suspects?'

He swiftly crossed the room, the candlelight throwing his shadow, lean and determined. Rían muttered to himself as he took down two framed Dalí prints, *The Persistence of Memory* and *The Elephants*.

While the printer spat out the pictures of Niamh talking to each suspect, Rían pulled out a large sheet of cardboard and wrote *TIMELINE* in black Sharpie.

7 p.m.	*Lecture begins.*
	Niamh in audience giving someone the dagger eyes.
7.45 p.m.	*Lecture ends. People begin to drift next door for drinks.*

Rían faced them like a lecturer in front of his classroom. 'Do we have a first sighting of her then?'

'She was in the restroom a few minutes after the lecture,' Allie said.

7.50 (approx.)	*Allie finds Niamh searching for her head-ache pills in the restroom. Isn't noticeably drunk at this point.*
8.05 (approx.)	*Jasmin talks to Niamh, who appears hostile.*
8.08	*Niamh talks to Rory. Timestamped.*
8.13	*Niamh talks to Lorcan. Timestamped.*
8.25 (approx.)	*Niamh emerges from the garden, angry.*
8.28	*Niamh talks to Javier. Seems intoxicated. Timestamped.*
8.35 (approx.)	*Niamh smashes a vase and runs out.*

'There we have it. All Niamh's known movements.' Rían stood back, examining his handiwork with a critical eye.

He'd stuck the printed photos of Niamh and all the suspects next to their times, circling them in red. 'The crucial time is between eight thirty and ten, when she was expected back at Latimer to meet Freddie. In that window, something happened to Niamh. She either went down to the shed of her own accord or was lured there. She consumed tequila and pills.' He pointed his marker at the picture of Freddie. 'Niamh would have gone willingly with him, because they were meant to meet anyway. She might have gone with Lorcan, maybe even Candice. It's hard to see how she would have gone willingly to the shed with Rory.'

'Unless she was unwilling,' Allie said.

'Diazepam doesn't interact well with alcohol,' Jasmin said, thinking of the small bottle of low-dose diazepam she was meant to carry for emergencies. She'd been prescribed it back in the summer, with a warning about how to use it safely, after a crippling panic attack on the plane back from Italy. 'Mixing the two is dangerous, maybe even deadly.'

'Something's bothering me about Javier,' Imogen said, paging through her notepad. 'Ah, there it is. Freddie claimed that Niamh was *arguing* with the waiter. Arguing is not quite the same as suggesting coffee. So which is true?'

'Freddie also said he stayed less than ten minutes,' Jasmin

said. 'But Javier talked to Niamh at eight twenty-eight, according to the picture. Then how did Freddie hear their conversation?'

'Interesting,' Imogen said. 'Maybe he was trying to insert a distance, since he and Niamh had a beef with each other?'

'Freddie lied. Not surprised.' Allie sounded angry. Jasmin looked at her curiously, but she was sitting with her knees to her chin, looking down at the wood whorls on the table.

'I'm with Freddie. I think they were arguing, and it wasn't about wine or coffee.' Damien got to his feet, checking the time. 'I've got to head into work, catch up tomorrow?'

'I should go too.' Jasmin winced, thinking about the homework she had to get through.

'I can drop you off,' Damien offered.

'It's out of your way,' Jasmin protested. 'I can walk.'

'Unless you're out of town, it won't add more than ten minutes. It's nearly dark.'

'OK. Great.'

Jasmin said her goodbyes while Damien changed into his work clothes, and then they went downstairs. His body brushed past hers as he unlocked a Golf that had seen better days. She felt again that spark, as she always did when he touched her. And from the way he lingered, she thought he might feel it too.

'It's my uncle's old car,' he said apologetically as they got in and shut the doors. 'There's a leak, so unfortunately that damp smell is here to stay.'

'It's fine. Thanks for taking me home,' Jasmin said. She hesitated, then added, 'Listen, is Allie OK?'

'She failed a test and missed another deadline. She might

get chucked off the course at this rate.' He sighed. 'She's not the only one struggling. Imogen is obsessed with this story. And she's desperate for her mother's approval.' He glanced at Jasmin. 'Don't tell her I said that, because she will probably kill both of us and then write a prize-winning article about it.'

'Noted.' Jasmin watched Damien for a moment as he changed gears while taking a corner. 'What about you? You seem on top of things.'

'No choice. I have to do well. My uncle's supporting me – kind of – and one of the conditions is that I get distinctions.'

'Alongside working at the gym?'

'Yeah. He became my guardian from when I was eleven. He resented it because he was young and ambitious and wanted to focus on his career, not be responsible for a kid. My aunt, she's a stay-at-home mum, did most of the day-to-day care, and I use that word loosely. Anyway, I won't bore you with a sob story, but he pays my fees. I pay for everything else.'

'That would keep you busy.'

'I don't have enough time to study,' he admitted. 'I might get a bit of reading done on my shifts. But with all that's been happening, I've been far too distracted. I'm worried, to be honest.' He gave her a tired smile. 'This has been a bit of a game, hasn't it? Finding out what happened to Niamh. Now though, I'm not so sure.'

'Should we be going off to Imogen's cottage then?' Anxiety knotted her stomach. For Damien, but also for herself. It was half-term this week, but with her Leaving Cert looming in the distance, Jasmin had to keep up with revision. She was ironically already behind with art and she couldn't afford to slip further back.

'Yeah! It's exactly what we need. Get away and let loose for a night. I'll drive up after work. Need a lift?'

'That would be great,' Jasmin said. 'My grandmother has this Halloween tradition she does every year and I'd like to help her with that first. I'll get the fuel.'

'You don't need to do that.' He turned into Jasmin's road, looking up at the tall trees barely clinging on to their green. In a week or two, they would be bare. 'Nice area.'

'My grandparents bought land here before it was built up,' she said. 'They gave my parents the site next door to build on.'

'You close to your grandparents?'

'Yes.' That ache in her heart again. 'Not my grandfather these days. He ... doesn't live here any more. Nor does my dad.'

He pulled into the drive and Jasmin reached for the door. 'Thanks. Hope you're not too late for work.'

'Sure. And ... Jasmin?'

She stopped with her hand on the door handle. 'Yeah?'

'Take a break from murder tonight, will you?'

TWENTY-TWO

Inside, Jasmin hung her coat in the hall closet and dropped her bag. Impatient, she pulled out her notebook. They'd learned a lot today, and she needed to sort her thoughts.

She started down the passage, looking over her notes as she walked. Of all of the suspects, she trusted Lorcan least. There was something she couldn't quite pinpoint that made her wary of him …

Nearing the kitchen door, she glanced up a moment too late. Dash sidestepped, trying to avoid her, but they collided. Her notebook fell to the floor, a loose page spilling open on the marble.

'Watch where you're going, Jas,' Dash said irritably.

Jasmin bent to pick up the fallen page. A tanned hand reached forward, picking up the notebook, which had landed face up and open. Her heart leaped as she looked up and saw who it belonged to.

'Javier,' she exclaimed. 'I didn't realise you were here.' She looked from Javier to Dash, wondering if Javier had been here in her home before. She shrank back instinctively, uncomfortable. He hadn't been upfront about talking to Niamh at the party – *why*?

Javier was looking down at her notebook, Jasmin realised, squirming as she saw the words, *Niamh and Merrick = affair. Since the summer?*

She snatched the sheet back, hastily standing up. If Javier or Dash noticed anything, it didn't show. She studied them both, seeing they were dressed for sport. 'You're off to the gym?'

'Yeah, we booked a hall to play six-a-side. Want to come? You can go to the torture chamber while we play.' Dash grinned wickedly. 'It's what you deserve.'

'Next time, maybe.'

'Suit yourself.'

Jasmin found Sonia in the kitchen watching a talk show on the tablet while she loaded the dishwasher. Theo Merrick was a guest. Jasmin sighed. Was he everywhere she looked? He was leaning forward, piercing eyes on the host.

'You're back late.' Sonia sounded pleased about it; she'd worried that Jasmin had seemed lonely earlier in the term. 'Where were you? Your dinner is in the oven.'

'I went to the library with friends and then we hung out after.' Jasmin nodded at the screen. 'What are you watching?'

'Oh – that science guy from the university. Theo Merrick.

171

He has a book out. About how wellness will save us, or something.' She poured herself a glass of red wine. 'Sounds miserable to me.'

'A book?' said Jasmin. 'He owns a company. And teaches. He's busy.'

'Impressive, isn't it?' Sonia watched the screen. 'Plus, he's hot.'

'Mam!'

Writing books, saving humankind, shagging students. Jasmin hadn't been convinced by Lorcan's protests.

'Let's face it, many of us *aren't* well. How can we be?' Merrick said from the tablet screen. 'The world is more chaotic than it has ever been. We've been living in crisis mode for years. A pandemic. Global climate breakdown. Humans today live with an enormous amount of constant stress. But what if we could be … better? What if we could be well again?'

The host laughed and smoothed her hair. 'Sounds tempting. And you have the answers?'

'I am a scientist. I don't *know* anything.' He gave a charming laugh. 'But I am looking, and I think that is what is most important. The hunt for discovery. For knowledge. Asking the right questions. I believe I am asking the right questions with my Wellness Formula.'

'Tell us, Professor Merrick,' the host said, 'what is the Wellness Formula?'

'The Wellness Formula is the blueprint for living an optimum life in the modern world. Guided by the very latest scientific advances, we take a holistic approach, one that challenges the usual assumptions around what we need to be in optimal health.' He chuckled again. 'I can't give away all my secrets. But it is unlike anything that's come before. Watch this space.'

'Sexy voice too,' Sonia sighed.

'I think he's creepy.' Jasmin turned down the sound. 'Listen, some friends have asked me away for the night – at the end of the week.'

'Where are you going?' Sonia dried her hands on a towel.

'To my friend Imogen's family cottage near Lough Drinagh. Nothing crazy, just five of us avoiding the Halloween madness.' Seeing the scepticism in Sonia's eyes, she added, 'They're all really sound. Imogen's mam is Síle Barrett, you know, the one who's always on TV.'

'Síle Barrett's daughter?' Sonia brightened. 'I suppose that's all right. Leave me names and phone numbers, OK?' She squeezed Jasmin's shoulder. 'You don't look so lost any more. I was worried about you.'

'Hey,' came a voice from the kitchen door.

Sonia and Jasmin were startled by Javier hovering at the doorway, holding his blue and white striped gear bag. 'I forgot my water bottle. Didn't mean to interrupt.'

'Not at all.' Sonia beamed at him. 'Nice to see you again, Javier. How's your course going? You're studying meteorology, aren't you?'

Jasmin stiffened. So he had been here before. 'No, environmental science.'

'Of course.' Sonia glanced at her. 'Jas keeps talking about doing something like that, don't you, Jas?'

Jasmin nodded awkwardly. Javier retrieved his bottle from the kitchen island and left. Clutching her notebook to her chest, she took off, calling after him.

'Javier.'

He stopped where the passage met the front hall and faced Jasmin.

'Did you know Niamh? Was she a friend?' she said. 'Is that why you tried to get her coffee that night?'

He gave a single nod.

She wanted to know how they met, what the nature of their friendship was, but she could tell by the tightness of his jaw that he wasn't receptive.

'Did she ask you to meet her at the McKellan?' Maybe Javier was the mystery friend Niamh had called the afternoon before she died.

Javier ran a hand through his hair. 'No. I was working and she just happened to be there. We – we hadn't spoken since the week before.'

'I'm sorry,' Jasmin said, seeing that talking about Niamh affected him. 'For your loss. And that you found her.'

Something worked over his face. Grief, she realised. For the first time, here was someone who was sad about Niamh's death. For all the *young lives taken too soon* or *such a terrible tragedy*, Javier seemed truly sorry for the loss of Niamh.

He nodded at her notebook. 'I couldn't help but see your notes. Running quite an investigation, aren't you?'

Jasmin flushed. 'I had some questions,' she muttered.

'I can tell. One thing,' he said casually, 'Niamh wasn't

having an affair with Merrick. She would never have been romantically involved with that prick.'

'How do you know?' Jasmin's eyes locked on his, and she saw the truth there. Javier didn't have an agenda like Lorcan and Freddie. He wasn't jealous that she'd taken more than her fair share of Merrick's precious favour.

'She wasn't interested. Niamh thought …' Javier shook his head, as if annoyed with himself. He took a moment, choosing his words. 'Sure, like everyone else, she was enchanted initially. Thought him a genius. But she changed her mind about him.'

A shadow crossed his face and Jasmin was sure he was holding back. Stopping himself from saying more.

'In any case,' Javier continued, his eyes flashing with anger, 'Merrick was way too old for her. I've heard the rumours, and I'm telling you with absolute certainty that they aren't true.'

Jasmin nodded, taken aback at his vehemence. 'OK.' Was he Niamh's maybe-boyfriend then? she wondered. Was that how he knew her so well? Was that why he seemed upset now?

'You were fond of her,' she said softly. 'Tell me about her.' She asked not for herself but for Javier. Because sometimes it helped to talk about someone you missed so badly you could scarcely breathe.

He let out an exhale. 'Niamh was the most determined person I knew. She could be unexpectedly funny and loved gory horror movies. She was great with children.' Javier's voice thickened with emotion. Jasmin could detect the faintest trace of an accent. 'We disagreed about something, a week before she

175

died, and I hadn't seen her since. I'll never forgive myself for not reaching out to her.'

'Why the disagreement?' Jasmin couldn't hide the flare of interest now injected into her words.

He shook his head. 'You really shouldn't be nosing around in this.' He shifted his weight to his other foot. He looked like he wanted to say more, but he didn't.

'It's just idle curiosity,' Jasmin said.

'That doesn't look like idle curiosity to me.' He gestured at the notebook, the loose pages sticking out untidily. 'That looks like borderline obsession.'

'What's Jas obsessed with now?' Dash said, stepping into the passage. To Javier, he said, 'You ready? I told Rory we'd be there in fifteen minutes.'

'Nothing,' Jasmin said, wanting to kick her brother. 'And I don't get obsessed.'

Dash scoffed. 'This one is like a dog with a bone. If Jasmin wants to know something, then she will.'

'Ugh.' She folded her arms. 'Would you ever stop?'

'Really?' Javier said. 'My niece is like that. Cute.' But it didn't look like he thought it cute, not in the least.

'More like ferocious. Come on.'

Before Jasmin could ask him anything else, Javier followed Dash. A moment later, she heard the door click shut.

TWENTY-THREE

Jasmin's face was ashen, with a blue cast to her skin. There were dark shadows beneath her eyes and her hair was long and stringy. Her eyes were wide and frightened, a patch of dead skin on her cheek. On her head was a black and burgundy wreath, and a tattered veil hung over her shoulders.

She opened the front door to Georgie's house, seeing a zombie and a dead soccer player on the front step.

'Show me your tricks,' she hissed.

'Can we see the monster's grave?' they chirped in reply.

'Only if you promise you won't disturb it.' Jasmin put a finger to her lips. 'Believe me, you don't want the monster to rise.'

Leading them down the twilit garden, she told them the story of the monster who wore human skin. Eamon had told it to her years ago, a retelling from *The Book of Monsters*. Down the candlelit path they went, Jasmin watching for hungry kings waiting in the shadows. They stopped at the fake gravestone between a cluster of trees, the house looming behind.

Georgie's house was large, the garden filled with mature trees. People said that it was haunted, and maybe it was. But not with shadows hiding at the top of the stairs or ghosts under the bed, or anything like that. The house was haunted with life and loss. It was haunted by Richard, who never came back. It was haunted by her grandfather, who had been larger than life. When Jasmin went near his office, she could still hear the *scritch-scritch* of the mice on their treadmill.

For the next hour, a whirl of sugar-scented children appeared at the gate, shrieking with delight when they saw Jasmin and asking her to take them to the monster's grave. Clammy little hands touched her dress, her veil, her wig, and Jasmin shared out sweets.

When there was a lull, she left the bucket of sweets hanging from the tall pillar outside. The dark had settled in, she was beginning to feel the cold and was glad to get inside.

She was near the kitchen door, which Georgie shut to keep the heat in, when she heard the sound of voices – a man, talking to Georgie. She pushed open the door, thinking she'd find Dash there with a cup of tea.

Theo Merrick was at the kitchen table.

The kitchen had changed since the day Georgie nearly died. Her grandmother had got an architect in, knocked out a wall, changed the oak cabinets and put in picture windows. It looked like a different room. Sleek, elegant, modern. This kitchen was pristine and white, like nothing bad had ever happened here.

But the old kitchen, the kitchen in her memory, remained a real and terrifying place for Jasmin. It was her nightmare room. The place she went when the panic set in. The place where the shadows with long fingers lived. In her mind, the old kitchen was still intact, and every mundane detail, the dried flowers on the window sill, the copper pans, pinned her inside. Sauce, dripping red down the oak. The ever-bubbling pot.

Now, seeing Merrick in Georgie's new kitchen, the vanilla cabinets and the picture windows disappeared. And she was back there again, in the old kitchen. On that day.

'Hello, Jasmin,' Merrick said. 'It's good to meet you again. I like your costume.'

'Why are you here?' Jasmin spoke without thinking. *Touch something cold*, she reminded herself as the panic fluttered its wings. She went to the freezer, wrenching the door open.

'Jasmin,' Georgie frowned at her, pouring tea from the pot into a cup, watching her open the freezer. 'Manners.' Georgie valued good manners above everything.

'Sorry. I didn't see anyone come in.'

Jasmin shook the ice tray, counting to ten in her head. She held an ice cube in her hand, feeling the stinging cold. She felt the panic settle. She looked at Merrick again, and he was watching her, his face inscrutable. She took in the large, expensive bouquet of flowers on the table as she sat down, the ice still clenched in her hand.

'You must have been down at the monster's grave,' Georgie said. 'You won't remember this, but Theo was one of your grandfather's PhD students.' Jasmin squeezed the ice cube, feeling it turn to water. 'It's been years since he's visited. Not since after …' Her voice trailed off and, as if by sleight of hand, the strong, assured Georgie that Jasmin knew disappeared. In her place was a woman who appeared unfamiliar – older, more fragile. Unsure of herself.

'You were made professor. A chair in Biomedical Science,' Georgie said, shaking herself and pasting on a smile for Merrick. 'I saw that in the local paper a few years ago.'

Merrick nodded graciously. 'Yes, yes I was.'

'Congratulations, that's quicker than most.' Georgie sounded impressed. 'And you're always on the TV, my daughter-in-law says. You must be doing very well.'

'I've been fortunate. I'm just sorry it's taken this long to come and see an old friend.'

'Nonsense,' Georgie said, beaming up at him. 'I'm sure you've enough to keep you busy. It's good of you to remember me after all these years.'

'I couldn't forget you, Georgie,' Merrick said, his hand reaching for hers. Jasmin couldn't bear it. Then his phone buzzed and he picked it up instead of taking Georgie's hand.

'Excuse me a minute,' he said, and went out. Jasmin got up and dropped the ice down the sink.

'I don't like him.' Jasmin spoke very quietly. 'He has a reputation at the university.'

'What sort of reputation?' asked Georgie.

Jasmin's own phone buzzed then. It was from Damien: **I got off early. There in ten?**

Merrick came back inside, apologising smoothly to her grandmother. 'Sorry about that. Gosh, it's good to be here, Georgie. I haven't been in touch with any of the old crowd, have you?'

'Not really,' Georgie said. 'Just some of the wives of the old guard, but I doubt that's who you mean.'

'I'm planning a reunion early next year.' He sounded warm, sympathetic. 'Feeling all nostalgic. Do you have any photographs of my cohort?'

'I haven't thrown anything out,' Georgie said. 'I could take a look, if you want?'

'I would be so grateful,' Merrick said. 'We could look through them together, if you like? I know the memories must be painful, but maybe … there might be some good there too.'

Georgie smiled. 'I'd like that.'

Merrick watched Georgie leave the room. Her steps sounded down the passage, then stopped outside Eamon's study. Jasmin glanced down at her damaged wedding dress. The veil falling on her thighs.

'You studied with my grandfather?' she said, gaining the courage to look up at Merrick.

'I did.' He was studying her openly now. 'I remember you, from when you were younger. Watchful little thing. Big eyes.'

'I don't remember you.'

Was that true? Jasmin thought back. There were always students passing through the house. Bunches of keen young

181

men and women who had long conversations with Eamon in his study or out in the garden when the weather was fine. He'd been a charismatic professor with acolytes. Not unlike Merrick now.

'I was one of many,' Merrick said. 'But there was just one of you. I remember – you loved mice. Used to study them for hours. We all thought you'd be an excellent researcher.' He took a sip of his tea. 'Is that what you plan to do, Jasmin? Research?' He smiled. 'When you finish school, of course.'

Jasmin shrugged. 'Maybe,' she said.

'I can still see you in the office on campus, back when it was Eamon's. His quiet little shadow. Your black eyes and black hair.'

'It was my favourite place.'

'Is that why you were there in my office, the other day?' Merrick said. 'Because of your grandfather?'

Jasmin swallowed. She was grateful for the face paint, because his gaze was penetrating. She shifted uncomfortably in her seat. 'When I saw his door, I needed to be inside. To be in his space again. It … brought him back to me, just a little.' Her words tasted like betrayal. Merrick was watching her greedily. 'Don't tell Georgie I was there, will you?' she whispered. 'It will hurt her. She doesn't like talking about him.'

'Are you sure about that?'

'This should cover all three years of your PhD,' Georgie said cheerfully as she entered the room carrying two old shoeboxes. Jasmin was relieved to look away.

'Hello, Dash,' Merrick said as her brother came in through the back door.

182

'Hey. Theo Merrick.' Dash greeted the older man with a polite smile. 'This is unexpected.'

Jasmin's shoulders tensed in surprise. How did Merrick know Dash? They were in the same faculty but different departments, and Merrick was a big fish.

'Called in to see an old friend,' Merrick said charmingly.

'Hey, Jas.' Dash chuckled at her costume. 'Come here, Grandma, and give me a kiss.'

'Who are you calling Grandma?' Georgie scolded him as she hugged her grandson. 'Tea?'

'Absolutely.'

Dash took out a cup, chatting easily with Merrick about his coursework. Jasmin wasn't sure why the interaction unsettled her, but seeing Merrick's eyes light up with interest as her brother spoke made her uncomfortable.

'I have to head off,' Jasmin said to Georgie, who was hunting through the boxes on the table. Jasmin waved at Dash and dropped a kiss on Georgie's cheek.

'Going to a party?' Merrick said.

'Something like that.' Jasmin hadn't the time to remove her face paint. She'd have to do it at Imogen's cottage.

Merrick followed her with keen eyes as she walked to the back door. She'd just stepped outside into the fresh, cool evening when she heard him call after her, 'Jasmin.'

She paused on the brick paving. 'What is it?'

He walked towards her, stopping still right in front of her. 'I'm looking for a project assistant.' He handed her a business card. 'I think you'll be perfect.'

Her eyes widened with surprise. 'You don't even know me.'

'You're diligent. You're like your grandfather. You are exactly what I've been looking for. It would look great on your college applications.'

There was something in the way he said it – *exactly what I've been looking for* – that made her wary. Jasmin couldn't compute why Merrick would want her, especially knowing that she was still at secondary. There had to be real students clamouring for the opportunity.

'What about Dash?' He was surely the more obvious choice. Then she cursed herself, she didn't want Dash working for Merrick.

'I'm asking you.'

'I – I'll think about it.'

'It will be good,' said Merrick, his eyes on Jasmin. 'Just like old times.'

TWENTY-FOUR

'Nice outfit,' Damien said, taking it in. His lips turned up in a smile.

'I like to be impeccably turned out,' Jasmin said with mock primness.

She'd had two minutes to dash home to retrieve the bag she'd packed earlier. Sonia had met her at the kitchen door, looking very pleased with herself as she'd handed over a large foil-wrapped dish in a thermal food bag. The car now smelt of melted cheese and garlic.

'Did you finish helping your gran?'

'I did.' Jasmin thought about Merrick in Georgie's kitchen and realised she didn't want to talk about him being there. She didn't want to explain how Merrick knew her grandfather and draw the past further into her present. 'How far is the cottage?'

'It's an hour away. The others got there early this afternoon.

The only rule is that we're not allowed to talk about murder while we're there.'

'Good rule.' Jasmin lifted her phone. She'd checked Imogen's Instagram earlier, and now she showed Damien the screen. It was a selfie of Imogen at Lough Drinagh and captioned, *November Eve. Let the games begin.* 'What does that mean?' she said. 'It sounds ominous.'

'Rían and Imogen have particular ideas about how Halloween should be observed.' Damien laughed lightly. 'Don't let them freak you out. We had a blast last year.'

They drove out of town, weaving their way through narrow country roads. Jasmin noticed the line of his shoulders, how tightly he held the wheel.

'You OK?' she said.

'I met my uncle and aunt for lunch today,' Damien sighed.

'How was that?'

'Tense.' He navigated a sharp bend. 'My uncle is not an easy man. He's hard to please.'

'And your aunt?'

'She's ridiculous. All she talks about is her beautiful house, her two children. How they won this prize or came first at that thing. She makes me feel like a nuisance.'

Jasmin didn't know what to say. He sounded raw, hurt and unusually vulnerable. She suspected that any kind of sympathy would make him clam up again.

And Imogen had taught her when to listen.

'There was one time,' Damien said hesitantly, 'when I was thirteen or so, and we were walking in the village. There was a

186

man on a bench, he looked really rough. Ill, on drugs, hurt maybe. He reminded me of my dad.

'When we got to the bench, my uncle stopped. I thought he might give the man some money. Instead, he said, "See, Damien, this is what failure looks like. This is what you would become if it wasn't for me."'

Jasmin took a sharp intake of breath. 'That's cruel.'

'He is cruel. He dropped a handful of coins on the ground, five and ten-cent pieces, and then made me walk away. When we got to the car, I found a five-euro note tucked into a door pocket. I lied, said I dropped something, and ran back and gave it to the man. When I looked up, I saw my uncle had followed me. I'd never seen such a cold expression on his face. When we got back, he took away my soccer ball, saying I owed him for the money I'd stolen.'

'He's awful.'

'Sometimes he was. Other times he was kind and funny. A friend. It messed with my head.' Damien's face was tight, eyes fixed on the dark road ahead. 'But I'm not a kid any more. Enough about them. When I finish my degree, I'll move away and never see them again.'

'Sounds like a plan.' Jasmin examined the radio, burning with curiosity. But Damien clearly didn't want to continue talking about his family. 'Does this play music?'

'Only CDs.' He pointed to the glovebox containing a stack of them. 'Those are my uncle's.'

'James Blunt it is then.' She pushed in the CD and pressed play.

They stopped for supplies, and then followed Imogen's directions into the foothills until they came to a farm gate. Jasmin hopped out, opening the old gate, which let out a squeaking sigh. Even in the dark evening, she could make out tall spruces densely packed all around them and, in the distance, light from the cottage shone down the narrow lane. They drove along the bumpy dirt road and Jasmin feared the old Golf wouldn't make it.

'You're here,' Imogen cried, throwing open the front door as they got out of the car. 'Jasmin, I like it. Very corpse bride. Come on in. We've got the fire going.'

Rían followed her out. 'Love this look on you, Jasmin,' he said, indicating a twirl with his finger.

Laughing, Jasmin obliged and he burst into applause.

Allie was on the rug by the fire, tossing nutshells into the flames. Her hair was pushed back with a band and she seemed content, like a little cat in its favourite spot. 'Hey, guys.'

'What's this?' Imogen said, opening the thermal food bag and seeing the large vegetable lasagne that Sonia had made.

'My mam insisted on cooking for us,' Jasmin said. 'That's what she does. I mean, she does a lot more, but she shows she cares by cooking.'

'Tell your mother that I love her,' Rían said, taking the dish and breathing in the aroma.

'This sure beats the frozen pizzas we brought. I'll put it in the oven.'

'I'll make a salad,' Imogen said. 'Damien, show Jasmin

her room. I've put her in the single. It's tiny, Jasmin, but Allie and I are more used to sharing with each other, aren't we, Allie?'

'That's right,' said Allie. The girls exchanged a soft look. Imogen was bending over backwards to reassure Allie, Jasmin thought. To make her feel special, important, loved. Allie was lapping it up.

Damien led her down the passage. The cottage was old, with thick walls and wooden beams above. The heavy wood seemed to soak up the light, and the low wattage, yellow glow didn't chase all the shadows away. Damien stopped at a door with a thick oak lintel and said, 'This is you.'

Jasmin opened the door and went inside. The room had a stone floor and whitewashed walls like a nun's cell. There was an armchair in the corner, the plaid worn and a little stained, and a small white sink in the corner. A selection of dusty paperbacks with garish 1970s covers sat on the little table beside the chair. She grinned. 'I love it.'

'We come here as often as we can,' Damien said, his gaze lingering. 'Nice to have you with us this time.'

'I'm going to change,' Jasmin said. She lifted both hands to her corpse-bride face and struck a pose. 'Time to become … Jasmin again.'

Damien shut the door behind him and she removed the costume and the face paint, taking her time to make sure it was all off.

When she was ready, she followed the smell of warming lasagne back down the passage to the living room. Her thick socks and leggings made her return quiet. She paused at the sound of Imogen's angry voice.

'Niamh was murdered. We owe it to her to find out what happened.'

'Actually, we don't.' Allie's voice was thinner, quieter. 'We don't owe her anything at all.'

'I do,' Imogen yelled.

The sudden silence was piercing.

Then Imogen said, more calmly, 'We have to do the right thing. If I am going to be a journalist with any kind of integrity, it means always finding the truth, no matter how inconvenient.'

'Is that what Mammy says? Those are mighty big shoes you're trying to fill,' Rían said. 'What if you don't need to fill them at all? What if you need to find a pair that's right for you?'

'I know what's right for me,' Imogen snapped.

'I don't know what's right any more.' There was a ghostly quality to Allie's voice. 'I don't know what's right or wrong or good or bad. It's all confused and I can't see my way out.' Her voice was shaking now. 'I just want everything to go back to how it was before. Before Niamh died. Before we spent all our time discussing murder. Before we met ...'

The words were a punch in the gut. *Before we met Jasmin*, Allie was going to say.

'I like her,' Damien said quietly.

'I know you do.' Allie sounded tired. 'I just want ...' then she paused, like the words were too difficult, 'things back to how they were.'

Jasmin leaned against the wall, taking a deep breath. After waiting a long moment, she noisily opened the door. Damien and Imogen were in the kitchen pouring drinks while Rían opened a bag of crisps. Allie was still at the fire, making her way through a bag of monkey nuts and dropping the shells into the flames.

'There you are,' said Imogen. 'You look almost human.'

Jasmin grabbed a water, then, steeling herself, sat next to Allie at the fire.

'Mind if I join you?'

'Of course you can,' Allie said brightly. 'Go on, grab a handful of nuts.' She held the bowl out to Jasmin. 'These always remind me of Halloween when I was little. My grandmother used to burn the shells and read the ashes. Every year she'd read out fortunes from the ash.'

'Can't imagine my grandmother doing that.' Jasmin smiled as she peeled a nut and tossed the shell into the flames. 'She's more … the culture supplement and crosswords.'

The other three in the kitchen had resumed their conversation, and let out a burst of laughter. Jasmin glanced up, noting how much more relaxed Damien was now. How their friendship could chase away the darkness.

'Yeah,' Allie said, her face softening. 'Nana was something of a witch, all right. She taught me to read runes, fortunes. Coins. It's traditional on November Eve to read fortunes.' Allie shook her little pouch of coins. 'Will I read yours?'

Jasmin hesitated. She didn't want to. But there was a challenge in Allie's eyes, so she said, 'Only if I can read yours.'

'Fair.' Allie inclined her head slightly. Her make-up was extra heavy tonight and she wore her leather trousers with a tight black top. She seemed a little more reckless this evening. There was an air of danger in the way she sat there, legs splayed and fixing her thickly lined eyes on Jasmin.

She shook the pouch and held it out. Ever so slightly she released a breath, and with it a few quiet words. 'I don't think I trust you.'

Jasmin flinched. She felt the words as if they were a slap in the face. In the kitchen, the others were laughing so uproariously Imogen was clutching her side.

'You can trust me.' Jasmin reached her hand in the bag. 'How many do I take?'

'For this, three.'

Jasmin took out the coins and placed them face down on the wooden floor. Allie turned one over. 'Past.'

It was the Noose, the same coin she'd pulled out the day Niamh died.

'This refers to Niamh. She looms large for all of us, but in different ways. What Niamh means to each one of us is not the same.' She closed her fist around the coin, as if it could tell her more. 'But it's not just Niamh. The Noose symbolises feeling stuck. Something – or someone – holds you and will not let you go.' Allie took a deep breath. 'Yes. It's a person. You're bound to a person and you can't move on.'

Jasmin pressed her lips together. She felt her grandfather's hand on her shoulder. Shadowy fingers snaking around her ankles. She shook herself; Allie was guessing, obviously. The shadows loosened their grip, slinking away. 'What does the present say?'

Allie turned the middle coin. It was a large stylised eye with a curling line below it.

'What is that?' Jasmin asked.

'The Watcher.'

Jasmin glanced up sharply. For, of course, the Watcher was her. She'd never told any of them that bit of family lore.

'This coin shows someone watching over you. A protector.'

Allie was wrong. It showed Jasmin watching everyone else.

'Someone is looking out for you and wants to keep you safe.'

Jasmin turned over the last coin. A demonic, horned face leered.

'The Demon. Or monster. It means there is danger in your future. A danger that you might not overcome.'

'I think that's enough, Allie,' Damien said mildly. He placed a bottle of wine alongside the salad on the coffee table and sat down on the couch.

'It's November Eve,' Allie said quietly. 'Divination is tradition for November Eve.'

'Maybe we'll save all talk of monsters and demons for later,' Imogen said. 'It's time to eat.'

'Jasmin's had her first reading from Allie,' Rían said, taking the hot lasagne from the oven. 'Now she truly is one of us, Crom Cruach help that poor child. Grab a plate, everyone.'

Jasmin took her plate of food and returned to the floor. 'How often does Allie read your fortunes?'

Imogen shook her head. 'Never. Not any more. It was … making me nervous.'

Rían agreed. 'We put an end to that ages ago. We don't mind big picture, general readings but never personal.'

'Damien?' Jasmin pushed. She'd seen the coins in Allie's hand just a few days ago.

'Tuesday,' he said reluctantly. 'When we were waiting for you guys.'

'You must have wanted something badly if you agreed to that.' Rían laughed while Damien shifted uncomfortably.

'What did they say?' Imogen asked, spooning hot lasagne into her mouth.

'I got that Demon one too,' Damien said. 'In my present. Danger for me tonight.'

'You better believe it.' Rían gave a maniacal cackle.

'And the Burning Heart in his future,' Allie muttered.

After they'd eaten, Jasmin took her empty plate to the dishwasher and washed her hands.

'You said I could read yours,' she reminded Allie. 'I'm ready now.'

Allie put her plate beside her and wiped her hands on a napkin.

'So you just look at the coins, search inside and say what your heart tells you. That's all.' She smiled. 'But not everyone interprets them right.'

Let's see how you do was the subtext.

She pulled out three coins and placed them down on the floor.

Jasmin turned the first coin, which showed an hourglass with time nearly up. 'Your time always runs out,' she said, the words coming easily. 'You're not getting what you want. It gets snatched from your grasp just as you reach for it. There's never enough time for you to get it right.'

The second coin was a heart but one that was fragmented into pieces. 'You're hurting. Badly.'

When Jasmin looked up at Allie's face, the truth there was so raw that Jasmin felt guilty at the intrusion. More words bubbled up, she had so much to say about Allie's hurt, but she made herself stop.

The third coin was an ouroboros, the snake eating its tail. The logo for Merrick's company. The image he'd shown at the lecture. The coincidence of seeing that image again in such a short time made Jasmin close her fist around the coin. It unnerved her. Merrick's symbol here, when they were trying to escape him.

'What does it mean?' Allie insisted, eyes fixing on Jasmin's. 'What's your reading?'

'You're trapped.' Jasmin's words were coming from somewhere else. 'You're stuck and you're never going to get out.' She opened her palm, the coin flat in her hand. 'You will die stuck.'

A loud banging sound from the front of the house interrupted them.

'What the hell?' Rían said while Damien let out a loud curse. They all rushed to the door. Jasmin had a deep dread in the pit of her stomach. She stepped out into the cold evening, peering into the darkness. They searched the distance, seeing nothing in the pitch black surrounding the house.

'This fell over,' Damien said, picking up what looked like a wide wooden board from the stone deck. As he raised it, Jasmin saw that it was a small folding table that must have been standing beneath the window.

'Tables don't just fall over.' Allie wrapped her arms around herself against the cold.

'Do you think someone knocked into it?' Imogen said. 'That's impossible. There's no one out here.'

Jasmin searched into the complete darkness.

'Maybe we shouldn't go out into the woods later,' Allie said, nervous eyes darting as she looked out too.

'Let's go inside,' Rían urged. 'It must have been a gust of wind.' He laughed. 'That's what they say in horror movies, isn't it? *It must be the wind*. And then it's an axe-wielding maniac in a clown mask.'

But there was no wind. Jasmin took a last look at the table, now back against the wall. It was heavy and unlikely to fall over for no reason.

'It's probably rotted at the side,' Damien said, 'and just chose that moment to give in.'

They all stared dubiously at the table.

'It's freezing out here,' Rían said. 'Let's clean up and get ready for the games.'

And they went in, shutting the door behind them.

TWENTY-FIVE

A short while later, they were back outside in the dark. They'd lit a fire in the pit out back and gathered around it, the heat of the flames warming Jasmin's face.

'This time of year is sacred to the old god Crom Cruach.' Imogen, in a vintage green cape, held out both hands over the flames like some arcane priestess. 'And we will offer gifts to Crom Cruach, although not human sacrifice as he might prefer.'

'Definitely no human sacrifice,' Jasmin confirmed, as if Crom Cruach might really be out there listening to them.

'We will present the gifts by placing them in the fire. But we have to earn the gifts first,' Imogen continued. 'And those who offer the most will receive the biggest favour.'

'How do we earn the gifts?' Jasmin asked.

'There are five gifts hidden in the woods behind the cottage. Five carved turnips.' Rían gestured to the thick trees behind them. 'We each take a torch and a sack.' He pointed at the chair behind him.

'My nana told me that carving turnips is more traditional than carving pumpkins,' Allie explained.

'Who hid the turnips?' Jasmin asked.

'We each hid one,' Imogen said. 'Damien hid two while you were changing. Obviously we can't retrieve what we hid, so you have an advantage, Jasmin.'

'But we are allowed to ambush each other and steal the gifts they might have found,' Damien said, eyes full of mischief. 'Don't trust anyone.'

'We'll work together again, won't we, Imogen?' Allie said.

'Maybe,' she said slyly.

'Any questions?' Rían said. 'No? We'll gather here in thirty minutes with our spoils. Whoever finds more than one will be Crom Cruach's favoured and wear the crown. Go!'

The word was gunfire. Grabbing a torch, Jasmin sprinted towards the woods.

Jasmin was fast. She heard the others behind her, their feet pounding on the hard ground. She heard Allie squeal as she stumbled on a stone. Some metres away, Rían overtook her, his long, lean legs powering forward. She picked up speed, glancing behind her to see Damien on her tail. He laughed as they raced for the trees.

Entering the woods, he veered sharply to the left. Jasmin stopped, catching her breath as she looked around her. The others had been here several times before and knew these woods. She didn't.

It was darker between the trees, the ground uneven. Jasmin stifled a giggle as she saw a figure dart from one tree to another, a beam of torchlight dancing in the distance. She jogged forward, flashing the light of her torch over the base of the trees.

In the distance, she heard Rían's wild laughter, then him roaring, 'I will get my revenge!'

'You'll have to catch me first,' Damien called cockily.

She moved away from their voices, creeping from one tree to another, deeper into the woods. A thick quietness had settled over the trees. Her heart was pounding and it felt good.

A low light glowed up ahead from the base of a trunk. Jasmin drew nearer to it, trying to make out what it was. A step closer, then another, and she saw the macabre features, the wide grimace with small teeth that were so perfectly human they made her shudder. The eyes curved upwards, giving the face a maniacal energy. The face was illuminated from the inside, glowing with menace.

It was only a carved turnip with a tea light inside. But it was far more menacing than any jack-o'-lantern she'd seen. The features were distorted, but not entirely unhuman. She had never seen anything more hideous.

'Jasmin.'

She whipped round to see Imogen in the distance, grinning and determined. Jasmin stepped in front of the turnip, guarding it with her body.

'Jasmin, let's be allies,' Imogen said. 'You can trust me, unless you want to run around these creepy woods by yourself.'

Jasmin shook her head. 'I don't trust you.' The same words that Allie had said to her.

'You can have that one,' Imogen said, holding up her hands in surrender. 'I won't try to take it.'

Jasmin hesitated.

'Seriously. It's yours to take. But we have to move quickly.' Imogen glanced behind her, alert. 'Rían's coming.'

'OK. Allies.' Jasmin reached down and lifted the turnip. She blew out the candle and dropped it into her sack. 'Let's get out of here.'

Imogen lunged at her. 'You fool,' she screamed like a banshee as she grabbed at the sack.

Jasmin leaped back, still holding the sack, laughing. 'You played your hand too soon, Imogen. Let me guess, this was the one you hid? You thought you'd wait for me to retrieve it and then steal it off me? I wasn't born yesterday.'

She sprinted away through the trees, leaving a cursing Imogen behind. She hadn't run this hard in so long and her body had missed being pushed to its limit.

When she'd put enough distance between them, she ducked behind a tree to catch her breath. Warmer now, she loosened her scarf slightly. She could hear the cries of the others occasionally echoing through the woods. The sound of laughter. A branch cracking as someone tracked through the woods. Jasmin darted to another tree.

She looked up at the tall spruces, the night forest. She had no idea which way the house was or what ground she'd already covered. She tried to gauge where she was from the direction of the moon, but she'd been a rubbish Girl Scout and nothing had changed.

'Jasmin.'

This time when she looked back she saw Allie.

'Jasmin, I want to talk to you.' Allie came closer. 'It's important.'

Jasmin laughed. 'Nice try, Allie.'

'Please.' Her face was pale in the torchlight. 'We really need to talk. Alone.'

Stifling another laugh, Jasmin turned and ran. She heard the distant call of her name as she left Allie behind. She went further into the woods. Seeing the glow of another turnip resting at the base of a tree, she jogged forward.

She was almost there when hands grabbed her, pulling her into a hard chest.

'Dammit,' she cursed. 'Let me go, Damien.' The chest wasn't lean and lanky like Rían's. It had to be Damien.

A gloved hand covered her mouth. She squirmed, trying to break out of the tight grip. She could feel the thin quilting of the jacket sleeve as it brushed her cheek. Her blood ran cold. Damien had been wearing his usual cotton military jacket.

Jasmin realised then, as the arms stiffened around her, that this wasn't her friend. This was a stranger. Blood pulsed in her ears as she struggled against the muscular chest, the strong arms. Her torch fell, the light blinking out. She screamed into the large hand covering her mouth, which only made him press tighter.

'You,' the voice rasped in her ear, rough and growly, like it was disguised, 'need to stop poking around. Or you will get hurt. Like Niamh.'

TWENTY-SIX

He shoved her away roughly, and catching his hands around her chunky knitted scarf it tightened around her neck for one terrible moment. Then Jasmin was released from the scarf and fell, her arm knocking into the turnip with its gruesome features. It seemed to mock her as it rolled away. The tea light was snuffed out, making the darkness complete. Her face hit something hard. The wind was knocked out of her. She turned and searched the darkness for the assailant, but he was gone.

After catching her breath, Jasmin sat up. She got to her feet, feeling a graze on her face, her body aching. She felt around for the turnip, for her scarf, for the torch, but it was too dark.

She staggered through the trees, not knowing where she was and feeling a mounting anxiety that no ice cube, no deep breaths, would stop. It was rising inside her, an avalanche of fear and dread. She saw Georgie's copper pans hanging from the trees. Oak cabinets superimposed over the darkness. The trees seemed to shiver and they became the kitchen on that day. Jasmin stumbled onwards, terrified that she could not outrun her panic.

Then she saw it. Light breaking through the darkness.

She ran towards it. She had to get out. She could feel the trees closing in, smothering her. She ran, feeling branches scrape her skin. A wildness descended upon her as she sprinted, ran as if her life depended on it, until she broke the treeline. She could still feel the weight of the hand on her mouth, the iron grip pinning her arms. She jogged to the fire, tugging off her jacket, taking gulping breaths.

Jasmin sank on to the ground, realising she was still holding the sack with the stupid turnip head. She rested her elbows on her knees, her face in her hands.

What the hell just happened? Who had grabbed her in the woods?

She turned sharply, hearing running feet. A wild war whoop as Damien ran to the fire, the others chasing him.

'We must be mutually favoured by Crom Cruach,' he said, emptying his sack as two turnips rolled like severed heads. 'You got two, didn't you? Rían found one.'

Jasmin looked up at him, her voice lost.

'You OK?' Damien frowned at her. The others reached the fire, chatting excitedly between them. He reached out a hand to help her up. 'Your face. You're hurt.'

Jasmin touched her hand to her temple and felt a graze. 'I'm fine,' she lied, taking Damien's hand. His grasp was comforting, grounding. He smelt of laundry detergent and that minty shampoo, and she was immediately comforted by his familiarity. 'All fine.' Her voice sounded strange and she cleared her throat. 'Got a little lost. Tripped.'

'You both won?' Allie said. 'Did you work together?'

'I didn't win.' Jasmin reached for her turnip head. 'I only found the one.'

'Then one is missing,' Imogen said, frowning at the sack. She finally looked at Jasmin. 'You're shivering.' She picked Jasmin's jacket from where she'd thrown it on the ground. 'Put this back on. Where's your scarf?'

'I lost it. In the woods.' Georgie had paid an unnecessary amount for the handmade chunky knit scarf and it was Jasmin's favourite. 'I'll search for it in the morning.'

'It's Crom Cruach's now.' Rían held out his hands in submission.

Jasmin took the jacket, her hand shaking with the aftereffects of adrenalin. The others looked at each other. She picked up her turnip from the ground and walked closer to the firepit.

'For Crom Cruach.' She threw it in.

Damien dropped his two turnips in after her and they all stared at the flames.

'You are the favoured one, Damien,' Imogen declared, throwing her arms up to the dark sky. 'Crom Cruach will protect you. He will watch over you and quash your enemies.'

Jasmin had to tell them but she couldn't find the words. The thickness in her throat made speech impossible. Her hands were clammy and her heart beat faster just thinking about talking through the attack. It pulled her back into the woods, trees closing around her.

'Jasmin,' Allie said. 'You're very fidgety tonight.' She nodded at Jasmin's jiggling leg.

Jasmin stopped jiggling.

From the deckchairs around the pit, they watched the flames die down. They were quiet now, lost in thought, but the silence was shared, bringing them closer.

Damien reached out a hand and placed it on Jasmin's thigh, lingering as he met her eyes. She hadn't realised she'd been jiggling again. He smiled at her, and it felt like the heat from his hand seared into her skin.

Rían stood up and stretched. 'I'm going to turn in.'

'Me too,' Allie said.

'I'm still bothered by the mystery of the missing turnip.' Imogen looked out to the woods. 'Jasmin, will you come with me to get my bag from the car?'

'You worried that Mr Turnip Head is waiting for you?' Rían teased.

'You laugh. We didn't give Crom Cruach his full offering,' Imogen retorted. 'I'd be worried if I were you.'

Jasmin followed Imogen around the side of the cottage to where the cars were parked.

Imogen turned to her. 'Is there something going on between you and Damien?' she asked bluntly.

'No.' Jasmin felt her face get hot.

'Good,' Imogen replied. 'Keep it that way.'

'I don't think that's your decision, is it?' Jasmin felt a flash of anger towards Imogen. She didn't mind her being bossy – but this was too much.

Imogen's voice softened. 'You don't understand. I'm trying to do you a favour. Damien is complicated. Fucked-up childhood, his parents were addicts and neglected him. He was sent to live with his aunt in some godforsaken village. I'm telling you this because Damien only knows how to be emotionally unavailable, that's all he's had his whole life. He doesn't let people in, and if you get involved you're on a road to heartbreak. Allie found that out the hard way. I don't want to see you hurt.' She sighed. 'I don't want to see her hurt either.'

'What do you mean?'

'She's noticed it too, the way you look at him. The way you look at each other.'

'I thought Allie was fine with their break-up. She said they were in a good place.'

Imogen sighed again. 'Maybe she is, maybe she isn't. But she's vulnerable right now and I don't want you to make things worse.'

There was a trudge of footsteps. Damien was coming round the back of the cottage, walking towards them.

'We've been tight long before you came along, Jasmin,' said Imogen softly. 'The four of us, we chose each other. Nothing comes between us. No one.'

'I see,' Jasmin said, tasting the bitterness of the words.

'Make it clear you're not interested.' The words were quiet, barely audible. Then Damien was there, grabbing Imogen's bag from the car and carrying it inside. Imogen hooked her arm in his and pecked him on the cheek. 'Thank you, darling.'

At the door, Damien let her ahead, saying, 'Come on, Jasmin. It's the night the ghosts walk, and you don't know what's out there. You shouldn't stay out here alone.'

TWENTY-SEVEN

Jasmin couldn't sleep. She kept thinking of those arms around her in the dark woods, holding her in place. The grinning turnips.

And when she managed to push the woods out, she'd hear Allie's words before dinner, *I just want everything to go back to how it was before.*

And then Imogen's voice, a whisper in the dark. *Nothing comes between us. No one.*

Eventually, at around two, she turned on the lamp. Her hand hovered over her school French novel that she'd optimistically packed. Instead, she got up, shivering in the cold, and took out her sketch pad. She got back into bed and started drawing.

Wrapped up in her thoughts, Jasmin allowed her hand to move freely. Without deciding to she had started drawing Allie. It was imperfect, but with the short, messy hair, the lined eyes staring back at her, it was clearly Allie.

Were they really worth it? Jasmin wondered, sketching and shading. Allie clearly didn't want her around, and Imogen, how dare she make demands like that? Hurt and anger and fear had knotted in her chest and she could barely breathe.

When she looked at the picture, she saw she'd altered Allie's image. Very lightly she'd added the impression of a skull to one side of her face – it was clear in the hollow eye, the sharp cheekbone above Allie's softer jawline. The teeth.

She'd made Allie a monster.

Hearing a light tap at her door, Jasmin got out of bed. Her feet were cold on the stone floor and she placed the sketch pad in her bag. Opening the door, she found Damien on the other side.

'You can't sleep either?' he said.

She shook her head, casting an eye over him, his defined arms and shoulders. His bed-messed hair. She felt suddenly reckless. 'Come on, let's be awake together.'

He came in and shut the door. There was only the narrow nun's bed in the room, so she sat sideways and patted the spot beside her for Damien to sit.

'Jasmin?' He sat beside her, so close that his leg pressed against hers.

'Yes?'

'What happened in the woods?'

She hadn't expected that. 'What do you mean?'

'I know something happened. You were visibly shaken. What was it?'

She felt her cheeks grow warm. That familiar squeeze of panic, like a fist in her chest. 'A man threatened me,' she admitted. 'He came out of nowhere, grabbed me and told me to stop poking around in Niamh's murder.'

Damien straightened up. 'You should have told us.'

'I wanted to,' she said, 'but I couldn't. My throat just closed up. At first I thought I'd imagined it. Like, who could it have been? Where did he come from? Did he follow us here?'

'He wouldn't have needed to follow us,' Damien sighed. 'Imogen announced it.'

'Her Instagram post.' Jasmin caught what he meant. She'd tagged the location.

'She might as well have posted a map to the house,' he said. 'I was worried when that table fell earlier. Do you have any idea who it could be?'

Jasmin dared to think back. 'He was strong. Rory perhaps, though it didn't really sound like him. But then, I got the sense that the attacker was trying to disguise his voice? It could have been Freddie. Or Lorcan at a push.' She leaned back against the wall. 'He overpowered me easily, and though I'm not tall like Niamh, I'm pretty strong, and sober. Niamh wouldn't have been able to fight back.'

'You think it was Niamh's murderer?'

'Who else would it be? Who else would want us to back off that badly?'

'Is there anything else you remember about him?'

Jasmin thought for a moment. 'His jacket was soft, one of those quilted ones, but not too puffy. He had thick gloves. He smelt damp, like he hadn't dried out his jacket after it got wet in the rain. Anyway, that's why I lost the missing turnip.'

'He took it?' Damien said. 'So it's his fault that our sacrifice is incomplete?'

Jasmin smiled, relieved for the levity. Damien's hand reached for hers, lacing their fingers together, and brought them both into his lap. It felt unbelievable to her that he was with her here. How close he sat. How his leg pressed against hers, their entwined hands resting on his thigh. Jasmin remembered those weeks when she'd watched him from afar, how he'd seemed enigmatic and unattainable. A distant dream.

She touched her fingertips to his cheekbone and his eyes held hers. Damien leaned closer. His voice was low. 'I really like you.' Then he leaned in to kiss her.

Of all her puzzles Damien was the most intriguing. More than Niamh's death, more than Allie's melancholy, Rían's forced joviality, Imogen's steel – Damien was the one she wanted to know the answer to. He was guarded. But when he kissed her, she felt he was letting her in.

'You've no idea how much I've wanted to do that,' he breathed against her skin.

He doesn't let people in.

She pulled back.

'What's wrong?' He looked at her warily.

'Just thinking about something Imogen said.'

'She warned you away from me, didn't she? Said that I'm troubled, that I can't keep a relationship?' He sighed and squeezed her hand. 'I guess she's right. But I want to prove her wrong.'

'What happened to you?' Jasmin said softly.

'It's like I said in the car. My uncle became my legal guardian when I was eleven. My own parents, they weren't doing such a good job.' He spoke lightly, but couldn't keep the pain from his voice. 'My dad drank, you know? And my mother …' He shook his head, and Jasmin's heart hurt for him. 'It wasn't good.'

She felt her heart ache as she studied his face for the child he'd been. From what he'd told her about his aunt and uncle, they didn't seem a whole lot better. 'You're making your own way. You'll be free of them all one day.'

He shook his head, forcing a smile. 'Enough about me. What happened to you? Don't say "nothing". I can tell. I can sniff out a miserable childhood.'

'My grandfather tried to kill my grandmother when I was eight.' Jasmin stopped. She hadn't meant to say that at all. But, now that she'd started, she felt compelled to keep going. 'I was right there. I didn't even notice until it was nearly too late. She was making pasta, my grandmother. I still can't eat spaghetti.'

'Jasmin.' Damien gently squeezed her hand again.

'I never saw it coming. My grandfather …' she paused, 'and I were close. I thought he was … the best man in the world.'

'Where is he now? What's he doing?'

'I have no idea. Prison, maybe. I don't want to know.'

Even talking about it made her feel a little sick.

Damien pulled her into his arms and they lay down on the bed. They fell asleep like that, holding on to each other. And

Jasmin knew they'd found something rare. She knew this because his darkness spoke to hers. Because she recognised her own monsters in him.

The next morning, Jasmin woke to find Damien reading her French novel. She lay on the bed, watching his face in repose. She itched to draw him, and instead committed his features to memory, the brows framing his eyes, the line of his jaw. Not taking his eyes from the book, his free hand reached for her, drawing her closer. She could hear Imogen and Allie chatting in the passage right outside the room.

'We should probably get up.' She sat up, but Damien dropped the book and pushed her back down again, chuckling as he wrestled her.

'Not yet,' he said. 'I'm not ready to go back just yet.'

She knew what he meant, the relentless cycle of work and study. 'Let's take a walk in the woods before we leave.'

'Good idea,' he agreed. 'But first …' He leaned in to kiss her and she wrapped her arms around him. From the kitchen came the sound of the others preparing breakfast, Imogen saying, 'No, not scrambled, you know I hate scrambled,' and Rían saying something that had her and Allie shrieking with laughter.

'Should we be helping them?'

'Later,' Damien said, his hand on her hip. 'We'll help later.'

She was so lost to him it barely registered when there was a knock on her door, then Rían calling, 'Jasmin, breakfast is ready!' Then in a lower voice, 'And tell Damien to hurry up. I haven't told the others he's not in our room.'

'There in a minute,' she called.

Damien lay back on the mattress, clasping both hands behind his head, while Jasmin pulled on her oversized sweatshirt. She ran her fingers through her hair and said, 'Maybe we should keep this to ourselves, just for now?'

'Are you trying to keep me your dirty little secret, Jasmin?' He drawled the words with a lazy charm, light and easy, but something in his eyes made her pause. It hurt him, she realised. She thought about his childhood, about how no one had seemed to want him, and she understood.

'When Imogen told me to leave you alone,' Jasmin went towards him, speaking gently, 'she also said it would upset Allie. I don't want to make things hard for her. Or you, actually.'

'You're not.' Damien got up from the bed. 'If anything, it's the opposite. I feel grounded when I'm with you.' He gave her a lopsided grin. 'Like I'm home. Like the sun is shining. The birds are singing. The stars exploding.' He placed his hands on her waist. 'I want more of it. Even though I don't deserve it.'

He drew her closer, his green eyes locked on hers. For the first time, the customary sadness there had been cast out. Jasmin felt a rush so intense it made her dizzy. It made her want to lean towards him, to say yes to anything.

'Jasmin!' They heard a call from the kitchen.

She broke away. 'Let's have breakfast. Then I need to find my scarf.' She opened the door, Damien behind her. In the passage, Allie was coming out of the bathroom. She paused a moment, then smiled brightly and said, 'Morning. Rían's made a fry-up. Hope you like fried eggs.'

When Jasmin took her place at the kitchen table, she said, 'I have something to tell you. Two things actually.'

Rían raised an eyebrow. Allie sawed at her bacon.

'First, I know we're not supposed to talk about murder right now, but I spoke to Javier. It turns out he knew Niamh. I got the impression they were close. He said they'd disagreed about something the week before she died – I don't know what. But he told me with absolute certainty that she was not romantically involved with Merrick.'

The others looked at her warily. 'What's second?' Rían asked.

'I was attacked last night in the woods. A man came out of nowhere. He grabbed me and told me to stop poking around or I would get hurt, like Niamh.'

Allie paled. Imogen's eyes grew huge. Rían looked like he'd eaten something unpleasant. Under the table, Damien's hand landed on her thigh, his touch warm and firm.

'This happened last night? Why didn't you say anything?' Imogen said.

'I was shocked,' Jasmin said. 'I couldn't.'

'I knew something had happened,' Imogen muttered. 'I knew it.'

'Do you know what this means?' Allie said.

'Yes,' Imogen replied. Her eyes were shining. 'It means we're on the right track. It means we're getting close, and someone doesn't like that.'

'No,' Allie exploded. 'It means we have to stop. No more playing Five Go on a Murder Adventure.'

'We can't simply give up,' Imogen raised her voice. 'That's what this guy wants us to do. Surely we aren't that easily scared off?'

'It's dangerous,' Allie said. 'We can go to the guards, tell them what we know.'

'They'll never take us seriously,' Imogen hit back. 'Look, Allie, you may be intimidated by some shadowy figure in the woods but I am not. If anything, this makes me even more resolved to find out what happened to Niamh.'

'Allie's right,' Rían said, all performance absent from his voice. 'This changes the game. Things have become a lot more dangerous.'

Imogen glowered at Rían, speechless. She pushed her plate away. 'Damien?'

'We need to be cautious,' Damien said. 'This person *killed* Niamh. They'll do whatever it takes to protect their secrets.'

Imogen stood up abruptly, her chair scraping the stone floor. She walked to the window and her fury was evident in the way she carried herself. An unpleasant silence stretched out.

'Fine.' She faced them again, her lips pressed together, and it was obvious it was not fine. 'On one condition. We go to the Verge gala dinner. And if you don't come with me, I will go alone.'

She walked out of the kitchen. The door to her bedroom clicked shut. Allie kept her attention on her plate, working through her mushrooms methodically.

'Should I go to her?' Jasmin said.

'Best leave her to herself for now,' Rían said.

Jasmin began clearing the plates and Damien got up to help.

'Careful with that one,' Allie said, stopping Jasmin from picking up a bowl. 'It belonged to Imogen's great-grandmother.' Allie lifted it from the table. 'It's cracked, see?' There was a small hairline crack running down from the rim of the bowl. It wasn't much right now, but in time it would spread and split the bowl in two. 'It won't last much longer before it's thrown out. No matter how much they care for it.'

Jasmin couldn't help thinking Allie wasn't talking about the bowl. She was talking about something else entirely.

TWENTY-EIGHT

The days passed quickly. Jasmin had a ton of revision to get through for her November tests the following week, so it only mildly bothered her that she didn't hear from Imogen or Allie or Rían. She didn't have time to dwell on it. Damien was either studying or working at the gym, so she didn't see him but they texted often.

The next Monday, Jasmin was surprised to find an email from Merrick, inviting her to come in to talk about the project assistant position. So he had been serious about the offer, serious enough to get her email address from Dash.

Jasmin read the details, which offered ten to fifteen hours a week, fitted in around her schedule. The pay was generous and on paper it seemed the perfect part-time job. She would be crazy to turn it down.

The question was – why her?

Maybe Merrick was simply doing her a solid. The

granddaughter of his PhD supervisor. One that he'd known when she was a child, even though she didn't remember him.

There was a single knock at her door, then Dash opened it and poked his head in. 'You've been working too hard. Want to come with me to the gym?'

'Sure,' Jasmin said, telling herself that she was going because she wanted to see Rory – Dash and his friends often arranged to train around the same time. She wanted to see if she could match Rory to the shadowy figure that had grabbed her in the woods. Nothing to do with Damien. Nothing at all.

Power Up was busier this evening and Jasmin made no pretence of using the machines in the cardio area. She went directly to the weight room and set herself up doing half-hearted stretches on the mat while watching Dash chat to the men between sets.

Rory wasn't there. Jasmin felt as sure as anything that it was him who'd been in the woods. Which meant that he was the likeliest candidate for murder. But again, the pieces weren't fitting.

'I see I'm not the lone wolf venturing forth with the investigation.'

Jasmin looked up to see Imogen delicately sipping from her water bottle straw. She was wearing leggings, which was utterly unexpected, and a pink headband.

'Nice outfit,' Jasmin smiled. 'It's convincing.'

'More convincing than you doing whatever it is you've been doing on that mat since I came in.' Imogen smiled. 'You're looking for Rory too, aren't you?'

'Yes.'

'He didn't come in on Halloween,' Imogen said. 'I got Damien to check the system.'

'Which means he could have been in Lough Drinagh.' Jasmin got to her feet.

'I also found out that Rory usually gets here around eight thirty on Mondays. It's now eight twenty-eight.' She grabbed Jasmin's arm. 'Come on.'

She let Imogen lead her through the cardio area towards reception. Nearing the doors, Jasmin saw Javier. She paused, curious. But Imogen was tugging her on.

'I knew you'd be sniffing around. You're just like me – bloodhound.' Imogen stepped back into the doorway of studio two, pulling Jasmin with her. 'There he is.'

They watched Rory swipe his membership card and walk through the turnstile. He entered the unisex changing village and they followed him, stalking down the rows to see where he'd leave his things. But he walked past the cubicles, disappearing into the communal men's changing room at the end.

'What now?' Jasmin said, lips twitching. 'Will we go in there and confront him?'

'Lord, no.' Imogen glared at the small silver pictogram of a man on the door.

A door banged somewhere unseen, and Imogen pulled Jasmin into the nearest cubicle. Keeping the door open a crack, they watched the men's changing room.

After a few minutes, Rory came out. He passed where Jasmin and Imogen hid, whistling a tune. Jasmin stared at him, trying to match his frame with the man who'd grabbed her the other night. She wasn't so sure any more. He seemed a little shorter, maybe too broad.

'Let's go,' Imogen said as Rory left. They went to the men's changing room and opened the door. A half-naked older man stood there.

They retreated hastily, Jasmin saying, 'Oops.'

'My eyes,' Imogen gasped.

They waited another minute, and when the man emerged from the changing room, Imogen said, 'It's empty now. Let's go.'

'What are we looking for exactly?'

'Proof. Maybe a petrol receipt saying that he filled up on the way, or one from a restaurant near there. He must have eaten, right? A guy that big needs to eat.'

'He's not a toddler. He can go a few hours without a snack.'

'Worst-case scenario, we get his house keys.'

'His *house keys*?'

'My gut says it was him who attacked you and killed Niamh. The man cheats on his tests. He doesn't care about anyone except himself. It's definitely worth searching his house again.'

Imogen led the way and they opened the door to the men's changing room. It was empty this time, and there was only one bank of lockers against the wall.

'He had a red gear bag.' Imogen hurried across the changing area, opening lockers one at a time.

Jasmin searched too. Most people didn't bother with padlocks, so it was easy to simply open and shut the doors when they didn't see the red bag.

But she did see a blue and white striped one.

'I found it.' Imogen was triumphant. 'Rory, you're one messy dog.' She continued to mutter under her breath as she went through his bag.

Jasmin knew that blue and white bag. She'd seen it the night Javier was at her house.

'Imogen, on a scale from one to ten, how unethical is this?' she said.

'Needs must, Jasmin.' Imogen mimed a gag as she looked through Rory's red bag. 'Needs must.'

Jasmin opened the zipper of Javier's bag. His clothes were folded neatly, but there was something that caught her eye. Something soft and cream-coloured.

She reached in and pulled out her chunky knit scarf. The one her attacker had pulled off her.

'Imogen,' she said in a strangled voice as she stared at it. They'd all gone walking the morning after, searching for the lost scarf outside Imogen's cottage, but to no avail.

'Mother of Satan,' Imogen breathed. 'Where the hell did you find that?'

'In Javier's bag.'

Something was wrong, she realised. Jasmin listened carefully. 'Imogen, do you hear that?'

'I don't hear anything,' Imogen replied, perplexed.

'Exactly.'

A moment ago, there'd been background noise. Now it had stopped.

'The shower!' Imogen stuffed Rory's bag back into the locker.

'Oh crap,' Jasmin said, and scrambled to replace her scarf. The sound of wet footsteps slapping on the floor came from around the corner. She paused, seeing the dark green quilted jacket hanging from the locker hook. The kind of jacket her assailant had been wearing. She smelt it now, damp, as if it had been soaked in the rain and shoved into a bag.

'What the hell?'

Jasmin turned reluctantly, feeling every bit the naughty schoolgirl who'd just been caught.

Then she saw who was standing there, a towel around his waist, just out of the shower.

'Damien,' she said, relieved.

Annoyed as a poked bear, he glanced from one to the other. 'You can't be in here! You guys are going to get me fired.'

'I can explain,' Imogen said.

'And you will,' Damien replied. 'But not here. I'll meet you at the smoothie bar.'

Imogen looked longingly at Rory's locker.

'You'd better go, Imogen, before someone else finds you here.'

'Fine.'

With a *humph*, Imogen strode to the door, looking so aggrieved that Jasmin had to hide her amusement. As though they hadn't sneaked into the men's changing room to snoop through untended belongings. Jasmin followed, but not before giving Damien a cheeky grin. Holding on to his towel with one hand, he caught hers with the other, tugging her towards him. He kissed her, before letting her go.

Imogen was outside the door, scribbling in her notebook. They stole through the unisex changing room, passing a pink-cheeked man clearly fresh out of the sauna, and into the wide bright corridor. Then Imogen halted.

'Oh crap.'

At the water fountain, Rory waited to fill his bottle. Imogen and Jasmin froze, deers in headlights, even though there was no way he could have known they'd been rummaging through his bag.

Rory did a double take when he saw Jasmin. Water bottle forgotten, he stormed over to her.

'I know you saw the tests,' he hissed. 'I didn't do anything wrong.' A thick vein in his neck pumped. His shoulder muscles were flexed.

'Pretty sure getting advance copies of class tests counts as something wrong.' Imogen put her hands on her hips.

He leaned closer to Imogen. 'So quick to judge.' His lips curled into a snarl. 'You know nothing.'

'Tell me then, Rory, what's your excuse?'

'Can we take this down a notch?' Jasmin said. 'Only people are looking.'

Rory gave a deep exhale. 'Sorry.' His eyes fluttered shut, and when he opened them again, he said, 'Look, I can explain.'

'Then do. I want to know why I have to work my arse off while you cheat your way through the course.'

'I have to pass,' Rory lowered his voice. 'You don't understand the pressure I'm under.'

'Then explain it to us.'

'I don't owe you anything.' Rory's anger poured off him like sweat in a sauna.

'Er, yeah you do. If you don't want me taking this to Mathieson.'

'Look, I have to graduate. I have to get control of my house and my money. Otherwise …' He shook his head. 'I need to get away.'

There was no hiding the urgency in his voice.

'Why?'

'I'm not trying to be top of the class or anything, OK?' he said. 'I want to get out of here, and it's not going to happen if I try to do it myself.'

'You can't be a journalist if you cheated your way through your degree.' Imogen was angry too. This offended her sense of professional integrity.

'I don't want to be a journalist,' Rory spat out. Jasmin noticed heads turning their way but Rory pushed on, oblivious. 'I chose this course because I *could* cheat my way through it. I don't care about the degree.' His tone was plaintive, and Jasmin heard the desperation there. She wondered what he wasn't saying. 'I want … to be free.'

'Did Niamh know about the stolen tests?' Imogen's voice was lower now.

Rory nodded. Misery was etched into his face. 'Niamh threatened to go to the School. She was going to spread rumours all over campus.' He looked defeated. 'I'm not smart like you, Imogen. I never wanted to come to university. All I want to do is run my own gym.'

Jasmin felt a sudden pity for Rory, the big hulking guy whose shoulders were now stooped.

'Please don't tell Mathieson,' he said in a small voice.

'I'll think about it.' And that was the only concession Imogen would make.

TWENTY-NINE

'Javier had my scarf,' Jasmin said again, probably for the fifth time, as they sat at a table. 'And there was a quilted jacket in the locker. I'm positive it's the one the attacker was wearing in the woods.'

Imogen nodded. 'It had to be Javier who attacked you.'

'Power Passion Triple and a Velvet Peach Shake,' said the woman behind the smoothie bar counter, announcing their orders.

'I'll get them,' Imogen said.

Jasmin traced a miserable finger down the edge of the table. Despite her reservations, she'd liked Javier. They'd both been there at the McKellan that awful day. Even though she didn't step inside the shed, finding Niamh had left an indelible mark on her. And she'd thought Javier had shared that with her.

But now she shut her eyes and saw Javier giving Niamh diazepam and telling her it was painkillers. Leading her down the garden to the shed. Offering her tequila straight from the bottle. And then, when she was too limp to resist …

'Javier was in our house,' Jasmin said when Imogen returned. 'I was telling my mam we'd be going to Lough Drinagh for Halloween. I dropped my notebook, and he saw that I'd been looking into Niamh's murder. That's why he told me that Merrick and Niamh weren't involved.'

'Are we thinking that Javier murdered her?' Imogen said.

'It fits, doesn't it?' Jasmin tried to think through the options without leaping to conclusions. 'Javier said he knew Niamh. He could be the maybe-boyfriend. Remember, no one actually saw the boyfriend well enough to identify him.'

'And it's always the boyfriend or the husband,' Imogen agreed.

'You two are in big trouble.' They glanced up as Damien approached their table, now dressed in a hoodie and joggers.

'Oh, you can't stay cross with us for long,' said Imogen.

'You working tonight?' Jasmin said, taking a sip from her Velvet Peach Shake.

'I was earlier,' he replied. 'Then I went for a swim.'

'Sorry about the snooping,' said Imogen sheepishly. 'I was so sure that it was Rory who attacked Jasmin in the woods. I had to find proof that he'd been out near Lough Drinagh. It was only a tiny little search through his bag. No one will know. It's not like there are cameras in the changing rooms.'

'What if he came in? What if he found you going through his bag?'

'It's not Rory we have to worry about,' Jasmin said. 'We talked to him just now. He seems desperate but …'

'… not a murderer?' Imogen finished the sentence. 'I got that too. I mean, if he can barely pass a test, is he really the right person to mastermind a murder to look like suicide?'

'Rory isn't stupid.' Damien folded his arms.

'Maybe not,' Imogen said. 'But we're currently looking at another suspect.'

Jasmin nodded. 'You know the scarf I lost when I was attacked? I found it in Javier's bag.'

'*Javier?*' Damien said. 'Javier attacked you in the woods?'

'Shh,' Imogen said. 'Keep your voice down.'

Damien ran a weary hand over the back of his head. 'The two of you aren't letting this go, are you?'

'I can't,' Jasmin said. 'I think about her. Niamh. She was a mess the day I saw her and I tried to help but I didn't try hard enough.' The cold shadowy touch, the king with hollow eyes who plagued her sleep. Jasmin knew she would not be free of this until she found peace for Niamh. 'I have to help her now. Even if it's too late.' She took a breath. 'Even if I have to do it alone.'

When they first started nosing around, Jasmin's motives were confused. She wanted to know what happened to Niamh, but more than that, she wanted to ingratiate herself with the friends.

It was different now. She didn't care if she did it alone. She didn't care if she lost her new, still unrooted friendships. She had to know what happened to Niamh. The truth mattered more.

A hand closed over hers. Imogen smiled at her. 'You don't have to do it alone.' Imogen wagged a finger at Damien. 'Come on, hands in. You know you want to.'

'This is so cheesy,' Damien muttered. But he placed his hand on top of Imogen's. 'You're not alone.'

'Imogen?' A cautious voice drew their attention. Walking by their table was Becky holding a large Power Passion Triple. 'I saw you two while waiting for my order, and then I was arguing with myself, should I, shouldn't I?' Becky gave a little chuckle and rolled her eyes. 'And here I am.'

Jasmin felt Imogen's restrained impatience. 'Is it something about Niamh?'

'Yes,' Becky said enthusiastically. 'I remembered something. A connection that I'd missed.' She glanced at Damien.

'It's OK, he's one of us,' Imogen said. 'You can talk in front of him.'

'Remember how I told you that I heard Niamh arguing with someone late at night? I heard him say, "You're going to regret this"? Well, I remembered that the guy had a very slight accent. You nearly wouldn't notice it, but it's there.'

The maybe-boyfriend. Jasmin was clutching her chair so hard that the sharp edges cut into her palms.

'Sorry,' Becky said. 'That sounded a lot more helpful in my head than out loud. His voice was distinctive – an Irish accent, but there's something beneath it. Something subtle that suggests he didn't always live here.'

'Actually, Becky,' Imogen said, looking ahead to the automatic doors. A man with a green quilted jacket and a blue and white striped bag was leaving the gym. 'That is very helpful.'

Later that night, Jasmin was clearing her desk, which was covered with textbooks and study notes, when her phone rang. She felt that warm tingle when she heard Damien's voice.

'You're still awake,' he said.

'Finishing some work,' she sighed, stacking her notes into a folder. 'Did you get your paper done?'

'I have a draft.' He hesitated. 'Do you want to come over?'

'Is this a booty call, Damien?' Jasmin teased, clutching the phone tighter, a host of butterflies alighting in her stomach.

He laughed. 'I've hardly seen you. I miss you.'

'Wish I could.' Jasmin didn't point out that they'd seen each other at the gym. She knew that's not what he meant. 'But tonight's no good.' She reached for a pile of pages at the edge of her desk.

'Another time.'

'I was not expecting to see you in the men's changing room today,' she said, finding Niamh's dragon pendant beneath the mess she'd cleared.

'I don't know how to tell you this but usually, in the men's changing room, you find men. In varying states of undress.'

'Hmm, tell me more,' she said, picking up the pendant and turning it over in her hand. Was there a way to get it to Niamh's parents? She examined it dubiously. It didn't look like anything of value.

'I'm afraid it might only encourage you. The start of a disreputable career.'

Jasmin laughed softly as she fell on to her bed. Her laptop was on her bedside table and she remembered Merrick's offer.

'There's something else I should tell you.' She fiddled with the dragon egg, running the soft pads of her fingers over the rough texture of the scalloped edges.

'Do I want to hear this?'

His voice. She could listen to his voice all night.

'I was offered a job, one I didn't apply for, as Theo Merrick's project assistant.'

She heard Damien's intake of breath on the other end. '*Theo Merrick* offered you a job? When did you even talk to him?'

'He was visiting my grandmother. I think I should take it.'

'I don't like it.' Damien was wary. 'It was Niamh's job, right? Merrick offered you Niamh's job. This is a bad idea.'

'It's perfect,' Jasmin argued. 'I can poke around, find out more about Niamh.'

'If you're looking for a job, I can see if there's anything going at the gym. They were looking for swimming instructors recently. They give the training and everything.'

'It's this job I'm interested in.'

He sighed. 'That's what I'm afraid of.'

'It was Javier who grabbed me in the woods, not Merrick,' she pointed out.

She felt a thin line hidden in the scalloped edges and turned the egg around to examine it. She pulled at the egg and it broke into two neat halves. Her mouth fell open as she stared at the pieces of the egg in her hands. The tiny SD card inside. The roaring in her ears blotted out everything that Damien was saying, his reservations about her working for Theo Merrick.

'... but we can talk properly tomorrow. What do you think?'

'Sure,' Jasmin muttered, hoping he wouldn't notice her distraction.

'Maybe you could come over in the evening?' he said.

'I'd like that.' *Wait*, she wanted to say. *I think I have Niamh's micro SD card.* But she hesitated. Damien sounded worried enough, now wasn't the time to add to it.

'Night, Damien.'

'Sleep well, Jas.'

The call ended and she reached for her laptop. Saying a quick prayer to the techno gods that the SD card wouldn't give her computer any viruses, she retrieved an adapter from her drawer and inserted it into the slot.

There were two folders on the card. The first was titled *Niamh ONE*, but Jasmin couldn't open it. It was encrypted, which meant there was likely something important on it. The second was called *Niamh TWO*. She clicked on the folder and saw that there was only one file inside. A video.

She opened it. After taking a moment to load, the video started.

The camera was badly positioned, catching a portion of a desk and a window behind it. Jasmin immediately recognised her grandfather's office. Merrick's office now. The camera shifted as if jolted, and the view changed. Now she saw, from a deeply unflattering angle, Merrick sitting behind his desk. She could only see his chin and mouth, but it was obviously him. That warm, calm voice.

' … and so what do they do when they've played the game and won but they're running out of time? The years have stacked up, they're nearing the end – but they're not ready to stop?'

'You have the answers, I'm sure,' a woman said. Niamh. Jasmin knew that voice too even though she was off-screen.

'I have every intention of finding the holy grail,' Merrick said. 'This will be my legacy. Ageing has always been the last, unconquerable frontier. Inevitable. From early adulthood, our bodies slowly begin dying. Brain cells die. Our bones weaken, cartilage thins. We wear out, our bodies giving in. We die. But the spirit inside wants to live.'

Jasmin rolled her eyes. He loved the sound of his own voice, Merrick.

'What exactly does this holy grail look like?' Niamh sounded amused.

'Countless studies show that injecting older rats with blood plasma from younger rats significantly extends the lifespan, the youth, of the older rat. What if we could replicate that with humans?'

'Could we?'

'Not easily. There's no single blood protein or stem cell population responsible for youth. And the youth-associated proteins become suppressed once they're diluted. There hasn't been a clear answer. Yet.'

'Well, obviously, because how could we even begin to test that safely on humans?' Niamh said.

'There are ways.' Merrick rubbed his chin as he spoke, and something about the way he said those words chilled Jasmin. 'You know there are. We've talked about this before.' Then Merrick shifted position, to the door, Jasmin presumed. 'Oh hello, Candice, come on in. We were just finishing in here.'

'Good morning,' came Candice's voice. 'Niamh, nice to see you.'

The camera wobbled. It was in a bag, Jasmin realised. Maybe positioned in a side pocket. And now that bag was lifted, giving a different view of the office, including a low-angle shot of Candice, who now touched a hand to Merrick's shoulder. Then the video stopped.

Jasmin pulled the SD card from her computer.

Niamh and Merrick, talking about the likelihood of finding an anti-ageing holy grail. About how you couldn't inject an older human with a younger human's blood – like rats.

Could you?

There are ways. You know there are.

What would Niamh and Merrick be arguing about? Imogen had wondered. *That's the million-dollar question, isn't it?*

Jasmin quickly searched Merrick's name and 'research' on her phone. She tapped her fingers while the screen loaded.

There it was. Phase two clinical trials for the Wellness Formula were scheduled for January. Clinical trials, Jasmin remembered this from her grandfather, involved testing on humans.

A hundred young people had signed up to the trials.

Jasmin played the video again. *What if we could replicate that with humans?*

There was no way on God's green earth that Merrick would have been cleared for highly experimental testing on human subjects. The clearance he would have obtained for the Wellness Formula would have been very specific and cautious. Scientific research didn't allow unsafe testing on people.

But what if you could hide your highly experimental testing behind something that had been approved? What if the Wellness Formula was a front for something Merrick would never otherwise be allowed to test and develop? It was deeply unethical.

What if this was what Niamh and Merrick had argued about?

It was true, there was no romance between Merrick and Niamh.

It was something far more sinister.

THIRTY

The afternoon was wet, drizzling rain settling on her skin like mist. Jasmin veered towards the Old Science, as she usually did. But today she did not stop to look at her grandfather's, or Merrick's, office window. Today she didn't pause or hesitate but walked straight to Merrick's lab on the ground floor. As if she had willed it, the door opened and a young woman signed for a parcel.

Jasmin peered inside. Lorcan wasn't there.

She went down the wood-panelled corridor until she came to the PhD rec room. Through the glass panel she could see Lorcan inside, drinking a mug of coffee. Under the harsh light she could see his eyes were underlined with shadows that had no business on the face of a twenty-five-year-old.

She pushed the door open.

'What do you want now?' He raised the large mug to his lips.

'When we spoke the last time, you said you'd seen Merrick favour other assistants. What did you mean?'

Lorcan gazed down at his coffee with the same intensity that Allie studied her coins. 'Why should I tell you?'

'Because something is very wrong. And you know it.' She sat on the padded chair beside him. 'I think you're hardworking and you hate that Merrick forces you to be dishonest.'

When Lorcan met her eyes, she saw something in them. Something more than fatigue. Maybe alarm, maybe relief.

'I don't lie for Merrick.'

'I think you care very much about the work you do, and the integrity of science. But being dishonest isn't only telling barefaced lies. It could be turning a blind eye to things you suspect aren't right. Merrick's grandiose ideas don't always fit easily with best practice, do they?'

Jasmin was part guessing, part remembering. Eamon Larkin had been similar to Merrick, ambitious and visionary, but frustrated. They dreamed of big discoveries and hated that they were constrained by rules and processes. Her grandfather had worked within the system, a caged lion, but Jasmin was increasingly certain that Merrick did not.

'You don't know anything, do you?' Lorcan gave a bitter laugh.

'I know that Merrick was trying to find ways around the rules about testing on humans. I know that very soon he'll run a clinical trial with a hundred volunteers.' She took a breath and then chanced her hand. 'If there is any chance that he might use the Wellness Formula trials as a way to secretly test some other hidden research on the people who sign up, we have to stop it.'

It was a shot in the dark, almost, but Lorcan's eyes went wide with shock. He stood up.

'We don't know anything of the sort.'

'You suspect it. You know that there are irregularities. You know that he's had unsuitable interactions with his project assistants, like Niamh. And I'm not talking about an affair.'

'What *are* you talking about?'

'Niamh knew things. Merrick talked to her.'

Lorcan went to the sink. He poured his coffee away and rinsed the cup. Then he turned back to Jasmin.

'I'm not saying that you're right,' he said, 'but if you were, what's there to do? If Niamh and the others agreed to be tested on, then that's what they chose.'

'What?' Jasmin heard a wild buzzing in her ears. 'Merrick tested on Niamh? With her consent?'

Lorcan paled, realising his slip. 'I didn't say that.'

She raised an eyebrow.

'I said *if*.'

'Lorcan, please,' Jasmin scoffed. 'You're playing word games. It's clear what you meant.'

He stayed mulishly quiet. But some of the fight left his eyes.

'It's completely unethical to experiment on students. Even if they appear to be willing,' Jasmin said. 'That's assuming they *were* willing.'

Lorcan's tightly pressed lips told her that he didn't approve of any of this.

240

'Either way, there's an obvious power imbalance. And you're implicated too, Lorcan. Imagine this all comes out five years down the line and you're working in some hotshot lab at a high-ranking university? You'll be guilty by association.'

He looked openly scared now. Jasmin had hit a nerve, so she leaned into it. 'Do you really want to build your career on Merrick's lies and manipulations? It's a terrible foundation, and it will cause your career to implode.' *And you could, you know, just do the right thing*, she thought. But that wouldn't have the same appeal to Lorcan.

He spoke quickly and quietly. 'There were others. Sometimes a star student that Merrick took under his wing. More often short-term hires who worked on specific projects or events for Verge, Merrick's spin-out company. There are usually two, maybe three, at any given time.'

'The project assistants.' Like Niamh. 'How does Merrick find them? Does he advertise for them?'

'That's actually a good question. I don't know how he finds them. Some kind of whisper network, I imagine.' He rubbed the bridge of his nose. 'They always seem to appear out of thin air. And they're always utterly smitten with him.'

Like Freddie, until Niamh screwed him over.

'But even then,' Lorcan went on, 'not all the project assistants get special treatment. Merrick seeks out the ones he likes best and makes them his favourites. Those who aren't favourites don't last the three months.'

'And all this happens right here? In front of the whole department?'

'Merrick's lab is here, so he conducts Verge business from here too. That's all above board, it's common enough.' He held up his hands as if to ward off possible objections from Jasmin. 'But they'd also meet at Ri—' He stopped, second-guessing himself again.

'At what, Lorcan?' Jasmin's ears pricked, as she suspected that Lorcan was about to admit to something that *was* unusual. 'Just say it.'

'Riverview. His old family home.' Rory's house. 'Merrick would meet his favourites there, in a more informal setting. To get to know them better. His stepbrother lives there now.' Which meant that no one would think twice about students coming and going.

'Rory doesn't mind?'

Lorcan shrugged, seemingly not surprised that Jasmin knew Rory. 'What can he do? Until Rory graduates, Merrick pulls the strings with his house and money. Everyone knows that.'

Jasmin remembered Rory's urgency that day at the gym. He'd told her he needed to graduate by any means necessary. Was it to get out from Merrick's influence? Did that make him more or less likely to have killed Niamh?

'Do you know who they are, these project assistants? Those he favoured?'

'I don't know their names. I work for the university and they work for Merrick.' His stand-offish tone made it clear that Lorcan kept a distance. 'There's a difference.'

'You have access to Merrick's computer?'

Lorcan shook his head. 'No. I'm not doing that. I'm not sneaking around his files. He'll know what was opened and when I'm in his office. Not a chance.'

He was a little weasel, Jasmin realised. Aware that something was amiss but too self-absorbed to actually do anything about it. She could feel her mouth turning down in distaste.

'There's nothing I can do,' Lorcan went on, fully convincing himself that this was true. 'I don't even know who the newest project assistant is.'

Jasmin let out a long release of breath. There really wasn't any other option.

'You're looking at her.'

THIRTY-ONE

Jasmin rapped on the blue door at the house on Burgess Street. Today it was answered by a housemate, who gestured her up the stairs before returning to his game. They were having a murder meeting – Imogen's words – but Jasmin was early, so she could steal some time with Damien. She passed by Rían's shut door, hearing what sounded like chanting monks inside.

'Hey,' Damien said as he opened the door in track pants and bare feet, and her heart did a little somersault. His hair was wet and he smelt of fresh laundry, obviously just out of the shower. His hand fell on her waist, natural and intimate, and she felt a pang of guilt that she hadn't been completely upfront. 'Come on in.'

Damien's room was much smaller than Rían's but had a large window overlooking the small garden. It was a simple, uncluttered space. Near the window was a desk with a laptop and textbooks stacked on the shelf beside it. A single desk chair. A room for working. A room for passing through. On the other side of the thin wall came the muted sound of recorded chanting, Rían's deep voice joining in.

'He does that a lot,' Damien said, grinning at the wall.

His hand still on her waist, he steered her to the bed. The indent of his head on the pillow suddenly made him seem vulnerable to her. It felt intimate, a snapshot of a moment when he wasn't working or studying or worrying.

'Damien,' she said, sitting on the bed. 'There's something I have to tell you.'

'It makes me really nervous when you say that.' He sat beside her. 'What is it?'

'I wasn't entirely honest with you. All of you.'

'Everybody has their secrets.'

'This shouldn't be a secret. And it's not fair to keep it from you. I'm not at the university. I'm still doing my Leaving Cert. I'm eighteen. I didn't lie about anything else, just that.'

Damien grabbed her hand and held it gently. 'I know.'

'You know?'

'That morning in Lough Drinagh. Your French novel has your school stamp in it.' He shifted closer. 'I don't care, Jasmin. There's only a year between us.'

'And you never said anything?'

He gave her a sad smile. 'I hoped you'd trust me enough to tell me.' He tugged her closer, folding her into him. 'You could tell the others,' he added.

'Maybe.'

'There's nothing you can't tell me, Jasmin. Nothing that would change how I feel about you. Nothing.'

'Same,' she breathed, and pulled him down on the bed.

'This is new for me,' he said. 'This intensity. I don't know what to do with it. How to be with it.'

'Same,' she said again. Then she kissed him, because that was the one thing she could do with this burgeoning emotion. She could kiss him and touch him. She felt a wild, irresistible urge to plug her heart into his. It was a madness, she knew, but it was a madness they shared.

Imogen arrived at seven, dramatically sinking to the cushions beside Damien as they gathered around Rían's coffee table. The room was bathed in candlelight and the chanting monks music had been switched for sweeping piano.

'Allie not coming?' Damien said. He was sitting across from Jasmin. Eyes on hers, his lips quirked up in that irresistible smile, making her heart flip again.

'She's meant to be.' Imogen arranged her full skirt so that it fanned out. 'She wasn't in her room when I left.' She looked at Rían and Damien. 'Jasmin and I have some important leads. We want to see this thing through, but we understand if the rest of you don't. After all, Jasmin did get attacked in the woods. Someone followed us there because they knew we were on to something. This is serious, I get that.'

'I'm in if you are. To keep an eye on you both, if nothing else,' Damien said, but Jasmin could see the worry in his eyes.

'Go on, so,' Rían said. 'Let's hear what you sleuths have been up to. Besides,' he pointed to the wall, 'we already made a murder wall.'

'Good,' Jasmin said. 'It wouldn't be the same without you.'

They told Rían what they'd learned about Rory and Javier, and he added the new information to the wall.

'Let's review our suspects.' Rían waved a comb at the murder wall, settling on the picture of Freddie. 'Freddie has a clear motive – revenge for Niamh ruining his career. But he was with his girlfriend for some of the night, giving him at least a partial alibi.'

'He could still have done it,' Imogen said, her eyes darting over the wall, looking at the pictures and the connections they'd formed. 'She could be lying to protect him.'

'Lorcan is by far the top contender in the most likely to be a psychopath category,' Rían said, his comb now jabbing Lorcan in the chest.

He's as slippery as an eel, Jasmin thought, still nettled from trying to talk to him. She was champing to tell them what she'd learned, but knew it would be wiser to wait for Allie.

'Javier has to be the maybe-boyfriend.' Rían's comb sought out Javier's image. 'He's admitted he and Niamh were friends. He knew Jasmin was nosing around, and he overheard where we were going that night. Besides, Jas found her scarf in his bag. Safe to say, we think he's our man in the woods, which immediately makes him the number-one suspect.' Rían rubbed his chin as if he had a full old-man-in-the-hills beard.

'Merrick has to be involved somehow,' Jasmin said.

Rían's bedroom door opened and Allie slipped in. She shut the door too quietly to be heard, staying at the wall in the unlit part of the room. Disapproval was etched into her face.

'Merrick couldn't have killed Niamh,' Damien rebutted, while Rían, who'd noticed Allie pressing herself to the wall, patted the seat beside him. Allie ignored him. 'He had that late dinner, remember, and we know she was intercepted before ten.'

'I know he was involved,' Jasmin said, tugging her laptop from her bag, 'because I found something important.'

'What?' Rían said.

'The night Niamh died, she dropped a necklace. A dragon's egg pendant. I picked it up, tried to give it to lost property before we found … then I forgot all about it. Last night, I discovered that the pendant contained a micro SD card.'

'What?' Imogen shrieked. Damien looked shocked, Rían wide-eyed. It was very gratifying, Jasmin thought.

'Jasmin, I'm dying here,' Rían said. 'What's on the card?'

'Two folders. One is encrypted. The other is a video.'

She flipped open her laptop, turning the screen for them all to see. Then she pressed play.

'It was never about an affair,' Imogen murmured when it was over. 'It was about living forever.'

'He told us himself,' Allie said as she peeled herself off the wall. 'That night at the lecture. He told us he was obsessed with immortality.'

'Glad you came, Allie,' Damien said, noticing her for the first time.

'Are you really?' Allie was pricklier than ever. Her hair was flat on one side, like she'd forgotten to brush it. Her eyeliner was smudged and her usual skinny leathers had been abandoned in favour of baggy jeans and a stained jumper. She narrowed her eyes at the murder wall.

'Allie,' Imogen said with dismay. 'You look, frankly, like shit in a box. Are you OK?'

'I thought we agreed we would stop.' Allie's voice rose, almost a wail.

'We can't stop now,' said Rían. 'Not when Jasmin just unleashed this twist!'

'Let's just go to Merrick's gala dinner as agreed, and we can talk next steps after,' Imogen said, but it was an obvious ploy to delay the inevitable. Her jaw was set. There was no way she was abandoning the investigation.

Allie walked right up to the murder wall, her eyes fixed on Rían's carefully arranged information. She whirled abruptly, and took a seat at the table.

'All right,' she said in a small voice. 'Just until the dinner.'

She doesn't like being left out, Jasmin thought. *Even though she's scared, she wants to stay together.* She felt a rush of exultation. She was the fourth now, she thought.

'So,' Imogen said, 'we think that Merrick is trying to replicate the rat experiments on humans, but since rats aren't humans, it doesn't quite work the same. He needs to find the right adjustment for it to work on humans. He can't know if he has the solution, unless he can test it on people.' Imogen let out a whistle. 'That's wild.'

'There's more. I spoke to Lorcan this afternoon.' Again, anticipation welled up in Jasmin. 'He made a major slip.'

'What did he say?'

'You're not going to believe this.'

'Jasmin, come on.' Rían touched a hand to his chest. 'My heart can't take the suspense.'

'Merrick used Niamh as a test subject. For one of his unethical experiments.'

'What?' Imogen cried.

'Lorcan says she agreed to it. Others too.'

'How could she possibly consent to something like that? The power imbalance is so huge!' Imogen was fired up.

'From what Lorcan said, Merrick sources carefully selected project assistants who adore him,' Jasmin explained. 'He lures them with his charm, confides in them until they are completely under his spell. Then they let him test his more experimental research.'

'And they agree to it?' said Allie disbelievingly.

Jasmin tried to remember Merrick's words from his lecture, something about the soldiers and the right cause.

'The soldiers were willing to die.' Jasmin reached for the memory. 'That's what he said in his lecture.'

For strong as the human impulse is to survive, it is also in the nature of humans to sacrifice themselves for the right cause.

'What?' Imogen's brow creased in confusion.

'The *Immortalis*,' Jasmin explained. 'At the heart of the story is the idea that we are hardwired to survive. But it is also our nature to sacrifice ourselves for the right cause. For the right king.'

'You remember that from the lecture,' Damien said.

'It made an impression on me.'

Did Merrick think himself a king? His chosen students a necessary sacrifice for some noble discovery? Was he equally excited by finding loyal, willing subjects, his own army of foot soldiers who would abandon reason and sense to follow him?

'They think he's a genius,' Rían said. 'So they'd believe they're the first to experience some unparalleled new medical breakthrough.'

'Or they don't know the whole story,' said Jasmin. 'They don't understand the risks.'

'What if Niamh didn't fully understand what she was getting into at first? And as she learned the truth of what was going on, she changed her mind?' Rían looked thoughtful.

'But she couldn't break out of Merrick's weird little cult.' Imogen's eyes were shining as the pieces clicked together. 'So she secretly gathered evidence, filming Merrick, getting him to talk. She hid it in the pendant she wore all the time. But Merrick must have realised what she'd done. He threatened her – she was scared. When she said, "He's a monster," she meant Merrick.'

'But it was definitely Javier in the woods,' groaned Jasmin. 'And he wouldn't do Merrick any favours – he doesn't seem to like him. So how does he fit in?'

'Somebody must be doing Merrick's dirty work for him,' Imogen said, frustration making her voice raw. 'But who?'

'What is this for?' Allie said, still distracted and staring into the middle distance. 'What's the point?'

'Excellent question, Allie.' Imogen jabbed a finger. 'Why is Merrick doing this? Is he taking shortcuts with the Wellness Formula?'

'Can't be the Wellness Formula,' Rían frowned. 'That's all documented and above board. He couldn't be secretly testing on students for that because it would mess up his results.'

'What if … ?' Jasmin thought about her grandfather and how rigorous he was. He'd taught her to keep careful notes, through their observations of the mice in his study. 'The Wellness Formula seems like genuine research that he's working on with Candice and other collaborators. The upcoming clinical trials are all legit, with everything as it should be – it will have withstood all kinds of scrutiny to get this far. But what if it's also a smokescreen? There is no better way to hide than in plain sight. What if beneath the cover of the Wellness Formula, Merrick has carved out room to explore the real discoveries he's interested in? What if he's stealing space within these legitimate trials to test them?'

'You mean use the upcoming clinical trials for the Wellness Formula to continue his unethical testing, but on a bigger scale than carefully selected project assistants?' Imogen said. 'And without informed consent?'

'He has a hundred young people signed up. We know he breaks the rules. What's to stop him?'

They fell silent, troubled by the idea of Merrick overseeing trials when he clearly didn't believe the rules applied to him.

'We need to look into this.' Imogen folded her arms. 'I'd be so pissed off if I signed up for a clinical trial and they were testing something secret and unorthodox on me. What if it causes long-term damage?'

'Maybe this was why Niamh changed her mind and wanted

252

to get out,' Allie said, distress making her voice thin. 'Maybe this is why she was killed.'

'We need more information,' Rían said. 'Can we speak to his project assistants?'

'I asked Lorcan to get me details. But he wasn't particularly keen,' Jasmin said.

'Wait. Does Merrick have a new project assistant?' Imogen said. 'We could approach him or her.'

Jasmin took a steadying breath. She looked up, seeing the resistance on Damien's face. 'Funny you should say that.'

THIRTY-TWO

'I should go,' Jasmin said. It was nearly eleven, and she hadn't told her mother she'd be home late. She was pushing the limits of Sonia's patience.

After the murder meeting, Jasmin had gone with Damien to his room. Just the two of them. She lay on his bed, resting against him, feeling his hand in the silky strands of her hair. She didn't want to leave, not yet. But she hadn't done her homework, and she was postponing the inevitable hurried catching up that was waiting for her. Reluctantly, she got up.

'I've been thinking,' Jasmin said, 'since Javier targeted me in the woods, it's probably not a good idea for me to keep the SD card, especially as I can't copy the encrypted folder. But I don't think it's safe for anyone—'

'I'll keep it,' Damien said immediately.

'It could be dangerous.'

'First, no one would know I have it. Second, they'd have to get past the weed-smoking gamers downstairs.'

'That's not the deterrent you think it is.'

'Then they'd have to fight off Rían,' Damien continued, 'and he's vicious. You try taking the last handful of crisps and see how he responds. By the time they get to me, they'll be mere husks.'

Jasmin handed it over and Damien locked the SD card in his desk drawer. He grabbed his car keys, then paused. 'You could stay the night?'

'I have school in the morning,' Jasmin said. 'Which reminds me, you never told the others my little secret.'

'Not my place to tell. You should though, they won't mind.'

'Allie would.'

'Allie's going through stuff. She gets like this sometimes.'

Jasmin wasn't sure if that was all there was to it, but Damien did know Allie better.

They drove home and he parked in the driveway. 'Will I see you tomorrow?'

'I'd like that,' she replied. He kissed her again, and then she was very late.

Jasmin floated up the path to the front door. It opened abruptly and Dash stood in the doorway, light flooding the path. He raised an eyebrow. 'Who was that guy?'

'None of your business, Dash.'

'I'll tell Mam you were snogging in the drive.'

'You won't.'

He gave her a stern look and she rolled her eyes. 'That was

Damien, you know him from the gym, and Rory's party. And before you say another word, he's barely a year older than me.'

He mimed zipping his lips. 'Go on in, you're in enough trouble.'

Sonia was waiting for her in the living room. 'Where were you?' Her hands were on her hips, feet planted wide, which was a bad sign.

'Sorry …'

'You didn't answer my messages.'

'I didn't check my phone.' Jasmin's neck warmed. She should have checked.

'This isn't like you, Jasmin,' Sonia said. 'I was glad when you made new friends after your old gang sided with Callum. But staying out on a school night, not letting me know … What's going on?'

'Nothing. I just forgot the time, that's all.' She always forgot when she was with them. It was like time in Faerie in the books she'd read, where one minute in the other realm was an hour or a day in the real world.

'Who were you with?'

'The usual crowd.'

'Were you drinking? Smoking weed?'

'No.' Jasmin rolled her eyes. 'You know I get panicky. I never drink much, if at all. And I'm far too anxious to take drugs.'

'That's true,' Sonia conceded. She softened. 'I miss you. I'm glad you've made new friends, but lately it feels like even when you're here you're not here.'

'I'm just preoccupied,' Jasmin said. 'Lots to do.' She added with faux brightness, 'I've decided to take on a part-time job.'

Sonia frowned. 'Is that a good idea, with how much you already have on?'

'It's only ten hours a week. I'll be working for Theo Merrick.'

'Theo Merrick? Oh wow.' Sonia blinked. 'That will look good on your CV, I suppose.'

'Really?' Dash said from the door. He'd been so quiet she hadn't realised he was still there. 'You're going to work for him?'

He looked annoyed, and Jasmin stiffened. She could see why this might irritate Dash; maybe he wanted to work with the esteemed professor. But she didn't want that. Not when she didn't trust Merrick.

'It's grunt work. Way below your pay grade.'

'I'm not jealous,' Dash shot back, and now he really was pissed off. 'Merrick approached me a while back.' And in a flash, they were children bickering over the Woody doll again. In her head, she heard the whiny sing-song voice, *but he asked me first.*

'Well, isn't it fantastic that you both made such a good impression?' Sonia said, sensing an argument brewing. 'Now, Jasmin, have you done your homework, or do I need to bring you a cup of tea?'

'Tea, please,' Jasmin said with a groan, dreading the school-work she still had to finish.

When she passed Dash in the doorway, he caught her arm. 'I'm worried about you.'

'I'm fine,' she insisted. Then something occurred to her:

'Hey, can I ask a favour? I have an SD card with an encrypted file that I want to open.'

'And?' Dash was frowning.

'Would any of your old school friends be able to help me with it?'

'I can ask. But do me a favour in return,' he said. 'Be careful with Merrick, OK?'

He disappeared before she could ask him what he meant.

Jasmin stood outside Rory's house on the canal.

In the afternoon light, she saw that it was much larger than she'd realised on the night of the party. Rory did a decent job of minding the garden too. The grass was neatly cut and the leaves had been gathered.

She wasn't here of her own accord; she'd been invited.

Merrick had asked her to an informal meeting at his old family home.

Riverview, where he brought his favourites.

She walked up the path, the cold autumn wind in her face. She missed her thick knitted scarf. She wished there was a way to get it back from Javier without confronting him about attacking her in the woods.

The door opened before she reached the end of the path. Merrick stood there, casual in a V-neck jumper and jeans.

'Come on in, it's chilly enough out there.'

She stepped inside, shrugging off her coat as Merrick moved to help her.

'I thought this was Rory's house.'

He arched an eyebrow at her. 'You've met Rory, I take it?'

She nodded.

'It will be Rory's house, when he graduates.' Something in Merrick's tone told Jasmin that he didn't see that happening any time soon.

She looked around the entrance hall. Through one door she saw the dining room with its heavy wooden table and chairs. No disco ball today. No sign of Rory either. Through the other was the living room, with dark brown floral furniture. The curtains were a green brocade, thick and heavy, and the room felt overdecorated and cloying, even more dated than she'd realised. This was the most unlikely home for a party-throwing, twenty-one-year-old gym nut. It was as if Rory didn't really live here.

'Rory likes having people around. Otherwise he rattles around in this big old house.' Merrick gestured for her to follow him. 'Candice and I have a flat in Carey Square.' Jasmin knew they were mostly fancy open-plan apartments. 'She's taken over the study there, so I keep my own little study here in my old family home. At least until it becomes Rory's.'

Jasmin was beginning to sympathise with Rory's urgency to graduate.

They passed through a door, then down a small passage to a bright room with picture windows that looked out on the back garden. Merrick placed a hand on the small of her back, leading her inside. 'Come, sit down. Coffee, tea?'

Merrick's 'own little study' was in stark contrast to the rest of the house, which felt frozen in time. This room had been

259

renovated, fitted with new windows and flooring. It was painted a soft white and contained stylishly modern furniture, including two geometrically pleasing armchairs in wood and brown suede. A glass trestle desk was in the corner of the room, the ergonomic chair beside it pushed out like Merrick had been seated there only minutes before. It was a sleek, minimalist room, but also lived in. The empty coffee cup beside the keyboard, the tin box of cinnamon mints, the open notebook and scattered pens. Merrick worked here a lot, Jasmin surmised.

Through the ajar door to an adjoining room she saw clear polycarbonate cages. For a second, she was back in her grand-father's study, moving to the drawer-style cages at the side of the room.

'Jasmin?' Merrick prompted. 'Can I get you anything?'

She was going to say yes, so he'd go to the kitchen and she could poke around his study. But then she spied a tray on the coffee table, already prepared with a ceramic coffee press, a silver teapot steaming at the spout and fancy biscuits.

'I'm fine,' she said, sitting on the armchair and glancing again at the adjoining room. There was not a sound from the cages. No quick movements at the corner of her eye. That was because there was nothing inside them, she realised.

Merrick watched her watching the cages, a hint of amuse-ment in his eyes.

'They're empty.'

But then why have a small room with cages adjoining your study? she wanted to ask, but it felt like Merrick was teasing her. Letting her observe, search for conclusions – it was a game to him. Jasmin waited, not saying anything, just as Imogen had done during their interviews at Latimer. Let him think he was interviewing her, but she was here for answers too. Hidden answers, the ones Merrick wouldn't realise he was giving her.

He took the chair directly across from her, as if they were playing a game of chess. He leaned forward, resting his forearms on his thighs, grinning at her. His sleeves were rolled up, revealing an expensive-looking watch. A lock of hair fell across his forehead. He was the complete package, Jasmin thought – warm, intelligent, handsome. And he made her skin crawl.

'I enjoyed calling in at Halloween,' he began. 'Georgie's in great form. She never slows down, does she?'

'No.' Jasmin smiled despite herself. 'She's the best. You know her from ten years ago?' She knew the answer, but she wanted to get Merrick talking. She already knew he liked the sound of his own voice.

'More than that. I completed my PhD here with your grandfather, graduated a few months before he ...' Merrick trailed off, and it was the first time Jasmin had seen him momentarily flounder. 'I did a postdoc abroad, and was lucky enough to return to a tenured job in Dublin. When I saw the opportunity to move back here, I took it.'

'I'm impressed you remember me.'

'Those days in your grandfather's study, talking late into the night, were something special,' Merrick said. 'Georgie would bake bread, and we'd eat it with cheese and mugs of tea and I would learn from the master. Hours would pass, and we wouldn't notice the time. You would come in and out, curling up on the sofa with your sketch pad or a book. It was your place in the world, as it was mine. You were part of the picture.'

Jasmin cocked her head. *Part of the picture.* It was a strange way of phrasing it, as if it were a classical painting that had been carefully composed. She heard the reverence in Merrick's voice, as if it had been some kind of sacred time.

His eyes had an almost dreamy cast. 'It's not really the done thing these days, bringing students into your home. But it is important to me, to have a similar place to share with my students, where I can talk to and inspire them late into the night, away from the university.'

'This room,' Jasmin said, understanding why it mattered to him.

'My time with Eamon, all those conversations in his study formed me. As a scientist, and as a man.' Merrick cleared his throat, like he'd revealed more than he intended. He pushed a white A4 envelope towards her. 'This is the contract. It's basic admin mostly, providing support to my office manager on campus. His details are all there.'

Jasmin reached for the envelope and placed it on her lap.

'Why me?' She tried to search beneath the charming smile, the pleasing facial features. 'You could have your pick of the best students on campus. Why would you offer this incredible opportunity to a secondary school student who you hardly know?'

'I do know you, Jasmin. I used to see you all the time. You were so careful and precise. You observed things like a true scientist. And not just the mice or whatever Eamon was trying to show you, but people too. You watched, and you understood.'

Jasmin frowned. *The Watcher.* 'I watched?'

'Yes. You kept yourself from the centre, but you saw everything. A child, but an old soul.'

No, thought Jasmin, shaking her head. She had become watchful and serious *after* Georgie had been attacked. Not before.

But Merrick was insistent. 'Absolutely. It was a rare, beautiful thing to see.'

It felt like the long-cherished pages of her family lore were being ripped apart. If Merrick thought her watchful, then her inability to fit in, to be condemned to the sidelines, wasn't because of her guilt at what happened to Georgie. She'd always been like that.

If she had always watched, then she would have been alert that day too. Which meant that no amount of vigilance would have stopped the attack on her grandmother. She felt a burning in her throat. It really wasn't her fault.

'Besides, you're his granddaughter,' Merrick said, oblivious to Jasmin's inner turmoil. 'I wouldn't be where I am if it wasn't for Eamon, and I'd like to return the favour however I can.'

The serpent eating its tail.

'You're smart,' he continued, not seeming to mind her silence. 'I could see that then, and I can see it now. Eamon always swore you'd follow in his footsteps and ...'

Jasmin was disoriented. She could swear she heard mice scratching and squeaking in the next room, and it was like she was eight again. Only a few minutes in, and her carefully planned conversational pieces were already derailed. *She* was derailed, her grasp on the situation slipping.

She had a sudden image in her head of the cages next door. Not empty, but with Niamh and Freddie and other unknown project assistants hunched inside.

'Excuse me?' she said, realising that she'd missed what Merrick was saying. She perched at the edge of her chair, as if sitting up straight would brace her.

'I hope you'll accept. There will be one month's probation to see if we're a good fit. If we are, the contract runs for three months, with the option of extension at my discretion.'

Her throat felt dry. She didn't want to do this. It felt like she too had fallen under his spell, but it wasn't pleasant and dreamy, worshipping a man like a god. No, this felt like she'd been drugged. Her head was swimming, her palms clammy. *Get a grip*, she told herself.

'That sounds good.'

He smiled. 'You're making the right decision. We're doing cutting-edge work here and I hope you'll be inspired by it.' He rubbed his jaw. 'I hope it will feel like what you had with Eamon.'

'You remind me of him.' Her voice was husky. That was the line she'd planned last night. She needed Merrick to trust her. To share intimacies with her the way he had with Niamh. She needed to flatter him, to make him feel they had a bond. 'You're both ambitious and more brilliant than the university deserves.'

His eyes went wide, then he chuckled. 'I don't think the university would agree with that.'

'He wanted to discover and explore. It frustrated him, all the admin and red tape. The processes that constrained and inhibited him.'

'You were so young, and yet you understood all this,' Merrick said. 'My instincts were right about you.'

'I never understood why he resigned,' Jasmin said. 'I always imagined it was his frustration at being held back when he wanted to soar.'

'You're partly right,' Merrick said, then hesitated. But she had seen it in his eyes.

'You know why,' she said, again feeling the rug pulled out from under her. 'You know why he resigned.' It was a few days before he had attacked Georgie, she thought. There had to have been a connection.

Merrick began slowly. 'There was a project your grandfather was working on. His life's work. His passion. Eamon had been doing independent research at home, which was in itself a problem for the university. He was obsessed, to the point that he went rogue, making choices that wouldn't have been approved. Someone discovered what he was doing and reported him. He was given a choice. Resign or be fired for conducting unethical research.'

Jasmin's hands held on to the suede chair. They felt slick with sweat. She wanted to stand up, walk out. Her heart was beating so loudly he must surely have heard it. *Her grandfather, conducting unethical research ... Someone reported him.*

Her stomach dropped.

You did this.

'Georgie,' she said in a whisper. 'It was Georgie who reported him.'

The missing puzzle piece from all those years ago. He'd been forced to resign because Georgie had reported his malpractice. And so he tried to kill her.

Merrick nodded. 'She was afraid for him. Perhaps she was right to be. Your grandfather had a brilliant mind. I don't think I've met anyone who has come close.'

This was a test, Jasmin realised. The project assistant was only part of it; there was more he wanted to offer, and he was currently interviewing her for *that*. If she failed, then the probation would put an end to things. If she passed, the nature of the job would be different.

She would have the job that Niamh had.

'I wish Georgie hadn't.' Jasmin held his eye. 'I knew him, you see. I knew that he could have done great things. I wish she'd stayed quiet.'

Merrick didn't respond, but she could read it in his face: *So do I.*

Jasmin held the moment. She let the silence linger and fill in what she wasn't saying out loud: *I can be lured to serve hungry kings. I am a willing foot soldier.*

'There's one other project assistant and you'll share duties with him. We're at a particularly busy stage with the clinical trial approaching.' He checked the time. 'He's fairly new. Only started a few weeks ago, but already one of the best I've had. You'll work well together.'

266

There was a knock at the door.

'There he is right now,' Merrick said, nodding to the door as it opened.

The door swung wide, and stepping into the room, wearing his green quilted jacket, was Javier.

THIRTY-THREE

'Javier Batista,' Merrick said. 'Meet Jasmin Malik. Our newest project assistant.'

Jasmin stiffened. She hadn't been this close to Javier since that night in the woods. Her heart raced and she rose from her seat. He looked as startled as she felt, but when he spoke he sounded calm.

'Hello, Jasmin, glad to have you on board.' The coldness in his eyes suggested that this was a straight-up lie. 'Theo, the event planner for the gala dinner called again.'

'She needs to speak to Candice.' Merrick sounded annoyed. 'Can you tell her that?'

As the men talked, Jasmin tried to gather her thoughts. She'd thought that Javier didn't like Merrick; he'd called him a prick when he dismissed the idea that Niamh could have been romantically involved with him. Had it been an act?

Because the reality was that Javier was Merrick's assistant.

And maybe, after booking flights and ringing the courier, he did a bit of murder for the good professor.

And with that one word, *murder,* Jasmin realised with a terrifying jolt, with a knowing deep in her bones that she was alone with the two men who were likely responsible for killing Niamh.

This time there was no warning: the panic that thrummed through her body was electric. She was limp with it. Wild palpitations from her heart echoed in her ears. Her head spun. 'Excuse me. I have to go,' she mumbled.

She fumbled her way down the passage.

'Jasmin?' she heard Merrick call but she didn't stop. She had to get away. She had to find safety, but suddenly the passage seemed labyrinthine and the exit felt too far away. Then she saw a glass door leading directly to the garden. Trying the handle, she was relieved when it opened. She walked briskly down the side of the house, taking deep breaths.

She'd just rounded the corner when she saw him, through the shrubs and half-bare trees in the dying afternoon light.

A man was standing in the road. He was caught in unexpected sunlight as the clouds momentarily shifted. A large bear of a man, though older than when she'd last seen him. His shoulders were stooped, his beard fully grey and his hair cut shorter than she'd ever seen it. He was gazing at the house, not seeing her in the shadows.

Standing on the narrow canal road outside Riverview was her grandfather.

As if entranced, Jasmin took a step towards him. Then another.

'Grandpa?' she croaked, not sure if this was a fever dream or if Eamon Larkin really was standing there.

With only that whispered word to guide him, he turned his gaze to look at her. He stared at her for a long minute, as if drinking in her features. His eyes, always expressive, showed a mix of emotions. First, unbridled joy. He loved her. She was his girl. Her panic eased. She stepped towards him, the wet grass soaking through her shoes and into her socks.

Then his eyes went cold. A flicker of alarm.

'There you are,' Merrick said from somewhere behind her. She turned to see him round the corner.

'Sorry.' She was a little calmer now. 'I have to go. A-a family emergency.'

'You left this behind.' Merrick handed her the large white envelope with the contract, which she'd forgotten. 'Welcome on board, Jasmin. We're thrilled to have you.'

She gave a weak smile and then hurried to the gate. But out in the road Eamon was gone. She checked up and down the street. Empty.

A little way down, a parked car started its engine. That had to be him. She sprinted to the car, hoping she could catch him.

But as she reached it, Jasmin stopped. It was Damien's car. He was in the driver's seat with Rían beside him. Imogen's face bobbed between the two front seats. Then Rían was out of the car, taking her bag and putting it in the boot.

'Get in,' he said gently, steering her to the passenger seat. He touched a comforting hand to her shoulder, like he knew she was shaken.

Jasmin slipped into the seat beside Damien. He moved his hand to hers, only briefly removing it to change gears.

'How did you know I was here?'

'I knew you were meeting Merrick,' Imogen said. 'We checked his lab and office, and you weren't there. Rían did the guesswork.'

'Rory's house,' Rían said grimly. 'Where he brings his favourites.'

'Javier was there,' Jasmin said. 'He's working with Merrick after all.'

'What happened?' Imogen said as the distance between them and Riverview grew. 'You have to tell us everything.'

'She's upset,' Damien said. 'Let's get a bite to eat first. We can talk after.'

'Fine. Did you see who was outside the house just before you came out?' Imogen sounded excited and Jasmin's heart stuttered another moment. But Imogen answered her own question. 'Eamon Larkin.'

'Who's Eamon Larkin?' Rían said.

'Remember the long read Allie and I did as a final project last year? We wrote about that mad professor. He was a big cheese at the university ten years ago. He tried to strangle his wife. Nearly killed her. I thought he was in jail.'

Damien's eyes met Jasmin's, and she saw the understanding there.

'Oh yeah,' said Rían. 'I do remember, vaguely.'

'But that's not all. A lot was kept hush-hush, men protecting men, old boys' club – you know how it goes. We did a bit of digging and found that Larkin resigned a few days before the attempted murder. There is a strong suggestion that the real reason was because he'd been conducting unethical experiments. He had these cages of mice at home, and he'd been running wild tests on them. He was a bit of a Victor Frankenstein, scientist gone rogue.'

'Wild tests?' Jasmin's mouth was dry. Phantom mouse paws ran up her shoulder to her neck.

'We talked to some of his students and rumour has it he'd been biohacking himself, basically turning himself into a super-cyborg-human with an unlicensed use of medicines. He did things like suppress his natural oestrogen levels, self-injecting home-made NAD IV infusions …'

'Sorry, what's that?' Jasmin's voice sounded small.

'A vitamin cocktail straight into the veins. All to make him physically superior. He really believed that this was the future. That in twenty or thirty years, we would all be medically enhancing our bodies.'

Jasmin felt sick. Her fingers tightened on Damien's.

'Mad, isn't it?' Imogen said, almost gleefully.

'People do it all the time,' Rían shrugged. 'Whether it's fillers to enhance their looks or supplements to increase their sporting prowess.' He wriggled his fingers. 'I wouldn't mind a cyborg hand. I'd never struggle to open a jar again.'

'It didn't turn out so well for Eamon Larkin,' Imogen said, and her breezy tone was a punch to Jasmin's gut. 'Disgraced, sacked, in prison. Probably all those hormones that made him snap and try to kill his wife. I heard it happened in front of their grandchild but couldn't confirm that rumour.'

'Will we call Allie to join us?' Damien said, trying to redirect the conversation. His hand squeezed Jasmin's again, the gentlest pressure, and she breathed through the dull ache in her heart.

It was a double exposure photograph. Her grandfather, but also not her grandfather. She didn't recognise the man who was so devoted to his science that he would medically adapt his own body. But she could believe it. Her grandfather had been a man who got things done. He had no fear. She knew he tested things on the caged mice in his office; it never occurred to her that it was illicit. But of course it was, because why else would he be doing it at home?

She felt small and stupid. Imogen knew so much more than her about her own grandfather. Why had she never thought to research it herself? But she knew why; and even now, she still couldn't.

Imogen was looking the case up on her phone. 'It says here that Larkin was sentenced to ten years, so he could be out already. Fancy seeing him outside Merrick's place.'

'It's interesting, isn't it?' said Rían thoughtfully. 'He sounds like he has a lot in common with Merrick. Making the body better, stronger, through the scientific method.'

Imogen tapped her chin. 'He was looking well, especially for a man who's been incarcerated for ten years. Maybe there's something to all this biohacking business.'

'Where do you want to eat?' Damien said, his tone clearly shutting down the current subject.

'Let's pick up something along the way,' Rían said. He rubbed his hands with relish. 'Then back to my room and the murder wall.'

'Oh! Forgot to tell you, Merrick will be on my mam's show tomorrow night,' Imogen said. 'She's doing a wellness special and he and Candice are part of the line-up.'

Jasmin scowled. She hated the thought of Merrick preening on the show, lapping up the attention.

They stopped to pick up spice bags, texting Allie and asking her to meet them at Burgess Street. By the time they bought the food, darkness had folded over the evening, sudden and too early, as it always did after Halloween.

On the ride back, they talked about Allie.

'She's spiralling,' Imogen said. 'I don't like it.'

'We've barely seen her,' agreed Rían.

Jasmin felt guilty. Like she was trying to replace Allie. They didn't need to jostle to be the fourth. There was room for both of them, if Allie would allow it.

Imogen's phone beeped and she let out a squeak. 'Well! Maybe things are on the up.' Her face shone as she looked up. 'Allie's out with a guy right now. Not holed up in her room. So maybe she's ready to turn a corner.'

'Our Allie, out on a date,' Rían said fondly. 'All grown up.'

But when they reached the house on Burgess Street, there was a marked Garda car parked right outside. The front door was open, letting the cold night in. They looked at each other in uneasy silence, then hurried inside.

The gamer boys were sitting around the kitchen table. They looked worried, but also excited, calling out when they saw Rían and Damien. 'Hey, you'd better check your things,' one of them said. 'We had a break-in.'

'A break-in?' Rían looked aghast. 'Here?'

A guard was standing in the doorway. 'You live here?'

'We do,' said Rían breathlessly. 'We've nothing worth stealing, so I don't know why anyone would bother.'

The guard shrugged. 'The burglar got inside but doesn't look like he had time to take much. Your friends came home and saw the kitchen window broken. We thought at first some of the rooms were trashed, but your friends assured us they'd left them like that.' He sounded bored, Jasmin thought. 'I'll come up with you and you can let me know if anything has been stolen.'

Damien nodded, and Jasmin noticed that he seemed tense. Anxious.

'When did this happen?' she asked the guard.

He checked the time. 'I'd reckon it's been ninety minutes, maybe two hours.'

'Thanks for rushing here,' muttered Rían.

'Let's go and check your rooms,' Jasmin said, slipping her hand into Damien's.

At the top of the stairs, Rían went to his room and Damien to his. The guard stood at the bottom of the stairs, waiting.

'You can go,' Rían said to the guard, coming out. 'Nothing's been taken.' But he looked worried.

'Yeah, my camera and laptop are both there,' said Damien.

When the guard left, Rían let out a stream of curse words.

'What?' cried Jasmin.

He flung open the door to his room. 'Look.'

Imogen and Jasmin rushed to his room.

'The murder wall,' Imogen cried.

Everything had been ripped off. All the pictures and connections they'd drawn. The timelines and theories that Rían had meticulously recorded.

'It has to be Javier,' Imogen spat. 'First attacking you in the woods, and now this.'

'He was at Riverview though,' Jasmin replied. 'No, wait, he got there well after I arrived. He'd have had time.'

Damien ran a hand through his hair. 'They broke into my drawer. Niamh's SD card is gone. They knew what they were looking for all right.'

Imogen groaned, sinking into Rían's desk chair. 'How could he have known about that?'

'I told Dash,' Jasmin said. 'About the card. I wanted him to ask his friends if they could crack the encrypted file. He might have said something to Javier.'

Imogen dropped her face into her hands.

'But how would he know it's here?' Rían pushed.

'Javier visits Dash at my house sometimes.' Jasmin felt like her head was swirling. 'If he'd searched my room, he might have thought to try here next.' They should have hidden it better, she realised, furious with herself.

Allie rushed in, her face bloodless. 'What's going on? I saw the guards driving off.'

'There was a break-in,' Jasmin said. 'They destroyed the murder wall and stole Niamh's SD card.'

'No,' breathed Allie.

Jasmin slumped on to the low bench. Damien sat beside her. His shoulders were hunched over, so obviously miserable.

'I should have found a better place to keep it.'

Jasmin placed a hand on his thigh and he tightened his hand around hers.

'Only the SD card was taken?' Allie said, her voice shrill. 'From your room, Damien?'

'What is going on with you, Allie?' Imogen said, studying her friend, the wide worried eyes again. 'You've not been yourself for days. Are you going to tell me?'

Allie's shoulders slumped. 'I cheated on a test, OK? I got the paper in advance and cheated. But I was caught.'

'Allie, no,' Rían said in dismay.

'I don't want to talk about it.' Allie held up a hand. 'It was stupid, so stupid, and I regret it. I'm going in to see Mathieson later this week.' Her face was tight, and Jasmin knew that Allie was eaten up with worry. 'We can talk after that. After I fix it.'

The silence in the room was uncomfortable. Rían shifted, clearly trying to stop himself from asking more questions. Jasmin was itching to know if she'd used the test paper she'd stolen from Rory's room. It seemed to fit.

'You can talk to me whenever you're ready,' Imogen said gently, and Allie nodded.

'Damien, can I check your room?' Allie said, changing the subject. 'Maybe they took something else?'

'Sure,' Damien stood up, frowning slightly. 'I'll come with you.'

Jasmin suspected that Allie didn't really want to check for theft, that she'd asked because she needed to escape, if only for a few minutes. To get away from Imogen's probing gaze, Rían's palpable worry. Maybe she felt Damien was the only person she could talk to about the test she'd stolen from Rory's room.

Damien touched Jasmin's shoulder before he left, an unconscious impulse, as if he couldn't resist. She felt it too, a near constant urge to touch. To hold.

'I'll get the food from downstairs,' Rían said as Damien and Allie left. 'Even a murderer breaking into my room can't change the fact I'm famished.'

When he left, Imogen let out a loud sigh. 'So, you and Damien. I see you ignored my advice. I wish it were otherwise, but it will end in tears.'

'Sometimes that's the price we pay,' Jasmin said lightly. 'Better to have loved and lost, and all that.'

'Your funeral.' Imogen scowled. 'Where's Rían? I'm starving.'

THIRTY-FOUR

The next evening, while she and Sonia tidied the kitchen, Jasmin received a message from Allie.

We need to talk. Meet me at the Deacy Library at 8.30.

Interesting, thought Jasmin. She worried it meant confrontation – about Damien, about how Jasmin had wormed her way into the group. Still, she had better see what Allie wanted.

'So go on, tell me about your interview yesterday,' said Sonia. 'What's the famous Theo Merrick like?'

Creepy, Jasmin thought. 'He's all right. Very pleased with himself.' She hesitated. 'Dash's friend Javier is working there too. Another project assistant.'

'He is?' Sonia surveyed the spotless kitchen. 'I like him. He was here only yesterday afternoon.'

'Hmm.' Jasmin really wasn't keen that Javier visited her house. But what could she do about it? Only keep watch. Always keeping watch. 'I'm going to the library. I won't be late.'

'But it's closed.' Sonia rubbed at a streak on an otherwise gleaming surface.

'The university library, to meet my friend Allie. She's a journalism student.'

'Oh,' Sonia said. 'OK. A university student. Are – are all your new friends older?'

'They're nineteen,' Jasmin minimised. 'We get on really well. I like them. I feel like I have a little gang again. You know how much I missed that.'

Sonia nodded but Jasmin could see that her mother was troubled that she was hanging out with an older crowd. But her old life, her school friends, all of that seemed so remote to her. Even though she sat in class every day, she didn't belong there.

But when she was at the Three Divas, or in Damien's car, or at Burgess Street, she fitted right in.

Most of the time.

'Does Georgie still have a visitor card for the library?' Jasmin said. She knew Georgie paid the membership fee so that she could revisit the literary classics and old films she loved.

'Ask her,' Sonia said. 'Need the car?'

'I'll bike it.'

Jasmin slipped out and headed next door. She found her grandmother and Benedict reading by the fire.

'Of course, dear,' said Georgie, rummaging in her handbag to retrieve the card. With her glasses on, she seemed older this evening. The lines on her face more pronounced, her cheeks a little more shrunken.

Jasmin had a sudden urge to throw her arms around her

grandmother and hug her. She remembered what Imogen had said in the car, about the mad professor trying to strangle his wife. In those stories, Georgie was always the victim, the poor wife who never saw what was coming.

But Jasmin thought Georgie was perhaps the bravest person she knew. Even a simple act like owning a university library card was a defiance. If Jasmin had been Georgie, she would have moved to the other side of the country. But Georgie held her head high, refusing to yield any territory. She would use the university library and stay friends with the other university wives. This was her house, her town, her place. She would not be cowed.

Jasmin remembered what Merrick had said, that it was Georgie who had reported her husband for unethical practice. Definitely the bravest woman she knew.

At eight twenty, Jasmin entered the university library. She swiped Georgie's card and went to the centre of the library. Its open design meant she could see the four levels all the way up to the ceiling and its glass dome. If she stood at the railing, she could see below to the basement level, where reference and periodicals were housed.

Allie hadn't said where in the library to meet but she clearly wasn't in the lobby. The lift pinged open and Jasmin stepped inside. There was a comfortable reading area with couches downstairs and she'd text Allie to meet her there. She was pulling out her phone when a hand reached inside the closing doors. The heavy steel doors stuttered and then opened enough for him to slip inside.

'Jasmin.' It was Javier. The doors closed behind him with a solid thud. She felt her stomach flip with fear.

'Are you following me?' She edged back, the metal rail digging into her back.

'What? Why would I … ?'

Jasmin felt cornered, and Javier must have seen the fear on her face because he held up his hands and stepped back. 'Sorry.'

'For what?' Her voice was brittle.

He looked at her beseechingly. 'Can I talk to you? Two minutes, that's all. Please.' There was something in his face, the rawness of his pleading.

'Two minutes. I'm meeting Allie.' She felt a horrible churning in her gut as the lift pinged at the lower level. 'She'll be along any minute now.'

They stepped out of the lift and towards the couches. Jasmin kept a distance between her and Javier, hugging her arms around her as she noted they were alone. Above, all four floors formed rings around them. She looked up to the glass dome, hearing a reassuring beeping from the loans desk.

'What do you want?'

'Don't work for Merrick. Don't take that job, please.'

'Why not?' Jasmin was blindsided. This was not what she'd expected.

'Merrick is … not a good man.'

'And you are?' She dropped her arms to her sides. She would not be intimidated. 'I know what you did.'

'What are you talking about?'

Without warning, the lights flickered. Jasmin looked around the windowless basement. Oversized reference books crowded the room but otherwise it was very empty down here. She felt the hairs on her arms rise. She felt the lightest touch of shadowy fingers on the nape of her neck.

With one last flash, the lights went out, plunging the building into darkness. Jasmin let out a cry, grabbing on to Javier's arm. Then she remembered that night in the woods and she thrust it away, a wild buzzing in her ears.

She stepped back, terror clawing at her as she searched for the exit signs. The shadowy fingers were lacing around her wrists now. She could smell the dank, ancient king. Feel his sour breath. She had no idea where the stairwell was.

The emergency lights were like small round eyes, emitting a weak, milky glow. From above, came the sound of voices, panicked and questioning. There had to be a generator, Jasmin reasoned, and it would kick in after a few minutes. *Stay calm*, she told herself as she took another step back.

She felt the cold touch of the old king as if he were right there, his fingertips on the nape of her neck. She shuddered. Might even have let out a little whimper.

A loud, assured voice boomed out. 'Due to a power outage, the library will be closing immediately. Please make your way to the main exit.'

'The stairwell is this way,' Javier said. 'Here, take my hand.'

He held it out but she didn't take it.

'I'm trying to help you.'

'Then why did you attack me in the woods?'

Even in the weak light, she saw his eyes shutter closed, the absolute dejection on his face. 'I was desperate. I'd seen your notes. You were asking too many questions, and I had to make you stop. I had to make you understand that this is very, very dangerous. If you don't stop asking questions, you're going to get hurt. Worse than hurt.'

'Is this meant to be a threat?'

'Niamh was murdered. And the people who had her killed will kill again. Better a scare in the woods than dead.'

'*Had her killed?*' Jasmin said. 'You mean Merrick.'

He swallowed.

'But Merrick couldn't have done it himself,' Jasmin continued. 'He has an alibi for the time she died. So who could Merrick have asked to do his dirty work?' Jasmin tapped a finger to her chin. 'What about his project assistant?' She narrowed her eyes at him. 'You.'

'You too, apparently.' Javier looked around. 'Can we get out of the dark and continue this conversation outside?' He gestured to a far corner where an illuminated green and white fire escape sign indicated the way out.

'Lure me to the stairwell so that you can murder me? I don't think so.'

'I'm not trying to murder you in the stairwell.' Javier let out a frustrated sigh. 'I don't want to murder you, or hurt you, at all.'

'I know you threatened Niamh.'

'I did not threaten Niamh.' Javier sounded genuinely perplexed. 'Niamh was my friend. She needed help and I let her down.'

'Becky heard you,' Jasmin hissed. 'You were in her room, and you said, "You're going to regret this."'

Javier ran his hands through his hair. 'Yeah, I did. We were arguing, remember, I told you we'd had a disagreement. But that was no threat. It was a warning. Niamh was tangled up in something dangerous and I wanted her out. She refused.'

'Due to a power outage,' the announcement repeated, 'the library will be closing immediately. Please make your way to the main exit.'

'Did you hear that?' Jasmin paused. Upstairs, the bustle had quietened. From a distance, there was a strange scraping noise. Jasmin couldn't tell what level it came from. The open space made the acoustics confusing. She glanced up, searching the shadows.

'The announcement? Everyone did, that's the point.'

'No.' Jasmin kept herself still. She had a heightened sense of alarm. 'Javier, something bad ...'

Get out of here, a voice inside her said. *Run.*

'Let's get out of here.'

That's when she saw it, a blur, an impossible shape in the shadows, dropping from above. The hard thudding noise. Something landed a few metres in front of her.

Run, her mind screamed. But she couldn't. She walked towards the dark shape, feeling a thick clot in her throat. Her heart was wild in her chest. The shadows were back, not just fingers but strong, thick arms, drawing Jasmin into their dark depths. Wanting her to lean into their embrace.

With shaking hands, she held up her phone, fumbling for the torch button. She was close enough now to catch the figure in its light. The fingers, slim and delicate. The stretched out arm. The unnatural position of the legs in their faux leather leggings. The thin face, eyeliner smudged. The head, smashed on the hard floor.

How fragile the human body was.

Jasmin put her hand on her mouth to stifle a scream.

It was Allie.

THIRTY-FIVE

There was a cry from above, a flashlight sweeping over the basement floor.

'Help us!' Jasmin called. 'Someone's fallen.'

What happened next was a blur. Security and library staff holding huge flashlights. Voices crying out. Hard shoes pounding down the stairwell. A hand on her shoulder and someone saying, 'I need to speak with you, if that's all right.'

'Her name is Allie,' Jasmin said. 'Allie Vaughn.'

She took a last look at Allie before stepping into the stairwell.

Outside the library was chaotic. Lights flashed on Garda cars. A small crowd of students gathered on the far side of the square. Jasmin and Javier were asked to give their witness statements. An ambulance arrived.

The next hour passed in odd staccato moments. Jasmin was here one moment, then somewhere else the next with no real sense of how. A guard offered to drive her home, but she declined.

Her hands were shaking as she held the bike handles and her skin was clammy in the cold November night. She stopped once to vomit. When she got home she tried to slip up to her room, but Sonia called her as she reached the stairs.

Her mother was in the living room with Georgie, watching a detective show they'd both become addicted to.

'Did you have a nice time?' Sonia ran an eye over her daughter. 'You don't look so good. Are you coming down with something?'

Jasmin shook her head, desperate to get away. She couldn't go through it again. Not tonight.

'Maybe. I'm really tired. Can we talk in the morning? Please?'

Sonia must have heard the raw plea in her voice because she nodded.

Upstairs, Jasmin took deep gulps of air. She could hear the gentle rumble of the two women talking, Sonia worried, Georgie soothing. Then she shut her door and sank to the floor. She sat there for a moment, resting her head on her knees.

After several minutes, she found the strength to stand up. She picked up her phone and called Imogen.

'Have you heard?'

'Of course I've heard.' Imogen's voice was clipped. 'It spread like wildfire on campus, and it's already online that a student …' She faltered. 'They're saying another likely suicide. That she was going to be chucked out for cheating so she … But I don't believe … I can't …'

'I saw her,' Jasmin whispered. 'I saw it happen.'

Imogen gave a sharp intake of breath.

'Imogen?' Jasmin said after a while.

'I'm here.' She sounded like she was far away. Her voice was empty. 'What happened?' she said after an eternity.

'She asked to meet me in the library. I couldn't find her. I ran into Javier and we were talking. Then the lights went out in the building and she … somebody must have pushed her.' Her voice hitched on the last words. 'They must have done.'

'Javier was there?'

'He was with me when it happened.' Jasmin swallowed. 'He couldn't have pushed her.'

'Why do you think Allie wanted to meet you?'

Jasmin remembered the night in the woods, when Allie approached her. *Jasmin, I need to talk to you. It's important.* Jasmin had thought it a ploy, but what if Allie really needed to get something off her chest? But why would she tell her and not Imogen?

'I don't know.'

'I've got to go,' Imogen said eventually. 'Let's speak tomorrow.' She rang off.

Jasmin brushed her teeth. She got under her covers and stared at the ceiling for a long time. She heard Sonia go upstairs to bed. The occasional car passed by, the sound of tyres on wet road.

Her phone buzzed. Damien.

I'm outside.

Jasmin went downstairs in the darkness. She opened the

door and there he was, standing out in the rain. In the outside light she could see his face was tight, his eyes red from crying. She let him in. Quietly, she led him up the stairs to her room.

He sat at the edge of her bed, his shoulders shuddering as she held him, his wet clothes on her dry skin. She didn't know what was tears and what was rain.

She listened for Sonia, in case her mother had heard them come up. Then, into the silence, she whispered, 'Stay here tonight.'

If Sonia found him there, she would be livid. Tonight Jasmin didn't care.

His arms wrapped around her, holding her as if he were sinking. Then she pulled back and peeled off his wet clothes, guiding him into the bed. She settled beside him, switching off the lamp.

Jasmin didn't sleep well that night. She woke frequently, seeing Allie's body on the library floor. She felt Damien's arms tighten around her, heard him shudder out of bad dreams, and she knew that he didn't sleep much either.

In the morning, Jasmin waited until Sonia left for work before bringing Damien downstairs. They kissed goodbye in the hallway. Promised to speak later.

She watched him walk away, head bowed.

'Want to tell me who that was?' Georgie's voice came from the living room.

'I didn't know you were here,' Jasmin said, hovering in the doorway.

'Clearly not.' Georgie shook her head, her chunky gold necklace glinting in the morning light. In her slacks and cashmere jumper, she was so familiar and comforting, despite the furrowed brow. 'Your mother asked me to check on you. What's going on, Jasmin? Sonia's worried. You were really out of sorts last night. And now sneaking a boy out of your room?'

'A girl was found dead last night,' Jasmin started and her voice sounded all wrong. 'At the university library. She's our friend. Was our friend. I was there last night, I went to meet her, and then …'

'Ah, sweetheart,' Georgie said, going to Jasmin and putting an arm around her, drawing her close. 'I heard it on the radio this morning. You knew her? Come here, pet.' Georgie steered her to the couch.

'Can we put the news on?' Jasmin said.

'Is that a good idea?'

'Please, Georgie.' She held back a sob. 'I need to understand.'

Georgie looked doubtful but she turned on the radio. It was the end of a discussion about a new bus corridor.

Jasmin sat down, still feeling that awful breaking in her heart that made it hard to even take in air.

Absently, Georgie said, 'Sometimes, knowing things can be dangerous.' Her voice was thick, and Jasmin was suddenly reminded of Allie's grandmother reading the future from the ashes of nutshells.

Jasmin studied her grandmother, whose lined face was worried. 'What do you mean?'

'Exactly that.'

Jasmin thought of Eamon's hands around her neck. Georgie had discovered what he was doing. She had used that knowledge to stop him. And he had tried to kill her.

'Now, you stay here while I get you a nice hot drink,' Georgie said, smoothing her hair.

Jasmin rested her head against the back of the couch, looking up at the ceiling.

Sometimes, knowing things can be dangerous.

Niamh had learned something, and now she was dead. Allie must have learned something, and now she was dead too.

Javier had been right: whoever killed Niamh would kill again.

Better a scare in the woods than dead.

Georgie returned with a mug of sugary tea and put it gently in Jasmin's trembling hands.

'I was there when they found the first student. Niamh Cunningham,' Jasmin admitted to Georgie. 'And then last night, I went to meet Allie and I saw ...' Her breath hitched.

The news alert sounded and Jasmin reached for the radio to turn it up. She listened to the headlines, then it came.

'... university when a second young woman was found dead on campus last night,' the reporter said earnestly, and Jasmin's stomach twisted into knots.

'The student fell five floors to her death. The young woman was said to be struggling with the demands of her coursework in the weeks leading up to the tragic incident. The university is increasing its mental health services available to students and appealing to them to reach out if in crisis ...'

Jasmin let out a loud gasp. 'They're making it sound like suicide. She did not jump!'

'Sweetheart.' Georgie put a tentative hand on her shoulder. 'Come now, let's turn that off.'

But Jasmin shook her head while some university official delivered the usual platitudes.

The news ended and the presenter's measured voice said, 'On the line to talk about this latest tragedy is Professor Theo Merrick, university chair and wellness expert. Professor Merrick, thank you for talking to us.'

Merrick's voice was sombre. 'First, I must express my heartfelt condolences to the Vaughn family for their tragic loss, and to the university community, who are deeply saddened by Allie's passing. And, I'm afraid, this young woman's death represents the real struggles young people are going through today.'

'So you believe this is a widespread problem?'

'It's an epidemic,' Merrick said solemnly. 'The welfare of our young is in a dire state. They are facing innumerable pressures, most of them entirely out of their hands, and it's causing unprecedented anxiety and mental health problems.'

Jasmin felt the scream deep in her stomach, then her chest, then her throat. But she stayed quiet. She let her grandmother put her arms around her and remained quiet.

THIRTY-SIX

She hadn't meant to go to the McKellan Galleries. Jasmin had started out walking, needing to get some air, and somehow she'd ended up here. The elegant Georgian facade was in front of her, and she felt eight years old again. Standing beside the man she adored.

She felt close to her grandfather here. Her grandfather when he'd been good, not the wild, feral man who'd tried to strangle Georgie. And today, she felt in desperate need of comfort.

Since Niamh's murder, when Jasmin laid her head on her pillow at night she saw the hollow-eyed king in her mind's eye. Now she felt him all the time, a heavy, constant presence who watched hungrily. He was always there: when she took the bus or when she walked to school. She felt him when she stood at her locker or in the garden at home. She was sure he was there. Just out of sight, maybe obscured by an evergreen bush, or on the other side of the street behind a car.

Rationally, Jasmin knew that there was no ancient, hungry king following her. But his constant presence was a portent, a harbinger of everything bad. And so many bad things had happened.

She went up the steps and inside the building. Seeing the gallery signs, she decided to follow a group of tourists to Rare Manuscripts. There, she paid the two-euro fee and stepped inside the temperature-controlled room to see *The Book of Monsters*.

It was in its glass cage, as if the book itself had to be contained in order to subdue the monsters on its pages. She shuffled behind a tourist family, who were warned by the attendant to put away their phones. They lingered at the glass and Jasmin tried to peer over their shoulders. She felt a sudden urgency, like if she could just see the book now, she would get the answers she needed.

Then the family shifted away and she saw the book, open to the same page as it had been before. The image of the ouroboros clear for anyone to see.

The serpent eating its tail.

Merrick's enduring sign.

She stared at the book for endless minutes. She could hear impatient shuffling behind her. The attendant asking visitors to keep moving along. But she couldn't. Her feet were rooted as she studied every tiny symbol. The careful, ancient lettering.

The king was behind her. She was sure of it. She had an irrational conviction that he was standing right there in the room, wearing an ordinary face, ordinary clothes. He felt like damp and shadows, like scuttling in the undergrowth.

It took a moment for Jasmin to realise that it was the scent that had got to her. A subtle smell, resinous and spicy, and so achingly familiar. It was the smell of her grandfather.

She raised her eyes from where she'd been transfixed by the book and looked up. In the glass, she caught the reflection of a tall man with short grey hair walking out of the room.

Jasmin whirled round and bolted for the door.

'Hey, watch it,' someone cried.

It was him. She was sure of it. Her grandfather.

He was visiting *The Book of Monsters* with her. Just as he'd done before.

She ran out of Rare Manuscripts, down the stone corridor, out of the front door. Only when she got to the front steps did she accept that if he had been there, he was gone now.

But it was the second time she'd seen him.

Was it really him? Why was he there? Was it for her?

Jasmin wrapped her arms around herself, shivering. If her grandfather was out of prison and he really wanted to see her, there were ways. He could talk to Sonia. He could wait for her outside school, or in the park she cut through every day on her way home.

But this felt different. He was watching, but from afar. Jasmin wasn't sure if she liked that. No one wanted to be watched by a near-murderer.

Or maybe it was simply habit patterns. She haunted the same places that he did because she was like him.

She missed him, she loved him.

He was a monster.

The oh-so gentle touch of the shadowy fingers nudged her down the steps and away.

Later that afternoon, Jasmin stood outside the house on Burgess Street. She didn't have that zing of excitement she'd felt every other time she'd waited outside the blue door. The sky was a flat grey today, no play of silver and white light.

Damien answered the door. His eyes were dull as he reached for her, holding her tight and kissing her.

'The others just got here,' he said as they started up the stairs.

'They're saying she jumped.' Imogen was standing in the centre of Rían's room. She was still in her coat. She looked as put together as always, her coat a sumptuous navy velvet, her neat bob shining. But her pale skin was almost translucent. There were blue-grey shadows beneath her eyes. For the first time, Imogen didn't exude purpose. She looked like a lost girl.

Rían was wretched. His clothes were rumpled, a far cry from his usual dapper self. He seemed absent, like he was somewhere else entirely.

'We went to see the dean this morning,' Damien explained to Jasmin. 'Told her that there was no way Allie would have jumped. She told us Allie was failing, at risk of exclusion. That she'd been caught cheating on a test, and that she'd been begging her lecturers for second chances, saying that she couldn't disappoint her family.'

'Her mam spoke to Imogen. Said they received a message from her,' Rían said. 'Right around the time she died. It said, "This is for the best. Please don't be angry with me."'

'Her murderer wrote it,' Imogen snarled. 'It's obvious. And it's cruel.'

Damien was pale. 'I don't know what to do.' He sounded helpless.

'We should go talk to the guards, together,' Jasmin said. 'Tell them the whole story.'

'You're right,' he said. 'But what *is* our story?'

'That Merrick killed her,' said Imogen.

'Merrick was in a TV studio with your mother last night,' Damien said. 'He has a rock-solid alibi, live on TV while hundreds of thousands tuned in.'

'Then someone who works for Merrick,' said Imogen. 'Javier.'

'Javier was with me when she fell,' said Jasmin. 'There's no way he did it.'

'You were with Javier?' Damien said, and Jasmin realised that they hadn't talked about the previous night. Damien and Rían knew she'd been there, but they didn't know the details.

'Allie asked me to meet her in the library. I don't know why. I was a few minutes early and bumped into Javier. He told me not to take the job with Merrick, that it was too dangerous. He apologised for the attack in the woods, and said he only did it because he was desperate for me to stop investigating. Said he was sure that Niamh's killer would kill again.'

'Sounds convenient.' Rían ran a tired hand over his eyes. It occurred to Jasmin how little she knew Rían. At first, she had found him the easiest of the four. He was exaggerated and dramatic, and never shy to say what he thought. But he was like a too bright light, difficult to look at and hiding things in its shadows. And tonight, when the light was subdued, she felt she was seeing him, the real Rían, for the first time.

'I agree with Jasmin. We should go to the guards.' Imogen pulled her lipstick from her bag. She applied it carefully, like she was putting on armour.

'I think we should wait,' Rían said slowly. 'The guards aren't going to listen to vague speculation. We have one chance to make a first impression, and we need evidence.' He gestured to the now empty murder wall. 'We remake the wall. We start from the beginning, going over everything carefully. Step by step. We know that Merrick is involved, but we don't know who's working with him. And killing for him.' His eyes glittered with emotion. 'We need to look again at Lorcan and Freddie. And Rory. They are all connected to Merrick. They all had issues with Niamh.'

The heaviness in the room was almost visible, like a thick grey mist fading them out.

'OK.' Imogen stood up and slipped an arm around Rían's waist. 'We go through everything again. For Allie.'

'For Allie,' Damien agreed, standing behind Jasmin and folding her to his chest.

Jasmin kept her eyes down. Because when she looked up, she saw Allie standing in the doorway in her leather mini and thick eyeliner. She could smell the musky perfume, unexpectedly heavy and old-fashioned, but a fragrance that had suited her. The cherry scent of the car freshener that always lingered in her hair. She could hear Allie's voice saying, *I don't know what's right or wrong or good or bad. It's all confused and I can't see my way out.*

THIRTY-SEVEN

Jasmin waited for Imogen outside Elizabeth House. She'd taken a second day off school, still reeling from Allie's death. Whenever she shut her eyes, she saw Allie on the library floor.

Imogen had spent the morning with Allie's parents. They were upstairs now, clearing out her room.

'They're in bits,' Imogen had said over the phone. 'Allie was the world to them.'

Sitting on the bench outside, Jasmin remembered that day she'd mitched afternoon classes. When she'd met Allie and Imogen outside Latimer. They'd all been energised, so sure they could find out what happened to Niamh.

Now, November had settled in and the dull grey was oppressive. Jasmin hated November. Dark and dreary, it seemed like a good time to die.

As she waited, she saw the young woman she and Imogen had spoken to at Latimer – Thuli. Imogen's summer romance.

'Hey, it's Thuli, right?' Jasmin said as she passed the bench. 'I'm Imogen's friend, Jasmin.'

'Is she OK?' Thuli said, perching at the edge of the bench. Her brown eyes were worried. 'I heard about Allie.'

'She's with Allie's parents now. They're clearing her room.'

'Ah,' Thuli said. 'She's soldiering on, isn't she? Keeping busy so that she doesn't have to sit with it.'

'Sounds about right.' Jasmin gave her a rueful smile.

Thuli sighed. 'Imogen and I had a glorious summer fling while we were both back home in Dublin,' she said. 'It ended before the summer did. We might have been together only a few weeks, but it felt like we'd known each other for a lifetime. I *know* her. And I know she wasn't doing some mental health survey when you were here before.'

'You saw through that?' Jasmin winced.

'That was so obviously Imogen prying into Niamh's death. She is insatiably curious. Of course she was looking for the story.'

'A bloodhound.' Jasmin remembered that first day she sat down at their table.

'I only met Allie twice, first when she came to Imogen's family home for a weekend in the summer. Then I saw her again the morning she died. We chatted. It's surreal, her last hours and we had no idea.'

'What did you talk about?'

'We got talking about Niamh, and she asked me if Niamh had been seeing anyone, if I knew anything.'

'I don't think she was.'

'*I* saw her with a guy.' Thuli said. 'I told Allie that. The way Niamh looked at him, she was totally into him.'

'Black hair, brown eyes?' Jasmin described Javier, wondering if their friendship was more than he admitted to. 'Hair on the longish side?'

Thuli shook her head. 'I told Allie I only caught a quick glimpse one night when I was going to the library and I saw them in passing.' She held out her hands. 'I couldn't pick him out in a line-up. He was good-looking, I guess. Muscular. Darkish hair? Can't really tell you more than that.'

Jasmin suppressed the strangled sound that wanted out. It might be Javier, it might not.

'The funny thing is that I saw him again,' Thuli said. 'The night before Allie died. In Messy Jack's. I'm ninety per cent sure it's the same man. His posture, the mannerisms. There's something about him that draws attention, but it's hard to put your finger on.'

'Did you get his eye colour?'

Thuli pulled a face. 'Couldn't say. Not in Messy Jack's.'

The lighting in the student bar was red and gave everything a surreal, under red water tinge.

'Anyway, what was really weird is that he was there, with Allie. So when she asked me that morning if I knew Niamh's boyfriend, I said no. But Allie did!'

'What?' Jasmin exclaimed. Then she remembered: *Our Allie, out on a date.* She had been out with a guy that evening, which wasn't something she did often. What if she had only

303

gone on a date because she'd wanted to follow a lead by herself? *Oh, Allie, what were you hiding?* Jasmin thought.

Out loud, she said, 'You told Allie you saw her with Niamh's boyfriend at Messy Jack's? What did she say to that?'

'She was shaken.'

'Thuli,' Jasmin said casually, 'it's probably nothing, but let's just keep this between ourselves, OK?'

'Sure.' Thuli nodded. 'I didn't mean to gossip.'

'Can I show you some pictures,' Jasmin said, 'and maybe you could tell me if you recognise him?'

'I can try,' Thuli replied, checking the time and getting to her feet. 'I'm leaving on a field trip this morning but will be back at the end of next week. Have to dash off now, let's get in touch, OK?'

Jasmin hesitated and then said, 'You and Imogen must have been great together. Do you mind if I ask why you broke up?'

Thuli sighed. 'We were great. But Imogen sees herself through her mother's eyes, with all her flaws accentuated. She doesn't like feeling vulnerable, so she comes over as hard and invincible. She needs to realise that she's enough.'

Thuli left and Jasmin watched her walk away. Then the door to Elizabeth House opened and Imogen emerged with an older man and woman. Allie's parents. Jasmin could see the grief bearing down on them as if it were a physical force.

Jasmin waited in the sunshine while Imogen hugged them both goodbye. She thought about what Becky had said. How she'd heard someone, Javier, arguing with Niamh. But Becky had also caught a glimpse of a young man in Niamh's room. They'd all conflated the two, because that had made sense.

But what if there had been two different men? One who Becky had heard – Javier. And another, just out of sight, who remained a mystery to them.

Getting to her feet as Imogen walked towards her, Jasmin suddenly knew why Allie had died.

Imogen swiped angrily at a tear, her other hand clenched in a fist. Jasmin saw the shuddering breath that ripped through her body, and her heart ached.

But talking to Thuli, Jasmin understood what Allie had discovered. What knowledge she had been killed for. Because the minute Allie pieced together who Niamh's maybe-boyfriend was, her fate had been sealed.

Sometimes, Georgie had said, knowing things can be dangerous.

And now Jasmin knew another dangerous thing.

It was midnight when Damien texted her. Jasmin lay flat on her back in her lamplit bedroom, her hair spread out on her pillow. She was thinking about Allie sitting in front of the fire, reading her coins. She remembered, with shame, her own reading of Allie's future: *You're trapped. You're stuck and you're never going to get out. You will die stuck.*

Her phone buzzed.

I'm outside.

Jasmin eased her way down the stairs, thinking how quickly this had become normal, that Damien would come to her late at night. Opening the front door, she put a finger to her lips and led him upstairs.

'You OK?' Jasmin said after she shut her bedroom door, turning the key to lock it.

'Not really.' Damien lay back on her bed.

She joined him and they lay there in silence for a while.

'That date Allie went on before the break-in. Do you know who he was?' Jasmin said eventually.

Damien considered for a moment. 'I don't think she said.'

'Would she usually tell you?'

'Yes,' he said. 'But Allie was different these last weeks. She was angry. I think she … might have liked me more than she'd let on.' He groaned. 'That makes me sound like a dick, doesn't it?'

'I'll hear you out,' Jasmin smiled at him. He was only saying what she'd suspected.

'I'm beginning to think that she'd played it casual, when we had our fling, and hid that she wanted more. To be honest …' He shook his head.

'What?'

'I feel bad saying this, but I thought she might have made the date up. To make me jealous.'

'She wanted more from you.' Jasmin felt a squeeze of guilt. And she could see in his eyes that Damien felt it too.

'It wasn't just that. It was everything. Her coursework, the cheating. She was becoming resentful of the roles that she and Imogen fell into.'

'With Imogen the main character and Allie the sidekick?'

'Yeah. At the beginning of term, Allie finally admitted to herself that she didn't want to be a journalist. She didn't have Imogen's appetite. Imogen didn't hide her disdain, did she? They were going through a renegotiation of their friendship, as were we. In time, everything would have settled. We would have found a way.'

Jasmin nodded. He was right. But Allie hadn't had time. 'I saw Thuli today.'

'The elusive Thuli who stole Imogen's black heart?'

'Thuli saw Allie out with a man the night before she died.'

He raised himself on one elbow. 'She did?'

'She recognised him. She'd seen him before – with Niamh. It's more than a little suspicious that both Allie and Niamh have been murdered, and that they were seen with the same man.'

'Did Thuli give a description?'

'Nothing specific. She's away for a week, but I'll show her the pictures of Lorcan, Freddie and Rory when she's back.' Jasmin turned on her side, watching Damien in profile. 'I don't think this was a regular date. Allie had to have been following a lead, one that she kept from the rest of us.'

There was a light tread in the passage. Jasmin listened as Sonia went down the stairs, probably for water.

'My grandmother saw you leave the other morning,' she admitted in a low voice. 'She told my mother, who wasn't too impressed.' Sonia hadn't said much because Jasmin was grieving, but she had not been happy.

'Should I go?' he whispered.

She put a finger to her lips as Sonia came back up the stairs, down the passage, then shut her bedroom door.

'No,' Jasmin said, a wild recklessness tearing through her. 'We'll be quiet.'

A month ago, she'd never have done it. She wouldn't have sneaked a boy into her room after she'd been warned not to. She wouldn't have risked her mother's anger. Her mother's trust.

Now, she reached for Damien, feeling bold. Finding the friends had changed her. Each one of them had made their mark on her, as sure and lasting as a tattoo.

Damien flipped her over on to her back, pressing down as his eyes devoured her. 'I've never felt like this before.' His lips brushed hers. 'I'm falling for you, Jasmin. Hard. My heart is yours, if you'll have it.'

Hands on her hips, he dropped his lips to her neck and Jasmin knew she had fallen too.

THIRTY-EIGHT

Jasmin woke early the next morning. Damien was still asleep and she went down to the kitchen, where Sonia was dressed for work and finishing her coffee.

'Are you ready to go back to school today?' she said.

'One more day?' Jasmin said, without much hope.

To her surprise, Sonia nodded. 'You need to take the time to grieve properly now. You've been close to the deaths of two young women.' She put her cup in the dishwasher. 'Go, be with your friends. Do something that Allie would have loved.'

Jasmin thought of Damien upstairs in her bed and felt like the worst daughter in the world.

Sonia left for work, and Jasmin went back up to her room, passing Dash on the stairs. Opening her door, she saw Damien on her bed, awake but deep in thought, and her heart gave a squeeze.

'Morning.' Jasmin felt suddenly shy, remembering the intimacy of the night. Their midnight discovery. She felt an invisible thread between them, binding them together.

'Come here,' Damien said, reaching for her.

'What are your plans today?'

'The usual,' he sighed. 'Classes, working. I'll take time off for Allie's funeral in a few days.' He smoothed back her hair. 'Can I ask you something?'

'What?'

'Stop working for Merrick. It's not safe. Please.'

She hesitated a moment, and from the disappointment in his eyes, she could tell Damien knew her answer. 'I can't.'

Before he could respond, her phone buzzed with a message. 'It's Imogen.' Jasmin sat up. 'She has something of Allie's and wants to meet.'

She texted back, agreeing to find them at the Three Divas later that morning.

'I've work this morning,' Damien said. 'But I'll drop you off first.'

They sneaked downstairs when Dash was in the shower. At his car, beneath the now sparse branches, Damien pulled Jasmin to him.

'Last night. It was everything.' His face was raw emotion, and she felt it too, that jolt of elation and desire and wonder.

He kissed her again, whispering how much he loved her, and his words made her spark and burst. She didn't care about the neighbours seeing, or someone getting out of their car a little way down the road, or the car door handle pressing into her as she traced the muscles in Damien's back. She couldn't get enough of him.

Drawing back from him, she sensed a figure in her peripheral vision. Turning, she saw Lorcan.

'What are you doing here?' she said, not at all happy that he was there, outside her home.

'I need to speak to you.' He glanced at Damien. 'Alone.'

'I'll wait in the car,' Damien said, glaring at Lorcan.

Jasmin shook her head. 'You'll be late. Dash is home, I'll be fine. Meet you later?'

Damien was clearly reluctant to leave, but Lorcan was fidgety, as skittish as a pony. Jasmin was worried that he would bolt and she wanted to know what he had to say. She gave Damien's hand a quick squeeze, and said, 'I'll be fine. I'll text you when he goes.'

She watched him get back in the car, then faced Lorcan. 'How did you know where I live?'

'Merrick has your address on file.' Lorcan shoved his hands in his pockets.

'Hmm.' He clearly didn't mind searching through Merrick's computer when it suited him. 'What do you want?'

'Can we go inside?' Lorcan scanned the road behind her.

Jasmin glanced back at the house. She didn't trust Lorcan. But Dash was home. She wouldn't be alone with a potential murderer. And she really wanted to hear what he had to say before he bolted.

'Did something happen?' She frowned. Lorcan's shirt was buttoned all the way to the top, like it was strangling him. 'You look terrified.'

'Please, can we go inside?' He looked around shiftily, like he was worried someone was watching. Jasmin relented.

She led him into the living room, brushing a hand against her phone in her denim skirt pocket.

'You remember our last conversation? That Merrick might be doing something dodgy under the cover of the Wellness Formula?'

'Of course.'

Lorcan pulled at his hair. 'I'm so close to finishing my PhD.' He groaned into his hands and Jasmin felt her patience dissipating. When he looked up, he said, 'I overheard him on the phone yesterday. I don't know who he was talking to.'

Jasmin sat beside him. 'What did you hear?'

'He was pissed off. He came into the lab last night, thinking it was empty but I was in the supply closet. I recorded some of the conversation.' With shaking hands, Lorcan pressed play on his phone.

'… which is what you were supposed to do.' Merrick's voice was low with fury. 'But you didn't, so I made my own arrangement. And now you think you can question that?'

There was silence while the other person responded.

'Look, you know the deal. You've always known it. You bring them in, butter them up. I give you what you want. Except, you haven't been holding up your end.'

There was a silence again.

'Niamh was a mistake, and that's on you.' Merrick sounded weary.

More silence.

312

'I see. Then we're going to have a problem. Just remember, you're in this too. You don't want to cross me.'

The recording ended. Lorcan's face was ashen.

'Merrick had someone recruiting the project assistants for him,' Jasmin said, trying to make sense of what she'd just heard.

'You asked how they heard about the job. Sounds like they were targeted. Now that I think of it, every one of them has been strong and fit. Glowing with health. It's always been about the testing.' Lorcan looked distressed. 'It's so calculated.'

'Do you have any idea who the recruiter might be? Someone you might have seen talking to Merrick?'

Lorcan gave her a withering look. 'He's Theo Merrick. Lots of people talk to him.'

Jasmin repressed her sigh. It was hard when your gods fell. Jasmin knew that only too well.

'The recruiter would likely be a student too,' she deduced. 'It has to be someone who can easily move between them and Merrick.'

She thought of Rory and his parties, the uncomfortable tug of war between him and Merrick. Maybe this was why Rory needed to cheat on his tests – so that he didn't have to bring in students as Merrick's human test subjects. And Rory matched Thuli's description of the man she'd seen out with Allie.

Lorcan bent over, dragging a hand down his temple and cheek. 'I wish this wasn't happening.'

'We need to take this to the guards,' Jasmin said urgently,

sensing that he was about to run. 'This is the proof we were looking for.'

'Not a chance.' He sat up. 'I got you this so you can do something about it. But it never came from me. In fact ...' Lorcan held up his phone and pressed the delete icon. 'I was never here.'

THIRTY-NINE

When Jasmin arrived at the Three Divas, Rían and Imogen were already there. She joined them in the alcove. Allie's seat was conspicuously empty.

Jasmin gave them a rundown of her conversation with Lorcan, including the deletion of the recording and his avowal to deny speaking to her.

'Coward.' A blue vein was visible beneath the pale skin on Imogen's forehead. 'It really is looking like Merrick specifically brought in the project assistants for the extracurricular activity. And they were carefully selected. Niamh and Javier both look strong and fit as anything. And he chose you. You look fit enough, Jas, despite your pitiful efforts at the gym. The perfect specimen of a young adult.'

'Well, thanks, I think,' Jasmin said. But Imogen was right, she'd always been good at sport, at least until she'd quit soccer back in September.

'I mean, if I were going to capture two humans and keep them in cages for my weird experiments,' Imogen continued, 'I'd probably go for Niamh and Javier.'

'I don't think he chose me because I'm fit,' Jasmin said. 'I think he chose me because of my—' She stopped abruptly. She'd been about to say 'grandfather'. 'My obvious physical perfection.'

'You forgot your irresistible charm,' Rían said with a hint of his usual spirit.

'We need to track down Javier again. Find out what he knows about the mystery recruiter,' Jasmin said. She paused, looking at Imogen. 'I didn't get a chance to tell you that I talked to Thuli.'

'My Thuli?' Imogen blushed faintly.

'Ooh, do tell.' Rían leaned forward. 'We never hear anything about Thuli. This is top-secret information. Can't believe you got to meet her.'

'Stop,' Imogen said, blushing deeper. 'This is why I don't tell you anything.'

'Yeah, it was while you were with Allie's parents and …' Jasmin glanced at Imogen, not wanting to say how distressed she'd seemed. How even though it was important information, it wasn't the right time. 'Remember when Allie went out on that date? Well, Thuli saw her at Messy Jack's with a guy. Here's the thing, Thuli was pretty sure she'd seen Niamh hanging out with this same man.'

'What?' Imogen exploded. 'Allie went out with Niamh's maybe-boyfriend? Wait, I thought that was Javier?'

'Becky mentioned two instances of Niamh with a potential boyfriend,' Jasmin said. 'One we know was Javier, and the other was a partial glimpse of an unidentified man.'

'And you think that partial glimpse was Merrick's recruiter?' Rían pieced it together.

'Yes. And I think it's Rory.'

'Back to Rory again.' Rían sighed. 'I feel like we're being played. Chasing our tails. Running an endless loop while Merrick laughs.'

'I know what you mean,' Jasmin admitted. 'It's like we're puppets and Merrick is pulling our strings.'

The urge to just give up and walk away gripped her. But then she looked at Allie's empty chair. Where she should be sitting, her legs pulled up as she fidgeted with her coins. Jasmin pushed on. 'We need to show Thuli pictures of him, Freddie, Javier and Lorcan.' Instinct told her not to cross Lorcan off just yet. 'Thuli's agreed to look at them when she gets back from her field trip. Or maybe we could email her?'

'I don't want Thuli involved.' Imogen bit her lip. 'She doesn't know what's going on. If she gets hurt, I'll never forgive myself.'

'But she could really help us,' Rían said gently.

Jasmin watched as Imogen battled inwardly. Her protective instinct towards Thuli against her desire to know.

'On one condition,' Imogen relented. 'I will do it, in person. I need to explain some of the context. And the danger. She can't agree to help if she doesn't know the risks.'

'That's fair,' Jasmin agreed.

'Do you think he was trying to recruit Allie?' Imogen said

in a small voice. Their coffees had long gone cold, but she lifted her cup and drank from it.

'I think Allie had a lead and followed it without telling us. She wanted to prove herself.' Jasmin regretted the words as soon as she said them. She hadn't meant it as a dig at Imogen, but Jasmin knew from her downcast eyes that it stung.

'If the recruiter does Merrick's dirty work,' Rían said thoughtfully, 'if he's the one who gets close, then he is likely to be Niamh's murderer. Who else could have lured her down to the shed and encouraged her to drink tequila? He must also have given her the diazepam.'

'And then he got close to Allie and killed her too.' Imogen's voice was husky.

'But he and Merrick are arguing on the phone,' Rían reminded them. 'So cracks are forming.'

Jasmin turned to Imogen. 'You said you found something of Allie's?'

Imogen reached in her bag and placed a phone on the table. It had a small shattering of glass in the corner.

'Allie's phone?' Jasmin exclaimed. 'I thought the guards or her parents would have it.'

'Yesterday morning, before we cleared her room, her parents wanted to see where it happened. They closed the library today, but we were allowed in. We went up to the fifth floor and her mam was in bits, holding on to the railing and sobbing. I tried to comfort her, and we were both sitting on the floor when I saw something under a trolley.'

'The phone?'

'It must have slid across the floor. Maybe in a struggle? I picked it up when Allie's parents were leaving. I did consider giving it to them, but I – I needed to look at it first.'

Rían snorted. They all knew there was no way Imogen would have given up that phone. Not before she'd had a chance to look through it.

She picked up the phone, and the pink skull on the back cover was so achingly Allie. She held it out, showing them the locked screen.

'I charged it up, and I've been trying to get in but I don't know the passcode. Allie tended to forget passwords, so I'm sure it will be something simple. But it's not her birthday. Or any of ours.'

'Sorry, but I have to head,' Jasmin said, realising the time. She had to catch up with homework. She was already so behind, and now she'd missed nearly a week of school.

'We'll walk out with you.'

Jasmin was getting to her feet when she saw Merrick enter the cafe. He was talking animatedly. And beside him, with his hand on the small of her back, was her grandmother.

Imogen snorted. 'Another poor sucker falling for his charm.'

Jasmin was rooted to the floor.

'Jasmin, my sweetheart, there you are.' Her grandmother smiled as she saw her. 'We were just talking about you.'

Imogen's eyes darted from Georgie to Jasmin.

'Georgie, meet Imogen and Rían.' Jasmin nodded to them, feeling anxiety knot her stomach. 'This is my grandmother, Georgie.'

'I am always thrilled to meet Jasmin's friends,' Georgie said. 'Imogen is such a beautiful name.' She made small talk with the friends, vivacious as always, while Jasmin looked for an opportunity to end the encounter. Merrick drew up behind Georgie.

'Hello, Jasmin. Looking forward to seeing you at the gala dinner later this week?'

'Gala dinner?' She remembered Imogen stealing invitations from Merrick's office, but so much had happened in such a short time.

Merrick frowned. 'Didn't Javier brief you? We need you to help out on Friday. Can you make it?'

'Of course.'

'I'll get Javier to send the details. He was supposed to have done that days ago. Now, Georgie, shall we get a coffee?'

'Black for me, dear. I'll find a table.' Georgie beamed up at Merrick, who went to place their orders.

'We're just leaving.' Jasmin hugged her grandmother. And then, quietly, so only Georgie could hear, she said, 'What's Merrick talking to you about?'

'Oh, just catching up. He asked about some papers that belonged to your grandfather. Some old research he was interested in. Told him I wouldn't have had a clue, unfortunately.' She smiled at Jasmin. 'Don't worry so much, darling. You go and have fun with your friends.'

Jasmin drew back, trying to read Georgie's eyes. 'I'll see you later,' she said. What papers could Merrick be searching for?

She followed her friends out of the cafe. 'Why was your

grandmother with Merrick?' Imogen said as they neared Rían's car.

'My grandmother knows everyone,' Jasmin said. 'He's probably after her money. Looking for investors.'

'Do all his potential investors call him "dear"?' Imogen said. 'They seemed like old friends.'

Imogen didn't even try to hide the suspicion from her voice. And Jasmin had to admit, in her shoes, she would be suspicious too.

FORTY

Later that afternoon, Jasmin was in her room. She was meant to be studying but she pushed her books away and picked up her sketch pad, flicking through her drawings. What had started as charcoal portraits for school had become her own personal project.

She paused at her portrait of Imogen. Like Allie, Imogen was rendered accurately on the page, with immaculate hair, heart-shaped face, intelligent eyes. The monstrous features were small, just a few scales on her neck, the teeth slightly too sharp, a suggestion of lizard in the eyes. The hint of something other threatening to take over.

Her beloved monsters. Her beautiful monsters.

Damien with a thick armoured skin, flexed muscles that were part stone, the slight suggestion of horns in his soft hair. Rían's features smudging into a chaos of shadow, part over-defined, part melted into shade. Pretty Allie, half her features overlaid with that of a skull, the hollow eyes, the grimacing mouth.

And what of herself, Jasmin wondered? What sort of monster would she be?

The true artist always leaves something of themself in their art.

Maybe the monster in her friends was all Jasmin.

Her phone buzzed with a text from Damien asking if he'd see her later. She smiled. He'd spent every night here since Allie died. He came around midnight and she'd quietly let him in, and they'd spend the night in each other's arms.

Packing her art away, she went next door to see Georgie. She still didn't like that her grandmother had been out with Merrick that morning.

Benedict was at the table, drinking a cup of tea and doing the crossword. The ordinariness of this afternoon scene calmed her.

'Jasmin,' he said, 'come and help me. This new crossword setter will be the death of me.'

Jasmin shook her head. 'You're not dragging me down with you, Benedict. Where's Georgie?'

He looked up from the crossword. A shadow passed his eyes. 'In the study.'

Jasmin caught her breath. For ten years Georgie had avoided that room. Until now. Until Merrick.

'Is she OK?'

Benedict hesitated. 'I think she is. I think this is necessary, if exceedingly uncomfortable for her.'

Georgie was sitting near the study window. She was talking on the phone, voice low. She glanced up, saw Jasmin, and ended the call.

'Who were you talking to just now?'

'Oh, just the girls, you know how they can go on.' She moved away from the window, slipping her phone in her pocket. 'This is a lovely surprise.' Her voice sounded strained.

'I thought we could take a walk.' Jasmin tried to keep her tone light. 'Maybe go down to the park?'

'Excellent idea. I've got a few things to finish up here first – I'll stop by for you.'

You'd have to know Georgie really well to catch it, but something was wrong. It was there in her voice. The way she couldn't quite meet Jasmin's eye.

'What things? Can I help?' asked Jasmin.

Georgie gave her a long look and then exhaled. 'I'm taking your grandfather's old things to Theo.'

Jasmin felt her skin prickle. 'Why?'

'I need this room for something else. A pottery studio, in fact. No point in holding on to these dusty old notes when there's someone actually interested in them.'

'You don't do pottery.' Jasmin folded her arms.

'Then now's a good time to start.' Georgie stood up. 'If you want to make yourself useful, then bring those boxes over there to the car.'

'Why Merrick?' Jasmin said.

'He adored your grandfather.' Georgie pulled the thick tape and sealed a box. 'When Theo was working on his PhD, he would come here all the time. He'd have dinner with us and we'd all talk late into the night. I think he deserves to have them.' She made for the door, stopping at the hall mirror. 'Load those in the car, will you? I'm going to put on my lipstick.'

'What if ... ?' Jasmin didn't know how to say it so she rushed in. 'What if Grandpa wants them back?'

Georgie paused, her top lip now a soft pinkish red. 'Jasmin, there's something I haven't told you and I should have. Your grandfather was released a few months ago.' She finished her bottom lip and then capped the lipstick.

Jasmin remembered him standing outside Riverview, and then her quick glimpse of him at *The Book of Monsters*. She'd shut down both experiences, stuffed them deep inside her. Wouldn't allow herself to think about it afterwards. Because even just thinking about him let him in, and she needed to protect her heart.

'Don't worry, Eamon won't come near us again.' Georgie's intelligent eyes searched Jasmin's face. 'He's moved to a remote village near the sea to be near his sister. But he was here, at the house, about a week ago.' Seeing the alarm on Jasmin's face, Georgie added, 'Dash and Benedict were here to chaperone. Eamon collected his clothes and personal items that were stored in the garage. I asked about all his old research and he didn't want any of it.' She let out something that was half exhale, half laugh. 'It's probably all out of date anyway.'

'Why didn't you tell me?' *Dash saw him and I didn't?* Jasmin felt a stab of jealousy.

'We were going to, Jasmin. Then your friend died and

you were distraught. You were always so close to your grand-father. He asked after you, but … we wanted to let things settle first.'

I wish I'd seen him, Jasmin thought. *I wish I could have seen him properly, just once more.*

'We don't stop loving people, even if they do terrible things,' Georgie said softly, heading towards the front door.

'What did he take?' Jasmin asked.

'He wanted only his art. His pens, paper and other supplies, and his drawings. The part of himself that he'd shared so easily with you. That I see in you.' Georgie's eyes were glistening as she opened the door. 'I think he's making a new start. No more science. And it's time for me to move on too. Make my yoga studio, let the light back into all parts of my home. Bring that box there, will you?'

Jasmin picked up the box and went outside into the grey day. The shrubs around the garden wall were still green, but around them naked trees reached their branches up to the lowering sky.

'Later we can choose some paint for my new music room.' Georgie popped the boot.

'You mean pottery studio?' Jasmin tucked the box into the corner. 'Or was it yoga?'

'Maybe I need a meditation room?' Georgie mused.

'Dance studio. Definitely.'

Georgie gave her an impish smile. And then they set off, the Rolling Stones playing a little louder than was seemly for a grandma.

A few minutes later, they turned into Rory's road and parked outside the now familiar house.

'This is the address,' Georgie said, squinting at the text message, several times magnified on her phone. She looked at the house dubiously. 'I expected something modern. Theo strikes me as the modern type.'

'He doesn't live here at Riverview,' Jasmin clarified begrudgingly. 'His brother does. Stepbrother. But Merrick seems to come and go as he pleases.'

The gate opened, and Merrick stepped into the road. He wore jeans and a jumper and an expression of unbridled glee.

He air-kissed Georgie while the boot popped. 'Don't you go doing the heavy lifting now. Leave that to me.'

He greeted Jasmin and reached for a large box while she took the smallest.

'Where is this going?' she said as she stepped inside the house. 'Your study?'

'They'll be stored upstairs. Leave it here and come into the kitchen. I've put the kettle on.'

'I'll carry it up, no problem.' It was a small resistance, refusing to do what he told her, but she'd take her victories where she could. Jasmin gave him a fetching smile and started up the stairs before Merrick could stop her.

At the old study-turned-gym, she looked down the hall, wondering if Rory was still cheating on his tests. Imogen hadn't reported him – not yet anyway. She stepped inside, remembering how she and Allie had hidden in there.

The gym equipment was messily stacked on the floor. A

used towel tossed on the bench. It smelt stale. But all she saw was Allie. Allie pacing the room. Allie studying the books on the shelf. She dropped the box and walked to the bookshelf, remembering Allie standing right there.

They'd had a moment that night. Allie had spoken honestly to Jasmin. *I never know what to say and I feel like this awkward lump, just standing there with a mouth full of teeth.* Jasmin felt her throat tighten.

She picked up the wobbly dog toy, remembering how Allie had played with it. She had knocked over a framed photo too. Cracked the glass.

Both the pictures on display had their glass intact, so Rory must have removed the one that Allie had cracked. Jasmin moved closer to study the pictures. She picked up one of an older man with the same strong jaw and bright eyes as Theo Merrick. His dad obviously, pictured with a sullen teenaged Theo, a woman and two girls, one older, one younger, who looked a lot like him, and a young child, Rory. Merrick's dad must have married Rory's mother – who didn't look a whole lot older than the elder daughter. Examining the photo, Jasmin was sure that Merrick and his sisters had resented it. They looked miserable in the picture, a decidedly unhappy family.

It didn't take a genius to deduce that the stepbrothers didn't have the best relationship even now, and that Rory begrudged Merrick for the withheld inheritance. It felt like Merrick's easy use of this house was a power move, meant to hold Rory in check. Jasmin wondered if Rory's many parties were a counterstrike.

Did their difficult relationship make it more or less likely that Rory was Merrick's recruiter?

'Jasmin? What are you doing here?' Rory said from the doorway. He held back from saying 'snooping again?', but the arch of his eyebrow suggested that it might have crossed his mind.

'My grandmother and I brought some boxes for Theo. My grandfather's old papers.' She put the photo down, thinking about this strange family that didn't seem to love each other. 'What's it like, having such a famous, high-achieving stepbrother?'

Rory stood behind her as she reached for the other picture, this time of an older Merrick, his dad and his sisters. They were cut from the same fabric, thick hair in varying shades of dark blonde and bright eyes.

He snorted. 'Let's just say we're very different.'

'What would he do if he found out you were cheating on your tests?'

Rory looked away, but she saw his jaw tic. 'He'd be delighted. He'd enjoy that I'd be kicked out of university. That I would have to let him come and go here, still the man in charge, until I'm thirty.'

'Those are Merrick's sisters?' Jasmin pointed to the women in the picture.

'Yeah, Helen and Nuala.' Rory shifted uncomfortably. 'Helen ran away before we moved in, but I've heard she's troubled. Nuala's no better than Theo. They never liked us. They've always been aloof and sneery, as if they're better. And it's not just me. You should see how they tr—' He shook his head. 'Trust me. They're not good people.'

Jasmin looked at him, feeling a tug of pity. Rory fitted uncomfortably within his family, and it seemed like Merrick was at least partly responsible for that.

'When Mam died,' Rory swallowed thickly, 'it wasn't easy, living here with them. When Riverview is transferred to me, I'll sell up and never see any of them again.'

Jasmin's heart swelled. The heat in his words made her realise that everyone saw only the tip of the iceberg. That his cheating on the tests had been an act of real desperation, and that he wasn't simply a lazy party boy looking for the easiest way out.

'I hope it works out for you.' She meant it.

And now she was second-guessing her certainty that he was the recruiter. It made her want to scream. With every step forward came a step back.

From downstairs, she heard the sound of Georgie calling. 'Jasmin, dear, we're leaving.'

'I hear you are his newest project assistant,' Rory said.

'Word travels fast.'

Again that tic in his jaw that made her feel that Rory had something more to say.

'Jasmin!' came Georgie's voice.

'You'd better go.' Rory stepped aside and their moment was over.

Jasmin bounded down the stairs and found Georgie and Theo on the front path. Georgie was mid-sentence.

'... settling down in a small seaside town. His sister has a house near the beach.'

'A small beach town.' Merrick exhaled loudly. 'This sounds so unlike the man I knew.'

'Well, he surprised us all,' Georgie said lightly, pushing her sunglasses down and hiding her eyes.

'I feel conflicted about taking these.' Merrick glanced at the remaining box. Hungrily, Jasmin thought. 'Won't he want his papers?'

'Oh, he didn't want them. He told me to get rid. Just took some of his art things.'

'And he left all his papers?' Merrick said incredulously. 'His research?'

'It will surely be outdated by now?'

'In some ways, but his thinking, his method. That's all here.'

'And all yours now.' She gestured to Jasmin. 'There you are. Shall we go?' She smiled at her granddaughter. 'I think we're done here.'

FORTY-ONE

Jasmin watched Georgie's car pull away from Riverview, feeling Merrick's eyes on her. She'd told Georgie she would go and see her friends and make her own way home. But now, beneath the weight of his gaze, Jasmin wondered if she was out of her depth. Taking a risk that she would regret.

She returned Merrick's gaze. 'Can we talk? It'll only take a minute.'

'Sure. Do you want to stay for a bite? Or a coffee?'

Monsters have to use their teeth, if they are to survive. Eamon's words from long ago echoed in her mind.

'No. This won't take long.'

He guided her inside. Entering his bright, modern study, Jasmin felt again that it was incongruent with the rest of the house.

She smiled sweetly. 'Actually, do you mind if I have that coffee after all?'

Mild annoyance flashed momentarily in his eyes but he was gracious as always. 'Of course. I'll make a pot.'

She watched Merrick leave for the kitchen, calling, 'Oat milk, if you have it.'

When his footfall faded, she took her phone from her small messenger bag. She opened the camera, setting it to video. She hit the record button and stuffed it back into her bag, with the camera lens showing. Just as Niamh had done before. She placed it on the floor, tilting up and facing the armchair across the room.

Jasmin wasn't naive. She knew she was up against a Goliath, that no one would believe a schoolgirl over the esteemed Professor Merrick. But she had to try.

Merrick came in with a French press filled with hot coffee and an apology. 'I'm afraid there's not much more than lean meat and beer in Rory's fridge. Will you take it black?'

'That's fine. Thank you.'

He sat on the armchair across from her, the same place he'd sat last time. She could tell from the folds in the light brown suede that it was his preferred seat. She nudged her bag with her foot to shift it slightly nearer.

'What did you want to talk about?' Merrick pressed down the coffee plunger.

'My grandfather.'

He looked up sharply.

'Everyone remembers him as this monster, the man who attacked his wife.' Jasmin let her voice crack. 'He's reduced to this cartoon villain, when he was so much more than that. *You*

333

remember him, the real him. You don't define him by his single terrible mistake.'

'You were close,' Merrick said.

'I never really got over him leaving,' Jasmin replied truthfully. 'I've always felt like something essential is missing.' Until recently. Until she met the friends. 'And not being able to even mention him … It's like I've been gagged all this time. The other day, in your office, it was … liberating. To simply *talk* about him again.'

Merrick poured their coffee. It smelt rich and nutty. 'Your grandfather wasn't only a scientist, he was a philosopher. He was a true scholar, in the purest sense of the word. His life's purpose was the search for knowledge.'

'*To think unfettered. To discover and explore, without constraint,*' Jasmin quoted as she took the cup of coffee. He'd first said that to her on her eighth birthday, but it became a mantra. 'He inspired me. That's also the reason I wanted to talk to you. You see, I've decided to follow in his footsteps.'

'You're applying here? To study science?'

Jasmin nodded. 'I want to continue the work he started.' She lifted her chin. 'His real work. The research that truly mattered to him, not what he did to keep the university administrators happy.'

Merrick was silent for a moment. When he spoke again, his voice was casual. 'Did he ever talk to you about it?'

'Yes, all the time. But there was only so much I understood. Or remember. He tried to make the mice live longer. We'd mark off their days on the board.'

'That's right.' Merrick stretched his legs out in front of him. 'Your grandfather asked me a question once: *Are you a king or a soldier?* I had no idea what he was talking about. He laughed. He told me to come back after I'd read the *Immortalis*.'

'The story of the monstrous king who sacrificed his soldiers to make himself supernaturally strong. From *The Book of Monsters*. Yes, he told me that story too. Many times.'

'Your childhood bedtimes must have been mildly terrifying.'

'When Grandpa did it, yes.' She leaned forward. 'But terrifying in a good way. In a way that makes us fully alive. Not safe and hiding. Grandpa wasn't like that. He didn't want me to be like that.'

'Your grandfather's private research was about enhancing the physical body,' Merrick said, 'making it stronger and more efficient. And one aspect of this was longevity. He wanted to slow down the ageing process. There's been a lot of money pumped into this in the last decade, and developments in stem cell research, with Klotho and Yamanaka factors. Things are moving. The human lifespan has, of course, been extended. But extending youth itself … restoring health and vigour … science has only got so far.'

'And that's what you want to do,' Jasmin said softly.

'Eamon lit a spark in me, all those years ago. I've made it my life's work to finish what he started. It's only a matter of time before a major breakthrough in anti-ageing. The research is right at the cusp.' Merrick regarded her steadily. 'Not for publications or glory. I want to know, and I want to know first.'

Raising the hot, bitter coffee to her lips, Jasmin understood. It wasn't immortality that Merrick prized. It was discovery. To join that elite, those who knew the mysteries others couldn't begin to understand. *Knowing*, this was Merrick's drug, the kingship he yearned for. And it looked like he would do anything to get it.

'Is that why you wanted my grandfather's research notes?'

'They'd give me insights into how his mind worked. Nudge me to ask the right questions.' Merrick was poised, elbows on the armrest and both feet on the ground. This was a man who was sure of himself. 'These days, it seems like his notes are the best way to sustain a dialogue with him.'

'You are so like him,' Jasmin said. Her heart was beating too fast. 'Refusing to be constrained or limited by rules.' She widened her eyes. 'I saw the last time I was here that you have cages in the room next door. Do you test on mice too?'

'I have,' he said, his eyes searching hers. 'But I'm beyond testing on mice now. I like that you ask questions.' He stood up. 'But if you want answers, you'll have to earn them. Along with my trust.'

Jasmin felt breathless. 'I want to win your trust. Tell me how?'

Merrick's smile was slow and cunning. 'You could start by giving me a blood sample. And you won't tell anyone that you've done it.'

'My blood?' Jasmin faltered. She was sure that this was highly irregular. That there were rules about blood-sampling for research, and that Merrick drawing her blood in his home study, while swearing her to secrecy, was not the proper protocol.

'Just a small sample to use in my experiments. Only if you

want to, of course. I won't do anything that makes you uncomfortable.'

Jasmin suspected that if she said no, she'd fail the first hurdle. That Merrick required his favourites to be comfortable with things that really should make them pause for thought. She exhaled. 'OK.'

'I'll be right back.' He got to his feet, then made for the adjoining room.

As she clenched her fist to ready a vein, she saw herself as if from the outside: in Merrick's chair, willingly giving him her blood. *For strong as the human impulse is to survive, it is also in the nature of humans to sacrifice themselves for the right cause.*

And here she was, willingly giving Merrick, the self-styled king, what he wanted. Because she believed it was for the right cause, even if hers wasn't aligned with Merrick's. But maybe this was how it started. You conceded your boundaries one by one, *for the right cause.* Until you found yourself lost down a dark road.

Is that what happened to Niamh? To Allie?

Jasmin adjusted her messenger bag so it would catch her on camera too, just before Merrick returned with a medical kit. He took blue gloves and a syringe from the kit, peeling back the seal on a vial. 'You'll just feel a pinch. Don't worry. I've done this many times.'

Jasmin glanced at the phone peeking out of her bag pocket, and hoped she'd framed it correctly.

'Why don't you want me to tell anyone?' she said. 'Not that I would. Just curious.'

He laughed softly. 'You certainly are. That's what I like about you.' He hesitated and she thought he wouldn't answer. But then he said, 'If this were official, I would need to do a risk assessment, get ethics approval, written consent and fulfil the various conditions the university demands. There would be a record.'

'You don't want a record of this?' Jasmin didn't flinch when the needle entered the vein in her arm.

'No.' His answer was short. She was pushing too hard.

When he was finished, Merrick carefully labelled the vial and put it in his kit. 'Good work, Jasmin. It means a lot to me to have you on board. Candice thought I was being foolishly sentimental by inviting you to be my newest project assistant, but I knew you were right for us.'

'I've earned your trust?'

'You've taken the first step.'

'When you said you were beyond testing on mice –' Jasmin got to her feet, sensing her time with Merrick this afternoon was ending – 'what did you mean?'

'What happens after the preclinical stage where you test on animals?' Merrick said.

'The clinical trials, where you test on humans?'

He gave one quick nod. 'Now, if you'll excuse me, I have to get back to work. The dinner starts at eight on Friday, I'll see you there at seven?'

She picked up her bag, pushing the phone out of sight. 'I'll be there.'

FORTY-TWO

On Friday evening at five thirty, Jasmin went up the stairs of the house in Burgess Street. She'd styled her hair and wore her faux fur and a silk little black dress, the one she hauled out when Sonia or Georgie made her go to a function.

'Jasmin,' Rían exclaimed loudly as she entered his room. 'You look …' He gave a chef's kiss, a touch too loud and too big. He wore a well-fitting three-piece suit in burgundy. His eyes had dark shadows beneath them and there was a brittleness to him. He tucked his stolen gala dinner invitation into the breast pocket.

'I'm glad you'll be there tonight.' Jasmin gave him a kiss on the cheek.

On the coffee table was a large picture of Allie surrounded by candles. Jasmin sat on the low bench, across from Imogen. The three had gone to Allie's funeral in Kildare the previous day. Jasmin had intended to go, but in an excruciating conversation, Imogen had asked her not to, saying that this was the best way she could pay her respects to Allie.

'When you're around, Damien only sees you,' Imogen had said. 'Give him a chance to say goodbye to Allie. Let her have that too.' She had been firm, though Jasmin had wanted to protest Imogen's reading of things. But she remembered Allie's reservations about her, and glumly agreed to do as Imogen asked.

'How was home?' Jasmin said to Imogen, who'd stayed two days with her mother.

'My mam wanted us to bond. She took time off work. My mother, who never cooks, made chicken soup. It was disgusting.'

'That sounds like she was trying to look after you,' Jasmin said gently.

'Look after me?' Imogen spat. 'She made me walk on the freezing cold beach, trying to get me to talk about my feelings.' Her outrage was almost comical. 'The only thing I feel is a burning fury for that prick Merrick.'

Jasmin looked at the murder wall, which had been created anew and was busier than ever. Post-its flapped untidily. Marker ink had been scratched on the wall itself, like Rían had been trying to find the formula for Allie's loss.

Jasmin accepted a small delicate teacup filled with flowery tea from Rían as Damien came in. He was wearing a smart shirt and slacks and a jacket that looked like it had been borrowed from Rían. Rían was taller and Damien broader so it didn't quite fit. He still looked painfully handsome.

'We're long overdue a murder meeting,' Imogen moaned,

clearly still disgruntled at her mother's attempts to coddle her.
'And at the top of the agenda today is cracking Allie's passcode.'
She took Allie's phone from her bag and waved it. 'Anyone have
any ideas?'

'I know Allie's code,' Damien sounded surprised. 'It wasn't
a secret. You know it too. We even joked what a useless passcode
it was.'

'Ah, that's right. I remember now.' Rían slapped his hand to
his head. 'What was it again? The last digits of her phone
number? Something stupidly obvious.'

'Well, I clearly wasn't there that day,' Imogen huffed. 'And I
wish your memories would have resurfaced a few days ago.
We're losing time.'

'Sorry, Imogen,' Damien said. 'I missed that you were
looking for the code.' His shoulders rose and slumped. 'I got
distracted.'

'I'm sorry too,' Imogen said immediately. 'I know. I don't
expect you to read every last message or hang on my every
word.'

'Touching, but maybe we should get into Allie's phone
before we have to leave for the dinner?' Rían curled his hand in
a move-it-on gesture.

'It's the numbers that correspond to the letters in her name,'
Damien said. 'Allie V. You know Allie could never remember
codes or passwords, so she kept it simple.'

His voice was raw with pain. Always the small details that
trip you up. Rían and Imogen were now lost in memories of
Allie and her inability to remember passwords.

'Nope, definitely don't remember that conversation,' Imogen said, waking up the phone.

'That is so Allie,' Rían said sadly. Fondly.

'Right, so two, five, five, four –' Imogen entered the numbers – 'three, eight … Mother of Satan,' she breathed out when she got in. 'It was right there all along.' She went straight to Allie's messages, finding her last message to her parents. *This is for the best. Please don't be angry with me.* Just as they'd been told.

It had been sent at eight thirty, which was the same time that Allie had fallen.

Had that message been sent before or after she went over the railing?

'Her last words were "Please don't be angry with me."' Imogen pressed the heels of her palms to her eyes. 'Jesus.'

'She never did like people getting mad at her.' Rían edged in closer, slipping an arm around Imogen and giving her a quick squeeze. 'Check the other messages.'

'Find out who she went out with that night,' Jasmin urged. 'When Thuli saw her at Messy Jack's.'

'The same fella Thuli saw with Niamh,' Rían added excitedly. 'Who is it, Imogen? He has to be in there.'

Imogen scrolled down, pausing at their group chat and others, past Allie's belly dancing chat, scrolling by the message thread between Allie and Jasmin arranging to meet at the library. Finally, Imogen clicked on a message.

She took a sharp inhale. Her eyes met Jasmin's.

'Who is it?' Jasmin said. 'Who did Allie meet that night? Who did Thuli see?'

Imogen put the phone down. Her face was stone.

'She was with Dash.'

The blood drained from Jasmin's head. She felt dizzy. Rían looked confused. Damien had a dawning horror on his face. Imogen looked cold.

Jasmin was on her feet, though she had no memory of standing up. Her fists were clenched.

'I should have known.' Imogen shook her head, her voice like ice. 'See, I thought it was odd, seeing your grandmother with Merrick at the Three Divas. They seemed like old friends. It made me curious, so I asked an acquaintance in the School of Fine Art and, of course, they'd never heard of you.'

'Imogen, wait,' Damien said. 'Slow down. Don't jump to conclusions.'

'So I did some more investigating,' Imogen went on as if she hadn't heard him. 'You lied. You're not an art student – you're still at school. Your grandmother is pals with Merrick because he was one of your grandfather's students. Your famous – no, infamous – grandfather, Eamon Larkin. Who went to jail for trying to kill your grandmother.'

'I didn't tell you –' Jasmin swallowed – 'because I was scared you'd think of me differently if you found out.'

'That's not all though, is it? Your brother, Dash, was out with Allie the night before she died. He was the one Merrick got to sweet-talk people for his trials. He got close to Niamh, recruited her, for Merrick. And then killed her, for Merrick. Allie was suspicious of you. And then out of the blue your brother got close to her.' Imogen choked back a sob. 'Your brother killed Allie, because you're one of them. You've been one of them from the start.'

'Imogen, that's not true,' Jasmin cried. 'If I was working with them, then why would I give you Niamh's SD card? Why would I help you at all?'

'The SD card that was conveniently stolen?' Imogen shrugged. 'I don't know how your sick mind works. Maybe you were trying to throw us off. Maybe Merrick isn't the bad guy after all. Maybe all of this comes back to your grandfather's illegal experiments. Maybe your brother is carrying on his work and you've been deliberately feeding us false information, pointing the finger at Merrick.'

Imogen was shouting now. Rían was hunched with misery. Beside him, Damien had gone pale with shock.

'What I do know is that I never want to see you again. Because if we hadn't met you, Allie would still be alive.' Her voice was pitched low, guttural. 'And believe me, I will make sure you pay.'

Jasmin stared at Imogen for an awful, endless moment. She felt the tapestried walls pressing in. She looked round at her friends – or at the people who had been her friends. She'd been wrong. This wasn't her place. There was no room for her here.

She turned and fled. Out of Rían's room, down the stairs and into the road. She was wearing heeled boots but she ran down the road, then the next, until her chest burned. In the distance was the bridge where she'd stood with Rían not long ago. *How do you think you'll die?* She took a deep breath, filling her lungs with air, then started running again.

Hearing a car approach slowly, Jasmin ducked into an alcove. It was Damien's car, crawling the streets. Looking for her.

Her heart flipped as she thought about their discovery. *Dash*.

Dash was Allie's mystery date and Niamh's mystery boyfriend? She clutched her stomach, trying to keep calm. Trying to ward off the dread.

She dialled Dash's number, but there was no answer.

Her eyes stung with unshed tears. She wouldn't cry. She would prove that it wasn't Dash. She had to. It couldn't be him. Not the gentle brother she'd known her whole life.

But she would once have said the same about her grandfather.

She didn't know what to believe any more.

The first drops of rain began to fall. She was going to walk to the McKellan, but it was raining.

But it's raining. The forbidden words she'd uttered that first night in Rían's room. Her punishment had been a rain dance. *We'll come with you, this time*, Damien had said, and it hadn't been a punishment at all.

But tonight was a punishment. This time she was out in the rain, alone.

She walked for a few more minutes, huddling into her faux fur, which was matting in the drizzle. Seeing a taxi approach, she hailed it.

'The McKellan Galleries, please,' she said to the driver and sat back in the seat, thinking about what she had to do next.

Jasmin gazed out of the window, watching the familiar landscape. This was Merrick's fault. If Dash was involved, it was because Merrick had forced his hand.

Merrick was the king, Dash was merely the soldier.

If she wanted to protect Dash, she had to get to Merrick.

FORTY-THREE

When Jasmin reached the event room at the McKellan, the place had been transformed. The large wooden dividers had been opened entirely, creating one large hall. Round tables had been set out with autumnal flower arrangements and tall tapered candles in silver candlesticks. She searched the room for Merrick, seeing only Javier talking to the catering staff.

'Jasmin, there you are.' Javier spotted her and beelined towards her, giving her a list of things to check. 'I need you to place the goodie bags, and then ...' he rattled off instructions.

'Who's doing the AV display?' Jasmin said, when she could get a word in.

Javier frowned and checked his clipboard. 'Someone from Candice's office.' He glanced to a window at the back of the event room. 'Thanks for reminding me. I should get the lighting set too.'

He bustled to the back of the hall, and a moment later he

reappeared in the window, talking to the woman there. That was the control booth, Jasmin surmised, where the AV display would play from.

The house lights dipped, then changed as Javier explored various presets. Jasmin got started on her tasks, the anger and dread still holding her in their grip. Dumping the last goodie bag on a chair, she marched over to Javier in the booth.

'We didn't finish our conversation in the library,' she said.

'Yeah, I know. How are you coping?' Javier surprised her with his gentleness. He put up a good front, but she wondered if he was as messed up about it as she was. 'I'm sorry about Allie, I know you were friends.'

'I don't think she liked me that much,' Jasmin said honestly.

'Does that matter?' he said. 'You spent time together. You were friends.'

'Why did you and Niamh argue that night?' Jasmin said, changing the subject. 'Why did you warn her that she would regret something?'

Javier drew her aside and glanced around, checking the door. 'I'm telling you this because I know you need answers. But this is a matter for the guards, and you and your friends have to stop your little investigation.'

'We … we're not doing that any more.'

'OK. Niamh had found something out, about Merrick,' he said, voice dropping even lower. 'She wouldn't tell me what, just that she was gathering information. That night she told me she'd got what she needed. I thought she was going to report him to the university ethics committee. But she told me she was going to blackmail him instead.'

'Blackmail?'

'I begged her to walk away. Take it to the dean. But she was adamant that she would use the information as leverage. I was furious. Scared for her. Told her it was too dangerous.'

'That she would regret it?'

'Yes.' He exhaled the word. 'We didn't talk again until the night of the lecture.'

'Freddie said you argued at the reception.'

'She was furious with me. Said I'd ditched her when she most needed a friend. I saw then that she was terrified. I think she'd realised that Merrick was a dangerous man. She'd met him in his office earlier and he'd lashed out at her. Before that she'd been optimistic, thinking she could take him down. That afternoon, he showed her exactly how much stronger he was. How much she stood to lose, if she went ahead trying to blackmail a man like him.'

That had been the afternoon Jasmin first saw Niamh, she realised. Niamh had been crying, scared. *He's a monster.*

'She was murdered because she'd threatened to blackmail Merrick,' Javier said. 'When I saw you doing the same thing, messing around in Merrick's business, I was desperate to stop you. Because I didn't stop Niamh.'

'You think Merrick killed her.' Jasmin felt relieved that someone else had seen it too, how sinister and dangerous he was.

Javier's voice was even. 'Of course he killed her. Or *had her killed* – because Theo doesn't get his hands dirty. You should

349

leave this alone, Jasmin. He will hurt you and anyone who gets in his way.'

'But you're working for him,' she said.

'I want him to pay for what he did to Niamh. As soon as I have enough evidence, I'm taking it to the guards.'

'So you can go snooping around Merrick's business but I can't?'

'He barely notices me,' Javier said. 'But he's wanted you on board ever since he noticed you at the lecture. It's a feather in his cap to have Eamon Larkin's beloved granddaughter involved.'

'Did you speak to Niamh that afternoon?' Jasmin thought of the anxious phone call that Niamh had made. 'Did you arrange to meet her at the alumni lecture?'

Javier shook his head. 'I was hoping to see her there, we obviously needed to talk, hopefully patch things up. But I hadn't arranged to meet her there.'

There was someone else then, someone that Niamh had in her confidence. Jasmin remembered asking Dash if he'd met Niamh over the summer, and his reply that he had. Her stomach squirmed. She thought again about the accusations that Imogen had hurled, accusations about her brother, and she thought she was going to be sick.

There was just one more question she had to ask.

'Javier, how did you hear that Merrick needed a project assistant?'

He frowned at her. 'Dash told me. Why?'

Dash told me.

Javier continued talking but Jasmin couldn't hear anything above the ringing in her ears. It felt like she was underwater, everything muted.

It had to end tonight.

And the only way was to take down the king.

FORTY-FOUR

In the restroom, Jasmin looked at herself in the full-length mirror, at her touched-up make-up, the mascara making her lashes long and thick. Shoving the tube back into her bag, she straightened her spine. She was ready. She would do this. She turned the corner, and stopped still. At the wash basins was Imogen.

Imogen narrowed her eyes. Jasmin put her hands on her hips. 'I thought friends would listen to each other before judging.'

'I guess we were never really friends.' Imogen shook out her wet hands and reached for the hand dryer. It blasted hot air, making it impossible for Jasmin to respond.

She turned away, refusing to let Imogen see the hurt on her face. She dried her hands and left.

The guests were mingling in the event room, slowly drifting towards their tables. They were an elegant audience with their expensive black suits, their silk and velvet, their bejewelled hands and necks. On a giant screen, a video played on repeat. Images of smiling, shining young people glowing with health.

Jasmin inspected the room, seeing Merrick with Candice, focused in a brisk discussion. Presumably last checks before he took the stage. Then she slipped into the control booth. Inside was a young woman in a fuzzy jumper, chewing gum and looking bored.

'I'm Jasmin, the new project assistant. Theo said you could take a short break. I'll cover for you.'

The woman frowned. 'Oh, but we're about to start.'

'Small delay. He said you should nip out for five minutes now. There won't be time later.'

The woman hesitated.

'Your choice.' Jasmin made to leave, anxiety tightening her chest.

'Fine, I'm starving.' She smiled and stretched. 'Candice seemed super-stressed.'

'They have a lot riding on tonight. The caterers are amazing,' Jasmin gushed, 'and if you're gone ten minutes, that's between us.' She mimed zipping her lips.

When the door swung shut, Jasmin quickly got to work. She pulled the computer towards her and opened her online storage.

Hearing voices outside the door, she moved fast, clicking to download the clip she'd recorded. She'd cut it to Merrick drawing her blood, admitting that he was breaking the rules.

Jasmin was sure that if she took it to the university it would be buried under the red tape of an investigation. She didn't have proof that he'd had Niamh killed, or that he planned to test on students. But she had enough to make him lose credibility.

If she played the clip here tonight, in front of his funders, it could hit Merrick hard. No one wanted to invest in a rule-breaking scientist, and it might be enough to stop the upcoming clinical trials.

Her heart was racing so fast she could hear it. She would add the clip to the presentation, hiding it three or four slides in. A soft ding indicated the download was complete and –

A hand closed on her wrist and she cried out in pain. Merrick pulled her away, shoving her hard against the wall of the small room.

His eyes were cold and furious as he reached for the keyboard. She launched at him and he pushed her back, harder this time, hitting her head against the wall. A little dazed, she watched as he deleted her video.

'You thought I didn't see you come in here?' he said with infinite calm as he worked. 'All guarded, with shifty eyes? You thought I wouldn't ask Susie why she'd left her post?'

Jasmin cursed herself for forgetting that Merrick saw everything. Even when it appeared that he wasn't looking.

'We are going somewhere quiet to talk.' He advanced towards her, slow and menacing. 'If you make any kind of scene, if you scream or shout or try to attract attention in any way at all, know two things. One, no one will believe you. Two, I will go after Georgie. I won't stop until I finish the job your grandfather started. If you value your grandmother's safety, you'll do as I say. Do you understand?'

She looked at him mutinously, refusing to answer.

'Candice is out in that room with Georgie right now. If we don't appear in the next few seconds, she will hand Georgie a glass of champagne that she's already drugged. Do you understand now?'

Jasmin nodded, her heart beating frantically. He slipped an arm through hers, holding her tight as they left the control room. It looked casual, arms linked with an old friend, but his grip was like iron. On the far side of the room, Jasmin saw Georgie with Candice, who was watching her closely, two glasses of champagne in hand. Jasmin took in a deep, ragged breath as Candice caught Merrick's eye but still held her position.

Jasmin crossed the foyer arm in arm with Merrick. He called hello to someone as they walked. Her head was beginning to pound.

'Smile,' he hissed at her as he waved to someone else. 'And stop looking at the floor.'

Jasmin looked up, and right into the faces of her three friends.

'Unbelievable,' Imogen said, hurt fighting the fury in her eyes.

'Jasmin,' Rían said, reaching out. Damien looked after her, frowning and troubled.

They disappeared down a passage. At the end, beside an outside door, they stopped at a room named the Eamon Larkin

Room. Jasmin had been so proud when her grandfather brought her to see it, only a few weeks before his hasty retirement.

'This seems fitting, doesn't it?' Merrick said, securing the door.

It was a study with a desk and armchairs. Cosy, with a fireplace and shelves of books. On the far side of the room was a pair of French doors. If they were locked, she could break the glass with one of the brass figurines. But how would that help? She couldn't fit through the neat wooden panes.

She felt a cold rage emanating from Merrick. She inched towards the French doors. They had to be unlocked.

The blow caught her off guard. She fell on the floor, ears ringing, the side of her face burning.

He wrapped thick black tape around her ankles and her wrists, then reached into her bag for her phone.

'What's the code?'

Jasmin shook her head, the dull pounding intensifying. The rough tiled carpet was itchy through her black tights and on her cheek.

'I'm not going to keep repeating the same threats,' he said with irritation. 'You've already caused a huge delay and I don't have time to waste. What is the passcode? Or must I ask Candice to bring Georgie here too?'

'Leave Georgie alone.' She told him the code and he found the video. He watched it, his face blank, then deleted it.

'Looks like I was completely wrong about you, Jasmin,' he said. There was disgust in his voice. 'You're nothing like your grandfather.'

'My grandfather might have broken the rules, but he didn't test on students,' Jasmin spat. 'He didn't think that other people were simply there for him to use and discard. Like Niamh. I know you were testing your own personal research on her. And I know you plan to continue your testing, under the cover of your Wellness Formula trials. What happened? Why did Niamh turn on you?'

Merrick's smile was cold. 'She thought she was getting early access to an approved Wellness Formula treatment. That's what I always tell them.'

'But Niamh discovered the truth.'

'She overheard me talking to Candice. And then she tried to blackmail me, which was a foolish move. She'd gathered evidence, apparently. I had to stop her.' He crouched down. 'And unfortunately, I'm going to have to stop you too.'

He looked at his watch.

'I really should get back to my guests. Do you remember the king in the *Immortalis*?' he murmured. 'How did he gain his vitality?'

'Through the sacrifice of the soldiers,' Jasmin said.

'The willing sacrifice. The older generation give life to the young, so should the young give life to the old. The serpent eats its tail.'

The young give life to the old. Jasmin understood then.

'You aren't simply testing on students,' she realised. 'You're harvesting them.' Her eyes widened as she realised Merrick's true purpose. 'That's what you're really after. That's why you took blood samples. And that's what you plan to do in the clinical trials.'

'Blood, and stem cells from bone marrow. You're smarter than Niamh.' Merrick sighed. 'It really is a shame it turned out this way. It would have felt more … complete, with Eamon's granddaughter at my side. Another serpent eating its tail.'

He pressed a piece of tape over her mouth. He shifted, and she choked back a sob when she felt him tie her bound wrists to the radiator. She was trussed up, immobile.

Turning out the lights, Merrick left the room and locked it.

The carpet was rough on her face. Her body was stiff from being bound and held in the same position. She lost track of how much time passed.

When a sound came, Jasmin wasn't sure if she felt relief or dread. It was the door opening quietly, allowing in a triangle of light for a too brief moment. Jasmin tried to move, but her range was limited and pain shot through her shoulder.

Unable to see, she strained to listen.

At the door, they waited. Hesitated.

Then quiet footsteps on the carpet. Slow, deliberate footsteps, edging closer to Jasmin.

Behind the armchair she curled into herself, knowing without doubt that this was danger. The menacingly slow walk. The insistence on darkness and silence. She knew also that it wasn't Merrick. Walking in the shadows wasn't his style: Merrick would have turned on the lights and given her another speech.

The footsteps paused. Her breathing was shallow. She made herself smaller, hoping, somehow, that they wouldn't see her.

Then all too quickly, shoes and trousered legs appeared in front of her. Smart black trousers, shoes that had seen better days. She made herself look up.

Relief flooded her body. Bending, he eased the tape from her lips.

'Damien,' she whispered. 'You came.'

He crouched down to her, reaching a hand to her face. He caressed her cheek.

'How did you get the key?' She lifted her bound arms. 'Untie me quickly, before Merrick comes back.'

'You don't understand,' said Damien. His eyes were unreadable. 'Merrick sent me.'

FORTY-FIVE

Damien smoothed the tape back in place over her mouth, softly, carefully. With a lover's touch.

Something thick and heavy was thrown over her, blacking out the already dark room. He lifted her in his arms, a groom carrying his bride. She wriggled, tried to scream, but he kept a firm grip on her as he crossed the room. She heard a key turn, a door open.

Jasmin felt the cold autumn night seeping through the thick cover. They were outside; Damien must have taken her through the garden door. She heard stones crunching beneath his shoes, then she was lowered on to a soft seat. She smelt the damp mould of his car. He must have moved it right outside the garden door, to reduce the risk of anyone seeing her.

'It has to look like an accident this time.' Merrick's voice reached her. She hadn't realised that he'd come out too. 'Can't have another suicide. Force the car down the embankment and into the river. Make sure she's dead. You'll need to be roughed up too. Move fast, there's a storm coming in.'

'I'll take care of it.'

'I'm sorry, Damien,' said Merrick softly. 'I know you tried.'

'You said you wanted Eamon Larkin's granddaughter, so I stayed on it.'

'Let me know when it's done.' Merrick sounded further away. 'Text the mother and say she's spending the night with friends. That will buy time.'

The car door shut. Then the driver's door opened, and after a moment the car started.

They'd been driving for two minutes when she felt the heavy cover tugged from her face. Damien had reached an arm back to pull the blanket away, but he didn't slow down or look at her.

An accident, she thought. That's what it would look like.

He couldn't stage it until he untied her. It would have to look realistic. And when he untied her, she would fight back. She tried to remember if there was anything in the car she could use as a weapon. Maybe there were tools somewhere? If she was quick enough, she could grab something.

Damien was driving fast now. Not knowing where they were and the high speed made that awful detached feeling take over. The panic settled on her, like a heavy weight squatting on her chest. Her breathing was shallow, quick, making her light-headed.

Three things I can touch, Jasmin remembered the technique her therapist had taught her. *My hands against each other, my cheek on the seat, the tape on my lips.*

A thought is just a thought. A thought can't hurt you.

But Damien can.

Three things I can hear. The car engine straining as he drives too fast. The silence inside the car. The ringing in my ears.

She wasn't doing this right.

Three things I can see: Damien refusing to look at me. Damien's hands on the steering wheel. The man who killed Niamh and Allie. Damien.

The man who wants to kill me.

It had all been a lie. He'd got close to her only to recruit her for Merrick.

He had killed Niamh. He had killed Allie, his friend.

He would kill her.

But Damien was anxious, Jasmin realised. He tried to hide it, but she knew him. She could tell by the way he held the steering wheel, hands locked at twenty to four. He looked into the mirror too frequently. He was afraid someone was following them.

Jasmin really hoped that someone was following them.

The ride was dark and interminable. They were driving on narrow country roads she didn't recognise and she had no idea where he was taking her. Suddenly, the car came to a stop and he got out, leaving the engine running. She heard a rusty squeaking, a sound she was sure she'd heard somewhere, sometime, before. Looking out of the window, she could only see the dark November sky.

Damien got back into the car and drove down a bumpy lane. When he stopped the car, Jasmin saw with a growing dread that she knew where they were. Imogen's cottage, near Lough Drinagh.

In the middle of nowhere. Not a soul around.

Damien got out of the car and opened the back door. He reached for her, gently lifting her. He carried her up the drive, pausing at the lockbox, where he collected the key.

Once they were inside, he placed her on the couch. The house was freezing, and Jasmin suspected that no one had been there since Halloween. Damien continued ignoring her and lit a fire. He opened a cupboard, rummaged around and eventually pulled out Imogen's mam's whiskey.

He poured two glasses, drank one quickly, then poured another and brought them over to where Jasmin sat by the fire.

'No one can hear you, so screaming is pointless.' He carefully removed the tape from her mouth. 'Drink this.'

'Do you give all your girls drinks before you kill them?' Jasmin said, trying for sweet but landing at choked.

'Looks like I do.' He rubbed the back of his head. 'Will you let me talk? Explain? If I untie you, will you run?'

She gave him a flinty look. Of course she was going to run.

He sighed. 'I know what I've done is unforgivable. But you wanted answers and we only have a few minutes.'

A few minutes before what? Panic ran down her spine.

'Why did you do it?' Jasmin said.

'Remember when I told you that my uncle had guardianship of me? Well, Theo is my uncle. My mother's younger brother.'

Jasmin thought of the picture she'd seen in the upstairs

study at Riverview. The older sister. What was her name again? Helen.

'Theo had just finished his postdoc in the US, and Nuala was newly married when my parents were deemed unfit. Theo took legal guardianship, and I was shunted between him and Nuala, like unwelcome baggage.'

Jasmin winced.

'Theo was too busy with his work, and Nuala had zero interest in me,' he continued. 'I was additional, an afterthought, and it became worse once she started her own family. I craved Theo's attention. I wanted him to notice me. To love me. At least when I was with Theo, he'd spend time with me. Talk to me. He paid me attention. But he could be cruel too. He liked to teach me lessons.'

Jasmin remembered the story of the man on the bench. How Merrick had insulted him, to teach Damien about failure.

'He called me his little monster. Taught me to inject his mice. Awful doses that would make them swell up, get sickly, writhe in pain. He made me observe them, take notes. He liked that I'm book-smart. Told me he'd pay for me to go to university. It was all I wanted in the world, to prove that I wasn't worthless. But then he told me that if I wanted to continue studying, and have him settle my fees, I needed to help out. Pull my weight. That seemed fair enough. He also insisted that we keep our relationship quiet. He said he'd explain why in time.'

'Everyone knows that he's related to Rory,' Jasmin said. But something else was clicking in her brain. Something Rory had said when they were in the upstairs study. *And it's not just me.*

You should see how they tr—. He hadn't finished the sentence, but Jasmin was now sure he'd been referring to Damien.

'If Theo could have hidden his relationship to Rory, he would have. Rory is a disgrace to him. But I suspect that's Rory's game, to strike at Theo with his loud parties and by being everything that Theo despises.' Damien exhaled loudly. 'When I started here, Theo told me the plan. That I needed to help him with his unofficial research. The kind the university would never let him carry out.'

Jasmin had sensed the callousness beneath Merrick's charm. Damien had been the stray dog that he'd kicked for fun, then fed and stroked to keep him trusting, only to kick him again.

Little monster. She thought about her grandfather, and how she had been his little shadow. Just as Damien had been Theo's. Different sides of the same coin. But Eamon had loved her, thought the world of her. She'd grown to his light. Damien had grown to Theo's darkness.

'At first, the jobs were harmless. Setting up the Riverview lab, driving around for him. Then he wanted something different. He was looking for a project assistant and needed someone smart and physically in good shape. They had to be risk-averse and open to manipulation.

'He knew I was good with people. I've always had a knack for that – for making people like me. I had to find good candidates, men or women, and charm them. Students who wanted careers in his field, who were dazzled by his name. Most didn't take much convincing.

'I would get close to them. Very close, with some. I'd allay their fears when Theo would explain that the rules didn't apply to men like him. Some wouldn't like it, or would want to tell their friends, and Theo would send them on their way when their probation was up. But others … they lapped it up. Kept it all secret.'

Or, like Niamh, they didn't have anyone to keep them grounded.

'When they were ready, he'd suggest an early course of a supplement that Verge was developing. I'd tell them that I'd already had the infusion, and it made me so much more alert and productive.'

'But in reality he wasn't giving them anything of the sort,' Jasmin said. 'Was he?'

'He gave them vitamin injections, nothing special. Sure, they felt more energetic. But it was a cover to draw blood samples, to research blood proteins. To harvest stem cells, because it's well known that young blood can offset ageing. He just had to figure out how exactly.'

Like the king in the *Immortalis*, drawing vitality from the young soldiers. Killing them so that he could live forever.

'You recruited Niamh.'

'Just before the summer, yes.'

'Did you sleep with her?' Jasmin winced. 'Is that how you recruited everyone?'

'That happened a few times. But Niamh and I, we flirted a little, nothing more. I started withdrawing from her in the summer, like Theo told me to. But he liked Niamh and she stayed longer than the usual three months. Then she started asking questions. Causing trouble.'

'It was you. Becky caught a glimpse of you from behind, arguing with Niamh. It was you that Niamh accused of only being there when it was convenient for you.'

'I didn't realise we'd been overheard. I never went to her room, except for that one time. We usually met in places where I wouldn't stand out. Where I wouldn't be noticed.'

Damien ran a hand through his hair.

'Then things got serious. Theo learned that Niamh had been compiling a file of evidence against him, documenting how he'd been testing on students and taking samples without their consent. They'd argued outside the Old Science. And again in his office when she admitted to secretly filming him.'

'And by doing that, she'd signed her death warrant.'

'Niamh called me, upset. She said she was leaving town and that Theo was a monster. She admitted she kept information that would destroy him on an SD card hidden in her pendant.' He took a deep breath. 'You heard her talking to me. I was the mystery friend.' He gave a humourless laugh. 'She didn't realise that I was working with Theo all along, until the very end. Until her final minutes.' His eyes fluttered shut momentarily, then he looked at Jasmin again.

'How did you kill her?' she said.

'Theo gave me clear instructions.' His voice was mechanical. 'I told Niamh that I'd be at the lecture and we could confront Theo when the event ended. I told her that we had to be careful, not play our hand too early. Niamh said she wanted money for her silence, but Theo would never let himself be blackmailed.'

Damien had let Niamh think she had an ally, but he was on Merrick's side all along. Jasmin felt like she had lead in her stomach.

'I picked Niamh up that evening. I took her pack of headache pills from her bag when she wasn't looking, knowing she would need them again after the lecture. She was highly strung and Theo was worried she'd cause a scene.'

Jasmin remembered Allie's recounting of Niamh searching for her headache pills in the restroom.

'When she came out of the restroom, I intercepted her, showing her that I'd found the pack of headache pills. I fed her three high-dose sedatives, which I'd switched out earlier. She didn't notice any difference.'

'Three?'

'It wasn't unusual for Niamh to increase the dosage. Then I watched. As the event photographer, it was easy.'

'You saw her talk to me?'

He nodded. 'I saw her avoid Candice, who was spitting mad with Niamh for daring to blackmail them.'

'Candice knew Niamh had evidence against Merrick?'

'Candice encouraged him to act hard and fast. They're well matched, that pair.'

Damien unscrewed the bottle of whiskey and topped up his glass. 'It was Candice who first suggested finding a more permanent solution.'

Jasmin remembered Candice crying in Merrick's office.

She had assumed afterwards that Candice had been crying because Merrick had an affair with Niamh. But no, Candice had been crying for herself. Because she had blood on her pretty, jewelled hands.

'Candice had slipped down to the garden for a smoke, and Niamh followed her. She demanded money and they had a bit of a tussle.'

Which was how Candice got the scratch on her cheek. The pendant clasp must have broken in the tussle. And then it fell while Niamh walked away, stumbling on the uneven paving.

'Theo was livid. He told me I had to get rid of her, that night. When she smashed the vase, I knew it was time to get her out of there. I told the others I was heading out to meet a girl from my Labour Law class, because they wouldn't ask questions about that. Niamh was waiting for me in another room. I told her that Theo would join us in the shed when he was done.

'We went to the shed. Theo had given me a bottle of tequila. It didn't take long before she blacked out.' When he looked at Jasmin, his eyes were rimmed red, his voice a whisper. 'I staged the scene.'

'You mean you lifted her body, which must have been a dead weight. You put a rope around her neck. You killed her, making it look like suicide.' Jasmin's voice hitched. 'Her family think she killed herself.'

'I know what I did. I think about it every day.' Damien's eyes were glassy. 'She woke up,' he added quietly. 'In the very last moments.'

Jasmin shuddered. 'What happened after?'

'I wiped the tequila bottle and diazepam pack, made it seem like only she had been handling them and put the pills back in her bag. I placed the note, one that Niamh had left for me at the gym the day after Becky heard us arguing.'

Jasmin felt sick. She didn't know what to say. Only earlier that same evening he'd been flirting with her as he took her picture. Brushing her hair from her face. All calculated, part of the plan.

'When we spoke, on the veranda, did you flirt with me because you saw me as a potential candidate?'

Damien hung his head. 'Yes.'

Jasmin shut her eyes.

'I didn't know you were Eamon Larkin's granddaughter then. Theo was so pleased when he found out. Told me what to do. And afterwards, I realised that I really liked you.'

'You told me you loved me.' Jasmin hated how small her voice sounded.

'I have never loved anyone but Theo. Until I met Imogen, Rían and Allie, no one had loved me. And then I met you. You changed everything. By the time we … I knew I had to get you out. Before it was too late.'

'You tried to talk me out of taking the job,' Jasmin said. 'Because you knew what he did to his assistants.' She looked him in the eye. 'But you never stopped Niamh, or any of the others.' Her chest heaved and her voice cracked. 'You're a monster.'

FORTY-SIX

You're a monster.

She'd flung the words at Damien with such violence that she expected him to be angry.

But his voice was even, quiet. 'I know what I am.'

Jasmin studied his face, thinking of her monster portrait of him. But there was nothing there that told of it. His bright eyes, sculpted jaw, nothing in his perfect symmetry hinted at the darkness inside.

'Why?' *Why didn't you say no, why didn't you report Merrick, why didn't you stop him?*

'I was a frog in a pot.' That lopsided grin again. 'Slowly boiled to death. When I first broke the rules for Theo, that gave him leverage over me, and it grew worse and worse, and for a long time that's all I knew.' He shook his head. 'I loved him. I thought he loved me. Since my childhood, no matter how cruel he could be, Theo was my sun and my moon. Anything he asked of me I gave without hesitation. Until recently.' His eyes fixed on Jasmin's. 'Until you.'

'Why did you kill Allie?' Jasmin would not let him in. 'Did he ask that of you?'

'She was too close to figuring everything out.' Pain was drawn into every feature. 'She confronted Theo in his office and he wanted me to get rid of her too. She realised something that night at Riverview, when she knocked over the photo.'

Jasmin remembered Allie's hand flinging out and hitting the picture, which fell to the floor, cracking the glass. It hadn't been there when Jasmin returned to the study.

'It was a picture of Rory, Theo and me, taken at Riverview. Allie didn't say anything in front of you – she was loyal, Allie was – but she confronted me about it. I told her that we were family but I barely knew him. She used her coins to confirm that I was telling the truth and I thought she'd let it go. But she didn't. She kept asking questions. Whether I saw Theo much now. Why it had to be a secret.'

'That was when she started behaving erratically.'

'Imogen was wrong about Allie. She would have made a good investigative journalist. She drove to Nuala's village one weekend, asked questions. Figured things out pretty quickly, that Theo pulled my strings. She never asked me if I killed Niamh. I could see the question in her eyes, but she didn't seem to want the confirmation. Despite everything, she believed the best in me. She wanted to help. She thought you might be the answer.'

'Me?' Jasmin said, tasting something bitter and metallic. A dark, burning mix of fury and pain seared her from the inside.

'She could see I was in love with you. She thought you could save me. So she told me she was going to tell you what she knew. We argued, that night at the library. Then the power went.' His jaw ticked. 'She fell.'

'It was an accident?'

'I didn't kill her, but Allie's death is as much my fault as Niamh's. If I hadn't argued with her...' He let out a shaky exhale.

'And you staged the scene, again.' Jasmin's voice was heavy with hurt and anger. 'You sent the message from her phone so there would be no further investigation. You made it so much worse.'

'I did what Theo told me to do. He didn't want an investigation. He didn't want anyone looking too closely at me and finding my connection to him.' The life had gone out of Damien's voice again, and Jasmin felt a hot, ugly scorn that was uncomfortably laced with sympathy. Because that was the only path he knew: do as Theo Merrick says.

Jasmin leaned forward. 'How much did you report back to Merrick, about what we were doing? The murder wall and our meetings? You told him everything about our investigation, didn't you?'

'No! I didn't tell him anything. I did what he ordered, but no more than that.' Merrick's good little soldier. 'Except for the SD card. I had to tell him about that.'

'You staged the break-in before coming to get me at Riverview.'

Damien nodded. 'I destroyed the murder wall. I did it to

scare you all, so that you would pull back. I didn't want you getting closer. It was driving me crazy, seeing you get closer while knowing that Theo would stop at nothing.'

'What now?' Jasmin said. 'You put me in the car and drive to the river? Give me diazepam first? Exactly how are you going to stage the accident?'

'I have a few ideas.'

He stood up, and moving with his usual athletic grace he drew closer to her. But somehow, even though she knew she was alone with a murderer, Jasmin wasn't afraid.

He took her hands, and with a box cutter gently sliced the tape. The familiarity of his touch mixed with her rising trepidation.

'Don't worry, Jasmin. You'll be OK.' Out of habit, he touched a hand to the side of her face, and then pulled back as if he'd burned her. 'Sorry.' He couldn't meet her eye as he cut the tape around her ankles. 'I won't hurt you. I can't. I'd sooner kill myself than hurt you.'

Jasmin stood up, her legs uncertain. She shoved him, and he let her. She felt a surge of fury flood her and she lashed out, thumping his chest with her fists. All her pent up fear and hurt unleashed as she yelled at him. He didn't fight her.

'I'm sorry, Jasmin,' Damien said. 'I'm so sorry. I was selfish to love you, to let you fall for me. But this, being with you, has been the best thing in my whole life. It has been everything.'

She was crying now, and he pulled her into his arms. His touch was comforting and repulsive. And she felt the old familiar confusion, this terrible guilt for loving a monster. For feeling what she felt, for someone who'd done something utterly unforgivable. Who'd crossed a line so red it was crimson.

'It will be OK.' He tried to soothe her and she wrenched herself out of his arms. She would not be comforted by him.

'If you're not carrying out Merrick's orders, what are you going to do?'

Damien reached into his pocket and pulled out a memory stick and closed it in Jasmin's hand. 'This is my video confession to Niamh's murder at Merrick's orders, and my role in Allie's death. I've included a letter, documents, emails, screenshots of text messages, to back up everything I say. I am going to drive my car into the river, just as Theo instructed.'

Jasmin realised what he was saying. 'Damien, no,' she begged. 'Don't. Please.'

She hated him. She loved him. She never wanted to see him again. She didn't want him to die.

'Turn yourself in,' she said. 'Tell the guards everything.'

'I would, if I could trust them,' Damien said. 'But I don't. If I turn myself in, I'll take the fall while Theo carries on doing what he's doing. They'll spin it that I was the jealous ex-boyfriend, and Theo will get a rap on the knuckles for cutting a few corners in his research. Men like him are never held accountable.' His eyes slid to hers. 'What if he comes after you?'

'That's a risk we'll have to take.' But he had a point. She could see Merrick giving one of his speeches, talking about Damien's failed romances, how he probably picked up toxic ideas about masculinity, while he, Merrick, was a pillar of the community.

'I think I know a way to make sure that this stops here,' Damien said.

From the door came the sound of a knock, gentle but firm. Jasmin's hand flew to her mouth; it had to be Merrick. He must have followed them.

The handle turned and the door opened. Jasmin couldn't tear her eyes away as a man stepped inside. A tall man, with a grey beard and buzz-cut hair.

'Grandpa,' Jasmin breathed. She froze, unsure. An endless moment passed while she drank him in. The body that was older and yet more muscled than it had been before. There was a tattoo on his neck, a rough ouroboros. His face was cragged and lined, his eyes sharp and wise. Still, Jasmin ran to him and threw her arms around him.

'Jasmin. My girl.'

She squeezed him hard, her throat too tight for words. She held him for an endless moment. When she pulled out of his arms, her face was wet.

'Why are you here?'

'Damien called me.' Eamon looked across the room to where Damien watched. 'He told me that you were in danger. Where else would I be?'

'I thought you were living in a small beach town on the other side of the country.'

'That's the plan,' Eamon said. 'But there was something I needed to do first.'

'What was that?'

'I have to stop Theo,' he said. 'I created him, you see. I taught him every wrong thing he's done. He's made himself so visible, I couldn't help but see him. I read the papers he's written, kept up with everything he's done. I had a terrible feeling that I knew where he was going with his research.'

'He has your research notes,' Jasmin said.

He laughed. 'Of course he does. I told Georgie to give them to him, and I told her why. All of it useless. Rabbit holes that will get him nowhere.'

'Georgie knows?'

'She called me. Told me that Theo had come over. That she was worried he was up to no good and she was determined to stop him. I told her I would take care of it. So I made an appointment with Theo. Pretended to be interested in what he was doing – admiring him, stroking that enormous ego. He invited me to come and see him at Riverview. He wanted me there, in his study, another eternal circle. When I saw you there, I knew that he'd orchestrated it deliberately. That using you was his way of proving that the student had surpassed the teacher. Then, yesterday, Damien found my number in Theo's study and rang me. He told me everything. He told me he was worried that Theo would hurt you.'

Jasmin stared at him. 'Damien called you?'

Eamon nodded. 'We met late last night. I knew then that we could help each other. We both want to stop Theo.'

'You have a plan?' She felt that foolish prick of pride. Her grandfather always knew what to do.

'We have to make it impossible for him to discredit Damien.' They both turned to where Damien stood. Jasmin looked at his hands. Hands that had killed. Hands that had touched her with love.

Eamon gave her a sad smile. 'For this to work, Damien can't survive.'

Jasmin swallowed.

He squeezed her hand, which still held the memory stick. 'Use this wisely. Theo Merrick must be stopped. Here's what I think you should do.' He told her his plan, with Damien helping her to understand.

'I don't like this,' Jasmin said, her voice smaller than she wanted.

'We have to go,' Eamon said. 'We don't have much time. There's a storm coming in. Mind yourself, my sweet girl.' Then he nodded at Damien. 'Say goodbye to my granddaughter.'

Eamon went to the door, and Damien came to her. 'I'm sorry. For everything.'

Words couldn't bring Niamh and Allie back.

He turned, then walked away. Jasmin watched him go, her stomach knotted with warring emotions. And she let him walk away, knowing she would never forgive what he'd done. That this would be the end.

He'd only taken a few steps when Jasmin rushed to him and threw her arms around him.

'I don't forgive you,' she said. But she held him close, feeling the warmth of his body for the last time.

'I know.' He whispered in her ear all the words she'd treasured before.

My heart is yours.

What a thing, she thought. To be loved not by one monster, but two.

They drew apart. He touched his hands to her face as if memorising it. Then he dropped a single, soft kiss on her lips.

'Goodbye, Jasmin.'

He joined her grandfather at the door. They both took one last, lingering look. Then they left.

FORTY-SEVEN

'This is going to change everything,' Imogen said, taking a deep breath as she pointed the remote at the TV.

They'd come to Jasmin's house, Imogen and Rían. They were in her lamplit sitting room, along with Dash and Javier.

It was strange having Imogen and Rían over. They weren't her friends, not any more. Jasmin wasn't sure they ever were. All they had to connect them was their shared, confused love for Damien.

None of them would forget that night, ten days ago, when Damien had taken her to Imogen's family cottage. After Damien and Eamon left, Jasmin had paced the cottage, her heart cut to ribbons, thinking about what had just happened. Eamon's last words to her. She knew she had to get back, that a storm was rolling in, but she was shaken. Unable to plan her way home.

Mind yourself, my sweet girl.

Not twenty minutes had passed when Imogen and Rían had burst in, breathless, saying, 'Where is he?'

They'd been furious, hurt. Imogen was shaking as she read out loud a letter Damien had left in her coat pocket, confessing to Niamh's murder. To his role in Allie's death. And saying that he'd taken Jasmin to the cottage to kill her on Merrick's orders.

Jasmin wasn't sure if they'd come to save her, or him.

Imogen had insisted they find him, despite the blustering wind. They'd all run out into the dark night. They got in Imogen's car, drove down the winding country roads as the rain started. They drove until they saw it: Damien's car in the rushing river. It had gone over the bridge, partly submerged, partly wedged between rocks. A door was wide open.

They'd all rushed down the embankment, screaming for Damien. Imogen tried to jump into the river, the fast unstoppable current, but Rían held her back. They called for help. They waited, the wind whipping at their clothes and hair, until the emergency services arrived.

There was no sign of Damien. He'd gone into the water close to where the river ran into the sea. They were told his body was likely to have been swept out into the ocean. The storm had made everything harder.

Imogen had showed the guards the letter he'd left her, which confessed to killing Niamh and arguing with Allie in the minutes before she fell to her death, but nothing more. Jasmin confirmed that he'd confessed the same to her.

They made no mention of Merrick. Yet.

Damien's written confession was all over the news the next

day, the handsome student killer with the soulful eyes. Merrick gave another sad speech on the evening news about student wellness. He made no attempt to contact Jasmin in the following days, but she remained wary. Alert. She was a loose end, which meant she wasn't safe. Maybe he thought her too afraid to speak out, after the horror of that night. Maybe he'd dismissed her as weak and ineffectual. She hoped so. She hoped his arrogance would keep him away, if only for a short while. Merrick would never suspect that he might be outsmarted by the boy he'd called his little monster.

Now, this evening, the TV was on and ads played in the background, the sound muted.

'I'm sorry,' Imogen said, still looking at the TV. 'For not trusting you.'

'So am I,' Rían said ruefully.

It turned out Dash had met with Allie the evening before she died. It really had been a date. They'd met briefly at Rory's party, and then they'd bumped into each other and arranged to have a coffee at the Three Divas in the early evening. But later, much later, Allie and Damien had gone to Messy Jack's. He'd been trying to calm her down, reassure her. That's where Thuli had seen them.

'I shouldn't have lied to you all in the first place,' Jasmin said.

She could see Javier and Dash from the corner of her eye, watching. They were on the couch, but alert. Ready to defend her.

Maybe Jasmin was less alone than she'd feared.

Merrick had offered a project assistant job to Dash around the time that Niamh died, but her brother had turned it down. When Javier heard about it, he'd asked if Dash would recommend him instead. Since the first days after Niamh died, Javier had suspicions, and working for Merrick gave him a chance to search for evidence. Jasmin was still peeved about the night in the woods, that he'd tried to warn her by scaring her, when he'd been running his own solo mission. He had returned her scarf though.

The theme music for Imogen's mother's show began. The guest was shown, Merrick smiling in his seat, ready to announce the launch of his groundbreaking wellness programme. Golden boy of the university – while Damien was a ghost.

'Merrick should be in prison,' Javier said.

Jasmin knew that there were many different kinds of prison. Many ways to be punished. She thought of Damien, and her heart ached.

'Has it started?' Georgie stood at the door. She stepped forward, placing a gentle hand on Jasmin's shoulder. She caught her grandmother's hand, the skin thin and lined.

This was the plan they'd set in motion as they watched the river, waiting for the emergency services. Eamon Larkin's plan, but Rían and Imogen didn't know that.

On the TV screen, Síle Barrett wore her customary designer trouser suit, immaculately coiffed with a shiny bob, like her daughter. She sat on a modern-looking leather armchair that was angled towards the guest chair, where Theo Merrick sat, his ankle crossed over his knee. He beamed back at her. He did not look like a man who'd lost his nephew, the child he'd raised, only ten days ago. There'd been no mention that the student who drowned was in any way linked to Theo Merrick. They hadn't found a body, the storm delaying the search, but Damien was presumed dead. The university didn't want to linger too much on yet another dead student and embraced the story of an accident. A nearly empty bottle of whiskey had been found in the car, and there'd been stern instructions about risky behaviour and the ills of binge drinking. Then Damien's letter – where he took the fall for Niamh and Allie's deaths – had surfaced, and Merrick was off the hook.

Imogen was nervous, Jasmin could tell. If this went wrong, her mother's career could implode. It was a huge leap of faith.

Síle was asking about the unfortunate series of student deaths at the university.

'It's tragic,' Merrick replied. 'Two young women dead at the hands of a troubled, violent young man, who then died in a car accident after a binge drinking episode. I hope that my research, the work I've done with the Wellness Formula, can help our young people live healthier, happier lives.'

'And what exactly is in this magic formula?' said Síle, raising an elegant eyebrow.

Merrick laughed. 'That's a trade secret.'

Síle nodded. 'So you're not, for instance, testing it on people – much like you would experiment on rats?'

Merrick blinked. 'Oh goodness no. That would be un-ethical.'

'Hmm. You're not carrying out tests on the same young

384

people you profess to care about without their express consent? And you're not harvesting stem cells to fuel your anti-ageing research?'

Merrick's smile went rigid. 'I'm not sure …'

'Professor Merrick, what exactly was your relationship with Niamh Cunningham, the first student to die so tragically?'

'I don't see the relevance of this question.' Merrick's eyes were livid.

'Maybe this will help explain.' Síle pointed at the screen behind them.

Suddenly, Damien's beautiful face filled their TV screen. Jasmin felt a deep ache in her heart as she looked into his sad green eyes.

This was his video confession. The real confession, where he told the full story.

'I am Damien McHugh and I am Theo Merrick's nephew and ward. I am recording this, in case anything should happen to me. At his instruction, I killed Niamh Cunningham and staged it to look like a suicide. This is only the tip of the iceberg of the terrible things my uncle has attempted to conceal. I have included documents, emails, text messages that verify the truth of this confession. I am so sorry for all the pain I've caused.'

The camera cut fast to Merrick, whose face was a mask of fury and confusion.

'You'll be hearing from my lawyers,' he snarled. He ripped off his mic and stormed off the set.

'This is an exclusive report on the secret anti-ageing experiments that Theo Merrick was conducting under the cover of his Wellness Formula,' Síle continued, ever the professional. 'We spoke to four students, who will remain anonymous. These students discovered, at great personal cost, that the much-loved professor is a monster. Let me start at the beginning, in October, when Niamh Cunningham ran crying from Theo Merrick's office ...'

Imogen slumped, limp, in her chair. 'She's good, isn't she?' she breathed, and Jasmin remembered the quiet words Damien had said in the cottage, when Eamon had told her his plan.

'*You have to promise not to tell the others. If Imogen believed I was alive, she wouldn't rest until she tracked me down. Tell them I had been drinking a lot. That I tied you up, but you found the box cutter and escaped. It was too late, I was already gone.*'

He'd been right. Imogen needed a story with an ending that couldn't be reversed.

'There's going to be some fallout,' Javier said, but Jasmin could see the relief in his eyes. He had gone to Síle with them, and provided corroborating evidence. He was finally avenging Niamh's death as best he could.

Georgie said, 'Well, then. I'm glad that's been taken care of. Not a nice boy, I always thought. I'd better go and see how Benedict is getting on. Goodnight, dears.'

She smiled at Jasmin, then moved to the door. Jasmin turned to watch, and Georgie glanced back. For one second, pain washed over her face, her eyes filled with sorrow. She nodded at Jasmin, saying, 'Talk to me, honey, if you need to. There'll be no secrets between us.' Because Georgie was the only other person who knew the truth about the night Damien's car went into the river. Her grandfather hadn't wanted Jasmin to carry it alone. And Georgie knew what it was to love a monster.

Dash turned off the TV. 'I knew there was something wrong about Theo Merrick. Always felt it.'

'I need to get out of here,' said Jasmin, her leg jiggling.

'I have to go home, my mother's going to call,' Imogen said. 'I need to tell her she didn't do a bad job at all.' The pride was clear in her voice. She finally seemed at peace with the career she craved, and her mother's greatness in that field.

'I'm going to head back too.' Rían hugged Jasmin. 'Don't be a stranger.'

'I'll come out with you,' Javier said.

'Me too,' Dash added. 'Where do you want to go?'

'Somewhere different,' Jasmin said. 'Somewhere I've never been before.'

Javier smiled. 'I'll see what I can do.'

She could hear Georgie and Sonia in the kitchen, the re-assuring hum of their voices. That familiar cadence. At the door, Javier waited for her.

There was a new lightness in her step, now that Niamh's murderers had been named. What had been hidden had now been forced to the light, and Jasmin no longer sensed the hungry king lurking in the garden. She no longer felt shadows reaching for her.

Her monsters were more ordinary than shadows and dead kings. And while she could never forgive them, she still loved them. It brought her some comfort that they'd found each other.

As she left the room, Jasmin's eye slid to the coffee table and the postcard, sent just two days ago, peeking out from under a book. If anyone picked it up, they'd see that it was a copy of a painted seascape. A place where the river met the sea. At the edge of the picture were the initials E.L.

If they flicked the postcard over, they'd see a small, rough ouroboros. And beneath that, only four words.

My heart is yours.

ACKNOWLEDGEMENTS

For kitchen conversations about possible and impossible things, thank you Cathal Seoighe, my professor husband, who once said, wouldn't it be fun to write a book about longevity and anti-ageing research? While I have of course taken much artistic liberty, I am grateful to him for answering my many questions, so that I could piece together the scientific background to this book.

As always, thank you, Claire Wilson my agent, for making the magic happen, and Safae El-Ouahabi.

Thank you, Ellen Holgate, Genevieve Herr and Katie Ager – I am fortunate to work with such brilliant editors. And thank you to everyone at, and with, Bloomsbury for yet again turning my words on-screen into a beautiful book that finds its readers. Thank you, Jessica Bellman, Emily Marples, Tim Hardy, Isabelle Tucker and the rest of the team, at every stage. Thank you, Michelle Brackenborough for the gorgeous cover.

It takes a village, and I am super grateful for the enthusiasm and support I've received from other writers, in Ireland, South Africa and the UK. I'm especially grateful for the enduring kindness, spanning many years, from Melinda Salisbury, Samantha Shannon, Katherine Webber, Deirdre Sullivan and S.A. Partridge.

A huge thank you to the book people, bloggers, influencers and sellers, who share online and in person. And lastly – thank you, dear reader, for picking this up and allowing me to tell you a story.

SAVANNAH IS CURSED.
DISCOVER THIS GRIPPING,
SOUTH AFRICAN FANTASY.

'A fiercely compelling, ferocious story'
KIRAN MILLWOOD HARGRAVE

DON'T MISS THESE
SPELLBINDING THRILLERS
BY MARY WATSON

'*The Wren Hunt* rings with ancient, subtle
magic, masterfully transmuted into words.
A tale that gets into your bones'

SAMANTHA SHANNON